DEEDS OF DARKNESS

1916: A young woman is found murdered in a cinema. Harvey Marmion and Joe Keedy set out to find the killer who so elusively fled in the dark. Before long, two more victims – are found dead. Meanwhile, Marmion's son Paul prepares for life on the front line as he marches to the Battle of the Somme. Suffering a vicious blow in No Man's Land, Paul is left blinded for the rest of his life. Marmion must come to terms with the permanent darkness of his son's life, while continuing to search for the brutal killer who only strikes in the dark.

DEEDS OF DARKNESS

DEEDS
OF DARKNESS

by

Edward Marston

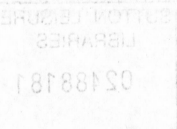

Magna Large Print Books
Long Preston, North Yorkshire,
BD23 4ND, England.

British Library Cataloguing in Publication Data.

Marston, Edward
    Deeds of darkness.

    A catalogue record of this book is
    available from the British Library

    ISBN   978-0-7505-4112-1

First published in Great Britain by Allison & Busby in 2014

Copyright © 2014 by Edward Marston

Cover illustration by arrangement with Allison & Busby Ltd.

Published in Large Print 2015 by arrangement with
Allison & Busby Ltd.

Magna Large Print is an imprint of Library Magna Books Ltd.

Printed and bound in Great Britain by
T.J. (International) Ltd., Cornwall, PL28 8RW

*This one is for my beloved grandfather,
Albert Edward, who fought in the Great War
and who resolutely kept its ugly secrets to himself.*

CHAPTER ONE

1916

War and Charlie Chaplin did not sit easily together in the mind of the Reverend Matthew Hearn. He had a rooted objection to cinemas themselves, but he saved his fiercest condemnation for the little actor who'd forged an international reputation by playing the part of a hapless tramp. Chaplin's popularity seemed to have no bounds. Songs had been written about him. Shops sold Chaplin merchandise. Music hall artistes impersonated him. But it was the way that Chaplin featured in comics and cartoon strips that rankled with Hearn. He believed that the minds of innocent children were being polluted and that was unforgivable. When he saw two parents approaching the cinema with their young daughter, he moved across to intercept them.

'Excuse me,' he said, politely, 'but do you think it's wise to take your child to see Mr Chaplin?'

'Yes,' replied the father, looking fondly at his daughter. 'Laura adores him. We had to bring her.'

'It isn't only Laura who enjoys Charlie Chaplin,' said his wife. 'We do as well. He makes us laugh until we cry.'

'That's my point,' argued Hearn. 'Should you be laughing at a time of national calamity? There's a war on – a dreadful, bitter, shameful war that's

11

killing our young men in untold thousands. Do you think that laughing at the antics of a clown is the most appropriate response to this crisis?'

The man shrugged. 'We like the films. They help us forget the war.'

'That's why Chaplin is so dangerous.'

'I want to go in, Daddy,' said Laura, fretting at the delay.

'Yes, darling,' said her father. 'I know.' He turned to Hearn. 'I'm sorry. We made a promise to our daughter and we can't disappoint her.'

'As you wish,' said Hearn, standing aside. 'But remember what I said.'

There was, however, no chance of their doing that. As they joined the crowd that converged on the cinema, the trio dismissed him from their minds. All that they wanted was the magic of another performance by a comic genius in the guise of a tramp, a man who could delight people of all ages and send them out of a cinema in a state of mild delirium. It was the same with everyone to whom Hearn spoke. They resented being stopped and brushed aside his objections to the entertainment they'd come to see. Of the dozens of cinema patrons he'd accosted, not a single one had been persuaded to turn back. It was dispiriting.

As he patrolled the pavement, Matthew Hearn cut an odd figure. A big, broad-shouldered, shambling man in his fifties, he looked less like a priest than a farm labourer in clerical garb. Beneath the wide-brimmed black hat was a gnarled face that was positively ugly in repose. What made him less threatening to newcomers was the low, gentle,

12

reasonable voice. It came from the heart.

A uniformed soldier approached him with a young woman on his arm.

'One moment,' he said, detaining them. 'Have you really thought about the implications of what you're doing?'

'We're going to the cinema, that's all,' said the soldier.

'But it's not all – that's the trouble.'

Hearn launched into his denunciation of Charlie Chaplin but his words fell on stony ground. With a protective arm around her shoulders, the soldier hustled his girlfriend past the priest and took her into the cinema. A policeman who'd watched the encounter sauntered over to Hearn.

'You're wasting your time, I'm afraid,' he remarked.

'They just don't realise what they're doing.'

'Yes, they do. They've come in search of some fun.'

'There's no place for fun when a war is on,' insisted Hearn. 'The soldier should have known that and so should the rest of them. Can't they hear the sound of artillery from across the Channel? Don't they read the casualty lists? Zeppelins are flying over London to drop bombs on us, yet all that they can do is to giggle at Charlie Chaplin.'

'Well, he is very funny,' said the policeman, admiringly.

'Are you saying that you *condone* what's going on in that cinema?'

'It's a free country, sir. You can't stop people doing what they want.'

'Cinemas are a source of evil.'

13

'I can't agree with you there.'

'They're places of darkness in every sense.'

The policeman looked at him shrewdly. 'Have you ever *watched* a film?'

'No,' replied Hearn, 'because I refuse to cross the threshold of places like this. Look at it,' he went on, pointing. 'Even the foyer is dimly lit. I'm told that it's almost pitch-black inside. That incites people to all sorts of improprieties.' The policeman smiled. 'That's not a cause for amusement,' he said, reproachfully. 'Your duty is to uphold the law. Cinemas are frequented by prostitutes who ply their vile trade in the darkness. Doesn't that concern you?'

'Yes, of course,' said the other, 'though I don't think you'll find many ladies of that kind at a Charlie Chaplin film. It brings in a family audience.'

'You may be wrong there, Constable. In the time that I've been standing here, I've seen two or three women slipping in there alone. Cinemas lure in unaccompanied females of questionable morality. And here's another one,' he added with a note of censure, 'that proves my point.'

An attractive, well-dressed woman in her twenties was hurrying towards the cinema. When she entered the foyer, she paused to check the time before buying herself a ticket. The policeman shook his head.

'You're mistaken there, sir,' he said. 'In a job like mine, you learn to pick out prostitutes at a glance and she is certainly not one of them. You're being very unkind to her. She's a respectable young lady who's simply come to watch a film.'

14

The woman in question handed her ticket to the usherette and was shown to a seat in the back row. She immediately removed her hat and put it on the seat beside her in order to reserve it. A news-reel was flickering up on the screen but she paid no heed to the information that appeared in large capital letters. Like everyone else there, all that she was waiting for was *The Floorwalker*, the latest film starring Charlie Chaplin. Once it was on, her friend would arrive. A concerted cheer went up when the main feature finally started and the accompanist began pounding the keys of her piano. Within seconds, the audience was shaking with mirth. The woman was only half-watching the scene in front of her. She was there for something more important than a film. Hope and expectation made her tingle. The feeling did not last. After several minutes, there was no sign of him and she soon had doubts that he would come at all. Her nerve started to fail her. He'd changed his mind or – worse still, she feared – he'd found someone else with whom to have an assignation. The very thought made her shudder. As time rolled on, the anticipatory joy she'd brought into the cinema slowly turned to acute embarrassment.

In a place where everyone else was rocking with laughter, she felt alone and utterly betrayed. She was on the verge of getting up and running out in tears when a shape was conjured out of the darkness. The man sat down beside her and reached out to hold her hand. She was so overjoyed that she didn't even mind the fact that her hat was being crushed beneath his weight. He was there.

That's all that mattered. He cared for her enough to honour his promise. She was ecstatic.

After kissing her hand, he stroked her arm then moved his attention to her thigh, caressing it with increasing boldness until she felt exquisite electric shocks all over her leg. He then put an arm around her shoulders, using the other hand to fondle her breast and make the nipple harden. It burnt with pleasure. By the time his lips met hers, she was giddy with sensation. She'd never been held and kissed like that before. It went on and on with gathering intensity and she lost all inhibition. Her surrender was complete.

Charlie Chaplin no longer existed. She was in another world but she was not allowed to savour its joys indefinitely. Her lover's kiss suddenly became a clamp across her mouth. His embrace tightened painfully. The hand that had explored her body with such practised skill now sought her throat and squeezed hard. Up on the screen, a chase scene was sending the audience into up-roar. Chaplin's tramp was trying to run down an upward escalator and staying more or less where he was. As they cheered, yelled and laughed uncontrollably, they almost drowned out the piano's rising frenzy. It was cruel on the woman. In the general pandemonium, nobody heard her struggle or saw her frantic attempts at escape. Resistance was pointless. The man was bigger, stronger and more determined than her. Sur-rounded by merriment, he stuck to his task, stifling her protest with his mouth and using both murderous hands to throttle the life out of her.

When she eventually went limp, he eased her

back in her seat, picked up her handbag, then vanished into the darkness.

She would have no need of the crumpled hat now.

CHAPTER TWO

'Who found her?'

'It was one of the usherettes. When the lights came up, everyone else left the building. The woman appeared to be asleep. The usherette shook her and she keeled over. It was obvious that she had not died by natural means.'

'What a grim discovery to make!'

'How on earth could it have happened?' asked the superintendent. 'The cinema was almost full yet nobody had the slightest inkling that a murder was taking place under their noses.'

'Charlie Chaplin is a powerful distraction.'

'I'll take your word for that, Inspector.'

Marmion was surprised. 'Have you never taken your children to a Chaplin film?'

'No, I haven't. As a matter of fact, they don't go to *any* cinema. However,' said Chatfield with a dismissive flick of the hand, 'let's forget my family for the moment and concentrate on the crime.'

'Do we have any more information, sir?'

'No, we don't.'

'Then I'd better get over to Coventry Street.'

Harvey Marmion had been summoned to the superintendent's office at Scotland Yard to hear about the murder. Claude Chatfield had taken the call from the manager of the West End cinema.

'Mr Brack was very agitated,' he said. 'I couldn't understand most of what he was saying.'

'That's understandable, sir. It must have come as a terrible shock to him. Apart from anything else, the cinema has had to close and turn people away. In view of what's happened, audiences might not be quite so keen to flock there now.'

'I'll want a full report as soon as possible.'

'That goes without saying, Superintendent.'

'And the commissioner is taking a personal interest in the case. Like me, he has grave reservations about the whole notion of cinema.'

'We must agree to differ on that subject, sir.'

'I'm not interested in your opinion, Marmion.'

'Then I won't presume to offer it.'

Marmion gave him a non-committal smile. There had always been unresolved tension between the two men and it had been intensified by the fact that Chatfield had been promoted over the inspector. The superintendent was a tall, thin, pale man in his forties with bulbous eyes set in a narrow face and warning signs of a bald patch. Marmion, by contrast, was muscular, well proportioned and had a full head of hair. His features were pleasant rather than handsome and they were now composed into the expression of resigned obedience that he always reserved for Chatfield.

'Well,' said the superintendent, irritably, 'don't just stand there, man. Get over to Coventry Street with Sergeant Keedy and find out the full facts.'

'Yes, sir.'

'Most important of all, solve the mystery.'

'Mystery?' echoed Marmion.

'Yes – why is it that a murder is committed in a crowded cinema yet we have absolutely no witnesses?'

'With respect, sir, that's not quite true.'

Chatfield's eyes bulged even more. 'Don't talk nonsense.'

'Nobody may have seen the actual murder,' explained Marmion, 'but we are all witnesses *after* the event. That was the killer's intention. He deliberately left his victim on display. It would have been much easier and far less dangerous for him to dispose of her in some quiet corner or dump her in the Thames. Instead of that,' he went on, 'he chose to do it in public, certain that his crime would soon be revealed in all its horror and that – when the newspapers report it tomorrow morning – the whole of London will witness what he did. That's the real mystery, sir.'

'What is?'

'Why does he feel the need to show off?'

Emmanuel Brack prowled up and down the empty foyer of the West End cinema and pulled intermittently on a cigar. He was a short, stout man in his forties with a face contorted by anguish. Dressed in an expensive, well-cut suit and sporting a bow tie, he wore gleaming black shoes that completed a picture of flabby elegance. He pulled out the white handkerchief from the top pocket of his jacket and mopped his brow. Through the glass windows, he could see the people outside, held back by uniformed policemen and wondering why they were unable to see the second showing of *The Floorwalker*. Wild rumours were already circulating, all of them detrimental to the immediate future of the cinema. Murder was bad for business.

When the detectives finally arrived by car, the manager rushed forward with gratitude and opened one of the doors for them. Marmion entered the foyer with Joe Keedy. There was a flurry of introductions and an exchange of hand-shakes.

'Thank heaven you've come, Inspector!' said the manager, still perspiring. 'This has been a disaster for me.'

'Forgive me if I reserve my sympathy for the victim,' said Marmion, crisply. 'Her situation is rather more serious than yours.'

'But I'm left to suffer the consequences.'

'Where is the body?'

'It's exactly where it was found. We haven't dared to move or touch it.'

'Good.'

'It was Mabel – she's one of our usherettes – who made the discovery. She almost fainted. Mabel is still recovering in my office and so is another member of my staff.'

'We'll need to speak to them in due course, Mr Brack,' said Marmion. 'First of all, we'd like to visit the scene of the crime.'

The manager stubbed out his cigar in an ash-tray. 'Follow me.'

As they fell in behind him, the detectives ex-changed a glance. Tall, good-looking and lithe, Joe Keedy had come to the same conclusion as

Marmion. Both of them had identified the manager as a self-important businessman whose only interest was in his cinema and who treated the death of a young woman as an ugly stain on his property that needed to be removed as soon as possible. Opening a door, Brack led them into the auditorium which was now blazing with light.

The corpse lay sprawled on the carpet between the rows of seats. When the usherette had shaken her, the woman had pitched forward onto the floor. Marmion and Keedy moved in for a closer look but the manager held back. It was Keedy who knelt beside the body to examine it. Before he joined the Metropolitan Police Force, he'd worked in the family undertaking business and grown wearily accustomed to the sight of death. He knew its unpleasant smells and its gift for disfigurement of its victims. Marmion was happy to let the sergeant carry out the inspection. He reserved his interest for the surrounding area.

Keedy looked up at him. 'She was strangled, Inspector.'

'Poor woman!' said Marmion. 'Even though she's slightly built, she must have put up some sort of struggle.'

'Why did nobody hear her?' asked the manager.

'It was because the killer chose the film with care, sir. Charlie Chaplin always generates a barrage of noise and laughter. It would muffle her protests and the darkness would hide the pair of them from prying eyes.'

Brack turned away in disgust. 'Can you get her moved, Inspector?'

'An ambulance will be on its way. But we'll need to take photographs before that,' said Marmion, beckoning the police photographer.

'I feel sorry for her, naturally but ... well, frankly, I don't want her here.'

Keedy stood up. 'We're looking for a strong man,' he decided, 'and one who was confident in his strength. He came here to kill and he succeeded.'

'He must also be something of a charmer,' observed Marmion. 'Back rows are normally the realm of courting couples. I doubt very much if they were strangers to each other. He might have persuaded her to come here willingly. The woman would have been completely unaware of his real intentions.'

'She's wearing a wedding ring.'

'I don't think we're looking for her husband, somehow. He wouldn't give himself away so easily. What we have here, I suspect, is rather more than the result of a marital tiff.' Marmion bent down to look under the seats. 'Something is missing.'

'If you mean her hat,' said Brack, 'it's in my office. Mabel found it on the seat beside the woman. It was crushed out of shape.'

'Is that all that the usherette found?'

'A dead body and a battered hat is more than enough, Inspector.'

Marmion stood up. 'Where's her handbag?'

'There was no sign of that. Perhaps she didn't bring one.'

'Then how did she pay the fare to get her here?' asked Keedy. 'And if she was coming for what she thought was a romantic tryst, she would certainly have brought a hairbrush and a powder compact.'

'I bow to your greater experience in these matters,' said Marmion.

There was a faint irony in his voice that went unnoticed by the manager. The detectives were not simply linked together by their profession. Keedy was engaged to Marmion's daughter, Alice, so he had now effectively become one of the family. It had not been an entirely welcome development to Marmion but he'd come to accept it in time. He moved back so that the photographer could start work and he began to rehearse aloud what might have happened.

'He brings her here with a view to killing her. He lulls her into a compliant mood. Having chosen his moment with care, he dispatches her and leaves her upright in her seat so that nobody notices anything untoward when the lights come on. By that time,' said Marmion, looking around, 'he's sneaked out of the cinema with her handbag.'

'It would be conspicuous,' Keedy pointed out.

'Exactly – so he'd take what he wanted then get rid of it.' He turned to the manager. 'Is there any other way out of here?'

Brack indicated some curtains at the front of the auditorium. 'That's the emergency exit.'

'Then he probably left that way.' A nod sent Keedy hurrying towards the curtains. 'If he'd gone into the foyer with a handbag, someone would have spotted him. He planned an alternative escape.'

They heard a metallic clang as the barrier was lifted on the emergency exit. A door creaked open. In less than a minute, Keedy came back through the curtains with a bag in his hands.

'You were right, Inspector,' he said. 'It was in the dustbin outside.' He gave the handbag to Marmion. 'Feel that leather. It's good quality.'

Marmion opened the bag and conducted a quick search of the contents.

'There are two things missing,' he said. 'The killer stole her purse and her house key. That gives us a possible motive for murder.'

'Do we know who she is and where she lives?' asked Keedy.

'This may tell us, Sergeant.' He extracted an envelope and looked at the looping calligraphy. 'Her name is Charlotte Reid and she lives – or, at least, she *did* live – in Bayswater.'

It was a paradox. Mabel Tyler actually found the dead body but it was Iris Fielding on whom the murder had the more devastating effect. All that she'd done was to sit in her booth and issue tickets to the patrons yet she felt horribly involved in the event. Alone with Mabel in the manager's office, she was still trembling.

'I must have *seen* him, Mabel,' she kept saying as she wiped away tears. 'I must have sold him – and her, of course – a ticket.'

'Try to put it out of your mind.'

'How can I? It's frightening. I'll have nightmares.'

Mabel had the same fear but she tried to control her emotions so that she could console her friend. Iris had the greater need. Mabel Tyler was a slight woman in her twenties with a birdlike habit of looking quickly in all directions as if afraid of danger. Twenty years older and several stone heavier, Iris Fielding was efficient at her job but uneasy when out of the safety of her little booth. Iris was married but Mabel remained resolutely single, even though she usually responded chirpily to male patrons who flirted with her. A troubling thought struck her.

'You only sold him a ticket, Iris,' she said. 'I must have shown him to a seat and even chatted to him. Think how *that* must make me feel. I helped a killer.'

'So did I,' wailed Iris.

Before the older woman could wallow in self-recrimination again, the door opened abruptly and the manager entered with Keedy. He introduced the sergeant to the two women. Mabel managed a wan smile of welcome but Iris simply dabbed at her moist eyes with a handkerchief.

'Sergeant Keedy would like to take a statement from both of you,' said Brack. 'Inspector Marmion is in charge of the case but he's supervising the removal of the body.' He heaved a sigh. 'We're closed for the rest of the day. Is it worth opening tomorrow, I wonder? What if nobody turns up?'

'I'm not sure that *I* will, Mr Brack,' said Iris.

'Well, I'll be here,' volunteered Mabel.

'Thank you,' said Brack. 'I'll leave you to it, Sergeant. I want to make sure that the corpse actually leaves my cinema.'

He went out through the open door and closed it behind him. Keedy took his measure of the two women before pulling out his notepad and pencil. Iris was seated and Mabel stood behind her. Keedy suggested that the usherette should sit down as well. When she did so, he perched on the edge of the desk.

'I'll start with you, Miss Tyler, if I may.'

'I was the first one to see him,' claimed Iris as if it gave her seniority. 'I sold him and the woman a ticket before Mabel even set eyes on him.'

'Can you give me an accurate description of the man?' asked Keedy.

'Well, no, I can't. He was just one of dozens of faces I saw.'

'Yes, I had a look inside that ticket booth. You can't see very much from inside there, can you? In other words, you're not really able to help us, are you, Mrs Fielding?' Iris looked hurt. 'Let's go back to you, Miss Tyler, shall we? I know that this will be something of an ordeal for you but I'd like you to tell me what happened from the moment you entered the auditorium when the film was over.'

Mabel cleared her throat, then told her story without embellishment. Keedy was thankful for her brevity and lack of self-indulgence. Iris, he sensed, would be far more melodramatic, intent on wringing full value out of her chance en-counter with the killer. He impressed on both of them the importance of not talking to the press.

'Will I have to appear in court?' asked Mabel, worriedly.

'I think that's highly unlikely,' said Keedy. 'What you've told me is useful but it's not evidence that will lead us to make an arrest.'

'What about me?' demanded Iris. 'Don't I get interviewed like Mabel?'

'Not unless you have something significant to add to what you've just heard. As you say, Mrs Fielding, faces flash past you. It would be impossible to remember any of them in detail.' He waited for a response that never came. 'If you do recall anything that might help us,' he added, 'you can contact Inspector Marmion or me at Scotland Yard.' He put the notebook and pencil away. 'Well, that's it, ladies. Thank you very much. Mr Brack said that you were free to go when I'd spoken to you. My advice would be to leave by the emergency exit. Word travels fast in London. Reporters will already be lurking in wait outside.'

'I don't mind talking to them,' boasted Iris.

'Well, I do,' said Mabel, firmly. 'Come on, Iris. We'll leave by the other exit. I never thought I'd hear myself saying this but, to be honest, I've had enough of Charlie Chaplin for one day.'

CHAPTER THREE

When the commissioner walked into his office, Claude Chatfield was seated behind his desk, poring over a document. He leapt instinctively to his feet. Sir Edward Henry waved him back into his chair.

'Sit down, Superintendent,' he said. 'You're not on parade.'

'Thank you, sir.'

'I just came to see if there was any more news.'

'I'm afraid not, Sir Edward.'

'Oh dear!'

The commissioner was an impeccably dressed man in his sixties with a curling moustache that matched his wavy hair. At an age when most men had retired, he had remained in a demanding post out of a sense of commitment and patriotism. Chatfield was ambitious enough to covet the position that the older man held but he kept his long-term aspirations well concealed.

'Policing the capital would be so much easier,' said Sir Edward, 'if every one of our vehicles was equipped with telephones. Detectives could then keep in touch with us at every stage of their investigation.' He gave a hollow laugh. 'It won't happen in my time, I know that. We don't have the appropriate technology and – even if we did – I doubt if our budget would stretch to it.'

'There is another problem.'

'Oh?'

'Some of our detectives would be reluctant to keep us up to date with what's going on. I'm thinking particularly of Inspector Marmion. When he's in charge of a case, he doesn't make contact with me as often as I'd like.'

'Marmion is a first-rate policeman. He gets results.'

'He might get them even more quickly if he took me fully into his confidence. I know what it's like to lead a murder investigation. I could be of help.'

'I'm sure that the inspector knows that.'

'He's been gone for well over an hour. I'd expect a telephone call by now.'

'Marmion will ring when he's good and ready.'

'He'd better,' said Chatfield under his breath.

The commissioner stroked his moustache. 'We'd better brace ourselves, I suppose,' he said. 'The press will have a field day over this. A woman goes to the cinema for what she believes to be harmless entertainment and she gets herself killed. It's going to be on every front page tomorrow.'

'That's why I need all the facts at my fingertips, Sir Edward. When I hold a press conference later on, I have to be fully briefed. As for it being a harmless entertainment,' he went on, 'I don't think that's how some cinema patrons view it. They're tempted by the opportunity to take full advantage of the darkness. Cinemas are a licence for lechery.'

'That may be so in some cases, Superintendent, and I share your qualms about the subdued lighting. But I still believe that most people go in order to see films. I read somewhere that almost twenty million cinema tickets are sold each week. Just think of that – twenty million!'

'We don't need to wait until the Germans invade us,' complained Chatfield. 'The American film industry has already done it. And this dreadful fellow, Charlie Chaplin – born and brought up in this country – is a major part of it.'

'In my view,' said the commissioner, 'we should be proud of that. Chaplin is one of our most prized exports.'

'He's a British citizen,' argued Chatfield, 'and of

29

an age when he should be fighting for King and Country. People who fill the cinemas over here to laugh at him should realise that. They ought to be ashamed.'

Sir Edward gave a wry smile. 'Then I suppose that I must hang my head along with the rest of them.'

'Why is that?'

'I belong to the misguided masses you've just condemned, Superintendent. I not only took my grandchildren to see a Charlie Chaplin film last year but – dare I confess this? – I thoroughly enjoyed it.'

The house was a neat villa in a tree-lined Bayswater terrace. When their car drew up outside it, the detectives got out to appraise the building. Marmion looked up at it with approval.

'This is the sort of place you and Alice need when you get married.'

'Then I look forward to receiving help from my father-in-law,' said Keedy, 'because I'm never going to afford a house like this on a sergeant's income.'

'You have to put something aside out of every pay packet, Joe.'

'I have too many bills to do that.'

'Then make economies,' suggested Marmion. 'Drink less beer and buy cheaper clothing. You don't *have* to look so smart all the time.'

'Yes, I do, Harv. It's a matter of self-respect.'

'Your job is to catch villains. They don't care two hoots if you're wearing a Savile Row suit or a loincloth with leather tassels on it.' They'd reached the front door now. 'I doubt very much if anyone is at home.'

'Let's see.'

Keedy left nothing to chance. He rang the doorbell and used the knocker. The noises reverberated throughout the house but they brought nobody to the door. When Keedy repeated the process, there was still no response. A woman walked down the street towards them. Short, fat and elderly, she had a motherly smile.

'Can I help you?' she enquired.

'Do you live here?' asked Marmion.

'No, that's where Mr and Mrs Reid live. I'm their neighbour. I live next door.'

'You must know the couple well, then.'

'Yes, I do – my name is Mrs Cinderby.'

'Then we're very pleased to see you, Mrs Cinderby,' said Marmion, taking out his warrant card to show her. 'I'm Detective Inspector Marmion and this is my colleague, Detective Sergeant Keedy.'

She was alarmed. 'You're policemen,' she gasped. 'Has Mrs Reid done anything wrong? I can't believe that's why you're here, Inspector. She's the most law-abiding woman in the world.'

'Where might we find Mr Reid?'

'Oh, you'll have to go to France for that. He's in the army.'

'I had a feeling that he might be,' whispered Keedy.

'We're anxious to speak to members of Mrs Reid's family,' explained Marmion. 'But our immediate need is to get inside the house. Mrs Reid has met with an accident, you see.'

31

'What sort of accident?' asked the neighbour. 'Is it serious?'

'I can't go into any detail, I'm afraid.' He checked his watch. 'You strike me as an observant woman, Mrs Cinderby. Have you noticed anyone outside the house in the last ... well, let's make it two hours or so?'

'No, I haven't, Inspector. I spent the afternoon with my daughter who lives in Swiss Cottage. I've just come from there.' The detectives looked disappointed. 'But I can help you get inside the house, if it's important.'

Keedy rallied. 'It's very important, Mrs Cinderby.'

'Then the person you want is Mrs Bond across the road.' She pointed to the villa opposite. 'She and Mrs Reid are good friends. Talk to Alma Bond – she keeps a spare key to the Reid house.'

A glance from Marmion was enough to send Keedy striding across the road. Mrs Cinderby was evidently a woman who was on friendly terms with her neighbours. Marmion pressed for detail.

'How long have Mr and Mrs Reid been married?'

'Five or six years, I'd say.'

'What does Mr Reid do for a living?'

'He's a civil servant, Inspector – or, at least, he was. Then he volunteered and they made him a lieutenant. Charlotte – that's Mrs Reid – is very proud of him.'

'Are they happily married?'

'Yes,' replied the woman with a measure of indignation. 'Of course they are. You only have to look at them to know that. They're wonderful neighbours and they adore each other.'

'They have no children, I assume.'

'No, that's something for the future.'

Marmion's heart lurched. Charlotte Reid's chances of motherhood had been brutally extinguished in the back row of a cinema. He felt sorry for her neighbour. Mrs Cinderby was going to have a profound shock when she learnt the truth and the same was true of Alma Bond. The close friend opposite would have no need of the key to the Reid household now. Marmion glanced across the road. Joe Keedy was having an animated conversation with an attractive, fair-haired woman in her late twenties. After taking a key from her, he held up a palm to stop her from trying to follow him. Whatever Keedy said was unable to appease her. Alma Bond stood outside her front door with her arms folded and watched intently.

'She insisted on letting us in,' said Keedy, rejoining Marmion.

'I'm glad that you kept her at bay.'

According to her, Mrs Reid went out shopping this afternoon.'

'I see. Let's take a look inside.' He turned to Mrs Cinderby. 'Thank you very much. You've been a great help.'

As he moved away, she plucked at his sleeve. 'This accident she's had,' she said, face furrowed with concern. 'It's bad, isn't it?'

'Yes, Mrs Cinderby. I'm afraid that it's very bad.'

'You're late, Matthew.'

'I got held up.'

'Did you have a long meeting at St Martin-in-the-Fields?'

'No,' said Hearn, 'it was mercifully short for once. On the way there, I made a point of going down Coventry Street to that cinema. People were streaming in. I felt that I simply had to point out the insidious effect that a film like that can have.'

'Oh, I do hope you were careful,' said his wife, anxiously.

'I was doing my Christian duty, my dear. I was denouncing an evil.'

'But that can be so dangerous sometimes.'

Beatrice Hearn was a plump woman in her fifties with a handsome face marred by the deep lines etched into her skin. She wore tiny spectacles and peered over them in consternation. When they were younger, she'd always admired her husband's bravery and willingness to stand up for his beliefs. Now that they were older, however, she wished that he would exercise more discretion.

'Remember what happened to the vicar of All Saints,' she advised. 'When he admonished that soldier who was relieving himself against one of the headstones in the churchyard, he was given the most foul-mouthed abuse. War has *changed* people, Matthew. It's coarsened them. The soldier threatened to hit the vicar.'

'I'll go on saying what I'm moved to say, Beatrice.'

'I'd hate it if anything happened to you.'

'I can look after myself,' he promised, giving

34

her an affectionate squeeze. 'I feel sorry for the vicar of All Saints. Tom Redwood is a wonderful man but he also happens to be rather short and slim. I doubt if a drunken soldier would dare to threaten me,' he continued, pulling himself up to his full height. 'He'd have more sense.'

The Reverend Matthew Hearn had just returned to his vicarage. After hanging up his hat, he looked in the mirror so that he could smooth down some wayward grey hair. When he planted a kiss on his wife's forehead, it failed to dispel her frown.

'What was the film?' she wondered.

'Does it matter? All cinemas are an abomination.'

'Why was the one in Coventry Street so popular?'

'Because it had had the gall to put Charlie Chaplin up on its screen,' he said with vehemence. 'You know my views on that gentleman. He's reputed to be one of the richest men in the film industry. I call that the wages of sin.'

'Everyone talks about him. One of the ladies in the Sewing Circle admitted that her husband always takes their children to any film that Mr Chaplin is in.'

'Then I'll have to talk him out of it, Beatrice. It's tantamount to heresy, in my opinion. His children's minds will be hopelessly warped. As for Chaplin,' he went on, grimly, 'he may have gone too far this time.'

'What do you mean, Matthew?'

'After my meeting, I went back to Coventry Street.'

'But that was only asking for trouble.'

'I didn't have to stop people going in there this time,' he told her, 'because the cinema had closed for the rest of the day. Police were on duty to turn people away. The crowd was very restive.'

'Do you know *why* the cinema was closed?'

'I'd like to think that it was the answer to my prayers, Beatrice, but I'm not that foolish. The rumour was that something terrible had happened inside there. An ambulance was just arriving when I got there.'

'Was somebody injured in the crush, perhaps?'

'It's worse than that. One man claimed to have heard two policemen talking. The word that they used was "murder".'

'Good God!' she exclaimed.

'I did warn them. I did foresee something like this.'

She was aghast. 'Someone was *killed* simply because they went to see a film?'

'Apparently so.'

'Don't go anywhere near the place again, Matthew,' she begged, grabbing his arm. 'You could be walking into jeopardy.'

'The danger was inside the cinema,' he reminded her, 'and you'd never get me going there. Well, perhaps they'll listen to me now. Instead of pushing me aside so that they can watch a film, perhaps they'll realise that cinema is, by its very nature, an abomination. It breeds corruption,' he went on, striking the pose that he routinely used in the pulpit. 'Charlie Chaplin is not the blameless entertainer they all say that he is. Today he was seen in his true light – as an accomplice in a murder!'

It took them seconds to confirm their expect-ations. The house had been burgled. Using the stolen key, someone had let himself into the Bayswater villa and left clear evidence of his visit. Drawers had been pulled out in every room. Cupboard doors had been flung open. The jewel-lery box in the main bedroom had been emptied. While Charlotte Reid was lying dead in a cinema, her home had been pillaged. After a quick tour of the house, Marmion and Keedy returned to the living room. On the piano that stood against one wall were some framed photographs. One of them had been taken on the wedding day of Derek and Charlotte Reid. The pair of them beamed happily at the camera as they stood outside the church porch. Their home bore the imprint of their characters. Until the burglary, it had been bright, clean, well kept and tastefully furnished. Keedy envied the couple. The villa had been an ideal place in which to start married life. He and Alice would be thrilled to own such a house.

'She was a good-looking woman,' said Mar-mion as he studied the wedding photograph. 'And her husband is a handsome man.'

'He's going to be shattered when he learns what happened to his wife.'

'Yes, Joe. It will be a double blow. Mrs Reid has not only been murdered, it looks as if she found herself an admirer while her husband was away. We'll need to take some of these photographs,' he continued, reaching for a frame. 'One of them will have to be released to the press.'

'What about their respective families?' asked Keedy.

'We know that her parents live in Yorkshire because that letter in her handbag was written by her mother. We'll have to contact the police in Pickering and ask them to break the sad news.'

'That woman across the road said that Mr Reid's family lived in Watford.'

'Then their address must be here somewhere. See if you can find it, Joe. The Reids seem to have been fairly organised people. There's probably an address book or some correspondence from his parents. While you're doing that, I want to take another look upstairs.'

'Why is that, Harv?'

'There's something very odd about this burglary,' said Marmion, removing the last photograph from its frame, 'but I can't put my finger on what exactly it is.'

Marmion left the room and Keedy began the search. The three drawers of the little writing bureau had been pulled out and thrown onto the floor, scattering their contents over the carpet. The lid had been pulled down and the much smaller drawers in the desk itself had also been yanked out. Keedy got down on his hands and knees to explore the debris. Above his head, he could hear Marmion moving around in the bedroom. It was not long before the inspector returned. Keedy had a present for him.

'Hey, presto!' he shouted, holding up a little red object. 'I've found the address book.'

'Well done, Joe!'

'What did *you* find, Harv?'

'It's more a question of what I *didn't* find,' said Marmion. 'What do you see when you look around this room?'

Keedy got to his feet. 'I see a bloody awful mess.'

'But it's an unnecessary mess.'

'Burglars often act out of spite, Harv. You know that. When they see a nice place like this, they can't resist spoiling it. Some of them have been known to piss over the furniture or drop their trousers and leave an even nastier memento.'

'I don't think that's the case here.'

'So what do *you* see?'

'I see the work of an amateur, someone who's trying to convince us that he was burgling the house. Is it really worth killing someone to ransack a place like this? There are hardly rich pickings here. No, Joe, he's trying to fool us,' said Marmion, thoughtfully. 'He didn't really come for the jewellery and any cash that might have been left lying about. The killer was after only one thing.'

'What was that?'

'It didn't register with me when we first looked in their bedroom but I had this nagging sensation. That's why I went back up there. Mrs Reid's underwear is missing. There's not a stitch of it left, Joe. That's what brought the killer here,' concluded Marmion. 'He came to collect some souvenirs.'

CHAPTER FOUR

Fingerprinting was an obsession with Sir Edward Henry. Once it had been established that every individual had fingerprints unique to him or her, he saw the immense potential as a source of evidence. He had experimented with it in Calcutta when he was Inspector General of the Bengal Police and a member of the Indian Civil Service. Advances in the technique of collecting and collating them were slow but steady and he'd watched developments with keen interest. When he joined Scotland Yard as Assistant Commissioner (Crime) in 1901, therefore, he set up a fingerprint bureau and the system immediately bore fruit. Some of the early results were so spectacular that they sent waves of alarm through the criminal fraternity. Sensible villains learnt to wear gloves while at work but, predictably, most of them were not sensible.

Harvey Marmion also knew the value of the fingerprints. Shortly after the ambulance had arrived at the West End cinema, a small team came in search of them. Marmion felt that the best examples of the killer's fingerprints were on the throat of his victim, but he nevertheless asked his men to check the seats adjacent to the one occupied by Charlotte Reid. He and Keedy had then been driven to Bayswater and seen the glaring evidence of a putative burglary. Since so many items had been handled then tossed on the floor, the killer's fingerprints would be everywhere. Marmion had therefore sent Joe Keedy off to the nearest police station in the car so that he could ring Scotland Yard and summon a second team to do the laborious work of taking fingerprints at the house. The inspector himself had gone across the road to talk to the best friend of the deceased. She had remained defiantly on her doorstep.

'Mrs Bond, isn't it?' he said. 'I'm Detective Inspector Marmion and my sergeant will have told you why we're here.'

'He made a point of *not* telling me,' she said, resentfully. 'What's going on?'

'Might we step inside for a moment, please?'

She considered the request, then stood reluctantly aside so that he could enter the villa. Its interior was identical to the one he'd just left, though it was vastly tidier. When they were in the living room, he waited for her to sit down then lowered himself onto the sofa opposite her. Alma Bond was a forthright woman with more than a touch of pugnacity.

'Don't lie to me, Inspector,' she warned. 'I'm old enough to be told the truth. According to Mrs Cinderby, there's been an accident. That wouldn't give you the right to search her house. Something is up and I want to know what it is.'

Marmion remembered the argument she'd had earlier with Keedy. Alma was fiercely loyal to her friend and had refused to hand over the key at first. She was also very apprehensive. When she'd looked across the road and seen the detectives flitting to and fro past the front windows, she

41

feared that something terrible had happened to Charlotte Reid. In a sense, she'd prepared herself for dire news, so Marmion saw no point in holding it back from her. On the following day, newspapers would be telling everyone in London and beyond that a heinous crime had taken place at the West End cinema. Alma deserved to be given advance notice.

He took a deep breath. 'It's my sad duty to inform you that Mrs Reid is dead.'

'Dead!' gulped the woman, putting a hand instinctively to her chest. 'That can't be true. Charlotte was so careful with traffic.'

'She was not killed in a road accident, Mrs Bond.'

'Are you telling me that she died of a heart attack or something?'

'No,' said Marmion, gently, 'that isn't the case either. That fact is that ... she was murdered.'

Alma Bond was a robust woman, but the news had the impact of a blow and she reeled from it. Marmion had to reach out and steady her. Tears welled up in her eyes and she kept shaking her head in disbelief. When he felt that it was safe to let go of her, he looked around the room.

'Do you have any brandy in the house?' he asked.

'I'll be all right,' she said, trying desperately to regain her composure. 'Just give me some time, Inspector. I can't take it in yet.'

'I appreciate that, Mrs Bond.'

'Just give me time.'

Marmion sat back and waited for a few minutes. He could see her wrestling with the implications of what she'd been told. The one thing she had not expected was that her friend had become a murder victim. When she finally spoke, her voice had none of its earlier truculence. It was barely a whisper.

'How did it happen?'

'Mrs Reid was strangled.'

She blinked in astonishment. 'No, no,' she protested, 'not that, surely. Who could possibly want to harm Charlotte? She was the kindest person I've ever met. Everyone around here liked her. I've lost count of the number of favours she did for me and for others. When it came to helping people,' she went on, 'nothing was too much trouble for her. You ask Mrs Cinderby. She always said that Charlotte was a saint.'

'Well, she may have to revoke her sainthood,' thought Marmion to himself. Aloud, he was more tactful. 'The two of you were very close, I hear.'

'We were, Inspector. We did everything together.'

'Then Mrs Reid would have confided in you.'

'Yes, of course,' she replied. 'And I shared all my troubles with her. That's what friends do, isn't it?' Realisation jolted her. 'But we'll never be able to do it again, will we? She's gone for ever. I just don't know how I'll manage without her.'

'You say that you shared troubles with each other,' he probed. 'What sort of troubles did Mrs Reid have, exactly?'

'She was in the same position as me, Inspector. My husband joined the army at the start of the year even though there was no conscription for married men at the time. Derek – that's Charlotte's husband – also signed up. Their regiments are both in France. You can see why we were drawn together,' she said. 'We were very lonely. Charlotte was worse off than me because I have a baby daughter to keep me company. I put her to bed just before you and the sergeant arrived here. Charlotte was like a favourite aunt to Jenny. I don't know how I'm going to explain to her that she'll never see Aunt Charlotte again.' She bit her lip as tears threatened, then she regained her full voice. 'Where did it happen? I want to know,' she continued as she saw his hesitation. 'Nothing can be worse than the fact of her death. Don't spare my feelings. I need the truth.'

'Very well,' he said, levelly. 'We believe that Mrs Reid might have been throttled by the man with whom she went to the West End cinema in Coventry Street.'

Alma Bond goggled. 'But she told me that she went shopping.'

'Evidently, you were misled.'

'Who is this man and why could he possibly want to kill her?'

'I was hoping that you might be able to give us some clues.'

'But I didn't even know she was going to the cinema.'

'Were you aware that she had an admirer?' Face blank, she shook her head. 'Are you sure about that, Mrs Bond? She was very attractive. We've seen some photographs of her. Mrs Reid was the sort of woman who could turn heads.'

'Charlotte was married, Inspector,' she said with emphasis. 'She never forgot that. She was

44

married to a man she idolised.'

'Yet – apparently – she went to the cinema with someone else,' he pointed out.

'I can't explain that.'

'In other words, you'd say that it was out of character.'

'Yes, I would – very much out of character.'

'Was she in the habit of going to the cinema?'

'No, Inspector. Charlotte and I have been a couple of times while my mother was babysitting but that was it. She'd never dream of going to see a film on her own.'

'That's not what she did in this case. In my opinion, it looks as if she might have accepted an invitation from a male friend.'

After grappling with the information, Alma glanced through the window.

'What did you find in her house?' she asked. 'Sergeant Keedy said that you wanted the address of Derek's parents but I had the feeling you were after something else. What was it?'

'The purse and the house key were missing from Mrs Reid's handbag. We had a strong feeling that the killer would come to the house itself – and he did. The place is in a dreadful state and several items are missing.'

'You mean that he was *there* – just across the street?'

'Yes, Mrs Bond. I'm hoping that one of your neighbours might have caught a glimpse of him coming and going. We'll soon be doing a house-to-house search for a possible witness.'

'This is frightening,' she said, cheeks shedding their colour. 'A man commits a terrible murder then burgles the house of the victim. What kind of cold-blooded monster is he? Thank heaven I didn't see him or I'd have gone over and confronted him. Just think – I could have ended up like Charlotte.'

'Fortunately, you didn't,' he said, soothingly, 'so don't let that possibility prey on your mind. We need to catch this man and to catch him soon. Without realising it, you may be able to help us. Let me repeat a question I put to you earlier, Mrs Bond. And before you answer, I advise you to think very carefully. Now, then,' he went on, measuring his words, 'were you aware that Mrs Reid had an admirer?'

'No,' she replied. 'No, I wasn't.'

She seemed hurt.

Claude Chatfield was even more irritable than usual. Having been forced to delay the press conference, he laid the blame firmly on Harvey Marmion. Now that the inspector had finally returned to Scotland Yard, Chatfield was able to issue much-anticipated information to the waiting reporters. Before he did so, he went to the commissioner's office. Sir Edward Henry glanced through the carefully worded statement.

'This is admirable,' he said, giving the sheet of paper back to Chatfield. 'You tell them enough for them to bite on without giving away too much. It's always important to hold back certain details from the press. They do like to sensationalise things.'

'Editors always think in terms of banner headlines.'

'It sells newspapers.'

'I just wish that I could have held the conference at the advertised time, but Inspector Marmion kept me waiting for hours before he finally got back here.'

'Marmion is always very thorough. It's one of his many assets.'

'I should have been in possession of the main facts much sooner.'

'These things can't be rushed, Superintendent.'

Chatfield fumed quietly. He was always looking for ways to criticise Marmion and was annoyed that the commissioner held the inspector in such high regard. He handed over one of the photographs taken from the house in Bayswater.

'This is a picture of the victim,' he explained. 'I've had copies made to release to the press. This crime will make people think twice about going to the cinema so blithely. It will at least have one positive consequence.'

The commissioner studied the photo with mingled interest and sadness.

'It's such a tragedy,' he said with genuine sorrow. 'She had her whole life in front of her and it's been snuffed out like a candle. What do we know of her family?'

'Her husband is in the army so she lives alone. Marmion is taking steps to contact Mr Reid through the War Office and to arrange for both sets of parents to be told what happened.' He took the photograph back. 'Thank you, Sir Edward.'

'Some embarrassing questions are going to be raised, I fear.'

'Quite so – what was a married woman doing at a cinema with another man? If, indeed, that's what actually happened.'

'Was the inspector able to find the answer?'

'No,' said Chatfield. 'Mrs Reid's closest friend appeared shocked to learn of the possible rendezvous and, even though she lives directly opposite, she saw nobody letting himself into the house. Nor, alas, did anyone else in the street, it seems. The killer came and went like a phantom.'

'What about fingerprints?'

'I knew you'd ask about that, Sir Edward. It's something I've tried to impress on Marmion. Fingerprints could give us the breakthrough we need. Several were collected at the cinema, though we've no guarantee that they belong to the killer. At the house in Bayswater, however, he left copious examples. We can match those with the ones found in Coventry Street.'

'Very good, Superintendent – you'd better go and feed something to those reporters. In situations like this, they get ravenous. No, wait,' added the commissioner as Chatfield moved away. 'Let me see that photograph again. It looked vaguely familiar but I couldn't remember why.'

Chatfield passed it over. 'Here you are, Sir Edward.'

'She's a very pretty young woman.'

'I think she was also very foolish.'

'Of course!' said the other, snapping his fingers. 'It's Edna Purviance.'

'Who?'

'She's the glamorous film star who appears in Charlie Chaplin's films.'

Chatfield sniffed. 'I wouldn't know about that.'

'Mrs Reid is not quite so arresting, mind you, but there's more than a faint resemblance. To start with, she has the same hairstyle as Edna Purviance.'

'The name is new to me, Sir Edward.'

'It's often in the newspapers, Superintendent. You obviously ignore anything that's connected to the film world.'

'I do so as a matter of principle,' said Chatfield, proudly.

'Miss Purviance is, in some sense, a mirror image of Chaplin. Both have gone from anonymity to worldwide fame. Chaplin has worked his way up from music hall, of course, so there's been a steady progression. In her case,' said the commissioner, 'the rise has been more meteoric. Charlie Chaplin met her by chance in a cafe and was struck by her beauty. He hired her immediately.'

'I find that rather troubling.'

'To some degree, I do as well,' said the commissioner, returning the photograph. 'But the film industry is a law unto itself. Strange things happen.' He smiled in apology. 'However, I'm sorry to have detained you so long. Speak to the press and, above all else, get them to appeal for witnesses to come forward who were at the West End cinema today and who may feel that they actually *saw* Mrs Reid and her companion.'

'Nobody sitting in the back row will have witnessed anything,' said Chatfield with candid disapproval. 'I've no doubt that they were otherwise occupied.'

Even without being told, Ellen Marmion knew that a murder had been committed. It was the one thing that made her husband late home in the evening. She just hoped that the case would, at least, keep him in London. A previous assignment had involved Marmion and Joe Keedy crossing the Channel and going to Ypres in order to arrest two suspects in a rape case before bringing both men back to face justice. A more recent investigation had taken them to a prisoner-of-war camp in mid Wales and kept them away all night. Ellen didn't mind how late it was before he finally turned up, even if it meant that she'd dozed off in her chair. What she hated was the thought of sleeping in an empty bed while her husband spent the night elsewhere.

With a cup of tea beside her on the table, she was knitting absent-mindedly and thinking about her son. Earlier in the year, Paul Marmion had come home from France on leave. Ellen had been delighted to see that he'd suffered no physical injuries but there were worrying changes in him. Something had happened to Paul during his time in the army. The happy-go-lucky son with the cheerful attitude to life had come back as a subdued young man who seemed to be nursing a secret he refused to divulge. The pleasure of seeing him was therefore tempered by the difficulty of talking to him about the war. When they saw him off at the railway station, his parents had been quietly disturbed, worried that a return to the front would change their son even more, perhaps to the point where they no longer recognised him as the child they'd lovingly brought up.

The approach of a car made Ellen sit up. The vehicle halted outside the house and she heard a car door opening and shutting. As the car drove off, there was the familiar sound of Marmion's key in the lock. She went into the passageway to welcome him and to receive a kiss.

'Who is it this time?' she asked.

'A young woman in a cinema,' he replied. 'You can read all the details tomorrow, Ellen. I'm afraid that Joe and I are going to be very busy.'

'Are you hungry?'

'I'm always famished during a murder investigation.'

'Then it's just as well I kept a meal for you in the oven.'

After hanging his hat on a peg, he followed her into the kitchen where a place had already been laid for him. Marmion sat down wearily. As Ellen took the meal out of the oven and set the plate down before him, he felt an upsurge of affection. His wife was so supportive and uncritical. He didn't need to discuss the new case with her. Indeed, he deliberately kept her ignorant of most of the work in which he was involved. She preferred it that way. Her philosophy was simple. Home was a place for rest and refreshment. When under pressure at Scotland Yard – and she could detect the signs already – her husband needed a temporary refuge.

'What have you been doing all day, love?' he asked, slicing a potato.

'Nothing really, I suppose, and yet time has flown past. I did some shopping, went to church

– it was my turn on the cleaning rota – then I spent the afternoon knitting socks and gloves, even though Paul said that the soldiers have already got enough of both.'

'It's the thought that counts, Ellen, the feeling that you and the others are doing your share in the war effort.'

'It also keeps us busy,' she said, 'and that's important. We mustn't brood.'

She sat back contentedly and watched him eat. Meals would be taken at irregular times from now on and he would often be preoccupied. Ellen accepted that without complaint. She'd been married to a policeman long enough to learn how to adapt to the extraordinary demands that his job sometimes placed on him.

'Oh, and I made a point of calling on Lena Belton,' she said.

'How is she?'

'She's still in a complete daze.'

'Any woman in her position would be,' he said, sadly. 'It's bad enough to lose one son but she lost two in the same battle. That must have been a crushing blow for poor Mrs Belton. And she no longer has a husband with whom to share her grief, of course. He died last year. She must think there's no justice in the world.'

'It's certainly shaken her belief in God,' said Ellen. 'When I asked her why we hadn't seen her in church for such a long time, she was very bitter. It turns out that she refused to see the vicar.'

'Then it's just as well that she's got a friend like you, love. At a time like this, she needs all the help and sympathy she can get.'

'She may need it, Harvey, but she doesn't accept it very easily. Lena didn't even invite me into the house. She kept me talking on the doorstep.'

'Ask her to come here for tea or something.'

'I did. She said she'd think about it – which means she won't come. What upset me was a remark she made as I was leaving.'

He forked another potato. 'Go on.'

'She said that *our* time would come. We'd never understand what she was going through, she told me, until we had a letter to tell us that Paul had been killed in action. I didn't like the way she said it,' admitted Ellen. 'Lena made it sound as if it was ... well, bound to happen. I've been worrying about Paul ever since.'

'You've been worrying about him since he joined up. We both have.'

'It's got worse since I spoke to Lena Belton. She frightened me.'

CHAPTER FIVE

From the relatively short police statement issued to them, the morning newspapers had concocted some lurid headlines and some blood-curdling stories. All of them had used the photograph of Charlotte Reid and some had also included a stock photo of the West End cinema. Importantly, every newspaper had made an appeal for potential witnesses to come forward. The response was good, but the people who turned up at Scotland Yard were, for the most part, unenlightening.

'I saw them, Inspector.'

'Are you sure?'

'Oh yes, I've always been observant.'

'That's encouraging to hear, Mr Davies.'

'I noticed right away that there was something peculiar about the man.'

'Why was that?'

'He was tall, thickset, wild-eyed and he walked with a limp. The woman with him was much shorter and very frail. I recognised her picture in this morning's paper. What struck me at the time was that they didn't really look as if they were a couple, if you know what I mean. They were ill-assorted. My wife said the same. It was almost as if the young woman was there against her will.'

'Thank you for your help, Mr Davies.'

'But I haven't finished.'

'*We* have, sir.'

'Let me tell you about the sense of menace I felt.'

'What I've heard is more than adequate.'

'Don't you want a full description of him?'

'We already have several descriptions of him, sir,' said Marmion, fighting off a yawn. 'Unfortunately, none of them tallies with the others.'

'But my wife and I were only feet away from him.'

'The sergeant will show you out.'

Joe Keedy already had the door open to usher

the witness out of the room but Graham Davies, a lean, lanky, middle-aged man with a rubicund complexion, had a vital question to ask first.

He grinned hopefully. 'Is there any kind of reward, Inspector?'

'Yes,' said Marmion, 'you have the reward of knowing that you did your duty. The sergeant and I are very grateful to you.'

Taking his cue, Keedy almost lifted their visitor out of his seat and propelled him out of the room before closing the door behind him. He rolled his eyes.

'I don't believe that he even went to the cinema yesterday,' he said. 'Did you smell the beer on his breath? He was just another pathetic drunk craving attention.'

'The limp is a new touch, though,' said Marmion, glancing down at the list in front of him. 'Two people have mentioned a moustache, three gave him a full beard and four put him in army uniform. Then there was the lady who said that his eyes were too close together and the man who told us that the killer was a hunchback.'

Keedy gave a dry laugh. 'A hunchback with a limp would never get into the army and – whether he had a moustache or a beard – he'd certainly have no appeal to Mrs Reid.'

'I agree, Joe. She'd be a little more selective than that. Mrs Bond insisted that her friend was faithful to her husband. It would have taken a very special man to lead her astray.' He rubbed his chin pensively. 'That leads me to one conclusion.'

'What's that?'

'They didn't go to the cinema *together.*'

'That's what I'm beginning to think, Harv. It would have been too risky. Mrs Reid would have been afraid that someone she knew might have spotted her. Going to the film on her own was one thing but, if she was seen in the company of a man, then tongues would begin to wag.'

'In other words,' said Marmion, 'the testimony of every witness so far is useless. They all claim to remember seeing a couple in the foyer. My guess is that the pair met inside the auditorium when the lights were down.'

'It makes sense. Mabel Tyler, the usherette, told me she'd shown three unaccompanied women to their seats and thought no more of it at the time. One of them had a French accent, apparently.'

'Did any of the women ask for a seat in the back row?'

'Two of them did – but Mabel never really saw their faces.'

'She'll see the face of one of them in this morning's papers.' Marmion sucked his teeth. 'We're getting nowhere, Joe. We need a filter system so that the liars and the time-wasters are weeded out before they even reach us.'

'Have you spoken to our beloved superintendent?'

'I tried, but you know what Chat is like. He went on about limited manpower and said that we were the only ones able to separate the wheat from the chaff.'

'It's been all chaff so far.'

Marmion grimaced. 'Blame the German Uboats. Their blockade is creating a wheat shortage.'

'Shall I bring in the next witness?'

'Make sure that he or she has something worth saying.'

'You mean that you don't want a bearded hunchback with a limp?'

'I just want someone we can actually trust.'

'Let me see what I can do.'

Keedy opened the door and went out. He was away for well over a minute. When he returned, he led in a burly man wearing a dog collar. Introduced to the inspector, the visitor gave him a firm handshake. There was a glint in his eye.

The Reverend Matthew Hearn was eager to be heard.

In another part of the building, Claude Chatfield was keeping the commissioner informed of the latest developments. Police in Yorkshire had contacted the parents of Charlotte Reid and broken the appalling news to them. Though it had distressed them beyond measure, the father had insisted on coming to London to view the body.

'He's a brave man,' said Sir Edward.

'We need a member of the family to confirm identification.'

'It's hardly in doubt, Superintendent. When someone has been strangled to death, they never look at their best but the photographs recovered from her house make it certain that the victim was Mrs Reid.' He pursed his lips. 'I hope that the father knows what he's in for.'

'He'll need someone to accompany him.'

'Do we know what train he's catching?'

'Yes, Sir Edward. I have the exact time of arrival.'

'Then you can arrange for Inspector Marmion to meet him at the station.'

'Actually,' said Chatfield, 'I thought that I'd do that.'

'You're far more use at Scotland Yard, controlling the investigation and deploying your men accordingly. Besides,' said the commissioner, 'Marmion is at his best in these situations. He knows how to talk to grieving relatives.'

Chatfield was affronted. 'I've had just as much experience.'

'The decision has been made, Superintendent.'

'The inspector is busy interviewing witnesses.'

'Sergeant Keedy can manage that on his own,' said Sir Edward. 'This takes precedence. When he gets to London, Mr Reid is going to be in a very delicate state. He needs careful handling.'

'That's what I would have given him,' said Chatfield, trying to conceal his disappointment. 'But it's your right to make the decisions. It's also important for you to speak to the press, Sir Edward. When we held that conference last night, several of them asked if we – the Metropolitan Police Force – had a position on cinemas. What they were really after was a statement from you.'

'Cinemas are a fact of life. Our position is that we accept them.'

'But do we approve of them?'

'Not when they become murder scenes,' said the commissioner, 'but that eventuality has – mercifully – never arisen before.' He narrowed his eyelids. 'What are you trying to get me to say, Superintendent?'

'I wouldn't dare to put words in your mouth, Sir Edward.'

'But...'

'Well,' said Chatfield, plunging in, 'it is an opportunity for pointing out the dangers of subdued lighting during the showing of films. We know for a fact that prostitutes make use of cinemas. The darkness is ideal for ... what they do.'

'I've heard the contrary argument put – that a little more illumination would actually make illicit sexual contact even easier.' Chatfield was shocked. 'I've no evidence of that, mind you.'

'Cinemas promote immorality.'

'What would you do about it?'

'Personally, I'd have them lit better and regulated more stringently. Where indecency was found to take place, I'd have the cinema closed down. In fact, Sir Edward,' affirmed the superintendent, 'if it were left to me, I'd find a way to put every cinema out of business.'

'Then you'd be jumping out of the frying pan and into the fire.'

'I dispute that.'

'Cinemas have been replacing music halls for years. If you stop people from watching films in a dark auditorium, they'll look for entertainment elsewhere. You were a humble constable when music halls were thriving,' said the commissioner, meaningfully. 'They created lots of problems for the police. How many times were you called in to break up fights or to throw out inebriated patrons? You've probably lost count.

Music hall audiences were far more boisterous than the people who attend cinemas. Do you really want to go back to *those* days again?'

Matthew Hearn came well prepared. He had committed his sermon to memory and delivered it with blistering sincerity. Marmion had to hold up both hands to stop the tidal flow of words.

'So you didn't actually enter the cinema,' he said.

'I refuse to do so on moral grounds, Inspector.'

'Then why do you think you can help us?'

'I saw her,' insisted Hearn. 'I saw the young lady whose picture was in the newspaper. She arrived on her own, checked her watch then bought her ticket. I was no more than six or seven yards away.'

'And you're certain that it was her?'

'Yes, Inspector – the policeman will tell you the same.'

'What policeman?' asked Keedy, ears pricking up.

'The one I talked to outside the West End cinema. He saw me trying to persuade people to shun the place and told me that I was wasting my time. Well, in retrospect, I was not. I warned that the cinema was a cradle of evil and so it has proved.'

'We need to speak to this policeman,' said Marmion. 'Sergeant, could you find out who was on duty in that area yesterday, please?'

'Yes, sir,' said Keedy, getting up from his chair and leaving the room.

'Let me be clear about this, Vicar. When you were in Coventry Street, you were engaged in some kind of crusade. Is that correct?'

'I was on my way to a meeting at the church of St Martin-in-the-Fields but I deliberately made a detour to pass the cinema because I knew what film they were showing. Charlie Chaplin symbolises the wickedness of the film industry. I simply had to speak out against him.'

'He gives audiences a great deal of pleasure, sir.'

'It's wrong to divert their minds from the horrors of war. Instead of worshipping someone up on a screen, people should be on their knees in prayer, asking for our soldiers to be spared death and mutilation.'

'It's a prayer I say daily,' admitted Marmion. 'I have a son at the front.'

'How would he feel if he knew the British public is idling its time away in pubs and cinemas?'

'Paul would approve. The first thing he did when he came home on leave was to go to a pub with a friend and he saw two or three films while he had the chance. It was a form of escape for him. It helped to revive Paul. People can't be hypnotised by the war twenty-four hours a day.'

'I could not disagree more strongly.'

'Would you close down every place of recreation?'

'Yes, I would – and I'd start with public houses.'

'You don't need to lecture me about those,' said Marmion, raising a palm. 'My brother is a major in the Salvation Army. We've had long arguments about the need for temperance. Let's return to Charlotte Reid.'

'It *had* to be her, Inspector. I mistakenly took

61

her for a prostitute until the policeman corrected me. He made me take a second look at her.'

Marmion's interest was kindled. Hearn was not the sententious priest he'd first thought. Instead of describing a couple, he was recalling a young woman who had arrived on her own. That supported Marmion's theory.

'What happened then, sir?' he prompted.

'Well,' said Hearn, 'it was not long before the film was about to start and everybody had already gone in. I was about to turn away when this man ambled towards the cinema. He glanced at the photographs on display outside then walked away. Shortly after, he turned around, went back to the cinema and bought a ticket. There was nobody else in the foyer.'

'Didn't you try to intercept him?'

'No, Inspector, I didn't realise he was going in until it was too late.'

'Can you give me a description of him?'

'It will be a very hazy one, I'm afraid. He caught me unawares.'

'Any details – however small – would be useful.'

'Then I can tell you he was of medium height and solid build. He was wearing a dark-grey suit and a hat pulled down over his forehead.'

'Age?'

'In his early thirties, I suppose, but I couldn't be sure.'

'Can you remember any facial features such as a moustache?'

'He had a sort of craggy handsomeness – for want of a better description – but no moustache. There was an easy confidence about him.'

'Thank you for what you have been able to tell me,' said Marmion. 'I wonder if you can help us even further.'

'I'll do all I can, Inspector.'

'I'd like you to look at some photographs of criminals who've come to our attention in the past for abusing or attacking women. One of them might just trigger a memory.'

'Then I'll be happy to see them.'

'Of course, we may be barking up the wrong tree. The man you saw may have nothing whatsoever to do with the murder. He may simply have seen the film on his own. When Miss Reid arrived, the real killer could have already been inside, waiting for her. However,' said Marmion, 'it's always worth checking, just in case.'

'Show me the photographs straight away. And incidentally, what's happened to the cinema?'

'The manager decided to keep it closed today. It was not a popular decision but, in the circumstances, I believe that it's the right one.'

'It is,' said Hearn with a smile of satisfaction. 'That information has made the journey to Scotland Yard more than worthwhile.'

Joe Keedy was in luck. When he discovered that Police Constable Allan Vernon had been pounding a beat that included Coventry Street, he also learnt that the man's shift did not begin until noon. Since Vernon lived within easy walking distance, Keedy left Scotland Yard and set off on a brisk walk. The constable lived in a section house that offered accommodation for unmarried policemen. The building was attached to the station house where Keedy had begun his career as a young constable. He had pleasant memories of his time there, though he was glad that he was no longer in the uniformed branch. Keedy was vain enough to want to choose his own clothing and not have to wear what all his colleagues wore.

When he made contact with Vernon, he introduced himself and explained why he was there. The constable was a fresh-faced young man with a ready smile.

'I'm sorry, sir,' he said. 'I haven't seen this morning's papers.'

'But you must have heard about the murder.'

'Oh, yes – I was there, keeping people back from the cinema.'

'Had you read the papers, you'd have seen a photograph of the victim. It was recognised by the Reverend Hearn who is vicar of a parish in Holborn.'

'Was he the man trying to stop people from seeing the film?'

'That's right,' said Keedy. 'He remembers talking to you – though he didn't know your name, of course.'

'I watched him for a few minutes. He was persistent, I'll give him that, but he changed nobody's mind. Given the choice between Charlie Chaplin and a sermon, you can guess which one they picked.' He grinned. 'I agreed with them.'

'The vicar claims to recognise the victim as the woman that both of you saw going into the cinema on her own.'

'Don't rely too much on his eyesight, Sergeant. He thought that she was on the game. Yet she was

64

a good-looking young woman who was obviously respectable.'

'Not entirely,' said Keedy under his breath. 'Right, then, PC Vernon – do up your jacket and fetch your helmet.'

'But I'm not on duty for over an hour, sir.'

'You're helping us with our enquiries. When you're fit to be seen in public, I'm going to march you to the nearest newsagent so that you can take a look at a photo of Miss Charlotte Reid. We need you to corroborate what the vicar told us.'

Allan Vernon brightened. Walking the beat was both tiring and repetitive. All that he ever encountered in the course of a normal day was petty crime. He was now involved – if only tangentially – in a murder investigation. It was something about which he could boast to his friends. His first task was to impress Keedy.

'I'll be with you in less than a minute, Sergeant,' he said.

Then he shot up the stairs as if he'd heard the starting pistol in a race.

There was a spring in his step as Claude Chatfield walked along the corridor to the commissioner's office. In response to a knock, he heard the invitation to enter and he went into the room. Sir Edward Henry saw the quiet smile on his face.

'You look like the bearer of good news, Superintendent.'

'That may turn out to be so.'

'You have a suspect?'

'We have two, Sir Edward. They were picked

out of the Rogue's Gallery by a vicar from Holborn who happened to be outside the West End cinema at the crucial time.'

He explained what Hearn had been doing there and how – when he saw the morning paper – he'd recognised the murder victim as the person he'd seen going to the film the previous day. The vicar had also described a man who was the last person to go into the cinema. Two villains had resembled the man.

'How reliable is the witness?' asked the commissioner.

'With regard to the victim, he's totally reliable. It transpires that he was talking to a police constable at the time. Sergeant Keedy had the sense to track the man down and show him the picture in the newspaper. The constable agreed that it was the woman they both saw entering the cinema yesterday.'

'What about the suspects?'

'We only have the vicar's evidence there,' said Chatfield, 'because the constable had moved on before this individual appeared. But the more he thought about it, the clearer the man became in the Reverend Hearn's mind. He picked out one suspect immediately and a second one after long consideration.'

'Do they look promising?'

'The first one does, Sir Edward. His name is Neil Gunney and he's had two convictions. One was for assaulting the landlady of a pub and the second was for a more vicious attack on the woman with whom he was living.' He screwed up his face in disgust. 'Gunney knocked her unconscious with her son's cricket bat.'

'In short, he has a record of violence against women.'

'He could be our man.'

'Have him brought in at once.'

'Marmion has already sent detectives to Gunney's last known address. All that we have to do,' said Chatfield, airily, 'is to wait for his finger-prints to be compared to those that were collected at the cinema and at the home of Mrs Reid.'

'This all sounds very promising.'

'Once we have a match – thanks to your Finger-print Bureau – we can book an appointment for Neil Gunney with the hangman.'

'Let's not count our chickens, Superintendent.'

'That's not what I'm doing, Sir Edward. I'm known for my caution. I never make hasty as-sumptions or yield to false optimism. But I have a strange feeling about this case,' said Chatfield with controlled excitement. 'It's an instinct born of long years as a policeman. The finger points at Gunney. If I were a betting man, I might even put money on it.'

'This is all down to Inspector Marmion,' said the commissioner. 'It looks as if congratulations may be in order.'

'*I* was the one who insisted that he gathered fingerprints.'

'He'd have done that as a matter of course.'

'Marmion doesn't always follow procedure.'

Sir Edward stood up. 'I'll go and see him right now.'

'He's not in the building,' said Chatfield, sourly. 'He went off to meet the father of the murder victim. You'll have to wait.'

Philip Christelow, the father of Charlotte Reid, was much older than Marmion had expected. When he met him at the railway station, the inspector put him in his early sixties though the visible signs of anguish added a decade or more. An accountant by profession, Christelow was a stooping man of middle height with clear blue eyes that stared out through a pair of wire-framed spectacles. He had an intermittent nervous twitch that made the spectacles dance on his nose. When he removed his hat in the car, he displayed a bald head that was wrinkled with dismay. Marmion said as little as possible. The worst was over. The father already knew what had happened to his daughter and he didn't press for details. The journey to the police morgue was thus conducted largely in silence.

As a rule, Marmion tried to avoid the morgue. If identifications of corpses needed to be made, he always asked Joe Keedy to accompany the relevant family members. The sergeant was at ease among the astringent odours and didn't baulk at the sight of the instruments for use in the autopsy. On this occasion, however, it was Marmion's duty to be there, to support a stricken father and to get a firm identification of the deceased. As he led Christelow into the room, his heart constricted. The body beneath the shroud looked so small and defenceless. He introduced Christelow to the pathologist then waited for the father to give the signal. The old man needed the best part of a minute to gather his strength before he nodded. When the shroud was drawn back to expose the head, Christelow gasped and seemed on the point of collapse. Marmion put a hand under his elbow to steady him. The cause of death was all too apparent. The sight made Marmion feel queasy. Livid bruises surrounded the neck. Pain and desperation were written into the face. Even after death, Charlotte Reid had not found peace.

When Christelow turned away, the pathologist covered the face once more. Marmion put an arm around the visitor and helped him out into the corridor, easing him down onto a chair and sitting beside him. There was a long, awkward silence. It was eventually broken by Christelow.

'Charlotte was our only child,' he murmured. 'She was a wonderful daughter.'

'I'm *so* sorry this has happened, sir.'

'What is the world coming to, Inspector? Can't a young woman do anything as harmless as going to the cinema without being set on in the dark by some fiend? Why did nobody come to her aid when this stranger launched his attack? *Somebody* must have realised what was going on, surely.'

Marmion winced. It was quite clear that Christelow was unaware of the full story. Hearing that his daughter had been killed, he assumed that it had been as the result of a random attack by an unknown man. The fact that she seemed to have encouraged the killer's interest in her would rob the father of a cherished image of a blameless daughter in a happy marriage. Marmion was not looking forward to confronting him with the truth.

'Take me away from here, please,' said Christelow.

'Where are you staying the night?'

'At my daughter's house, of course – I wouldn't dream of staying anywhere else. It holds precious memories for me. Apart from anything else, I was able to lend Charlotte and Derek some money to buy it.'

'We'll take you there right now, Mr Christelow.'

Marmion was grateful that the father had not seen the house in disarray after the burglary or his memories would no longer have been quite so precious. The team of detectives who'd harvested fingerprints at the house had – following Marmion's instructions – tidied it up as best they could. It was at least in a fit state to receive a member of the family. No words were spoken on the drive there. Christelow lacked the energy to initiate a conversation and Marmion was content to leave him to mourn in silence. When they reached the house, the old man looked up at it as if he'd never seen it before. He had to be moved gently towards the front door. Marmion carried Christelow's suitcase and put it down when he took out the key to let them in.

They were met by a sense of vast emptiness, a house in mourning for a beloved occupant. Christelow had to force himself over the threshold. Picking up the suitcase, Marmion followed him into the living room.

'The killer burgled the house, I'm afraid,' he explained, 'so a number of items are missing. As for the empty picture frames,' he went on, indicating them, 'you can have the photographs back. We borrowed them for a short while but left the frames.'

'Where's the best one?' asked Christelow, plainly disturbed.

'They'll all be returned to you, sir.'

'Why did you take the photograph in the large silver frame? It stood on the mantelpiece. Charlotte's mother and I paid for her to have it taken. We have a copy of it on our sideboard at home. It was a beautiful photo of our daughter.'

'I'm sorry,' said Marmion, 'but there was no photograph on the mantelpiece.'

'Yes, there was. It's always stood there. It had pride of place.'

'I've no memory of ever seeing it, Mr Christelow.'

'Where is it?' yelled the old man with sudden rage. 'I want it back!'

Propped up on some pillows the man lay on the bed with a glass of whisky in his hand. He stared at the photograph in the large silver frame and smirked.

'Here's to you, Charlotte!' he said, raising his glass.

Then he took his first, celebratory sip.

CHAPTER SIX

When he'd first visited the house, Harvey Marmion had been examining the scene of a crime and had gone through his usual routine. It was different this time. He felt like an intruder in someone else's home. His instinct was to leave but he felt that he should stay for a while to offer some moral support and, if possible, acquaint Philip Christelow with the notion that his daughter may have willingly agreed to meet in the cinema the man who went on to murder her. The father had flopped into an armchair and sat there in a daze, too listless even to remove his hat. Marmion went off into the kitchen to make a pot of tea. It gave him something to do and might allow Christelow the time he needed to recover from the profound shock of seeing his daughter at the mortuary. Everything that Marmion needed was there, including a tray on which to put the teapot and the two china teacups. Adding a sugar bowl and a milk jug, he put a spoon on each saucer then carried the tray into the living room. Christelow had now taken off his hat. He rallied slightly at the sight of the tea.

'Thank you, Inspector,' he said. 'You're very considerate.'

'It's the least I could do, sir.' Marmion put the tray down on the table. 'In any case, I'm rather in need of a cup of tea myself. Do you take milk and sugar?'

'Yes, please – two spoonfuls of sugar.'

Marmion poured tea for both of them, added milk and sugar then handed one of the cups over. He sat in the chair opposite Christelow. Now that it had been restored to something like its original condition, it was a cosy room with an oval mirror over the mantelpiece and some tasteful paintings on the walls. Marmion could imagine Derek and Charlotte Reid occupying the very seats that he and Christelow sat in. He stirred his tea and wondered when he should introduce a third person into the marriage.

'Do you have any children, Inspector?' asked Christelow.

'Yes, sir, I have a son and a daughter.'

'How old are they?'

'They're both in their twenties, sir. Paul is in France with his regiment and Alice has joined the Women's Police Service.'

'Dear me! Are you happy that your daughter is in such a dangerous job?'

'To be honest,' confessed Marmion, 'I'm not and I was against the idea at the start. But Alice is a determined young woman with a mind of her own. As for danger, she's not likely to court that in the way that male officers do. Policewomen have very restricted duties and are not involved in tackling desperate criminals.'

'Danger lurks everywhere for a woman,' said Christelow, bitterly.

'We do our best to keep the streets safe for them, sir.'

'It's a pity you don't do the same in cinemas.'

73

'Your daughter's murder is an isolated case. We've had assaults on women in cinemas before but never anything like this.'

Christelow frowned. 'Why didn't Charlotte go to the cinema with a female friend – that Mrs Bond across the road, for instance? I know they're very close. My daughter would have had someone to protect her.'

It was time for Marmion to grasp the nettle. He took a firm grip. 'Our belief is that Mrs Reid felt that she *did* have someone to look after her.'

'What are you talking about?'

'She went to the cinema in order to meet a male acquaintance.'

'That's nonsense!' protested Christelow. 'Charlotte would never do that.'

'The evidence points that way, sir.'

'What on earth are you suggesting, Inspector?' demanded the old man with outrage. 'Are you claiming that she actually *knew* her attacker? I refuse to accept that. We brought our daughter up in a strict Christian household. She would never behave in the way you're implying. While Derek is away in the army, Charlotte would have no reason whatsoever to look at another man.'

'I can only tell you what seems to have happened.'

'Well, I'm not interested in your speculation. It's not only upsetting to me, it's very insulting to Charlotte. I *know* her, Inspector, and you do not. Put yourself in my position, man. How would you feel if similar allegations were made about *your* daughter in the wake of her death?'

Marmion backed off. 'I'd feel very much as you

do, Mr Christelow.'

'Then let's hear no more of it.'

'I was simply trying to prepare you for what might appear in the press.'

'I'd never trust a word that newspapers say. As for you, Inspector, all I require you to do is to catch the man who committed this foul murder. Please spare me any theories about Charlotte's private life because I find them abhorrent.'

'I understand, sir.'

There was another long silence, even more awkward this time. Marmion took the opportunity to drink his tea. Christelow merely stared into his cup. When he finally spoke, his eyes were glinting behind the spectacles.

'I think I'd like you to leave.'

Joe Keedy had never found the uniform worn by members of the Women's Police Service to be very flattering. In his view, it deprived them of their femininity and their individuality. There was one notable exception. When he left Scotland Yard by the main entrance and saw two women constables walking towards him, he picked out Alice Marmion at a glance. She somehow turned the uniform into eye-catching attire. They were delighted to see each other but – since fraternisation on duty was frowned on by their superiors – they settled for a smile. Alice's companion melted discreetly away so that her friend could have a private moment with Keedy.

'Where are you going?' she asked.

'We've just had a call from detectives sent to

pick up a suspect,' he explained. 'They've got him cornered but are not quite sure what to do.'

'Why is that?'

'He's climbed up on the roof.'

'Be careful, Joe! I don't want you climbing up there after him.'

'I'm hoping to talk him down.'

'What if he refuses to come?'

He grinned. 'I'll think of something.'

Alice was an attractive woman in her twenties with sparkling eyes and dimpled cheeks. Tall and shapely, she radiated good health. When she looked nervously in both directions, Keedy laughed.

'They can't arrest us for talking to each other, Alice.'

'Gale Force can do worse than that,' she warned. 'In her eyes, I've got two major defects. One is having a famous father. The other is being engaged to a dashing detective sergeant.'

'I can't believe that Inspector Gale called me dashing.'

'That was my word for you, Joe.'

'Well, it's an accurate one because I really have to dash. Apart from anything else, I've been able to commandeer a car. That's a real treat.'

'Where's Daddy?'

'He's taken the victim's father to identify the body of his daughter.'

'Daddy always gets depressed when he has to do that.'

'It's all part of the job, I'm afraid.'

'Do you have evidence against this suspect?'

'He's just given us some by avoiding police

arrest. Not that we were going to arrest him at first,' he went on. 'We just wanted a friendly chat with Mr Gunney. I was going to arrest and charge him afterwards.'

She was wistful. 'When will I see you again?'

'It will be whenever I have free time, Alice.'

'That's always in short supply during a murder investigation.'

'You know the ropes. Someone gets killed and out comes the midnight oil.'

'When this is over, I want us to do something special to make up for being apart so much.'

'I know just the thing,' he teased, 'we can go to the cinema.'

She pushed him playfully. 'Go away,' she said, fighting off the urge to kiss him. 'And, whatever you do, don't get up on that roof.'

'We want this man,' he said. 'I'll do whatever it takes.'

When he left the villa in Bayswater, the police car was still parked at the kerb. Marmion was just about to get into it when he saw the curtain twitch in the front room of the house opposite. Since he had an excuse to call on Alma Bond, he took it in the hope that it might lead to something else. When he knocked on the door of her house, it was opened immediately. Alma was holding a drowsy one-year-old in her arms.

'Hello, Mrs Bond,' he said.

'Was that Charlotte's father I saw going into the house?'

'Yes, and that's why I came over. He's just identified the body and that's always a harrowing experience for a parent. If you could spare a moment, I think he'd be glad of a friendly face and the chance to speak about his daughter to someone who knew her well. Would that be possible?'

'It would have to be later on, when Jenny's in bed.'

'There's no hurry. Mr Christelow is staying the night.'

'I'll get one of the neighbours to step in for an hour or so.'

'Thank you.'

It was clear that she was not going to invite him in this time. However, she'd lost the belligerence she'd shown on his previous visit. He hoped that it was because she'd had time to reflect on what had happened.

'I'm afraid that I inadvertently upset him,' he said.

'How did you do that, Inspector?'

'I suggested that his daughter had gone to the cinema to be with a man she supposed to be a friend. Instead – well, we both know the rest.' He looked at her quizzically. 'Do you still adopt the same stance as Mr Christelow?'

'Yes, I do – but it's not a stance. It's what I believe.'

'It's what you *want* to believe, Mrs Bond, but that's a different thing. How will you feel when the full truth finally comes out?'

'I'll be … disappointed in Charlotte.'

'So you accept the possibility that she did go to the cinema to meet someone?'

She was defensive. 'I didn't say that, Inspector.'

'I think you know more than you're telling me,' he said with a challenging stare. 'To that extent, you're deliberately obstructing a police investigation.'

'No I'm not,' she retorted.

'Do you know what I see when I look at you, Mrs Bond? I see a good neighbour and a loyal friend. I also see a shrewd woman who'd be attuned to the slightest change of mood or behaviour in Charlotte Reid. If someone had come into her life – even on a casual basis – you'd have been subtly aware of it.'

'Charlotte never mentioned another man to me,' she asserted.

He sensed that there was more to come and waited patiently until she was ready to divulge some information. She struggled with her conscience before she reached a decision. The baby, meanwhile, had dozed off on her shoulder. Alma rocked her daughter gently to and fro.

'The marriage was not as happy as I told you,' she said at length.

'Mr Christelow seems to think that they lived an idyllic life.'

'That's how it may have looked to him, Inspector.'

'How did it look to you?'

'They wanted a family. Derek was very keen on the idea and so was Charlotte. She was very excited when she confided their plans to me. But, as you well know, nature can be very cruel sometimes. They tried and tried. It was all in vain.'

'Did Mrs Reid undergo hospital tests?'

'She subjected herself to all sorts of examinations. My blood ran cold when she described some of the procedures. At the end of it all,' said Alma, hugging her daughter close, 'she was told that she could never bear children.'

'That must have knocked her for six.'

'Charlotte described it as a death sentence – and, in a way, of course, it was. She and Derek could never recover from the blow. They were deeply hurt and felt somehow inadequate.'

'I'm sure that you did your best to reassure them.'

'I tried to reassure Charlotte but I was never close to Derek. He was always a bit aloof with me. Anyway, she did her best to get used to the idea but he didn't. That's when the trouble started.'

'What sort of trouble, Mrs Bond?'

'Derek stayed late at work most nights and went on to his club. That's what he told her, anyway. They just stopped doing things together.'

'So a rift developed – it's a familiar pattern.'

'I'm certain it's one of the reasons that Derek joined the army. He wanted to get away from home. Charlotte did all she could to stop him but there was no holding him. He blamed it all on her, you see,' said Alma, shaking her head. 'He told her that he'd never have married her if he'd known she was barren.'

Marmion glanced over his shoulder. Philip Christelow, he thought, was probably reminiscing about happier times he'd spent in the house. Unknown to him, his daughter and her husband had effectively been living separate lives.

'I'd never say any of this to her father,' said Alma, earnestly, 'and I hope you won't tell him either. He's a nice old man. It would break him.'

'You can rely on me, Mrs Bond. As it happens, I doubt very much that he'd want to speak to me again – until we catch the man who killed his daughter, anyway.' He lowered his voice. 'What I'd like to hear about are the consequences.'

'Consequences?'

'Mr Reid couldn't cope with bad news so he drew away from his wife then actually left the country to get clear of her. How did she react to that? She must have been very angry but also very saddened. As a consequence,' said Marmion, 'she would either have become increasingly gloomy or ... she might have looked for male attention else-where.' He leant forward slightly. 'Is that what happened?'

'She told me nothing and named no names, Inspector.'

'Yet there was something, wasn't there?'

'Yes,' conceded Alma, shifting the baby to the other arm. 'There were small things at first – a new lipstick, a change of hairstyle and so on. Then she became a little distracted. Charlotte would talk to you for a few minutes then her mind would wander as if she was thinking about something else.'

'Something else – or *someone* else?'

'I've told you all I know,' she said, guilt-stricken at having been forced to betray a friend. 'Please don't come again, Inspector. It's hard enough coping with the fact that Charlotte was killed. Don't harass me any more.'

Stepping back into the house, she closed the door firmly in his face. Marmion didn't mind in

81

the least. He'd got what he came for and was content.

Keedy arrived at the house to find one of the detectives standing outside it. The other, he learnt, was in the garden to stop the suspect from escaping by that means. Neil Gunney was invisible from the front elevation and Keedy was grateful for that. Had he been visible to the whole street then a crowd would have gathered and it would have hampered the detectives. Keedy was taken through a side door to a large, neglected garden with an apple tree at the far end. It screened the house from the gaze of neighbours and made the little drama about to be played out a more private affair.

Neil Gunney fitted the description given by the Reverend Matthew Hearn. He was a chunky man in his thirties with the sort of rugged features that some women found appealing. When he'd heard the detectives banging on his door and saying they needed to talk to him, he moved fast. To escape what he feared would be his arrest, he'd clambered out of his flat on the top floor and got up behind the dormer window, intending to stay there until the visitors had gone. The landlady unlocked the door to let the officers go into the room but they saw no sign of Gunney. What gave him away was that he dislodged a loose slate and it fell past to the ground with a crash. The detectives went down to the garden to investigate and saw him up on the roof. They failed to persuade him to come down of his own accord. While one of them acted as sentry, the other went to the

82

nearest police station and rang Scotland Yard. As a result, Joe Keedy was there.

The sergeant decided to open negotiations with the suspect.

'Are you Mr Gunney?' he called.

'Who's asking?' grunted the other.

'I'm Detective Sergeant Keedy and I'd like to invite you to have a chat back at Scotland Yard. You'll find it rather more comfortable there.'

'Say what you have to say, then bugger off.'

Keedy laughed. 'Did you hear that, chaps?' said Keedy. 'He likes me.'

'We couldn't get him down,' admitted one of the detectives.

'It's easy. We send for the fire brigade and hose him off the roof.' He raised his voice. 'How would you fancy that, Mr Gunney? We'll use a hose to shift you. The fall might kill you but at least you'd be nice and clean.'

'You can't do that!' roared Gunney. 'It's against the law.'

Keedy became serious. 'What did you do yesterday, sir?'

'That's my business.'

'Did you, by any chance, go to the cinema?'

'No, I didn't.'

'Did you meet a young lady there?'

'No, I didn't.'

'Can you explain your movements yesterday afternoon?'

'I was busy.'

'Come down here and tell us why.'

'Leave me alone.'

'He's a right bastard, sir,' said one of the detectives. 'I'd half a mind to start hurling stones at him and knock him off his perch.'

'There's a much easier way to get him down than that,' announced Keedy.

He went in through the back door and was instantly met by the landlady, a fleshy woman in her fifties with a surging bosom and a quivering apprehension. When Keedy had introduced himself, she pleaded with him.

'Don't blame me, Sergeant,' she said. 'I didn't know what sort of a lodger he was. I'm very careful who I let my rooms to. I run a good, clean house. We've never had trouble with the police before.'

'What sort of a lodger is Mr Gunney?'

'He's been very quiet and well behaved so far. I've no complaints. He's out most of the day so I see very little of him.' An involuntary smile touched her lips. 'He bought me some flowers for my birthday.'

'I'd like to see his room.'

'He keeps it very tidy. It's the biggest one on the top floor. I'll take you up.'

'I can manage on my own, thank you. It's unlocked, I take it?'

'Yes, yes, I unlocked it for the other gentlemen. The funny thing is that I didn't realise that Mr Gunney was even up there. I thought he'd gone to work.'

'What sort of work would that be?'

'He's an insurance agent,' she said.

Keedy thanked her for her help then ascended three long flights of stairs to the top floor. A smell of damp greeted him and there was no carpeting in the passageway. Since Gunney's room over-looked the garden, it had to be the one directly ahead of him. He opened the door and stepped in. The landlady had been right about its tidiness. Keedy began with the wardrobe and was sur-prised to see two suits of good quality hanging in it. There was a small sideboard and he opened each of its drawers. Hidden away underneath a pile of socks was a bottle of unopened brandy. After looking in every corner of the room, Keedy got down on his hands and knees and peered under the bed. Two large suitcases lay side by side.

He yanked both of them out. The heavier of the two contained several more bottles of brandy and a canteen of silver cutlery. The other one had an expensive carriage clock, some silver candlesticks and an assortment of smaller items. What Keedy did not find was the stolen underwear belonging to Charlotte Reid. One thing was clear to him. The man up on the roof was not a killer. He was a thief who kept his booty tucked neatly away under the bed until he could dispose of it. Keedy put his head out of the window.

'Can you hear me, Mr Gunney?' he asked.

'I've got nothing to say,' replied the man.

'This is the best brandy I've tasted in years. I think I'll toss a bottle to each of my colleagues. They deserve it after watching you up there all this time.'

'Don't you touch my brandy!' howled Gunney. 'That's stealing.'

'Then you'd better come down and take it from me.'

85

'It's private property.'

'Yes and I'm wondering who it really belongs to.'

'It's mine.'

'Then I'll have another sip while I'm waiting. You don't mind, do you?'

'I bloody well do.'

Gunney's rage was greater than his fear of arrest. There was a scraping noise above Keedy's head, then a leg came into view. Gunney was an agile man who'd clearly been accustomed to climbing on roofs. Dangling from the edge of the dormer, he got a foot on the window sill, grabbed the stone surround then lowered himself into the room. He stared in dismay.

'Where's my brandy, then?'

Keedy gave him a benevolent smile then held out some handcuffs.

'I'd like you to try these on for size, sir,' he said.

Claude Chatfield was a man who backed his instincts and he hated being proved wrong. When faced with the possibility that he'd made a mistake, he was loath to admit it. He vented his frustration on Marmion.

'You're keeping me waiting too long for information.'

'I apologise for that, Superintendent.'

'I'm at the hub of this investigation. I need the facts at my fingertips.'

'I've brought you the two reports as soon as I could,' said Marmion. 'I've only just returned from Bayswater and Sergeant Keedy has not long finished interviewing Neil Gunney.'

'I still think he's our prime suspect.'

'The sergeant and I take another view, sir.'

'He was seen at the cinema by the vicar and identified from a photograph.'

'With respect, sir, it's a question of class. Gunney has a kind of vulgar charm for a certain sort of lady but I don't think it would have the slightest appeal to someone as refined as Mrs Reid.'

'There's such a thing as attraction of opposites, Inspector.'

'Thank you for pointing that out, sir,' said Marmion with light sarcasm. 'That possibility never occurred to me. The fact is that all we can do is to charge Neil Gunney with the theft and possession of stolen goods found in his flat. It won't take us long to discover where that haul came from.'

Marmion was careful not to mention the absence of lingerie in Gunney's flat. The man who stole it from Charlotte Reid's home would most certainly keep it, along with the framed photograph of her. Marmion's initial report of the burglary at the Bayswater villa had deliberately omitted any reference to stolen underwear. It would have scandalised Chatfield and sent him off into a tirade against sexual perversion. Though the missing lingerie gave an insight into the character of the killer, Marmion didn't want the information made public. The victim's parents had already had enough indignities heaped upon them. The revelation that their daughter had been consorting with a man of such bizarre tastes would have been wounding. Newspapers would pour salt liberally into the wound.

'I should have tackled him,' said Chatfield, tapping his chest. 'I know how to get the truth out of even the hardest villain.'

'We have the truth, sir, and we have the evidence to convict him.'

'Gunney has blood on his hands. He killed that poor woman.'

'There's only one way to substantiate that claim and it's to get a match with fingerprints. We have Gunney's on file and they're being compared with the mass of examples lifted at the Reid house. I hope that your instinct is sound, Superintendent.'

'It's never let me down before.'

'It would certainly save us a great deal of time and trouble to discover we actually had the culprit in custody. Mr Christelow might actually have a good word to say to me then. But I, too, have instincts.'

'Then you can keep them to yourself,' said Chatfield, fussily. 'And please stop questioning my line of reasoning. You're right in the middle of this case, Marmion. That often means you can't see the wood for the trees. I can take a more detached and dispassionate view of things. That gives me an advantage over you.'

'You already have that by virtue of your rank, sir.'

'Gunney is our killer.' He rubbed his hands with glee. 'Have him taken to an interview room. I'll soon have a confession out of him.'

'That may be so,' conceded Marmion, 'but I warn you that it certainly won't be a confession of murder.'

He turned to leave Chatfield's office, but his

exit was blocked by the sudden appearance of Sir Edward Henry. Having entered the room without knocking, the commissioner waved a piece of paper in the air.

'It's just as well you didn't place a wager on it, Superintendent,' he said. 'You were wrong. This report has come from the Fingerprint Bureau and it puts Neil Gunney in the clear. There's no match whatsoever between his prints and those that belong to the killer. The same goes for the other suspect picked out by the Reverend Hearn. The fingerprints we have on file from him are nothing like those collected in abundance from the victim's home.'

Marmion smiled inwardly at the glazed expression on Chatfield's face.

'Take heart, Superintendent,' he said. 'We can all make an honest mistake.'

'I'm still not convinced that it was a mistake,' said Chatfield. 'Gunney could still be our man. Look at his record. He preys on women and assaults them.'

'I'm afraid that a number of men are in the same category, sir. They prefer to hand out a beating in private so that nobody can see them. Our killer struck in a public place. That takes bravado.'

'It also takes a cold, calculating ruthlessness,' said the commissioner.

'That rules out Gunney straight away, Sir Edward. This case won't be solved as easily as that. The vicar's evidence was useful but not conclusive. There's no proof that the man he saw going into the cinema on his own was, in fact, bent on murder.'

'That's a salutary reminder, Inspector.'

'It looks as if the trail has gone cold,' said Chatfield, ruefully.

'Don't be downhearted, sir,' advised Marmion. 'We still have several avenues to explore and we may yet have reliable witnesses who were at the cinema. With the exception of the Reverend Hearn, those who've come forward so far have been of no use at all but there may be others with genuine evidence. People don't always remember things until they've had time to reflect. Let's not give up hope so easily.'

'I never give up hope,' asserted the superintendent, thrusting out his chest. 'You may recall a murder case I led back in 1912 – the victim was a man named Arthur Bramhill. We had virtually no evidence to go on but I refused to give up. Three years later, I sent the killer to the gallows.'

'Your tenacity was admirable, sir.'

'I'd like a somewhat quicker resolution in this case,' said the commissioner.

'I think I can guarantee that, Sir Edward.'

'Are you that confident, Inspector?'

'It's not a question of my confidence but that of the killer. To all intents and purposes, he got away with it. More to the point, he's enjoying the publicity he obviously craves. He's tasted celebrity,' said Marmion, 'and I'm sure he'll want some more of it. This is not the last we've heard of the killer of Charlotte Reid. He'll be back. He'll want another victim.'

The young woman had been gazing at the painting for several minutes, studying every detail as she sketched on her pad. After watching her with interest, the man strolled over and stood beside her.

'You have excellent taste,' he said. 'That's my favourite painting as well.'

CHAPTER SEVEN

When British armies fought in places like India, the Crimea and Africa, they were engaged in distant events that had no immediate resonance on the home front. This war was different. It could be heard, it could be felt and, as German bombs were dropped with increasing regularity, its acrid smell became familiar. Housewives might not be directly involved in the hostilities but, every time they went shopping, they were aware of the food shortages brought about by the limited number of imports reaching Britain. Many items became scarce, some almost disappeared from the shelves and others lacked their earlier quality. The country was by no means close to starvation levels but every household felt the impact of the shortages. One way to counter it was to get up early and be first in the queue.

'Good morning, Lena.'

'Oh, hello.'

'The queue will stretch around the block before the shop opens.'

'People are hungry.'

'I don't think much of this new type of margarine,' said Ellen Marmion. 'If there's not enough butter to go around, they should at least find something that tastes nice.'

Lena Belton shrugged. 'I just take what I can get.'

'They say that rationing is not far off. In a sense, I suppose, it's already here because we're only allowed so much of this and that. Do you remember the outbreak of the war when some people flew into a panic and bought large quantities of everything they could get hold of? Oh,' said Ellen, penitently. 'Sorry to bring that up. It was thoughtless of me.'

She chided herself for being so tactless. At the start of the war, Lena had had a husband and three sons. Only the youngest boy remained. It had not been kind to talk about events a couple of years earlier and stir up raw memories. Lena Belton was a round-shouldered woman with grey hair peeping out from beneath her hat and a face pitted with the pain of loss. Ellen had known her for years and seen her hit by the recurring deaths in the family. Anxious not to upset her, she tried to think of a neutral topic of conversation but it was Lena who spoke first.

'I saw your husband's name in the paper yesterday.'

'Yes, Harvey is leading another murder investigation.'

Lena was bitter. 'Why do some people have to *kill?*'

'I wish I knew.'

'You're not even safe watching a film.'

'It's unsettling.'

'Do they know who did it?'

'Not yet, but Harvey won't give up until they find him. He's working all hours at the moment and so is Joe Keedy, of course. That's really upset Alice. She knows that she won't see much of him until this case is solved.'

'How is Alice?'

'She's well, thank you. As you know, she joined the Women's Police Service.'

'I thought she liked being a teacher.'

'She did,' said Ellen, 'and I wish she'd kept her job, Alice was good at it. Oddly enough, I bumped into the headmaster of the school yesterday. He's as worried about food shortages as we are. Every morning he has the children reciting a poem by Rudyard Kipling.'

'Why does he do that, Ellen?'

'It's called "Big Steamers" and it lists all the foods that ships bring us from overseas. Mr Poole – that's the headmaster – has a son in the merchant navy so the poem means a lot to him.'

There was a concerted cheer as the shop door opened and the butcher emerged in an apron to lift his straw boater and give his customers a wave of welcome. The queue surged gratefully forward. Ellen and Lena never reached the shop in the first move but they were only yards short of the front door. It was Lena who brought up the war this time.

'Patrick wanted to go in the merchant navy,' she said.

'I never knew that.'

'His brothers were keen on the army but he always preferred the sea.'

'How old is he now, Lena?'

'He's almost seventeen.'

'Patrick is such a big, strapping lad, he could pass for twenty or more. When he gets to eighteen, he'll be conscripted. He can go in the Royal Navy then.'

'No he can't!' snapped Lena, eyes blazing. 'What a stupid thing to suggest! I've lost two sons to this war, I'm not going to lose a third. Whatever happens, Patrick will not be another useless sacrifice.'

Ellen was startled by the sheer venom with which she spoke. Lena Belton was adamant. One son at least would survive. Ellen suddenly felt uncomfortable standing next to her. She was glad when there was another surge and the pair of them got inside the shop itself and they were able to see what was on sale.

Though he arrived at Scotland Yard earlier than usual, Joe Keedy found Marmion already at his desk. After poring over a newspaper, the inspector flung it aside in disgust.

'Have you seen that article, Joe?'

'I haven't read any paper yet.'

'Don't bother with this one. It's pure drivel. I TALKED TO A KILLER. All she did was to sell him a cinema ticket. She makes it sound as if they had a long conversation about everything under the sun.'

Keedy picked up the newspaper. 'Are you talking about Iris Fielding?'

'Didn't you warn her to keep her mouth shut?'

'Yes, Harv, but I had a horrible feeling that she

94

wouldn't listen. The usherette had more sense. Mabel Tyler wouldn't do anything like this,' he said, scanning the article before giving a snort of annoyance. 'Yet she probably exchanged far more words with him.' He put the newspaper down. 'What has the morning brought us?'

'I daresay we'll get a few more bogus witnesses from the cinema but I'm still hoping for reliable new information from one of the patrons.' He picked up a sheet of paper. 'I've already had one nice surprise.'

'Where did it come from?'

'I'm not quite sure because his handwriting is atrocious so I can't really decipher his name. He's a window cleaner who happened to be working at the rear of a property in Coventry Street on the day in question.'

Keedy took the letter from him. 'Did he *see* anything?'

'He may have done, Joe. He mentions a man leaving the cinema by the emergency exit and crouching over the bin before putting something in it.'

'It must have been the handbag.'

'He doesn't mention that. His view must have been obscured. But the man then walked right past him. Window cleaners tend to have sharp eyes. They need them for peeping through bedroom windows.' They shared a laugh. 'What do you think, Joe?'

'His writing is worse than mine,' replied Keedy, handing the letter back, 'but he could be useful. Why didn't he pop in and tell us what he saw?'

'He's a working man. Time is money. He can't

afford to take an hour or more off to give us information that may turn out to be useless. At least we know where to find him today because that's a bit I can read. He'll be up a ladder in Leicester Square, cleaning the windows of the Cupid cinema. I think that you and Mr What-ever-He's-Called should have a chat.'

'I'll get over there this morning. And I'll make a point of passing the West End cinema on my way. If it's reopened and Iris Fielding is there, I'll give her a flea in her ear. What else have you got in line for me, Harv?'

Marmion sat back in his chair. 'I've been thinking, Joe.'

Keedy chuckled. 'I've never known a time when you're *not* thinking. My brain switches off when I leave here but yours keeps whirring away like a motor.'

'How did she meet him?'

'Charlotte Reid?'

'Yes, a relationship of some sort had obviously developed if she'd reached the point where she agreed to a rendezvous in the cinema with all that that implied. It was a big decision for her and not one to be taken lightly. So who was he and how did he wheedle his way into her affections?'

'We've no way of finding out. Mrs Reid didn't confide in anyone, and her friend, Mrs Bond, is as much in the dark as we are.'

'I remembered something her father told me,' said Marmion. 'He stressed that his daughter was raised in a strict Christian household. That means she would have been a regular churchgoer in Bayswater. Find out what church she went to and see what activities she engaged in.'

'She'd hardly have met her future killer at a church social.'

'Stranger things have happened.'

'I fancy that their friendship began elsewhere.'

'We need to build up a fuller profile of her, Joe. What did she do in her spare time? Where did she go? Speak to that neighbour of hers, Mrs Cinderby. She'll be able to help you. But don't bother with Mrs Bond,' said Marmion. 'I'm afraid that I exhausted her as a source of information.'

'Yes, she's a spiky lady, isn't she?'

'She was knocked sideways by the murder of her friend, but she was also more than a bit resentful that Mrs Reid hadn't even hinted that she had an admirer. Alma Bond is one of those women who like to know everything.'

'Right then,' said Keedy. 'So far I've got a nameless window cleaner and a dear old lady who lives next door to the victim. Is there anyone else, Harv?'

'Knock on doors in Bayswater. We heard how ready Mrs Reid was to help her neighbours. They'll all have something to tell you about her. Collect more pieces of the jigsaw so that we can fit them into place.'

'What about you?'

'I'll wait here until lunchtime in case any more so-called witnesses turn up.'

Keedy's face ignited. 'Does that mean I can have your car?'

'Yes, you can – but only if you bring it back in one piece.'

'What about Mr Christelow? He may still be at

the house.'

'Then give him a wide berth, Joe. He takes the same view as Mrs Cinderby. He thinks his daughter is a saint.'

'All fathers are ignorant of what their daughters are really like.'

Keedy blurted out the words before he realised what he was saying and he wished that he could take them back. His romance with Alice Marmion had been kept secret from her parents until the moment when the couple felt they were ready to reveal the truth of the situation. Marmion had severe reservations about Keedy as a son-in-law and not only because he was some years older than Alice. The sergeant had had a number of girlfriends in the past. Marmion didn't want his daughter to be gently discarded after a certain length of time like her predecessors.

'I'm sorry, Harv,' said Keedy. 'That wasn't a dig at you.'

'It's a fair point. I don't know Alice as well as I'd like to but I know her a damn sight better than Mr Christelow knows *his* daughter. Saints don't go to the cinema with strangers while their husbands' backs are turned,' said Marmion, pointedly. 'And there's something else to consider. Nobody ever achieved martyrdom by watching a Charlie Chaplin film.'

Life as a policewoman had been a continuous education for Alice Marmion. It had given her a detailed knowledge of the geography of central London and introduced her to the darker aspects of the capital. It had also helped her to understand the difficulties faced by her father and by Joe Keedy. Everything looked fine on the surface but she had glimpsed the crime and corruption that bubbled underneath. The huge influx of refugees from Belgium or France and the prevalence of soldiers and sailors on leave created a host of additional problems. London could be too vibrant at times. New clubs had opened up everywhere, prostitution was rife and – even with their watered beer – pubs were as popular as ever. Walking the beat was a far cry from the ordered world of the little school where she'd taught for a number of years.

Taking a deep breath and adjusting her uniform, Alice tapped on the door.

'Come in!' called a voice from inside the office.

Alice entered the room. 'Good morning, Inspector.'

'Ah, you've arrived at last, have you?'

'I was told that you wished to see me.'

'I do, I do,' said Thelma Gale, scrutinising her to see if there was anything in Alice's appearance with which she could fault. 'Shut the door.'

Alice obeyed the order then stood in front of the desk.

Inspector Gale was a stout woman of unprepossessing appearance who looked as if she'd been born in uniform. Her face was untouched by cosmetics and her hair was brushed back from her forehead and held in a tight bun. She exuded authority.

'Stand up straight, girl,' she said, 'and try to look more purposeful.'

'Yes, Inspector,' said Alice, drawing herself up.

99

'How many times must I tell you? We're on a mission. Policewomen are tolerated rather than respected. We must prove that we can do the job every bit as well as our male counterparts. Don't you agree?'

'Yes, I do.'

'Nobody is in a better position to understand that than you. Look at your father. Look at Sergeant Keedy. Wouldn't you like to see women doing the real detective work that they do?'

'I would, Inspector.'

'We should never settle for being second class,' said Thelma, slapping the desk with a palm. 'I believe passionately in the rule of law which is why I denounced the work of militant suffragettes. We'll never make advances by smashing windows in Oxford Street or slashing paintings in the National Gallery. That's vandalism. The women who did that were trying to achieve a noble objective by violent means and that was a mistake.' She glared at Alice. 'Well, speak up. Don't you have an opinion on the subject?'

'I believe that women should have the vote,' said Alice, firmly, 'and the war has given us the opportunity to prove our worth.'

'It's an opportunity that we must seize with both hands.'

It was a familiar theme and Alice had heard her return to it again and again. All that she could do was to stand there and listen. There was an underlying enmity between the two women. Alice admired the inspector for her efficiency and dedication but resented the way that Thelma Gale picked her out for undeserved criticism. Keedy always explained away the inspector's attitude as an example of a plain and undesirable spinster being jealous of Alice's youth and beauty, but there was another side to Thelma's envy. She resented the fact that Alice had privileged insights into real policing denied to her. As a result, she was often singled out for the full blast of the woman known to everyone under her command as Gale Force.

That morning, however, the gale was no more than a soft breeze.

'How is the murder investigation going?' asked Thelma, sweetly.

'I have no idea, Inspector.'

'Come, come – your father must have let slip something.'

'I haven't even spoken to him since he began work on the case.'

'Sergeant Keedy would have discussed it with you.'

'He has more sense than to do that, Inspector,' said Alice, resolutely, 'and I have more sense than to ask him. All I know is what I read in the newspapers. As it happens, I've hardly seen the sergeant since the murder took place. He and my father are working all hours. They're under great pressure from Superintendent Chatfield to solve a case that is – for obvious reasons – very disturbing.'

'It may have one positive effect,' said Thelma, sharply. 'Women will now be far more careful when they choose to go to a cinema with a man. However, that's not what I wanted to see you about.' She looked at the paper in front of her. 'I've been working out the new shift patterns and I'm glad that you won't be distracted by the pleasures of your social life.'

'What do you mean, Inspector?'

'I'm transferring you to night duty.' She smiled malignantly. 'I'm afraid that you'll be seeing even less of Sergeant Keedy for a while.'

Toby Ruggles was a ginger-haired man in his fifties with an unshaven face and piggy eyes. Joe Keedy found the window cleaner squeezing out his chamois leather into a bucket of water. Ruggles was smoking a cigarette. When he heard that he was speaking to a detective, he rolled the cigarette from one side of his mouth to the other but never removed it.

'We got your letter, Mr Baggles,' said Keedy.

'It's Ruggles – Toby Ruggles. Can't you read?'

'Thank you for making contact. Tell me what you saw.'

'It's all in the letter.'

'I wanted to make sure that you were a real person. We get lots of hoax letters at a time like this. Some people seem to enjoy giving us misleading information and sending us off on the wrong track.'

'I'd never do that, Sergeant.'

'That's good to hear.'

'This is my territory, see?' said Ruggles with an extravagant gesture. 'I've cleaned windows round here for years.' He jerked a thumb at the cinema behind him. 'The Cupid is my favourite.'

'The West End is much bigger and grander.'

'Yeah – but the manager is much stingier. They

102

pay me well at the Cupid and I get two free tickets every time. Me and the missus started coming here when it was known as the Palm Court. God knows why they changed the name.'

'Let's go back to the day of the murder.'

'If you like,' said Ruggles, shaking his head so that he shook off the ash at the tip of his cigarette. 'I was at the back of Coventry Street, cleaning a window.'

'How far away from the West End cinema were you?'

'Fifteen or twenty yards at most. I was up my ladder.'

'What did you see?'

'Well, it's like I said in my letter. This bloke comes out of the emergency exit and I thinks to myself that it's a funny thing to do. I mean, it's a Charlie Chaplin film. They're always good. When he opened the door, I could hear the laughter inside. Why was he leaving before the film was over?'

'Go on.'

'There was this bin outside and he lifted the lid. Because he had his back to me, I couldn't see what he put inside. Next minute, he legs it down the street and goes right past me.'

Keedy produced his notebook. 'Could you describe him to me?'

'Yeah – I got two good eyes, Sergeant. You need them in this business to see that you've done a proper job. I don't cheat like some of the others. They never get right into the corners, especially on first-floor windows which the customer can only see from below. They get their money's worth from me.'

'I'm still waiting for that description.'

'He was shorter than you – but not all that much – and he had the same sort of shape. I reckon he was about the same age as well, Sergeant. In fact,' he went on, removing the cigarette so that he could emit a throaty laugh, 'it might almost have *been* you.' Dropping the cigarette to the floor, he stamped on it. 'He wore this grey suit. It was smart but not as good as yours, and I noticed how clean his shoes were. I mean, they were gleaming.'

'You saw nothing of his face, I assume,' said Keedy, jotting down the details.

'He was wearing a hat so I only saw a little,' said Ruggles, 'but he could shift, I can tell you that. I've never seen anyone walk that fast.'

'Was anyone else about?'

'Yeah – there was quite a few people but they didn't take any notice of him. I did, Sergeant. That's why you got that letter from me.'

'It's very public-spirited of you.'

'If truth be told, it was the missus who made me write it.'

'Please thank her on my behalf.'

Ruggles began to roll himself another cigarette. Closing his notebook, Keedy walked away. The chat with the chain-smoking window cleaner had produced one valuable fact. His description of the killer was almost identical to the one given by the Reverend Matthew Hearn. Charlotte Reid *had* gone into the cinema first. In all probability, the last person to enter it was the man who intended to strangle her to death.

The morning had been largely unproductive for Harvey Marmion. He interviewed two people who claimed to have been at the cinema on the fatal day but learnt nothing of value from either of them. Superintendent Chatfield then descended on him and badgered him for more information that could be released to the press. To get rid of him, the inspector promised that he would have something new to say about the killer at the end of the day. Left alone in his office, he wondered what on earth it could be. There was a tap on his door and a policeman showed in a visitor. Well dressed and well groomed, the newcomer was in his late thirties. Marmion wondered why he was so diffident.

'May I help you, sir?' he asked.

'I'm not sure,' said the man.

'Have you come about the appeal in the newspaper?'

'Yes, I have.'

'Then please sit down,' said Marmion, indicating the chair.

The man sat down. 'I can't stay long.'

'What was the name, sir?'

'It's ... Mr Smith.'

'Then I'm grateful that you came to see me, Mr Smith.'

During his career as a policeman, Marmion had met scores of people who gave the surname of Smith. Some were genuine but most wanted anonymity. The visitor was one of the latter. Marmion respected his feelings.

'Were you at the West End cinema on the day

concerned, sir?' he said.

'We were, Inspector – that's to say, I did go there with a friend. We like Charlie Chaplin films. The place was quite busy so the usherette showed us to the back row. We wanted to sit much closer but there were no two seats together.'

'I understand, Mr Smith.'

'Before the film started,' said the other, 'this young woman was shown to a seat in the back row. The usherette's torch lit the woman's face for a split second and I saw how pretty she was.'

'Are you telling me that it was the woman in the newspaper photograph?'

'It could very well be, though I didn't get a proper look at her. It was dark and there were two empty seats between us and her. Then the film started and all our attention went on that. After a while – out of the corner of my eye – I saw this man take the seat on the other side of her. She made a noise as if she were pleased to see him. They were only four or five feet away from us.'

'This is very valuable information, sir,' said Marmion, encouragingly. 'What else do you remember?'

'Not a lot, Inspector, because we were so engrossed in the film. But they didn't seem to be watching it at all. They were ... very close together and that went on until the man suddenly disappeared. I don't know why. When the lights went up, the woman seemed to be asleep – though how anyone could nod off during a Chaplin film, I can't imagine. We left her there and went out at the other end of the row.' He gave a nervous laugh. 'That's all I can tell you, sir.'

'It confirms what we suspected, Mr Smith.'

'We were horrified to read what had been happening so close to us.'

'Your friend must have been extremely upset.'

'Yes, Inspector, she was unable to come to work next day.' The man rose to his feet. 'Talking of work, I must get back to the office but I felt that I had to come. Do you know who he is? Have you identified the killer yet?'

'Let's just say that your testimony is a big step towards an arrest, Mr Smith.'

He offered his hand and was met by a clammy palm. 'Goodbye, sir, and thank you.'

The visitor looked as if a great load had been lifted from his shoulders. Marmion watched him go then made a few notes. Two things were evident. The man was married – he was wearing a wedding ring – and his companion in the cinema was not his wife. He'd also lied about not wishing to sit in the back row. Marmion's guess was that he employed the woman he took to the film. If he was the boss, he'd be able to take time off during the afternoon. It was not Marmion's business to pry into their relationship. All that he wanted was a genuine witness and he'd just heard testimony from one who'd sat uncomfortably close to a murder.

Mrs Cinderby was thrilled to see Joe Keedy again. She not only invited him in, she plied him with cups of tea and home-made biscuits that were tastier than any he'd eaten before. She was lonely. That was why she was so glad of company. Because it was a fine day, her husband had gone off to his bowls club. From the way she complained about his desertion, Keedy had the impression that it was his regular escape route. Calling on the old lady saved him a great deal of time. She was able to tell him all that he needed to know about Charlotte Reid's many activities at the church. When she was alive, she'd been a dedicated parishioner who was on the flower rota and who helped to prepare refreshments in the church hall after certain services.

'She loved that church, you see,' said Mrs Cinderby, fondly. 'She and Derek were married there.'

'We were told that she was very popular with the neighbours.'

'Oh, she was, Sergeant.'

Off she went and all that Keedy could do was to marvel at her knowledge of the rest of the people in the street. She went down one side then worked up the other, listing the families with which Charlotte had had a close connection. It was almost as if Mrs Cinderby had conducted a census. Alma Bond was picked out once again as the dead woman's bosom friend and the old woman spoke kindly of her. What was clear to Keedy was that there was a strong sense of community in the street. Many families had sent off young men to the war and, in a few cases, some had either lost them in action or received them back home with their crippling injuries. Everyone was drawn together by adversity.

Keedy was deeply grateful. He wouldn't have to bruise his knuckles by knocking on door after door. Most of the information he needed had been kindly provided by Mrs Cinderby.

'I saw the inspector bringing Mr Christelow here yesterday,' she said with evident disappointment, 'and I hoped that I'd be able to speak to Charlotte's father. My husband and I got to know him quite well, you see. But he wouldn't even answer the door. He just wanted to be alone. I wasn't even able to offer my condolences.'

'I'm sorry to hear that,' said Keedy, closing his notebook and rising from the chair. 'Thank you for everything. You've been a godsend, and those biscuits of yours would win prizes.' She tittered. 'I've learnt everything I needed to know so I'll be on my way.'

'It was a pleasure to see you again, Sergeant.'

Mrs Cinderby showed him to the door and opened it for him.

'She was a busy woman,' he said. 'I don't know how she fitted in so many activities. Mrs Reid seems to have known almost everyone in the street.'

'Oh, she had friends elsewhere as well.'

'Really? You didn't mention those.'

'There was Mrs Stothart, for instance. She lives on the main road. She and Charlotte saw each other every week. They went to art classes together.'

CHAPTER EIGHT

'That's unfair, Alice!'

'Someone has to do it.'

'Yes, but why must it be you?'

'There's an easy answer to that, I'm afraid.'

'Inspector Gale is picking on you again.'

'I've learnt to live with it, Mummy.'

'You ought to complain to your father.'

'That's the last thing I'm going to do,' said Alice, firmly. 'First of all, he has no authority where the Women's Police Service is concerned. Second, it's exactly what Gale Force *wants* me to do. Then she'll be able to taunt me with the fact that I'll never make a policewoman if I run off to Daddy like a cry baby.'

'What about Joe? Couldn't he have a quiet word with the inspector?'

'Joe would never do it and I would never ask him. It's something I must sort out for myself, Mummy. And the night shift is not as bad as it sounds. I'll be coming off duty at midnight.'

'Yes,' said Ellen, anxiously, 'but think how bad London can get after dark. I remember the sorts of things that your father had to deal with when he was in uniform on a night shift. I'd hate you to be caught up in that kind of trouble.'

'I'll be fine, don't worry. And there will be two of us, remember.'

Ellen Marmion was not reassured. She was very

pleased when her daughter called at the house after work. Her chances of seeing Alice had been rather slim of late, so it was in the nature of a treat. Over tea and cake, they caught up with each other's news.

'You won't see much of Joe if you're on duty every evening, Alice.'

'That's one of the reasons the inspector did it. Not that I'd hope to spend much time with Joe while this investigation is going on,' said Alice, resignedly. 'He's like Daddy. He gets completely immersed in a case. Even when I'm with him at times like this, his mind is elsewhere. However,' she added, 'that's enough of my moans. What sort of a day have you had?'

'Well, it got off to a difficult start, to be honest.'

'Why – what happened?'

'I met Lena Belton in the queue at the butcher's,' recalled Ellen. 'She's always been a bit prickly but she was downright rude this morning.'

She told Alice about the friction that had taken place and how the other woman had stalked off without saying another word to her. Knowing that her mother would never give offence deliberately, Alice was upset on her behalf.

'I don't think she was angry with you, Mummy. It's the situation she's in.'

'Yes, I know, and she has my full sympathy. But it's not easy to feel sorry for someone when she bawls at you in public like that. And I'm not the only one. Lena had a row with Mrs Mitchell last week.'

'Mrs Mitchell *never* has rows. She's a harmless

old thing.'

'Lena Belton doesn't think so. When Mrs Mitchell invited her round for tea, Lena turned on her and said she didn't need people poking into her private life. It really hurt Mrs Mitchell. She was at the butcher's this morning,' explained Ellen. 'When she saw me under fire, she waited outside to have a word with me.'

'What did she say?'

'Well, it turns out that Lena has sent Patrick away.'

'Whatever for?' asked Alice, mystified. 'In her situation, the one thing she needs is companionship. Does she really *want* to live alone?'

'Apparently she made Patrick give up his job at the brewery and packed him off to a cousin of hers who has a farm. Patrick has been there before and likes working with animals.'

'That still doesn't explain why he's gone.'

'Lena doesn't want to lose her only living son, Alice. Now that we're being bombed more often, she thinks that London is too dangerous. So she sent Patrick off to Warwickshire because she believes he'll be much safer there.'

Alice could understand the logic behind the decision. She knew the Belton family well. As a teenager, she'd gone out for a time with Norman Belton, the eldest of the three boys, and she'd felt a sharp pang when she heard of his death. When the name of Gregory Belton, the other brother, joined the list of those killed in action, she'd been shocked and sympathetic. Alice thought that Patrick would be drawn even closer to his mother but that, it transpired, was not the case. He was being exiled to the Midland countryside for his own protection.

'This war could drag on for years,' Alice predicted.

'That's what Paul said and he's in the best position to know.'

'They could still be in need of fresh blood when Patrick is old enough to be called up. What's going to happen then, Mummy?'

'I dread to think,' said Ellen. 'The navy is going to have to fight tooth and nail against Lena Belton to get her last son into uniform. She swore that Patrick was not going to suffer the same fate as his brothers – and she meant it.'

Marmion and Keedy had just finished pooling their information when Superintendent Claude Chatfield marched unannounced into the inspector's office.

'Have you prepared that press statement yet?' he demanded.

'Sergeant Keedy and I are in the process of working on it, sir,' said Marmion.

'I need it on my desk in half an hour.'

'It will be there, Superintendent.'

'Wouldn't it be better if the inspector issued the statement himself?' asked Keedy, artlessly. 'After all, he's at the very heart of the investigation and can field questions more easily.'

'I can do all that's necessary,' said Chatfield, peremptorily.

'Inspector Marmion knows how to handle a press conference. And there's another factor to bear in mind, sir. After solving that case involving

113

the deaths of five munition workers, he's held in high regard by the newspapers.'

The superintendent bristled. 'Are you saying that I'm *not?*'

'No, no, sir. It's just that the inspector has ... a special skill.'

'If I do,' said Marmion, defusing the argument, 'it's because I've learnt from watching the superintendent in action. He's the right person to give the statement to the press and we must make sure it's accurate.'

'Thank you, Inspector,' said Chatfield, only partially mollified.

After shooting Keedy a look of utter disdain, he strode out of the room. Marmion closed the door after him before the pair of them dared to laugh.

'That ruffled his feathers, Joe.'

'I hate it when Chat behaves like that. It's not all that long ago when you and he were the same rank. Power has gone to his head.'

'He's not entirely to blame,' said Marmion, tolerantly. 'You know how the system works. The commissioner puts pressure on him. Chat leans heavily on us. We take it out on our detective constables and they probably go home and kick the cat. Policing revolves around the structure of command.'

'You'll be telling me next that it's in the nature of the beast.'

'It is – and Chat is the beast.' They laughed again. 'Let's finish the statement and get him off our back.' He looked down at the paper in front of him. 'We can release details of his height, age and appearance. Both the vicar and the window

114

cleaner agree that he was well dressed.'

'Toby Ruggles mentioned his gleaming shoes.'

'Yes, I wondered about that, Joe. We're looking for a man who's strong enough to kill, bold enough to do so in a cinema and who takes care to polish his shoes. What does that tell you?'

'He might have been in the army.'

'Or in the police force,' said Marmion, thoughtfully. 'When I was a young constable, our sergeant was a stickler about appearance. He always inspected our boots. And if you dared to wear your helmet at the wrong angle, you got a mouthful of abuse that would turn the air blue.'

'I'm not so sure about him being a copper, Harv,' said Keedy. 'We're trained to *save* lives not to take them.'

'There's always one bad apple in the barrel.'

'We've just met him – Superintendent Chat.'

Marmion read through what he'd written then looked up at Keedy.

'Tell me about that woman in Bayswater – Mrs Stothart, was it?'

'That's right – Christine Stothart. She's a nice lady, though she brews the most evil cup of tea. It was like drinking engine oil,' said Keedy. 'Anyway, she and Mrs Reid went to the same church and became good friends. When they saw an advert for art classes at a local school, they decided to try them out. It was only one evening a week but they were surprised how much you can learn in two hours. And they always had plenty of homework.'

'Did they use oil paints?'

'No, it was only watercolours.'

'I always fancied being an artist in my spare time,' said Marmion, reflectively, 'but I never have any. The only painting I ever do in our house is when I give up part of my holiday to decorate a room.'

'Mrs Stothart was quite honest about it. She said that Mrs Reid had far more flair than her. And she took a real interest in art, going off to galleries and so forth. She usually went on her own because Mrs Stothart has two children so she didn't have the same freedom of movement.'

'That raises an interesting question, Joe,' said Marmion, scratching his head. 'If Charlotte Reid was so keen on art and she was given regular homework, why didn't we see any of her paintings at the house?'

Sitting at the table, the man opened the portfolio and went through the paintings one by one. Some were mere sketches in charcoal and others were only half-finished, but all of them betrayed real talent. It was the completed paintings that aroused his interest. Charlotte Reid knew how to use watercolours and get the best out of them. While he admired her skill, however, he deplored her choice of subject. She had painted a bowl of flowers, a basket of fruit and a black cat basking on a mat in front of a blazing fire. There were also some uninspiring landscapes. He put them back in the portfolio and closed it before tying the ribbon. Then he glanced at the silver-framed photograph of the artist that stood on his mantelpiece.

'Oh, Charlotte,' he said with real regret. 'You

should have come to me, my darling. I couldn't teach you *how* to paint but I could certainly have told you what subjects to choose.'

As he stepped into the corridor, Marmion saw the pair of them walking towards him. Sir Edward Henry looked as spruce as ever while Chatfield had an air of unassailable self-satis-faction.

'The commissioner complimented me on the way I held the press conference,' he said. 'You might pass on that information to Sergeant Keedy.'

'I'll make a point of doing so, sir,' said Marmion.

'You must take some of the plaudits, Inspector,' observed the commissioner. 'It was, after all, your statement that was read out.'

'Thank you, Sir Edward.'

'Unfortunately, the press always want instant results.'

'They won't get them, I'm afraid. This case will take time to solve. When the new information appears in tomorrow's newspapers, we should – with luck – have more witnesses coming forward. Now that we're certain he left by the emergency exit,' said Marmion, 'we might have jogged a few memories. According to the window cleaner's evidence, there were other people about when the killer made his escape. Until they're told, they don't realise that they've seen something that may be of great use to us.'

'The trouble is,' moaned Chatfield, 'that when they *do* realise it, they don't always come forward. Some people fight shy of actually helping the police and I don't just mean the criminal class.'

'That's true, I fear. By the way, I notice that it didn't take long to reopen the West End cinema.'

'No, Inspector, and it was against my advice.'

'Mr Brack is in business, sir. He needs patrons.'

'Well, the numbers will certainly be down today – and it's the same with the other cinemas. They've all seen a drop in attendance since the murder. People have been frightened off.'

'It all comes back to the subdued lighting,' said the commissioner. 'It's the reason I went to the press conference today. The superintendent gave me wise counsel. He suggested that I might clarify our position – the Metropolitan Police – to the reporters.'

'What did you say, Sir Edward?' asked Marmion.

'I told them that I'd written to the Cinematograph Exhibitors Association of Great Britain and Ireland to suggest that a dark auditorium could, in some cases, constitute a threat to the moral probity and comfort of their patrons. As a matter of urgency, I emphasised, they should look into the matter. I sent a copy of my letter to the Home Secretary.'

'That's a sensible move, Commissioner.'

'I think it's long overdue,' said Chatfield. 'Cinema is a social canker.'

'You should go to church in Holborn, sir,' said Marmion. 'The Reverend Hearn told me that he was preaching a sermon on that very topic this Sunday.'

'You're forgetting that I'm a Roman Catholic, Inspector.'

'Of course – I'm sorry, sir.'

'So I should hope. What is Sergeant Keedy doing at the moment?'

'He's carrying out some vital research, Superintendent.'

'And where is he doing it, pray?'

'When I heard that it was open again,' said Marmion, easily. 'I sent him to the West End cinema.'

'What on earth did you do that for?' asked Chatfield, almost puce with anger. 'The sergeant is supposed to be on duty, not idling his time away by watching Charlie Chaplin.'

'I wanted him to put himself in the killer's place, sir. He's going to sit in the same seat as the man, watch the film and choose the best moment in it to launch his attack – except that there won't actually be one, of course. Then he's going to leave by the emergency exit.'

'What possible purpose can that serve?'

'We're trying to get inside the mind of the killer, sir.'

'I endorse your initiative, Inspector,' said the commissioner.

'*The Floorwalker* runs for twenty-four minutes,' Marmion pointed out. 'In that limited amount of time, a man caught a young woman off guard and strangled her to death. That means he'll have been to the cinema before and seen the film. Everything was planned in advance. Sergeant Keedy is going to re-enact the crime.'

'I should have been informed beforehand,'

119

snarled Chatfield.

'You just have been, sir.'

'It's a ludicrous idea.'

'I take issue with you there,' said the commissioner. 'The inspector may have hit on a novel approach. Sergeant Keedy may well discover something useful.'

The first thing that Joe Keedy did when he got to the cinema was to give Iris Fielding a verbal rap over the knuckles for talking to the press. She was suitably abashed. He then thanked Mabel Tyler for doing the opposite and resisting the temptation to see her name printed in the newspapers. Emmanuel Brack was on hand to give him a complimentary ticket. The manager was in a despondent mood.

'I expected this film to be a sell-out,' he complained, 'but patrons have just dribbled in. Some of them have come just to stare at the place where the murder happened rather than to watch the screen. They're ghouls, Sergeant.'

'We always get some people like that, sir.'

'One thing, anyway,' said Brack, decisively. 'It won't happen again. I've turned the lights up slightly and told the usherettes to patrol the aisle more often. And if anyone tries to escape through the emergency exit, they'll walk straight into the security man I've stationed there.'

'You're closing the door after the horse has bolted, Mr Brack.'

'I'm doing it to give myself peace of mind.'

'Fair enough, sir.'

The manager went off to open the door to a

group of four people, bowing and beaming at them like an overzealous uncle greeting his nephews. Keedy asked Mabel Tyler to show him to the seat next to the one taken days earlier by Charlotte Reid. The usherette went through the standard procedure and used her torch to guide him to the back row in the gloom. In his mind, he sat beside the murder victim. Apart from a couple at the end of the row, it was unoccupied. That suited Keedy. He watched the newsreel up on the screen then noticed the surge of interest when the credit sequence for the main film appeared. He was soon laughing along with the rest of the audience.

Charlie Chaplin was thoroughly engaging as a tramp in a department store but Keedy remained detached. He watched and waited. Minutes after the film had begun, someone glided out of the darkness and lowered herself down beside him. The woman dispensed with introductions. Easing her shoulder gently against his, she put a hand on his thigh. Keedy immediately moved it away. She purred into his ear.

'If you'd rather wait,' she said, 'I know a place we can go to afterwards.'

'So do I,' he whispered. 'It's called Scotland Yard and I happen to work there as a detective sergeant.'

The woman disappeared in a flash and Keedy was amused. On balance, he decided, it might be better not to mention the incident to Alice. Concentration restored, he waited for the moment when he could commit murder. It came when the laughter that had bubbled continuously throughout reached a pitch of absolute hysteria. Keedy turned to the seat beside him, throttled an invisible woman, then calmly got up, walked down the side aisle and slipped through the curtains that led to the emergency exit. Pushing the door open, he stepped out and blinked in the light.

The burly figure of a security guard confronted him with a raised palm.

'What do you think *you're* doing, sir?' he growled.

Keedy smiled. 'I've just strangled a young woman in the cinema,' he said, 'and I'm making my escape.'

Harvey Marmion sat in his office and studied the post-mortem report. It was an aspect of his job that he least enjoyed because it recorded the unnatural death of a victim and that always saddened him. On the other hand, autopsy reports could sometimes be replete with valuable clues that pointed his way towards an arrest. Unhappily, that was not so in Charlotte Reid's case. She had been throttled by a powerful man against whom she had been helpless. That was all that was revealed. Marmion knew that her father would ask about the report and there was one consolation that could be offered to Philip Christelow. There was no sign of sexual violence on his daughter. It was a huge relief.

Christelow was still at the house. Joe Keedy had established that when he went to Bayswater. Marmion wondered if he should pay the man a courtesy call. It was still early evening and Christelow might be more amenable to discussion now

122

that he'd had time to absorb what had happened to his daughter. He would want to know about the autopsy, the date of the inquest and when the body could be released for burial. There was an additional reason to visit him. Now that he had finished with the borrowed photographs of Charlotte Reid, Marmion felt that they should be returned to their rightful place at the house.

What prevented Marmion from driving immediately to the Reid house was the nagging thought that Christelow still needed more time to accommodate the idea that his daughter was not the faithful wife of his imagination. At all costs, the inspector wanted to avoid another distressing scene with Christelow. It might be kinder to leave the man, for the time being, in the false comfort of his memories of his daughter.

When the lights went up and the patrons filed out of the auditorium, there was a buzz of pleasure as they recalled favourite moments in the film. For the vast majority of people, Charlie Chaplin had banished all thought of the crime that had occurred at the West End cinema earlier that week. Up on the screen, the tramp had unwittingly solved a crime of a different kind and emerged as a hero.

Once they had all gone, Mabel Tyler was the first usherette to come into the auditorium. Her heart missed a beat when she saw that one person was still there, sitting upright and motionless in his seat. Terrified that she'd stumbled on a second victim, she was about to call the manager when she saw a slight movement of the head. It

123

was enough to calm her nerves and make her walk towards the man. She put her hand gently on his shoulder.

'The film is over, sir,' she said. 'It's time to leave.'

The man turned to her as if in a daze, tears streaming down his face.

It was Philip Christelow.

'Welcome back, Joe.'

'Thanks.'

'How did you get on?'

'It was an interesting exercise, Harv.'

'What did you learn?'

'Well,' said Keedy, 'the first thing is that I'd never make a killer. I was only engaged in make-believe but my hands were shaking and my blood was racing. The killer must have ice in his veins – not to mention intense concentration.'

'You mean that he wasn't distracted by the film?'

'Yes, and that's a major achievement. Charlie Chaplin was hilarious. It was all I could do to keep my mind on why I was there.' He chuckled. 'There was another distraction to cope with as well.'

'Oh, what was that?'

'I was a man sitting alone in the dark, Harv. I was fair game.'

He told Marmion about his fleeting encounter with the prostitute. They were in the inspector's office and Marmion was amused, smiling as he imagined the woman bolting when she learnt that she was seated beside a policeman. At the same time, however, he was a little uneasy, all too aware that Keedy took Alice to the cinema on occasion. What the sergeant got up to in the dark with his daughter Marmion didn't know and he tried to clear his mind of pointless speculation.

'You were right, Harv,' said Keedy.

'I usually am.'

'He'd been there before. He'd watched the film and got the lie of the land, so to speak. I picked out the exact moment when he must have struck. The noise was deafening. If Charlotte Reid had screamed her head off, nobody would have heard her in the middle of that tumult. It was the same with the escape route,' he went on. 'The seats were adjacent to the side aisle. Once I'd dispatched my victim, I was out of that auditorium in a few seconds. If I'd driven down the aisle on a motorbike, nobody would have been any the wiser.'

'Then what happened?'

Keedy told him about the brush with the security man and Marmion laughed.

'I hope that he had a sense of humour, Joe.'

'Luckily, he did,' said Keedy. 'I thought it was a waste of time to have him there, but he did stop another crime from being committed. At an earlier showing of the film, a youth had crept out to the emergency exit and opened it so that his friends could sneak in free. The security guard foiled his plan. He not only stopped the friends from going in, he threw out the youth who'd actually bought a ticket.'

'It's a petty crime compared to the one we're investigating.'

'That's what I told him.'

'What about the killer's movements when he left the cinema?'

'Thanks to Toby Ruggles, I knew which direction he took so I went exactly the same way. I timed myself. Within twenty seconds, I was lost in the crowd in Piccadilly Circus. He left nothing to chance, Harv.'

'So it seems.'

Keedy became serious. 'What I'd like to do is this,' he said. 'I feel that I stumbled on something but I'm not quite sure what it is. With your permission, I'd like time to think it over, then I'll be able to give you a fuller account.'

'That sounds like a good suggestion to me, Joe.' There was a knock on the door and Marmion looked up. 'Come in.'

The door opened and a uniformed policeman popped his head in. 'There's a gentleman asking to see you as a matter of urgency, sir,' he said.

'Is it connected with the murder?'

'Yes, it is, Inspector.'

'Did he give a name?'

'He's the victim's father – Philip Christelow.'

Marmion was on his feet at once. He told the policeman to fetch the visitor then suggested that Keedy left the two of them alone. The sergeant quit the room. A minute later, Christelow was shown in. Marmion was shocked by his appearance. Pale and drawn at their first meeting, the older man was now haggard, his complexion a ghastly white and eyes like twin pools of despair. Marmion had to help him into a chair. He closed the door after the policeman had gone then sat

126

behind his desk, opening a drawer and taking out the bottle of whisky and glass that he kept for emergencies. After pouring a tot, he took it across to Christelow.

'I don't drink,' said the other, waving it away.

'This will help, sir, I promise you.'

Marmion held it to his lips and met with no resistance. Christelow took a first sip and, although he pulled a face, he was encouraged to take a longer sip. Marmion put the glass into his hand then returned to his own chair. There was a protracted silence. The visitor seemed to revive slightly but he said nothing. It was Marmion who eventually spoke.

'I'm glad that you came, sir,' he said, indicating the photographs on his desk. 'I'm able to give these back to you and there are a number of things that we need to discuss.' After waiting for a comment that never came, he pressed on. 'Why did you wish to see me, Mr Christelow?'

'I wanted to apologise to you, Inspector.'

'No apology is called for, sir.'

'I think it is.'

'It was not my intention to upset you when we last met. If anyone has to say sorry, then it should by rights be me.'

Christelow shook his head. 'Do you know where I've been?'

'No, sir, I don't.'

'I went to the West End cinema.'

Marmion was alarmed. 'Was that altogether wise?'

'In one sense, it was very unwise because I was profoundly disturbed. In another sense, however,' said Christelow before taking another sip of whisky, 'it was sobering. It told me things about my daughter that I didn't know.'

'Have you ever *been* to a cinema before, sir?'

'No, I haven't. We sometimes have lantern slides in the church hall but they're of a very different nature. Also, I have to say, the audience sits there in respectful silence. People don't start screaming like a pack of wild monkeys. I couldn't believe the behaviour that I witnessed.'

'As it happens,' said Marmion, 'my sergeant was there at the same time as you. He mentioned the ear-splitting noise of laughter but gave the impression that people remained in their seats.'

'It was a scene of abandon, Inspector, and I felt thoroughly shaken by it. I was horrified to discover that my daughter had taken part in such an event. I saw nothing in the film to justify it,' said Christelow, sternly, 'but, then, to be frank, I was not there to watch Mr Chaplin. I wanted to learn something about my daughter.'

'And did you do so, sir?'

'Sadly, I did, and that's why I felt an apology was overdue.' Christelow looked into the glass then drained it in one gulp. He winced at its impact. 'What I learnt was that Charlotte may have been a victim but that she was also – to some extent – a willing victim. Of her own volition, she went to that cinema to meet a man in the darkness. Only one motive could have taken her there. She trusted him.'

'Your daughter might also have loved him, sir.'

'What was happening all round me was not love,' said Christelow, curling his lip. 'I could *hear* their

128

animal grunts during the newsreel. When my eyes grew accustomed to the dark, I could even see them as they embraced each other and...'

His voice tailed off and he closed his eyes tight, unable to find words to express his feelings. Marmion sympathised with him. For someone who lived in a provincial backwater, coming to London was in itself a daunting experience. A first-ever visit to a cinema had been an abrasive event. Since it was the place where his daughter had been murdered, it had a gruesome significance. Marmion could understand what impelled him to go but the consequences had been too much for Philip Christelow. He was suffering at a deep level.

When he finally opened his eyes, the man had clearly reached a fearful decision.

'I'm going back to Yorkshire,' he said, bluntly. 'Charlotte is no longer my daughter. I want nothing more to do with her.'

CHAPTER NINE

He wore a different suit this time but Olive Arden recognised him immediately. Totally absorbed, he was feasting his eyes on a painting by Stubbs. He looked even more handsome in profile. Olive was uncertain whether to approach him or to leave him in peace. In the end, she did neither. Becoming aware of her presence, he turned to face her, producing a dazzling smile of surprise.

'Hello,' he said. 'We meet again.'

'Yes, this is the third time.'

'I didn't expect to see you in this gallery.'

'To be frank,' she explained, 'I was just stretching my legs. I've been standing in front of a Turner so long that I was aching all over.'

'Turner's a difficult artist to copy.'

'I took the easy way out. I was sketching *The Fighting Temeraire*.'

He laughed. 'That was clever of you.'

On the two previous occasions when they'd met at the National Gallery, he'd restricted himself to a few comments so that he didn't frighten her away by showing her too much attention. This time, however, she seemed to want some conversation, holding his gaze deliberately. Olive was a plump woman in her early twenties with a homely appearance and close-cropped dark hair. She wore a long blue skirt that needed ironing, a red blouse and a loose-fitting coat that gave her a slightly raffish air. A hat with an upturned brim was balanced on the back of her head. Under her arm she carried a sketchbook. At their first encounter, he discovered that she was a student at the Slade School of Art. At their second, he'd done little more than exchange greetings. It was time to befriend her properly.

'You were lucky not be a student when Henry Tonks was at the Slade.'

'Yes,' she said, 'I've heard that he could be very strict.'

'By all accounts, he could make wounding remarks to young artists.'

'I'm told that he joined the army.'

130

'He did,' said the man, knowledgeably. 'Before he worked at the Slade, he was a doctor and reverted to that profession last year to join the Royal Army Military Corps.'

She was impressed. 'You seem to know a lot about him.'

'One picks up gossip in my line of work.'

'Oh – and what's that?'

'I work in the art department of a major auction house.' His smile broadened. 'That's why I keep sneaking off here. I just love to see genius in action.'

Olive was glad that she'd bumped into him. He was polite, well spoken and took an interest in her work. She was happily unaware of the fact that this was no chance meeting. He had spotted her earlier and, when she set off on her walk, he'd contrived to get ahead of her so that Olive would believe that she'd found him by accident. He looked back at the painting.

'George Stubbs was one such genius,' he observed.

'The horses are so lifelike.'

'If you look at equine portraits by artists in previous centuries, you'll see that they're always out of proportion. Stubbs did his homework properly. He acquired a dead horse, set it up in his studio and stripped away the skin to that he could see every bone, muscle and sinew. That's what I call a professional approach. But I'm holding you up,' he said with a gesture of apology. 'You'll want to get back to Turner.'

'There's no hurry' she said, 'and I enjoy hearing you talk about paintings.'

'Thank you.'

'Did you study at an art college yourself?'

His smile was self-effacing. 'I can only *sell* paintings – not create them.'

'I don't think any of mine will ever sell,' she confided.

'That sketch I saw you doing was first-rate.'

'Yes, but I was only copying what someone else had painted. I can't seem to find any inspiration myself.'

'That will come in due course, Miss... Oh dear!' he said with a grin. 'Here we are, chatting away like old friends and I don't even know your name.'

'It's Olive,' she said, brightly. 'Olive Arden.'

Like every other detective, Harvey Marmion knew the importance of gathering evidence in the wake of a murder with speed and thoroughness. The first twenty-four hours were critical, giving the investigation direction and establishing momentum. His early hopes in this instance, however, had been dashed. They had a description of the killer but it could fit vast numbers of men and, though details were given in every newspaper, the response was disappointingly poor. Three people had come forward to claim that they'd seen the man at the rear of the West End cinema at the time in question but they could only give vague impressions of him rather than key details about his appearance. The truth was that the killer had vanished into the maelstrom that was London. It was like looking for a grain of salt on a sandy beach.

Claude Chatfield was quick to blame Marmion

for the lack of progress. When they met in his office that morning, the superintendent was at his most astringent.

'What am I to tell the commissioner?' he demanded.

'You may tell him that we are doing all we can to solve the crime, sir.'

'I see few visible signs of that, Inspector.'

'As you well know,' said Marmion, 'gathering evidence takes time and sifting through it requires patience. Murder cases are rarely resolved in a matter of days and that's all we've had so far.'

'What worries me is how you're deploying your men.'

'Have there been any complaints from them?'

'No,' retorted Chatfield, 'they're too dog-loyal to their master. Because you've had a measure of success in the past – and more than your fair share of luck, I should add – they foolishly imagine that the great Inspector Marmion is the paragon of Scotland Yard. And it's not true.'

'I agree with you wholeheartedly.'

'Your career has been riddled with errors.'

'We're all prone to make those, sir,' admitted Marmion, 'but, in my defence, I will point out that every murder case in which I've been involved has resulted in the conviction of the killer or killers. Need I remind you that two of the murders *you* investigated still remain unsolved?'

Chatfield reddened. 'That's neither here nor there.'

'It does show that even the best horse stumbles.'

'I'm not a horse,' snapped the other, 'and I didn't stumble. I may have made a few minor

133

misjudgements but I used my detectives effectively. I certainly didn't try to solve a crime by sending them off to watch a film.'

'It was only one man, sir.'

'There's a huge difference between work and leisure.'

'Sergeant Keedy was able to combine the two.'

'And did anything new come to light?'

'I believe that it did, sir. We understand the killer much better now.'

'Don't bother to *understand* him, man – just arrest the fellow.'

'We first need to know how he thinks, how he moves, what his motives are.'

'And all this was put up on a screen in the West End cinema, was it?' said Chatfield with heavy sarcasm. 'What was the film called – *How to Solve a Murder?* Are you going to call Charlie Chaplin as your star witness?'

Marmion pretended to laugh. 'That's very funny, sir.'

'I take the same view of cinema as the Reverend Hearn. It's sheer wickedness made manifest.'

'That's what you may say in the pulpit, sir, but who gets to hear you apart from us? Unlike you, the Reverend Hearn was prepared to declare his objections in public. In doing what he did, he exposed himself to abuse, ridicule and the possibility of assault.'

Chatfield blenched. 'Are you advocating that I stand outside that cinema?'

'On the contrary,' said Marmion, 'I'd urge you to go *into* it and actually watch a film. You might even surprise yourself by enjoying it.'

134

'How dare you!'

The superintendent looked as if he was about to explode. Before he could do so, however, the telephone rang on his desk and he snatched it up as if it were a club with which he could belabour Marmion. As he heard the voice at the other end of the line, Chatfield went from blind fury to obsequious fawning. The commissioner had rung. The argument was over.

Seizing his opportunity, Marmion waved a farewell and slipped out.

Until the end of the week, Alice Marmion was still on a day shift in central London. She and her companion, Peggy Lassiter, walked around their beat, giving directions to strangers, intervening in strident arguments and generally helping to keep the capital city ticking over without incident. Inspector Gale had told them that the mere sight of their uniforms would have a calming effect on the citizenry. That was not their experience. Army and navy uniforms were everywhere and the young men inside them were inclined to be celebrating their leave by drinking too much beer. When they resorted to rowdiness, they were not calmed by the sight of two attractive women in police uniform. They tended to jeer, tease, challenge and try to embrace them. Some of the crudely flirtatious comments they were forced to hear had been shocking at first, but they were now able to shrug them off without embarrassment.

Though a little younger, Peggy was bigger and bulkier than Alice.

'I've had a poor haul today,' she joked. 'I only had one proposal of marriage.'

'Then you're lucky,' said Alice. 'I've had lots of proposals but none of them included marriage.' They traded a laugh. 'We're sitting targets, Peggy.'

'It could get worse on the night shift.'

'That's why Gale Force assigned us to it.'

'I prefer to think she trusted us to handle difficult situations.'

'It's more a question of disliking us enough – me, anyway – to want to inflict punishment. All that we can do is to take it on the chin and get on with it.'

'It will certainly broaden our education, Alice.'

'That's my worry.'

'Just imagine what some of these soldiers will be like after dark.'

Alice made no reply. Her attention had just been diverted by the sight of a woman she knew coming out of a recruiting station. Lena Belton was evidently in a bad mood. When she came into the street, she turned to glare at some of the many posters pasted onto the wall. Large and colourful, they all appealed to a sense of patriotic duty and urged the men of Britain to sign up there and then. Alice thought for a moment that Lena was going to tear one of the posters down. In the end, the older woman simply wheeled away in disgust. After excusing herself from her friend, Alice went over to intercept Lena.

'Hello, Mrs Belton,' she said.

'What?' Lena needed a moment to recognise her. 'Is that you, Alice?'

'Yes, this uniform is hideous, isn't it?'

'It's not as hideous as an army uniform.'

'None of us asked for this war to start, Mrs Belton.'

Lena was aggressive. 'What do you know about it?'

'I only know what my brother has told us and it was very depressing.'

'Well, at least he was still alive to talk to you. My two lads are not. They saw these evil posters and were tricked into throwing their lives away. Well, it's not going to happen to Patrick,' she went on, jabbing a finger at Alice. 'I've just been to tell them that. I asked for a guarantee that my younger son – my *only* son – wouldn't be called up when he came of age and they said that he couldn't dodge conscription.'

'You've sent Patrick away, I believe.'

'He's gone to my cousin in Warwickshire. They're not having him.'

'Does he want to join up?'

'It's not a question of what *he* wants, Alice Marmion,' shouted Lena. 'It's a question of what *I* want. Patrick will do what his mother tells him. Norman disobeyed me and so did Gregory. It won't happen again.' A sneer came into her voice. 'There was a time when Norman was fond of you, wasn't there? He had hopes – not that I ever shared them, mind you. Well, you might want to know this,' she said, putting her face close to Alice's. 'When Norman was killed, they sent back his effects. There was a photo of you among them. I saw what you'd written on the back – before I tore it up and threw it in the bin.'

Turning on her heel, Lena walked off. Alice was

deeply hurt.

When Harvey Marmion was summoned to the superintendent's office, it was left to Joe Keedy to go through the rest of the responses triggered by the latest appeal in the newspapers. Three people had actually come in person to Scotland Yard, each with a different memory about the man they'd seen leaving the West End cinema by the rear entrance. Since one of them wore thick glasses and blinked incessantly, the detectives had discounted his evidence at once. What remained was a small pile of letters, notes and – in one case – a drawing. Keedy examined the coarse artwork. It was a picture of a young woman being attacked by someone who was recognisably Charlie Chaplin. After scrunching it up, Keedy tossed it into the waste-paper basket.

The correspondence handed in that morning was not much more useful. There were some extravagant, and easily dismissed, claims from people who tried to name the killer. Another person who'd been outside the cinema recalled how fast he'd walked in the direction of Piccadilly Circus. And a detailed account of the murder itself was from someone purporting to be the killer. Having sat in the cinema during a showing of the film, Keedy realised that the 'confession' was a complete fabrication. He was still reading it when Marmion came into the office.

'Any joy?' he asked.

'There's plenty of joy, Harv, but not because we've had anything of the slightest value. I just have to laugh at some of the drivel that's come

138

in.' He held up a sheet of paper. 'This is a confession.'

'Who sent it?'

'He calls himself Jack the Strangler.'

'Then I could have done with him just now,' said Marmion, taking the letter from him. 'If there was ever a candidate for strangling, it's Chat. He had the nerve to accuse me of making slow progress.'

Keedy hooted. 'That's rich, I must say. Whenever he ran an investigation, snails used to overtake him in droves. Yes,' he conceded, 'Chat usually got results but only because he always chose good sergeants who did most of the work.' Marmion shot him an old-fashioned look. 'I didn't say that *you* were like that, Harv.'

'It's just as well.' He put the letter on the desk. 'Jack the Strangler has obviously never strangled anyone. If you listen to him, Charlotte Reid was throttled with a tie – just like the other three victims he says he's dispatched in a cinema.'

'Some people have strange fantasies.'

'Except that – in the case of our killer – it was no fantasy, Joe. It was real. He obviously thought about it beforehand and planned meticulously. Well, you found that out when you went there yesterday.'

'I did,' said Keedy, 'and I stayed awake thinking about that film last night. Then it finally struck me. He didn't just choose a cinema to draw attention to his crime. It wasn't only the darkness he sought.'

'Then what was it?'

'It was the excitement, Harv. When he saw that

139

film beforehand, he knew the tremendous excitement it stirred up. I wasn't even watching properly and I felt it. The audience went wild and the piano was thundering away. It was the kind of heady excitement that you and I feel when we're chasing a villain,' he explained. 'It makes your blood race and gives you the feeling you can do *anything*.'

'I'm not quite sure what you're saying, Joe.'

'The killer *used* that excitement. He fed off it. When he strangled Charlotte Reid, he was in a state of exhilaration that gave him extra power and pleasure. Let me put it more bluntly,' said Keedy. 'It wasn't just murder for him. It was a sexual act.'

Having chosen his vantage point, he enjoyed a cigarette while he waited. Founded over forty years earlier, the Slade School of Art was a breeding ground for some of the finest artists of their generation. Its reputation was unrivalled. It was not long before the students began to drift out either in groups or in pairs. They were in high spirits and there was a certain amount of horseplay. The watching figure admired and envied their bohemian air and sense of freedom. He was waiting for Olive Arden to appear. When she eventually emerged, she was with two other female students. There was no sign of a boyfriend. Olive was too plump and too plain to attract serious male interest. Reaching the gate, she waved goodbye to her two companions then set off alone in the opposite direction. The man waited until she was well clear before he sauntered after her.

With a bag slung over her shoulder and a sketchbook under her arm, Olive walked through a rabbit warren of streets until she came to a row of terraced houses in a run-down district. Raucous children played violent games. Cats hissed at each other and dogs sniffed in the gutters. Producing a key, Olive let herself into a house and disappeared. The man was content. All his suppositions about her had been proved correct. Olive Arden was a loner. Judging by her accommodation, she was short of money. With no social life to enjoy, she was condemned to lonely evenings in a bedsitter. She was susceptible to flattery.

As he walked away, he made his decision. Olive would be next.

When she came out of the library, Ellen Marmion had a couple of books in her bag. She was such a regular visitor there that the librarian had joked that they'd soon run out of books that she hadn't read. Since the start of the war, she'd turned even more to the comfort of romantic fiction, relishing the escape it gave her from anxiety about her son. In the stories that she read, couples met, fell in love and, after enduring a series of setbacks, they married and lived happily ever after. That was not the path Paul Marmion was destined to take. When he joined the army, he'd had a girlfriend who promised to wait for him until he was demobilised but that promise slowly withered away. When he was home on leave the previous year, he was so tetchy with

141

her that the relationship was put under intense pressure and it had broken apart irreparably. Ellen was sad that her son would not have the relatively untroubled courtship that she and Marmion had enjoyed. In some ways, even though they were hampered by Victorian social values, circumstances had been more favourable to them. Paul was in a different world. His mother wondered if he'd ever find a young woman who'd put up with the morose and angry person he'd become.

Ellen made an effort to think about her daughter instead and was instantly soothed. Alice had found her future husband and – even though Marmion still had vestigial doubts – her mother was delighted in her choice. Joe Keedy was a good man and a fine detective. Alice would one day be married to an inspector who led his own investigations. Ellen suspected that her daughter would get to hear far more about Keedy's work than she ever did about Marmion's cases. It would draw the couple together even more.

Lost in thought, Ellen didn't see who was walking towards her until Lena Belton was only yards away. Ellen came to a sudden halt. Lena stopped reluctantly.

'Hello,' she grunted.

'Oh, I'm glad I bumped into you, Lena,' said Ellen. 'I'm sorry about what happened in the butcher's shop. I should have had more sense.'

'Yes, you should.'

'I meant no harm.'

'Everyone says that.'

'I hope you'll forgive me.'

'Your time will come, Ellen.'

'What do you mean?'

'Our soldiers are dropping like flies,' said Lena, tartly. 'Sooner or later, Paul's turn will come. Then you'll understand how I feel.'

Ellen was shaken. 'Don't wish Paul's death on me. That would be cruel.'

'I'm just facing facts.'

'Lots of them will survive.'

'Yes, but what will they be like when they come home again? They'll be ghosts of what they were, Ellen. Look at your son. He's not the Paul Marmion who used to play with my lads. He's already lost that nice girl he used to go out with. He frightened her off. That's what war does to them,' she went on, nastily. 'If it doesn't kill them or send them back with arms or legs missing, it gets inside their heads and destroys them that way. One way or another, you've lost your son.'

A busy day left Harvey Marmion little time for reflection but when he finally had a moment alone that evening, he recalled what Joe Keedy had told him. At face value, it seemed odd that a man who was about to commit murder from sexual motives should choose a Charlie Chaplin film as the place to do it. *The Floorwalker* had been a good, wholesome comedy, aimed at a family audience and guaranteed to produce both laughter and a strain of pathos. On the other hand, Marmion conceded, there could be something intoxicating about the excitement it created. It was not only when chasing criminals that he'd felt that overwhelming exhilaration.

143

He'd experienced it when standing on the terraces of a football ground and watching the winning goal being scored by his team. It had been impossible not to be carried away by the uninhibited joy of the fans and the dizzying sense of power they all shared.

If Keedy's suggestion was right, they were dealing with a strange man. He took sexual pleasure from the murder of Charlotte Reid yet he somehow remained icily cool. Moreover, he chose a public place in which to strike. Murders that involved a sexual element were not unknown, but they usually occurred in private and the victims were left with clear evidence of the excesses to which their killers had been driven. That was noticeably absent in the present case. Charlotte Reid had been left in such a position that she'd aroused no suspicion among the patrons leaving the cinema. Even the usherette had assumed that the woman was simply asleep.

Something else, however, had to be weighed in the balance. When Marmion had searched the victim's bedroom, he'd discovered that her underwear had been removed. On the following day, he'd learnt that a framed photograph of her had also been stolen. The killer wanted souvenirs. It now appeared that the woman's artistic efforts had also been spirited away. Having murdered her, the man pretended to commit a burglary in order to have a memento of what she looked like, what she wore next to her body and what came into her mind when she picked up a paintbrush. Charlotte Reid was a prized possession that was going to be cherished.

As he turned over the evidence in his mind, he was grateful that he'd kept crucial parts of it from the superintendent, a deeply religious man with firm ideas about moral behaviour. Marmion remembered how shocked Chatfield had been when they'd worked together years before on a case that involved a series of beatings administered to young women. When the culprit was eventually caught, he boasted that each of the women had been sexual conquests and that he'd cut off wisps of their pubic hair to add to a bizarre collection that ran into double figures. Chatfield had been so horrified at the case that he'd asked Marmion to conduct the interview with their prisoner. In time, of course, the full truth about the present investigation would emerge and the superintendent would demand to know why he was not told earlier about the sexual element. Marmion decided to cross that bridge when he came to it.

Keedy had agreed to say nothing about what he'd felt in the cinema. In the hands of the press, an already sensational story would be whipped up into something even more feverish. Such publicity would be unhelpful and distracting. Newspapers would have their day when the killer was finally behind bars and his motives came fully to light. Given the way that the crime had been committed and the comparative ease with which the man responsible had disappeared, Marmion was bound to wonder how long it would be before that time arrived.

His meditation was cut short by a rapping on his door.

'Come in!' he called.

A uniformed policeman entered. 'You have a visitor, sir.'

'Who is it?'

'Lieutenant Reid.'

It took Marmion a moment to realise that it had to be the husband of the victim. He got up quickly from his chair and came around his desk.

'Send him in at once.'

The policeman went out. Moments later, he brought Derek Reid into the office then closed the door as he left. After brief introductions and a handshake, Marmion and the newcomer were left to appraise each other. Reid accepted the offer of a seat and the inspector returned to his own chair.

'Let me say that you have my deepest sympathies, sir,' said Marmion. 'To lose your wife at such a young age must be unbearable. To lose her in these circumstances only makes things worse.'

'I'd like to know exactly what "these circumstances" were, Inspector.'

'What have you been told so far?'

'I'm aware that Charlotte was killed in a cinema, of all places,' said Reid, crisply, 'and I've seen some of the newspaper reports. They don't tell the full story, of course, and that's why I'm here.'

'It was good of the army to release you, Lieutenant.'

'Fortunately, I have understanding superiors. But I haven't been given that much time. There's a strict limit on the amount of compassion available.'

'You don't need to tell me that,' said Marmion,

ruefully. 'My son was home on leave recently but had to return to the Somme before he got back into any kind of routine at home. Not that my experience can match yours,' he added, apologetically, 'but I do have some idea of the demands that war makes.'

Having seen photographs of Derek Reid at the Bayswater house, Marmion had some idea what to expect. The man had clearly aged and a once-handsome face was now lined with fatigue and despair. He spoke with the voice of a good public school education. He cut a striking figure in uniform. His back was ramrod straight and his clear blue eyes warned that he'd not be fobbed off with insufficient information.

'Go on,' urged Reid. 'I've been at the front, Inspector. I've seen thousands of soldiers killed before my eyes. I'm not so battle-hardened to be able to take the death of my wife in my stride but I don't need you to soften the blow.'

'Your father-in-law said something rather similar.'

'Mr Christelow is a resilient man. He can cope with anything.'

'I beg to differ, sir.'

'Oh?'

'I'll come to that in due course, sir.'

Marmion bought himself a little time by shuffling the papers on his desk before opening the folder that contained his case notes. Once he started, he gave a concise recitation of the main facts, listing all the neighbours and friends to whom he or Joe Keedy had spoken. Reid's face was immobile. When it was all over, his voice had a sharp edge to it.

'You've missed several things out, Inspector.'

'I deliberately missed one important fact out,' said Marmion, 'because I didn't wish to provoke the emotional reaction that I got from Mr Christelow. Now that you've heard the outline of the case, I can tell you with certainty that Mrs Reid knew her killer and went to the cinema with the express purpose of meeting him there.'

Reid looked surprised rather than shocked. 'Really?'

'And there's something that I felt unable to tell your father-in-law.'

'Don't hold it back from *me*, Inspector.'

'The killer stole your wife's key so that he could let himself into your house. When he left, he took a number of items with him.' Marmion took a deep breath before he pressed on. 'They included your wife's underwear.'

Reid needed a few minutes to absorb the information. Hitherto, he'd remained calm and undemonstrative but an expression of disgust now appeared. His eyes had a look of profound dis-illusionment. When he finally spoke, there was a slight tremor in his voice.

'Do you have any idea who this man is?'

Marmion was honest. 'No, sir, we don't,' he said. 'But we will do before long. That's not an idle prediction, Lieutenant. It's a heartfelt promise.'

CHAPTER TEN

Joe Keedy knew the value of checking and double-checking his notes. Facts which had seemed unremarkable at the time when he collected them from witnesses could suddenly spring out at him and take on a new importance. Though it had happened during previous investigations, however, it did not occur now. There were no gems hidden under the accumulated dross. After suppressing a yawn, he stretched his back then rose to his feet and slipped his jacket on again. He straightened his tie in the mirror, combed his hair and walked along the corridor to Marmion's office. Keedy followed his normal routine, tapping on the door before opening it and going in. When he saw that the inspector had company, he immediately apologised and backed away.

'No, no,' said Marmion, 'please stay and meet Lieutenant Reid.' He turned to his visitor. 'Sergeant Keedy has been involved in the case from the start. It is he who has been gathering intelligence from people in Bayswater.'

'How do you do, Sergeant?' said Reid, getting up to shake his hand.

'I'm sorry we meet at a time like this, sir. May I offer my condolences?'

'Thank you.'

When the two of them had sat down, Marmion

explained what had so far been discussed, signalling to Keedy with a glance and a change of inflexion that he was to be careful what he said. While the inspector talked, Keedy weighed up their visitor and felt an upsurge of pity for the man. In addition to the loss of his wife, Reid had been forced to accept that her loyalty to him was very much in question. Alma Bond had claimed that Charlotte and her husband had drifted apart, but that was not in evidence at the moment. Patently, Reid was a grieving spouse, desperately trying to reconcile what he'd learnt about his wife with the image of the woman he'd married. The formality of his pose could not conceal the pain he was feeling.

'Was there a post-mortem?' asked Reid.

'I have the report here,' replied Marmion, extracting it from the folder, 'and you're at liberty to study it. I'd intended to show it to your father-in-law but he was in great distress and stalked out of here.'

'That doesn't sound like him, Inspector.'

'His visit to the cinema was too much for him to bear.'

Reid was stunned. 'He's never been to the cinema in his entire life.'

'That's why he reacted as he did,' suggested Keedy. 'But I fancy that he felt obliged to see the film during which his daughter had lost her life and it had a disturbing effect on him.'

'It was more than disturbing,' said Marmion, sadly. 'Not to put too fine a point on it, Lieutenant, he was a broken man. When he was compelled to acknowledge that his daughter had ...

gone to that cinema with someone other than her husband, he more or less disowned her. Mr Christelow didn't even stay to ask when the body could be released. He went straight back to Yorkshire.'

'Nobody can disown their own child,' said Keedy. 'It's unnatural.'

'He'll come round,' murmured Reid.

'I sincerely hope so,' said Marmion. 'You don't want an awkward situation like that.' He leant forward. 'Is there anything else you'd like to ask us?'

'Yes, there is. I'd be interested to know what Sergeant Keedy was told by our neighbours when he spoke to them.'

'They were universally sympathetic,' said Keedy, 'and they spoke of Mrs Reid with affection and respect. Mrs Cinderby worshipped her.'

'She's been a good friend to us.'

'Her comments were extremely helpful.'

'What about Mrs Bond?'

'She was less forthcoming,' admitted Marmion. 'Mrs Bond felt that we were hiding things from her so I told her the plain truth. She's very protective of your wife's memory. I had some ... uneasy moments with her.'

'Alma can be outspoken on occasion.'

'The sergeant and I both found that out.'

'What did she tell you?' As soon as Marmion began to recall his conversation with the woman, Reid cut him short. 'That's not what I'm asking you, Inspector. I want to know what she told you about ... Charlotte's friend.'

'She told me nothing at all, sir, because she had

151

no idea that he existed.'

'I find that incredible. Alma and my wife were very close.'

'Nevertheless, Mrs Bond was not your wife's confidante – in this matter, at least. It came as a real blow to her.'

Reid gritted his teeth. 'It's come as a blow to me, Inspector.'

There was a pause. Reid seemed to go off into a reverie, allowing Marmion and Keedy to have a silent conversation with their eyes. Keedy now had a clearer idea of what exactly their visitor had been told.

Reid looked up. 'Could I have a little time on my own, please?'

'Of course,' said Marmion.

'I've had one too many surprises since I came here, Inspector.'

'Sergeant Keedy will show you to his office, Lieutenant. Stay in there as long as you like. There's a lot for you to mull over.' He offered the report. 'You don't have to read this, sir. It might only add to your distress. In my view, however, you have a right to know the full details.'

'Thank you, Inspector.'

Getting to his feet, he took the report then followed Keedy out of the room.

Since there was no hope of seeing Joe Keedy, and since she would soon be spending her evenings on duty, Alice Marmion paid another visit to her mother. She was given a cordial welcome. Talk immediately turned to the subject of Lena Belton.

'When was this, Alice?'

'This morning – I was on my beat with Peggy Lassiter.'

'And you saw Lena coming out of a recruiting office?'

'She didn't so much come out,' said Alice, 'as storm out. You could almost see the flames shooting out of her nostrils.'

'What did she say?'

'They turned her down, Mummy. When she demanded that they didn't conscript Patrick when the time came, they showed her the door. I was going to point out that she went to the wrong place but she didn't give me time to get much of a word in. Mrs Belton will have to go to the War Office instead.'

'Are they likely to grant Patrick immunity?' asked Ellen.

'I don't know. It seems unlikely. Some families have lost three or four sons. There was a Lancashire woman mentioned in the paper the other day who'd lost all *six* of her sons in action. How on earth can she cope with a tragedy like that?'

Ellen was pensive. 'There's another aspect to this, Alice.'

'What's that?'

'Well, you remember what Patrick was like as a boy.'

'I do,' said Alice with a laugh. 'His brothers were lively enough but Patrick was a bundle of energy. I remember watching him in a football match once. He never stopped running.'

'Do you think he'd actually *want* to join the army?'

'If he wasn't so afraid of his mother, he'd have joined already though I fancy that it would have been the navy. He looks old enough and he's certainly got enough fire in his belly. Left to himself, Patrick would want to avenge his brothers.'

'He might well resent his mother wrapping him in cotton wool.'

'I'm sure he does.'

Ellen sat back on the settee. 'You obviously caught her at a bad time.'

'Yes,' said Alice, 'she was actually quite spiteful to me.'

'Spiteful?'

'It was that business with Norman. Yes, I went out with him for a while but it was never very serious. Norman was too full of himself for me. But we did ... spend time together and I did let him have a photo of me. He even got me to write something on the back and I saw no harm in that. It was silly, I suppose.'

'You were never silly, Alice.'

'Then I was unguarded,' said her daughter. 'It turns out that Norman had that photo in his wallet when he went off to war. Mrs Belton found it among his effects. She made it sound as if I sent him off with a broken heart.'

'She's just casting around for someone to blame.'

'Well, I wish she'd find another target.'

'She already has done,' said Ellen. 'It was me.'

'Don't tell me you had another row with her.'

'I met her on my way back from the library and she just took against me. Lena has lost a husband

and two sons in a short space of time. What she sees in me is a woman with a healthy husband, a lovely daughter and a son in the army who's so far managed to escape injury. She's seething with envy.'

'What happened to her is not *your* fault, Mummy.'

'She makes it sound as if it was,' said Ellen. 'Lena just had to strike out at me. She warned me that it would be Paul's turn next and that, even if he wasn't killed or wounded, he'd come back as a complete stranger.' She exchanged a worried look with Alice. 'The awful truth is that she's right, Alice. When he was home on leave, he *was* already a stranger. What on earth is the war doing to him?'

The bombardment had gone on for days and it was deafening. German lines were being pounded mercilessly. Racked by exhaustion and numbed by boredom, Paul Marmion leant against the side of the trench and cleaned his rifle absent-mindedly. Then a miracle happened. The noise ceased abruptly. During the brief silence that followed, the haunting strains of 'Pack Up Your Troubles in Your Old Kit Bag' came from a mouth organ played nearby. Paul heard nothing.

Derek Reid needed only twenty minutes to regain his composure. When he came back to Marmion's office, he was poised and alert. He handed over the autopsy report.

'Did you read it, sir?' asked Marmion.

155

'I read enough of it.'

'I'm told that you were a civil servant,' said Keedy.

'I was, Sergeant,' replied Reid, pulling himself up. 'It's the reason I joined the Prince of Wales's Own Civil Service Rifles.'

'Have you seen action?'

'The regiment was at Festubert and at Loos. I joined too late for either.'

'Where are you based now?'

'We're near the Somme.'

'So is my son,' explained Marmion. 'He's expecting something very big to happen before too long. As you well know, they've been building up their strength there for weeks. I think Paul said there was something in the region of three-quarters of a million men.'

'It's something of that order,' said Reid, 'but, as you can imagine, my mind is not exactly on the war at the moment.'

'We understand, sir.'

'Thank you for all that you've done.'

'The time to thank us is when we have this man in custody,' said Marmion. 'We won't rest until we've got him.'

'What are your plans now, Lieutenant?' asked Keedy.

'I intend to spend the night at home,' replied Reid, 'then I'll have to make contact with my family and with my wife's parents. I can't say I'm looking forward to a trip to Yorkshire but ... well, there are fences to mend.'

'You can tell them that their daughter's body is now available for release.'

'There may be some negotiating before I do that.'

'Mr Christelow seemed like a reasonable man.'

'Yes, he's a decent old fellow but very ... old-fashioned in his attitudes.'

'My children say the same about me sometimes,' said Marmion with a world-weary smile. 'But if you're going to Bayswater, I'll organise a car for you.'

Reid shook his head. 'Thanks all the same but ... I'll make my own way.'

'I used the spare key to let your father-in-law into the house. I daresay that he returned it to Mrs Bond before he left.' He opened the door. 'Goodbye, sir. If there's anything else we can do, just ask.'

'I will, Inspector.'

After giving each of them a farewell nod, Reid went out of the room.

'He bore up extremely well,' said Marmion, closing the door. 'If he's been at the front, he'll have been used to hearing explosions but he was still rocked by the bombshell about his wife's apparent infidelity.'

'Any husband would be, Harv.'

'Allegedly, Reid and his wife led separate lives. That will rankle with him. Because he showed no interest in her, she looked for it elsewhere – or that's how it appears. He must accept that, to some extent, he's to blame.'

'He's probably too busy blaming Mrs Reid at the moment.'

'I'm afraid so,' said Marmion. He thought of the superintendent. 'We'll have to tell Chat about

157

his visit, of course, but we don't want the press knowing that the victim's husband is back in this country. They'll hound him for interviews. The sooner he goes off to Yorkshire, the better.'

'Do you think he'll persuade his in-laws to attend the funeral?'

'Mother Nature will do that for him, Joe.'

When he got to the house, Derek Reid looked up at it with misgiving. Memories of happier times spent there had been soured by his wife's murder and by the revelations that came with it. He swung round, crossed the road and knocked on the door of the villa opposite. It was not long before Alma Bond appeared.

'Derek!' she exclaimed.

'Hello, Alma.'

'You're the last person I expected to see.'

'The army is not *that* hard-hearted,' he said.

'Come in, come in.' She stood aside so that he could step past her, then closed the door. 'You picked a good time. I've finally got the baby asleep. Let's go into the living room.' He put his bag down and followed her. 'Well,' she said, running an eye up and down him. 'You do look smart in that uniform.'

'I don't *feel* very smart at the moment,' he confessed.

'No, of course not – I'm so sorry about what happened, Derek. I'm still in a daze, to be honest.' She indicated a chair. 'Do sit down. We've lots to talk about. Is there anything I can get you?'

'No, thanks.'

'I've got some sherry.'

158

He sat down. 'I don't want anything at the moment, Alma.'

'Very well.'

She settled into the armchair opposite him and inspected him more closely. The strain was obvious. He looked hunted and worn out. Alma wanted to put a consoling arm around him but something held her back. Instead, she gave him a supportive smile. Without preliminaries, he asked the question that had been burning away at the back of his mind.

'Did you *know?*'

'No, I didn't.'

'I'd rather have the truth. I won't hold it against you.'

'You've already heard it, Derek. I swear to you that Charlotte didn't say a single word about ... meeting someone else. That might mean that it had only just happened. I can't say.'

His gaze was steady but she met it without turning away. After a moment, he seemed to accept her word and sat back. He glanced around the room to see if there'd been any changes since his last visit there. His eyes met hers once more.

'Could she have told anyone else?' he asked.

'There's no question of that happening.'

'How can you be so sure?'

'I know Charlotte.'

'I thought I did.'

'Have you been to the police?'

'Yes,' he said. 'I met the detectives in charge of the case – Inspector Marmion and Sergeant Keedy. They seemed very competent.'

'I didn't like either of them, to be honest. The

159

sergeant wouldn't tell me the truth and the inspector questioned me as if I was a suspect.'

'What did you tell him?'

'I told him that I was very surprised,' she replied, 'and shocked. I'd never have expected it of Charlotte. Life is hard for a lot of us here. It's not very nice, living alone while your other half is in the army. You wake up every day afraid of getting bad news and you go to sleep praying that your husband is safe. Charlotte made the best of it and she had a lot of commitments at the church to occupy her mind.'

'Unfortunately, there were not enough of them.'

'Don't think too badly of her, Derek.'

'If you want the truth,' he said with a gesture of helplessness, 'I don't know what to think. My head is in a whirl. I'm hoping that a night back home will help me to get things into perspective.'

'I suppose you know that your father-in-law came here.'

'Yes, the inspector told me about his visit to Scotland Yard.'

'Mr Christelow came in for a cup of tea but that was about all,' she said. 'Before I knew it, he'd disappeared. He didn't even bother to knock on the door to tell me that he was going. He just dropped the key through the letter box.'

'I'll need to speak to him.'

'You look as if the first thing you need is a good night's sleep.'

'I can't even imagine sleeping when I'm in this state, Alma.'

There was a considered pause before she blurted

out her question. 'What's it like over there?'

'Don't you get any letters from Nigel?'

'Oh, you know my husband,' she said with a dismissive laugh. 'Nigel always makes light of everything. If you read some of his letters, you'd think he was over there on holiday instead of fighting in a war.'

He was bitter. 'Well, it's certainly no holiday, I can tell you that. The best description is that it's hell on earth and the chances are that it's going to get much worse.' He lifted a warning hand. 'Don't get me started on the war, Alma. Some of the things I've seen are ... well, let's just say that they'd turn your stomach.'

She became practical. 'What about the funeral arrangements?'

'They can be made now, I suppose,' he said, uncertainly. 'The body is ready for release, though somehow I don't have any urge to set things in motion.'

'Charlotte's parents will want a say in it.'

'That's in dispute at the moment. Before I can contact an undertaker, I have to go and sort things out with them.'

'I'd like to help as much as I can.'

'Would you?' he said, gratefully. 'That would be wonderful, Alma.'

'Charlotte was very popular. A lot of people will want to come.'

He sighed. 'That means I'll have to listen to them trotting out the same trite phrases time and again. And I'll have to wear the face of a bereaved husband.'

'Isn't that what you *are*, Derek?'

161

'I don't know,' he confessed. 'I feel as if I'm in limbo.'

She stood up. 'Would you like that glass of sherry now?'

'Yes, please, I think I would.'

When she went off to the kitchen, Reid put his head in his hands and gave in to momentary despair. He then spotted something out of the corner of his eye and bent down to retrieve a baby's rattle from beneath the armchair opposite. After looking at it wistfully, he put it aside. Alma came in with two glasses of sherry and handed one to him. He rose to his feet.

'What are we going to drink to?' he wondered.

'We could drink to the time when this is all over and done with.'

'Good idea!' They clinked glasses and sipped their sherry. 'I'm involved in war on the Western Front and another kind of battle on the domestic front. This one promises to be the worse.'

'No,' she said, touching his arm. 'Don't think that. The pain will ease in time. You won't go on torturing yourself, Derek. You're too sensible to do that. The thing I always admired about you was your self-control.'

'Where has it gone, I wonder?'

'It's still there. You haven't really changed.'

He looked at her fondly. 'Neither have you, Alma.'

'We'll miss Charlotte terribly,' she said, 'but there's one thing to remember.'

'What's that?'

'She'll never find out about *us*, will she?'

He drank some sherry and watched the smile

spreading slowly over her face.

'I've been thinking about what you said, Joe.'

'I've said a lot of things.'

'You talked about a feeling of excitement in the cinema.'

'I was putting myself in the killer's shoes.'

'It's happened before.'

'What has?' asked Keedy.

'He wouldn't be the first man to get sexual satisfaction out of murdering a woman. Does the name of Neville Creswick mean anything to you?'

'I've got a vague recollection of him. Didn't he beat women up?'

'Yes,' said Marmion. 'He battered them while in the act of making love to them. I remember him telling me that it heightened the pleasure. He was talking about *his* pleasure, of course. I don't think any of his victims had quite the same thrill. One of them was in hospital for three weeks.'

It was late evening and they had stayed at Scotland Yard to review the evidence gathered so far. Marmion sifted through his memories of earlier cases.

'Then there was the notorious Dr Thomas Neill Cream,' he said.

'Everyone remembers him.'

'My father was a bobby at the time. On the day that Cream was hanged, they all went down the pub and had a drink to celebrate.'

'He poisoned his victims, didn't he?'

'Yes, Joe. He made full use of his medical training. Strychnine was his favourite tipple for the prostitutes he preyed on. When he'd had his

163

money's worth from them, he bumped them off.'

'Was he the one who was cross-eyed?' asked Keedy.

'That's the chap. An optician wrote to *The Times* with the barmy suggestion that Cream only became so perverted because of his eye defect. If it had been corrected by surgery when he was a child, Cream would have been a model citizen.'

'I don't believe that. Evil is bred in the bone. It doesn't matter about your eyesight. We used to have a vicar with a bad squint. He didn't feel the need to slip off and poison women.' He checked his watch and realised how late it was. 'What put Dr Cream in your mind?'

'It was the impulse he had to chase publicity,' said Marmion. 'He was known as the Lambeth Poisoner but his life of crime actually began in America. He served ten years in prison for the murder of a man whose wife was Cream's mistress. The poison used in that case was also strychnine.'

'What's this about seeking publicity?'

'He took stupid risks in Chicago, taunting the police, and he did the same thing here. Having killed a number of women, he made an offer to Scotland Yard to name the Lambeth Poisoner for the small fee of £300,000.' Keedy laughed aloud. 'It's true, Joe. At one point, he complained to the police that he was being stalked. There was this passion for self-advertisement in him. I think that Charlotte Reid's killer has it as well.'

'Dr Cream didn't murder his victims in a public place.'

'I still think there's a similarity.'

164

'What about that other case you mentioned?'

'Neville Creswick also resembles our man in one respect.'

'Do they both have a glass eye and wear a ginger wig?'

'They're collectors,' argued Marmion. 'When they commit a crime, they take away a trophy of some sort from their victims. We know what happened at that house in Bayswater. He's probably still gloating over his spoils.'

'I've forgotten what Creswick collected,' said Keedy.

'He removed hair from each of the women, Joe, and it didn't come off their heads.' The sergeant was startled. 'Yes, that's right. It couldn't get more personal than that. I worked on that case with Chat. He was appalled at what we found. He called Creswick a complete moral degenerate.'

'I'd call him a dirty bugger.'

'But you see my point, don't you?'

'Yes, Harv, I do.'

'Creswick and Cream were two of a kind,' said Marmion. 'Once was never enough. They simply had to go on, finding victim after victim. That's why I'm convinced that our man will strike again. In strangling Charlotte Reid, he got our attention. He'll find a way to keep it.'

With a glass of wine on the table beside him, he fondled Charlotte Reid's drawers and looked up at her photograph. Olive Arden would not have such sensuous underwear and he might have to accept that. But there were other souvenirs he could take from her. All that he had to do was to find a place of darkness.

Notwithstanding her brush with Lena Belton, the visit to the library had been a productive one. Ellen Marmion had chosen a novel that was so enthralling, it banished all thought of sleep and imposed a temporary deafness on her. Only when her husband was standing directly in front of her did she realise he'd finally come home.

'Oh!' she said, sitting up. 'I didn't hear you coming in.'

'Then it's just as well I'm not a burglar.'

'I was enjoying my book so much, Harvey.'

'I wish that I had the time to read a novel,' he said, enviously. 'The only fiction I get to see these days is in the statements given to me by villains. Some of them are born writers. They dream up the most beguiling stories.'

'What kind of a day have you had?'

He flopped into an armchair. 'It was a tiring one.'

'Have you made any progress?'

'Yes and no, Ellen. I'd say "yes" but Chat would say "no". But, then, we look at the case in very different ways.'

She reached for the newspaper beside her. 'You're off the front page.'

'That suits me,' he said. 'I don't like it when the press are breathing down my neck every minute of the day. If the war has pushed us to the inside pages, it's all for the best. Attention has shifted elsewhere.' Ellen offered him the paper. 'No thanks, love, I've already seen it. Chat made me read all the newspaper reports. He was irritated by the fact that I got mentioned more times than he did.' He loosened his tie. 'What about you, Ellen – good day?'

'Bits of it were good.'

'Then tell me about those. I could do with cheering up.'

After slotting the bookmark into place, Ellen put the novel aside and talked about their daughter's visit. Marmion was pleased to hear what Alice had had to say. He was less happy when he heard that both women had had a clash with Lena Belton. Ellen tried to play down the sharpness of her exchange with Lena.

'Stop making excuses for her, Ellen.'

'You have to remember her situation.'

'We've been making allowances for her situation ever since her two sons were killed. She's not the only mother who's mourning deaths on the battlefield. There are three or four in this street alone. I feel sorry for the woman,' he went on, 'but you mustn't let her throw your sympathy back in your face.'

'It wasn't quite like that.'

'And why did she have to be so nasty to Alice?'

'That's just her way.'

'Then her way is wrong and she's unfair to you and Alice. I'd completely forgotten that she and Norman Belton were friends for a time. I always thought he was rather uncouth. Also, he didn't like me.'

'It was only because you caught him smoking in the garden shed.'

'I wasn't worried about the fag,' he explained. 'Most kids of that age try to smoke. No, I was

167

angry because he'd stolen the packet from his father.'

'You frightened him off, Harvey. He stopped seeing Alice after that.'

'Oh, I don't think it was my doing, love. I fancy that Alice had already given him his marching orders. Norman soon found someone else.'

'Yet it was our daughter's photo he took with him to France.'

'We only have Lena's word for that.'

'She can be spiteful, I know, but she's not a liar.'

'No,' he conceded, 'that's true. My advice is to steer well clear of her. Let someone else bear the brunt of her resentment.'

'I can't just dodge out of the way if I see her coming towards me.'

'You can and you should, Ellen.' He got to his feet. 'It's time for bed.'

Picking up the book, she rose from her chair. 'Tell me some more about the victim's husband,' she said. 'Did you say that his regiment is near the Somme?'

'Yes, and he feels that there'll be a major battle before long.'

'Oh dear – Paul could be right in the middle of it.'

'So could Lieutenant Reid. When he's sorted out everything here,' said Marmion, 'I have a feeling that he'll be glad to get back to France. There's nothing left for him here except an empty house with unpleasant memories.'

Alma Bond let him talk. She plied him with more

168

sherry and he poured out his troubles. What stopped the flow was the sound of the clock, chiming the hour.

'Goodness!' he said. 'Is it that late? I'm so sorry to keep you up.'

'I've been interested in what you were saying, Derek.'

'Thank you for listening. It's been a great help, Alma.'

'Without knowing it, you've helped me as well.' She reached out to touch his arm. 'You don't have to go, you know.'

CHAPTER ELEVEN

Alice Marmion leafed idly through a magazine and looked at the photographs of recently married couples. One of the bridegrooms was in uniform but the rest were not. She was reminded that the arrival of conscription had accelerated a number of romances. Since only single men had been liable to compulsory call-up at first, there were those who married quickly in order to escape being shipped abroad to take part in the war. Because conscription of married men had now been brought in, that avenue had been closed. Sooner or later, Alice realised, the smiling bridegrooms she was looking at would all be drafted into the armed services. Their married life would be brutally short.

As she studied the brides, she felt pangs of

envy. She and Joe Keedy had moved from close friendship into a full-blown romance and on to a formal engagement. Yet the actual wedding was still some distance away. They had decided to wait so that they could save up to buy a house. The delay was irksome.

Alice put the magazine aside and started to undress. Before she could remove the first garment, however, she heard a sharp tap on her window. She ran to the curtain and tugged it back so that she could gaze down. There was a figure in the gloom and, even though she could not see him clearly, she knew that it was Keedy. Her heart lifted instantly. After waving in acknowledgement, she switched off the light and crept quietly out of her room. In less than a minute, they were strolling arm in arm through the darkness.

'I never dared to believe that you'd come,' she said.

'You should have had more faith,' he told her. 'If it wasn't for that she-dragon of a landlady, I'd have shinned up the drainpipe and climbed in through the window to give you a surprise.'

'Male friends aren't allowed inside the house after a certain time.'

'I wouldn't be a male friend, Alice. I'd be an interloper.'

'That's even worse. You're supposed to obey the law.'

'I always do. Breaking the rules set by a cantankerous landlady is another matter altogether. They're not legally enforceable.' He paused to give her a warm hug. 'It's wonderful to see you again.'

'Yes,' she said, kissing him. 'I was just thinking about you.'

'I should hope so,' he said, laughing.

'Don't be so conceited, Joe Keedy.' They continued their walk. 'I was looking at some wedding photographs in a magazine.'

'Ah, I see.'

'I kept wondering how long it would be before *our* wedding.'

'We agreed to wait, Alice.'

'Yes, I know.'

'And, unfortunately, we can't put an exact time limit on that wait. I know it's frustrating, but it will give us time to get to know each other better.'

'I've known you for years, Joe!'

'Not in this way,' he argued. 'I'm still finding out new things about you.'

'They'd better be *nice* new things,' she warned.

'They always are. In any case,' he added, 'this is not only about you and me, Alice. I still haven't worn your father down completely.'

'Daddy's given his approval.'

'That's just a form of words. Deep down, he still has worries about me and he's not happy that I'm so much older than you.'

'The age difference is meaningless when you love someone.'

'*We* know that – your father doesn't.'

'He's *accepted* you, Joe. You're one of the family now.'

'I don't always feel that.'

They came to a corner and crossed the road. Keedy changed the subject.

171

'How are you getting on with Gale Force?'

'She's put me and Peggy on the night shift. You can guess why.'

'It may not be a form of punishment, Alice,' he reasoned. 'Perhaps your inspector is simply showing trust in you. She'll surely want to put her best women on duty in the dark because that's when real trouble is likely to erupt.'

'It's personal with Gale Force,' said Alice. 'She keeps criticising me.'

'The superintendent keeps criticising me and your father but that doesn't mean he has no respect for us. Chat only has to look at our record. It's his job to yap at our heels all the time.'

'The inspector doesn't just yap, Joe, she *bites*.'

'I'm not surprised,' he said, putting an arm around her shoulders. 'You're a very edible young woman.'

'Mummy suggested that *you* had a word with Gale Force.'

'Heaven forbid!'

'That's what I told her.' They walked on in silence for a while. 'How is the investigation going?' she asked at length.

'It's moving very slowly, Alice.'

'Have you had much help from the public?'

'Oh, yes,' he said, rolling his eyes, 'we've had a lot. The trouble is that ninety-five per cent of it has been entirely useless. Our most reliable witnesses have been a window cleaner who was up his ladder at the time and a vicar who stood outside the cinema trying to stop people getting in. You can guess what his sermon will be on this Sunday.'

'Why did he want to stop people going in?'

'He thinks that cinemas are dens of iniquity.'

'They provide good entertainment, that's all. I love watching films.'

'Then let's make a date to see one as soon as we can.'

'When will that be, Joe?'

He puffed his cheeks. 'Who knows?'

'Will it be before or after we're married?'

'You may well ask, Alice. It's in the lap of the gods.'

Harvey Marmion arrived at Scotland Yard that morning in the belief that Claude Chatfield would be waiting to ambush him. As it turned out, the superintendent was having a long discussion with Sir Edward Henry. Grateful to be spared another confrontation for a while, Marmion went through his post and read a number of letters from people claiming to have reliable information about the killer of Charlotte Reid. Since none of them was remotely helpful, they ended up in the waste-paper basket. Marmion next addressed his mind to his case notes, going through them with meticulous care. The superintendent soon burst in.

'I want a word with you, Inspector,' he said.

'Good morning, sir.'

'Why on earth didn't you tell me?'

'Tell you what?'

'Charlotte Reid's husband was here yesterday.'

'That's right,' said Marmion. 'He'd been given compassionate leave by his regiment and came in search of details about the murder of his wife.'

173

'I should have been informed.'

'There's nothing you could have told him that Sergeant Keedy and I were unable to pass on to him. As it happens,' he said, inventing what he saw as a permissible lie, 'I did suggest that he came along to your office but the lieutenant was in too much of a hurry. He even refused the offer of a car to take him to Bayswater.'

'Is he coming back again?'

'No, sir – I suspect that he'll be travelling north today. Now that the body can be released, he has to discuss the funeral arrangements with his wife's parents. As you saw in my report, Mr Christelow left here in what I can only call a state of turmoil. He said that he disowned his daughter.'

'That was a shameful thing even to contemplate.'

'I agree, sir.'

'The parental bond should never be broken.'

'How would you react in similar circumstances?'

'Even by your standards,' said Chatfield, scornfully, 'that's a crass question. Neither of my daughters would ever *be* in such circumstances. They don't befriend strangers and they don't have the slightest inclination to go to a cinema. You, on the other hand,' he continued, 'have a daughter who doubtless does watch films, most likely in the company of Sergeant Keedy.'

'My whole family enjoys the cinema, sir.'

'Would you disown Alice if she ended up like Charlotte Reid?'

'For all sorts of reasons,' replied Marmion, 'that would never happen. But since you ask a

174

question, the answer is that I'd love and support my daughter no matter what happened to her. A father has responsibilities that can never be shuffled off. I just don't understand Mr Christelow's position.'

'What about his son-in-law?'

'Lieutenant Reid thinks that he can talk him round.'

'I'm asking about the position *he* takes, Inspector. Some husbands would recoil in horror when they learnt what their wives had done behind their back.'

'Mrs Reid didn't set out to get herself murdered,' Marmion reminded him.

'She committed an act of betrayal.'

'That's only a supposition, sir. We don't really know what sort of a relationship she had with the man. It may have been a casual friendship, something that she never intended to go beyond a certain point. To portray her as an adulteress,' said Marmion, forcefully, 'is both unfair and, very possibly, inaccurate.' Chatfield ground his teeth. 'As for Lieutenant Reid, he behaved with dignity. When I told him what had happened, he didn't for a moment threaten to disown his wife.'

'That's all to the good,' muttered Chatfield.

'Nor did he flinch from hearing unpleasant details.'

'He's a soldier. War toughens a man.'

'Everyone is vulnerable in some way.'

'I'm not.'

Marmion smiled. 'It's one of the many respects in which you're unique, sir.'

'Are you being facetious, Inspector?'

175

'You know me better than that.'

Chatfield subjected him to a long, searching stare then brushed an imaginary speck of dust from his sleeve. He straightened his shoulders.

'If he does come back here,' he said, reinforcing the order with a wagged finger, 'I insist on being told at once. I'd value a word with Lieutenant Reid.'

'You may have to wait a while,' said Marmion. 'He has a prior commitment in Yorkshire with his in-laws.'

Derek Reid had always liked Pickering. He thought that the town had ineffable charm and great character. Indeed, he and his wife had talked about retiring there in their old age. Though they'd enjoyed living in London, the slower pace and the proximity of open countryside gave Pickering a special appeal. Reid felt nothing of that appeal when he alighted from the train and walked the hundred yards to the house. Unsure what sort of welcome he would get from his wife's parents, he braced himself before ringing the doorbell. He could hear footsteps, then the front door was opened wide.

Philip Christelow peered at him with an amalgam of surprise and dismay.

'Derek!'

'Hello, sir.'

'What are *you* doing here?'

'We need to talk.'

Olive Arden was disappointed. Though she searched through all of his favourite galleries, there was no sign of him. When she left her flat that morning, she did so in the hope of meeting him once again and talking about art. He usually arrived about lunchtime and she schooled herself to be patient before she went looking for him. Olive could imagine all sorts of reasons that might have kept him away, not least the demands of his job, yet she still felt somehow thwarted. She hoped that he hadn't just flitted into her life and out again. She'd miss him badly. Olive took a last look around then she gave up and trudged back to the gallery where she'd been sketching all morning. Without realising it, she passed within feet of him. After she'd gone, he emerged from the corner in which he'd been hiding and smiled.

Olive was desperate to see him. It was time.

'What sort of a reception do you think he'll get, Harv?' asked Keedy.

'I don't know.'

'Lieutenant Reid seemed like a decent man in a rotten situation. The last thing he needs is for his wife's parents to turn their backs on him.'

'They're turning their backs on their daughter, Joe.'

'All she did was to go to the cinema.'

'Mr Christelow comes from the same school of thought as the Reverend Hearn. The film industry is anathema to them. In the eyes of her father, Charlotte Reid was guilty of a double sin. She went to see a film that aroused the audience to a pitch of hysteria, and she had an assignation with another man.'

'Millions of people go to the cinema every week.'

'I wish I was one of them.'

'What century is Mr Christelow living in?' asked Keedy in disbelief.

'It's easy to dismiss him as an old fuddy-duddy,' said Marmion, 'but there's something else at stake here. It's the bond between father and child. I talked about it with Chat earlier on. For once, we were in agreement.'

'No man should turn his back on his daughter.'

'What if it had been the other way round, Joe? Suppose that *she'd* been the killer and the man had been the victim. Should he still stand by her?'

Keedy was emphatic. 'Yes, Harv, he should. A father should support his children whatever the situation. Well,' he said, 'you'd support Alice if she murdered a man in a cinema, wouldn't you?'

Marmion chuckled. 'I somehow doubt if that eventuality would ever arise.'

'It was a theoretical question.'

'Then here's a theoretical reply. Yes, I *would* be in Alice's corner. Obviously, I'd condemn what she did but it wouldn't blind me to my duty. I love her too much to walk away from her.' He winked at Keedy. 'It might be safer if you didn't take her to the cinema for a while, Joe.'

'Chance would be a fine thing.' Keedy glanced towards the door and lowered his voice. 'Have you mentioned those two cases to Chat yet?'

'No,' admitted Marmion. 'I certainly won't mention Neville Creswick to him. Chat was scandalised by that investigation. He still bears the scars. As for Dr Thomas Neill Cream, he'd see no connection whatsoever between a cross-eyed poisoner and a strangler in the dark.'

'Both committed a sex crime.'

'I'm not ready to spring that word on the superintendent yet.'

There was a lull in the conversation. Keedy was just about to say that he'd seen Alice the previous night but something held him back. Apart from the fact that he and Alice had a private life of their own, he suspected that Marmion would not wish to know about every meeting they had with each other. The inspector had been badly bruised by the fact that the romance between his daughter and his colleague had developed in secret. Yet all that Keedy and Alice had done was to fall in love when they were unattached to anyone else. It had been natural and unforced. If a father could endure such pain at a necessary deception, how much more pain would he suffer had his daughter been murdered in a cinema by a complete stranger?

Keedy began to have a residual sympathy for Philip Christelow.

There was one source of relief. Esther Christelow was so distraught at the death of her daughter that she'd taken to her bed. She was upstairs at that moment, being tended by a neighbour. It meant that Derek Reid and his father-in-law were uninterrupted. They got off to a tricky start. Christelow had invited him into the house but had refused even to talk about the funeral at first. Reid tried another tack.

'What did you think of Inspector Marmion?'

'He was very understanding.'

179

'I thought he was a good man. He inspires confidence.'

'Is he any nearer to solving the crime?' asked Christelow.

'No,' said Reid, 'but it's not for want of trying. The policeman I met when I first arrived at Scotland Yard told me about Marmion's past successes.'

'I don't want to hear about them, Derek.'

'It might give you hope.'

'Nothing can do that,' said Christelow with uncharacteristic sharpness. 'I'm done with the whole thing. That's why I couldn't wait to get away from London.'

The older man sank back in his chair with his arms folded. Reid looked around the room. It was large and well proportioned. The furniture was serviceable rather than stylish and the floral pattern on the wallpaper was starting to fade. It was a home for people who abhorred change. They found it safe, cosy and reassuringly familiar. Reid had liked it when he was first taken there years before. It had quaint features that he'd commented on and the well-polished cup on the mantelpiece had given him something to talk about to his future father-in-law. Philip Christelow was a dry, conscientious, unexciting man who had shrunk in size over the years. The cup he'd won in a bowls tournament was the one indication that he had a sporting interest.

Having come all the way to Pickering in a draughty train, Derek Reid was determined not to leave empty-handed. He decided to shock his father-in-law.

'Charlotte and I used to go to the cinema occasionally,' he said. 'In fact, we saw a film on the night before I joined the army. We enjoyed it.'

Christelow shuddered. 'That's not what *I* call enjoyment.'

'But you've only ever seen one film.'

'That was more than enough.'

'You can't count that,' said Reid. 'Given the associations that place had, you couldn't possibly enjoy the film. It must have been an ordeal for you.'

'It was.'

'Then it's unfair to judge the cinema on that basis.'

'I'll never watch another film as long as I live, Derek, so don't try to persuade me otherwise. Charlotte was brought up with healthy pursuits. She didn't need to join the kind of howling mob I saw watching that little tramp.'

'If it was my fault for introducing her to films, then I apologise. I couldn't foresee that this would happen.' Reid sat on the edge of his chair. 'Look, I'm sorry but we need to discuss the funeral arrangements.'

'You make them, Derek. My wife and I will not be attending.'

'Would you spurn your own daughter at a time like this?'

'It was Charlotte who spurned us – and the life we wanted for her.'

'That's ridiculous,' declared Reid. 'I can't think of a more dutiful daughter. She was always talking about you and her mother. And nobody could have been more involved in the local church.'

181

'She broke her marriage vows, Derek. Doesn't that worry you?'

'Yes, of course – it's worrying and it's hurtful.'

'Then how can you conceive of forgiving her?'

'She was my wife,' said Reid, earnestly.

'Then why didn't she behave like one?' asked Christelow. 'While you were away, fighting for your country, Charlotte formed an attachment that should never have existed. Change places with her for a second,' he went on, urgently, 'and you'll see what a heinous sin she committed. You're a respectable married man, Derek. You abide by your sacred vows. You'd never *dream* of looking at another woman.'

Reid's face was motionless but his stomach was churning away.

Ellen Marmion let herself back into the house and went straight to the kitchen. Having been on her feet throughout the afternoon, the first thing she wanted was to sit down with a cup of tea. As she filled the kettle and put it on the gas stove, she became aware of the stillness of the house. Alice had tried to persuade her to take in a lodger so that she had some company but Ellen had wanted to keep the empty rooms that belonged to her children. She nursed vain hopes that Alice would one day yearn for the comforts of home and Paul would need his room when the war was finally over. There was even the possibility, of course, that Alice and Joe Keedy might want to move in temporarily after their marriage. It was what she and Marmion had done at the start of their wedded life. It had not been a happy

182

arrangement. While her parents were unfailingly kind and obliging, they were always there. The lack of privacy eventually drove the newly-weds out to a place of their own.

When the kettle had boiled, she warmed the pot before putting in the tea. Then she set everything out on the table and waited. When she glanced up at the clock, she wondered what time her husband would be home that evening. The thought of submerging herself in her book cheered her up. It would defeat time once more. Before she could pour her tea, she heard something come through the letter box. It was several hours too late for the postman. Curiosity got her up from the chair. Lying on the mat beside the front door was a copy of the evening newspaper. The banner headline jumped up at her with the ferocity of a wild animal.

BATTLE OF THE SOMME BEGINS

Ellen knew the implications at once. Her son was engaged in a battle that was fraught with peril. Casualties were inevitable. Someone had taken grim satisfaction out of delivering the news to her.

It must have been Lena Belton.

'He must have gone to ground,' decided the commissioner.

Marmion disagreed. 'I don't think so, Sir Edward.'

'There's no proof that he even lives in London.

183

The killer could be almost anywhere in the country.'

'I doubt that,' said Keedy. 'If he doesn't live here, he wouldn't have been able to draw Mrs Reid into what she thought was a friendship. That takes time.'

Marmion nodded. 'She was not the sort of person who'd talk easily with strangers. Her neighbours spoke of her as being self-possessed and very guarded.'

'Then how did this fellow penetrate her guard?' asked Sir Edward.

'We don't yet know,' replied Marmion. 'Sergeant Keedy has been looking into the social activities in which she was engaged. Most were related to the church. We think that it's highly unlikely that she met the killer in that way because she'd have done so when other people were around. When they saw the description of him in the newspapers, they'd have been able to identify him at once.'

The three of them were in Marmion's office. Sir Edward Henry was restive. The failure to identify the killer had exposed the police to criticism in the press, complaints from the public and angry telephone calls from the owners of the capital's many cinemas who were distressed at the fall in attendance as a result of the murder. It was important to restore confidence at the earliest opportunity and that could only be done by the arrest and conviction of the killer.

'It's a terrible thing to say,' confessed Sir Edward, 'but this latest turn of events at the Somme may work to our advantage. We'll be able to get on and solve the crime without having the press watching our every move.'

'Inspector Marmion might take a different view,' said Keedy.

'Really?'

'His son's regiment will be in combat.'

'Yes,' said Marmion, seriously. 'You'll understand why I can't see the battle as a useful distraction.'

'And nor should I,' said the commissioner, quickly. 'I do apologise for passing such a remark. It was obtuse and insensitive. Please forgive me, Inspector.'

'The news is not unexpected, Sir Edward, but it's nonetheless troubling.'

'I can imagine.'

'With regard to the murder,' said Marmion, 'the sergeant has provided an interesting suggestion and I'm happy to endorse it.'

'Thank you, sir,' said Keedy before turning to the commissioner. 'There was one thing that Mrs Reid appears to have done by herself. She developed an interest in art. She and a friend of hers – a Mrs Stothart – used to go to art classes together. It seems that Mrs Reid had the greater talent and dedication. Wanting to learn from the Old Masters, she went off to various art galleries on her own.'

'Think of it, Sir Edward. An art gallery is, by definition, a place of safety. It's the last place you'd expect a killer to be lurking. Visitors have a shared interest,' Marmion pointed out. 'A casual remark from a stranger would not cause offence.'

'That's a plausible argument,' said the commissioner.

'There's something else that came to light,' said Keedy. 'Mrs Stothart told me that they were given homework at their art classes. They were asked to draw sketches or produce watercolours before the next session. Mrs Stothart had over a dozen in her portfolio but we didn't find a single painting at the Reid household.'

Sir Edward pondered. 'The killer stole them?'

'What other explanation is there?'

'Was the woman *that* talented?'

'I don't think so, Sir Edward,' said Marmion. 'He didn't take them because they had outstanding artistic merit. Paintings are highly personal things. They tell you a lot about the artist's mind and character. That's what he was after, in my view. The killer wanted a special memento of Charlotte Reid.'

He had also stolen his victim's underwear but Marmion was not going to release that information just yet. Missing artwork was enough to interest the commissioner. He began to think through what he'd just been told.

'An art gallery is not entirely a safe environment,' he contended, 'because a nimble pickpocket can prey on visitors mesmerised by a particular painting. But it is a place where a woman could venture alone without undue fear. I can see why Mrs Reid was attracted to galleries.'

'Pickpockets have been known to frequent such places,' conceded Marmion, 'but the war has done us a favour in that respect. It has taken lots of villains out of London and into uniform. My guess is that women and older men form a majority in any art gallery. That would have comforted Mrs Reid.'

'Quite so – it was a good suggestion of yours, Sergeant.'

'Thank you, Sir Edward,' said Keedy.

'Though I still find the killer's choice of venue rather perplexing.'

'I don't. I sat through that film in the very same seat and I can vouch for the pandemonium that was created. It was bedlam in there. And even though the lights had been turned up very slightly, it was still impossible to see clearly anyone more than four or five feet away.'

'Nevertheless, the man took an unholy risk.'

'It was both a risk and an incentive,' Marmion put in. 'He revelled in the fact that it was a public crime. I think it gave him an extra thrill.'

'It was a very perverted thrill,' observed the commissioner.

'Yet it's one that he'll wish to repeat, Sir Edward. He's an exhibitionist.'

'Surely, he won't strike in a cinema a second time.'

'No, he'll choose another location, I fancy.'

'And it may well be in a public place,' said Keedy. 'Darkness won't only be found inside a cinema. The possibilities are endless.'

'There are two things about which we can be fairly certain,' concluded Marmion. 'The second murder will take place in London and it's only a matter of time before it happens. I don't think that even the battle of the Somme will take attention completely away from us.'

It was easier than he'd anticipated. Olive Arden didn't need the slow, careful, inch-by-inch courtship he'd had to use on Charlotte Reid. The art student was more eager and less fearful of consequences. Once he gave her his gift, the friendship was sealed. It was an expensive art book he'd bought in Foyles and it delighted her. Because she could never have afforded to buy it herself, she was overwhelmed by his generosity. When he told her that he had a library of such books at his home, Olive agreed to go there on the following evening. He met her outside the National Gallery and they walked for less than fifteen minutes before they reached the house. She was impressed by its size.

'Do you live here *alone?*'

'My wife died last year.'

'Oh – I'm so sorry.'

'Let's not talk about that,' he said, smoothly. 'You came to see my library and the best way to do that is with a drink in your hand.' He opened a door and took her into a room lined with book-cases on three walls. 'These are the art books,' he told her, pointing at one wall. 'You're welcome to borrow any that catch your eye.'

Olive gasped. 'I couldn't do that!'

'I'll get you that drink.'

There were lots of books to examine and Olive enthused about each one, drinking far more wine than she realised and running out of superlatives for some of the illustrations she found. Charlotte Reid would never have visited his home like this or – when he flirted gently with her – responded so willingly. When she was slightly tipsy, he got

Olive to admit that she'd had a brief romance at the Slade but it had ended rather abruptly. From the way in which she talked about the young man in question, he sensed that Olive was not a virgin.

He could have taken her there and then but he had other plans. When it was dark enough, he offered to walk her back to her lodgings. Olive protested that it was a long way to go and that she couldn't possibly trouble him.

'It's no trouble, darling,' he said, softly. 'It will be a pleasure.'

CHAPTER TWELVE

By the time the detectives got to the park, the area had been screened off and a ring of uniformed policemen were keeping curious members of the public away from the scene. The Home Office pathologist needed little time to determine the cause of death. Clearly, the woman had been strangled to death. She was sprawled on the grass behind some bushes. Her clothing was in disarray.

Taking charge of the investigation, Harvey Marmion had his first sight of the victim. He and Keedy began to make instant deductions.

'I think that he's struck again, Joe.'

'You did feel that it would be somewhere in public,' said Keedy, looking around, 'and there's nowhere more public than a park.'

Marmion sighed. 'This poor woman is very different to his earlier victim.'

'She looks a fair bit younger.'

'Mrs Reid was dressed more smartly.'

'I don't see a handbag or anything that might tell us her identity.'

'Search the vicinity,' said Marmion. 'Last time, he took what he wanted then threw the handbag away. He may have done the same again.'

'Are we *certain* it's him, Harv?'

Marmion ran a hand across his jaw, then walked around the corpse. 'We shouldn't make hasty judgements, of course, but ... yes, I think so.'

'She's chunkier than Mrs Reid. Why didn't she fight back?'

'To answer that, you only have to remember Neville Creswick.'

'You mean that he beat her into submission?'

'No,' said Marmion, lowering his voice, 'I mean that they were, in all probability, having intercourse when it happened. Look at the position she's in and the way that her skirt is lifted up. I suspect that the killer took his pleasure and throttled her either during the encounter or afterwards.'

'In that situation, a woman would be completely off guard.'

Keedy spoke with such easy confidence that Marmion was jolted. During his time at Scotland Yard, the sergeant had been relentlessly teased by colleagues about his supposed conquests. Having heard the taunts directed at his sergeant, Marmion didn't want his daughter to be simply the latest one to provoke banter in the police canteen.

'Find that handbag,' he ordered.

No sooner had Keedy moved away than the police photographer arrived. Having been called to many murder scenes, he was not affected in any way by the gruesome sight. As far as he was concerned, it was one more job to him. Marmion gave instructions and the man took photographs from a variety of angles. Throughout the process, the inspector was uncomfortable, wishing that they didn't have to leave the victim in such an undignified position. He was glad when the photographer went and he was able to cover the body.

When Keedy eventually came back, he was carrying a small bag.

'He'd tossed it into some shrubs,' he said. 'It's not as expensive as the one that Charlotte Reid owned.'

'Do we know who she is?'

'I'm afraid not, but we know where to find out. There's a card in here. She's a student at the Slade School of Art so my guess about the art gallery may have been closer to the mark than I dared to hope.'

'Is there a house key in the bag?'

'It's missing, Harv. But her purse is still here. There's not much in it.'

Marmion took the bag from him and looked through its contents. All that he found were the basic items that any young woman might carry. The purse contained little money. He handed the bag back to Keedy.

'Who found her?'

'It was one of the park keepers.'

'Name?'

'He's called Jimmy Riddle and I daresay he's been ribbed about it all his life. Some parents ought to think twice before they name their kids. Alice and I will make a point of doing so.'

Marmion felt another jolt. Had they got as far as talking about a family?

Jimmy Riddle was a short, bow-legged individual in his early fifties with a face like a pickled walnut and the eyes of a frightened rabbit. When the detectives approached him, he whipped off his peaked cap and stood to attention. Marmion took care of the introductions and assessed the man as he did so.

'I understand that you found the body, sir.'

'Yes, I did, Inspector,' said Riddle. 'In my years as a keeper, I've found all sorts of strange things in this park but never anything like this. To be frank, I just didn't know where to look.'

'Well, you can look at *me* now,' said Marmion, fixing him with a stare. 'I'd like you to tell us exactly what happened and at what time.'

'Oh, I can tell you the time. The first thing I did was to look at my watch.'

'That was very enterprising of you.'

'I knew it might be important.'

Jimmy Riddle gave his statement with the nervous alacrity of a man who'd been rehearsing it ever since he'd realised that he'd stumbled on a murder scene. The crime had taken place in an area of St James's Park that he described as his territory. He'd arrived for work, started on his customary patrol then walked towards the place where they were now standing. He flashed an apologetic smile.

'I'll be honest,' he admitted. 'I was caught short so I slipped behind the bushes for a piddle and I saw her lying there. That's not unusual, mind. I've found young women before, dead drunk on the ground or just sleeping. This one was different – it was them marks on her neck, Inspector, and she wasn't lying natural, if you know what I mean.'

'What did you do then?' asked Keedy, looking up from his notebook.

'I called one of my colleagues to come over and keep people away then I ran as fast as I could and told the first copper I came to.' He pulled out his pocket watch. 'That would have been at precisely 7.28 a.m.'

'Thank you, Mr Riddle,' said Marmion. 'You've been very helpful.'

Keedy glanced at him again. 'Was anybody about at the time?'

'Yes, a lot of people walk through the park in the early morning. Some are on their way to work and others are just having their daily exercise.'

'Was anyone in this particular vicinity?'

'No, Sergeant – that's why I sneaked around here for a piss. You don't do that kind of thing with an audience now, do you?'

Superintendent Chatfield acted with commendable speed and efficiency. When he got back to Scotland Yard, Marmion discovered that additional detectives had been assigned to him. Chatfield was in a mood that verged on the benign. Marmion could never remember a time when the man had been so considerate and softly spoken.

193

'You've had time to think things over, Inspector, so I must ask the obvious question. Are we looking for the same man or not?'

'I believe that we are, sir.'

'What do we know about the victim?'

'We know precious little beyond the fact that she's a student at the Slade. I sent Sergeant Keedy over there to break the sad news and find out all that he could about the young woman.'

'What's your initial response?'

Marmion hesitated, then decided that the truth could not be hidden.

'I'm afraid that Neville Creswick came to mind, sir.'

Chatfield stiffened. 'Don't talk to me about that devil! He was a brute.'

'The killer has traits in common with him, sir. Until it's confirmed by the autopsy I can't be sure but my guess is that the young woman was seduced into having intercourse with him and was subsequently strangled.' He cleared his throat. 'It may not, however, have been subsequently. You may recall that Creswick–'

'Yes, yes,' said Chatfield, interrupting, 'there's no need to remind me of the details. I know that some men do behave in that bestial way. I can't understand their perversion but I'm not unaware of it. I just don't like dealing with fiends of that kind.'

'The killer is only interested in women, sir. You're quite safe.'

Ordinarily, Chatfield would have fired back a riposte but he ignored the joke altogether and pressed for full details. Marmion explained what had happened to the victim and how he and Keedy had followed the usual procedures. He took the opportunity to praise the sergeant for suggesting that an art gallery might have been the venue at which the killer met his victims.

'Yes,' said Chatfield. 'The commissioner mentioned that to me.'

'We know that Charlotte Reid visited galleries and an art student would surely have done the same. That could be the crucial link between the two women.'

'It appears to be, I grant you, but the link could be illusory.'

'Don't worry, sir. We won't rush to judgement but I sense that we are looking in the right direction. Only time will tell if I'm correct.'

'You usually are,' said the superintendent with unaccustomed warmth. 'Well, Inspector, you now have more men at your disposal.'

'I'll brief them immediately, sir.'

'Wait a moment.' He put a gentle hand on Marmion's arm. 'You arrived here this morning and left straight away to go to St James's Park. You won't have had time to see the morning paper, will you?'

'No, I haven't. Are the press taking more pot shots at us?'

'The shots are not being fired by the press, Inspector.'

Chatfield handed him the newspaper lying on his desk and Marmion glanced at the headline. He realised why the superintendent was being so kind towards him. A frightening statistic had come back from the battle of the Somme.

195

19,000 BRITISH DEAD ON FIRST DAY.

'It doesn't mean that your son is among them, Inspector,' said Chatfield.

The Slade School of Art had been founded in 1871 with money left by Felix Slade, a wealthy art collector from Yorkshire. It opened in the newly built north wing of the quadrangle of University College, London. Joe Keedy was not academic by nature so he felt a little out of place in such surroundings. Since it was July, he was surprised to see so many students about during the holiday period and wondered why the young men had not been conscripted. The news he brought caused understandable horror and consternation among the few members of the teaching staff who were there. From the description he gave of the deceased, they were able to identify her as Olive Arden, a keen young artist who had stayed on beyond the end of the summer term to continue her studies. None of them knew very much about her background but they directed Keedy to Olive's best friend at the school. Fortunately, Millie Duxford was on the premises.

Expecting to meet another student, Keedy was startled to discover that Millie was one of the models employed at the Slade and that she was posing for a couple of young artists. What the sergeant first saw, therefore, was a full-bodied woman in her thirties with dyed hair brushed up

196

at the back and held in place by some slides. While he was slightly taken aback, she did not bat an eyelid at the appearance of a stranger. It was only when Keedy was introduced to her that she reached for her dressing gown and slipped it on. They adjourned to a nearby room where they could be alone.

Keedy pointed to the chairs and they both sat down. Millie was worried.

'This is not about my landlord, is it, Sergeant?' she asked.

'No, Miss Duxford.'

'I promised to pay the rent I owe him but I can't do it at the moment.'

'Forget about your landlord,' he said quietly. 'I need to speak to you because I understand that you're a friend of Olive Arden.'

Millie brightened. 'Oh, yes – we see a lot of each other. Olive is a wonderful artist. I think she's going to be famous one day.'

'I'm afraid that won't be possible.'

'Why not?' She saw his expression and she quailed. 'Has something happened to her?' He chewed his lip. 'Don't keep me in suspense, Sergeant. I want to know.'

'Earlier this morning,' he explained, 'the body of a young woman was found in St James's Park. It's my sad duty to tell you that it was Olive Arden.'

Millie was aghast. She had the look of someone who'd strayed inadvertently onto a railway track and suddenly realised that a train was hurtling towards her. Tears welled in her eyes and she began to tremble. Keedy reached out to take both her hands between his palms. She made an effort to adjust to the news.

'Are you telling me that Olive was ... *murdered?*' she whispered.

'I'm afraid so.'

'This is terrible – it's unbelievable!'

Sensing that she was about to give full vent to her grief, Keedy tightened his grip on her hands. He leant forward and spoke with quiet authority.

'We need your help, Miss Duxford,' he said. 'Until I came here, I didn't even know who the victim was. I still have no details of where she comes from, why she was at the Slade, what sort of social life she had and where she lives. You're in a position to give me all the answers.'

Millie nodded. Pulling her hands away from him, she used the back of one of them to stem a tear. Keedy took a handkerchief from his pocket and offered it to her. She thanked him with a smile then dabbed at both eyes.

'I didn't come prepared for this,' she said, indicating her dressing gown. 'Not that it makes any difference, I suppose,' she added, sorrowfully. 'Even if I'd been properly dressed, I'd still have been knocked senseless by the news.' She returned his handkerchief. 'Are you absolutely sure that it was Olive?'

'I'm afraid that I am.'

'Then I'll help you all I can to catch the bastard who did this,' she promised.

Keedy had his notebook out. 'Tell me about Olive.'

The story poured out of her. Millie Duxford had a kind of rough-hewn beauty that was arresting at close quarters. When he'd seen her holding a pose, Keedy had been fleetingly reminded of the image of Britannia, proud, indomitable and wholly unselfconscious. Though poorly educated, she provided the relevant facts without meandering off into personal digressions.

Olive Arden, it turned out, was a second-year student at the Slade. She came from the Isle of Wight where her late father had been a sculptor of some renown. What she and Millie had in common was that they were both chronically short of money and took it in turns to help each other in emergencies. Both of them had done all manner of menial jobs in order to survive. At one point, Olive had even tried her hand as a pavement artist.

'It rained almost every time,' said Millie. 'It was cruel. As soon as she'd finished a chalk drawing, the skies opened and it was washed away.'

'Did she have any close friends apart from you?'

'There was Hugh, of course, but that didn't last long. Olive was very hurt, him being her first, so to speak. She thought that he felt the same as her but he was...' She gave an expressive shrug. 'I had her crying on my shoulder for weeks.'

'When was this?'

'Oh, it was before last Christmas.'

'Has she had any other boyfriends here?'

'No,' said Millie, 'that business with Hugh put her off. Also – and I have to be honest – Olive wasn't the sort of girl who knew how to ... make the best of herself. Yet she did start to make friends with one man.'

'Oh? Was it someone here at the Slade?'

She shook her head. 'It was a man she met at the National Gallery.'

The installation of a telephone at his home had made Harvey Marmion's work much easier. Instead of being summoned to Scotland Yard by a policeman sent to fetch him, he simply lifted the receiver and listened to the superintendent's voice. While Ellen could appreciate the advantages of having the instrument, she also bewailed its main disadvantage. It sometimes rang insistently in the middle of the night. Crime was not specifically a daytime activity. If an emergency arose in the small hours, then a call was immediately made to Marmion. It meant that he was the person who invariably answered the call. There were many occasions when Ellen wished that she could contact him at work but she'd always held back in the past, knowing that there was strong official disapproval of any detective making or receiving personal calls.

Now, however, she was desperate to speak to her husband. When she dialled the number, she was put through to his office and relieved to hear Marmion's voice at the other end of the line. Fearing a slight reprimand for ringing him at work, she was instead thanked.

'I was just about to get in touch with you, Ellen,' he said.

'Were you?'

'I thought you'd have seen the morning paper by now.'

'It was put through the letter box.'

'Why? We don't have it delivered.'

'I think it was Lena Belton again.'

'This has got to stop,' he said, angrily. 'Just because she suffered losses, it doesn't mean she can goad us when Paul goes into combat.'

'Did you see the figures, Harvey?' she whimpered. '19,000 killed.'

'They may be inaccurate.'

'Whatever the number, it's an enormous one. The bombardment is still going on. I mean, it's happening far away in France yet people in places like Kent and Surrey can hear the noise clearly. Paul is right in the middle of it all.'

'We don't know that, Ellen.'

'He told us that there was a huge battle brewing.'

'His regiment might not even have been deployed as yet.'

'It's bound to be at some stage,' she said, fearfully.

'Then we must pray that Paul comes through it, love,' he said, trying to reassure himself as much as his wife. 'Paul's a good soldier. He won't do anything foolhardy and he spoke well of his officers. Don't torment yourself, Ellen. All that we can do is to ... keep hoping. As for Mrs Belton,' he went on, 'if she pushes any more newspapers through the door, she'll get a visit from me.'

'Thanks for talking to me,' said Ellen. 'I was afraid you wouldn't be there.'

'I have to leave very soon, love. We have another crisis.'

'Don't be too late back. I need you.'

'I'll do my best.'

'Goodbye, Harvey – and thank you.'

'Goodbye.'

She heard the receiver being put down at the other end of the line. Grateful that she'd managed to speak to her husband, Ellen wasn't really comforted. Marmion was as worried about their son as she was but he had more self-control. She replaced the receiver and went into the living room. Picking up the newspaper, she looked at the front page again. The death toll was high yet it was only a fraction of the total force launched against the Germans in a mass attack. There was still hope. Snatching up the paper, she took it into the kitchen and put it in the bin under the sink. Her husband wouldn't need to confront Lena Belton about what she'd done. Ellen vowed that she would accost the woman.

Millie Duxford looked different when fully dressed. She let her hair down and put on a pair of spectacles. She then led Joe Keedy on a twisting journey through the streets. When they reached the house where Olive Arden had lodged, Marmion's car was standing outside and attracting a lot of interest from a group of noisy children. Using the telephone at the Slade, Keedy had contacted the inspector to tell him the name and address of the second murder victim. Marmion had gone straight to the house where she'd lived.

'We don't have unlimited transport,' Keedy explained. 'When the inspector has the car, I have to walk.'

'That's not fair,' said Millie.

'I've been telling him that for years.'

'It's not much of a room, I'm afraid, but it was all that Olive could afford, and the landlord was very good to her.'

'Did she walk to and from the Slade every day?'

'She was a student, Sergeant. She had to save her pennies.'

They were still chatting when Marmion emerged from the house. Glad to see Keedy, he was introduced to Millie and surprised to hear that Olive's best friend was an artist's model. Much of what the sergeant had found out had already been gleaned by Marmion from the landlord.

'He said that she was his favourite lodger,' recalled Marmion. 'Her death has really upset him. He just couldn't take it in.'

'Neither could I,' interjected Millie. 'I still can't.'

'We're still working on assumptions to some extent, though. Ideally, we'd like the next of kin to identify the body but the mother lives alone on the Isle of Wight and Olive's brother, it seems, is in the navy.'

'That presents us with a problem,' said Keedy.

'No it doesn't,' volunteered Millie. 'I'll do it.'

'Are you sure you'd be up to it?'

'I'd be doing it for Olive, Sergeant. The sooner you know for certain that it's her, the sooner you can go in search of the black-hearted villain who murdered her.'

'Thank you, Miss Duxford,' said Marmion. 'Can you come with us now?'

'Yes, of course.'

'Then please step into the car. I'd like a word with Sergeant Keedy.' He opened the door for Millie to get in, then closed it after her.

'She's been a great help, Harv,' said Keedy. He nodded at the house. 'What did you find in her room?'

'I found what you'd expect to find in a student lodging. In her case, however, there was a significant omission.'

'Let me guess – her portfolio had disappeared.'

'That's right, Joe. He didn't take any underwear this time and he didn't leave the place in a mess.'

'Didn't the landlord hear sounds of an intruder?'

'What he heard was the sound of a key being put into the lock shortly before midnight. Assuming it was Olive, he turned over and went to sleep again. He didn't hear anyone leaving the house. What about you – any leads?'

'Thanks to Millie, we could have a very good one. When I got to the Slade, by the way, she was posing in the nude for some students. She's got an amazing body, Harv,' he said with a nudge in his voice. 'I was distracted for a moment.'

Marmion was stern. 'What did she tell you?'

'Olive had met an older man at the National Gallery. He gave her a present, apparently. It was an art book. Millie says that the girl was over the moon. She agreed to see him yesterday evening.'

'Do we have a name for the man?'

'Yes – it was Lionel.'

'Did Millie have any idea who he was?'

'All that Olive told her was that he works in the art department of an auction house.' He snapped his fingers. 'We've got him, Harv.'

'Don't get too excited, Joe. It's never that easy.'

Sir Edward Henry was disturbed to hear of the second murder. He knew that it would give certain elements in the press a weapon with which to attack him and, by extension, the whole of the Metropolitan Police Force. Editors were already claiming that it was no longer safe to go to the cinema. The new accusation would be that the police were unable to guarantee the safety of the public in the city's parks. And since the two murders appeared to be linked, there would be dire warnings that a ruthless killer was on the prowl in London in search for female victims. At a time when reassurance was needed, fear and panic would be spread indiscriminately. The commissioner took his anxieties to Claude Chatfield's office.

'We must do our best to restore calm, Superintendent,' he said.

'The press conference has already been arranged.'

'Then I'll make a statement myself before Inspector Marmion takes over.'

'I'm best placed to cope with the press, Sir Edward.'

'You've incurred too much displeasure. Excellent as your performances have been in front of them, they haven't satisfied the demands for information. You were actually pilloried in a cartoon this morning.'

Chatfield scowled. 'I thought that very unjust, Sir Edward.'

'It was. On the other hand, it was an excellent likeness of you. Be that as it may,' said the commissioner, 'I'm taking you out of the firing line for a while. The inspector is much better at dodging the bullets. He has a gift for dealing with awkward reporters and he's actually been to the scene of this latest murder.'

'Nevertheless, I'd like to be there, Sir Edward.'

'We'll go together. Marmion will need the support of some top brass.'

They continued to discuss the case and look for parallels with the murder of Charlotte Reid. Minutes later, they were joined by Marmion himself. He was able to furnish fresh details of the crime. Chatfield was shocked.

'The victim was merely a *student?*' he asked. 'The man must have been years older than her.'

'Relationships with such an age difference are not uncommon,' said Marmion, thinking of Keedy and Alice. 'What links the two women is that they were both vulnerable. Charlotte Reid was lonely because her husband was abroad in the army and Olive Arden had been deeply upset by the break-up with her boyfriend. She told her friend that she was afraid that nobody would ever take an interest in her again. I daresay that she was flattered by the attention she got from this man.'

'At least we have some idea about who he was,' said the commissioner.

Marmion was guarded. 'That remains to be seen, Sir Edward. All that we have is a Christian name. I've sent detectives to all of the main auction houses in search of an employee called

Lionel. It may be a futile exercise. I can't believe that the killer would give himself away by disclosing his real name.'

'Have the girl's family been informed?' asked Chatfield.

'Yes, sir – I telephoned the police on the Isle of Wight. They will make contact with the victim's mother. The father died some years ago. From what Miss Arden's friend told us, the mother is not in the best of health.'

'We need someone in the family to identify the body.'

'We have the next best thing,' explained Marmion. 'The friend I mentioned is a woman named Millie Duxford. She appears to be the closest thing that Miss Arden had to a family in London. Miss Duxford has already been a great help to us and has offered to view the body. Sergeant Keedy has taken her to the morgue so we will get a firm identification very soon.'

While she'd been quick to volunteer her help, Millie Duxford grew increasingly apprehensive when they reached the morgue. During his years in the family undertaking business, Joe Keedy had seen the impact of extreme grief many times. Relatives viewing the remains of a loved one had been known to faint, suffer a heart attack or become hysterical. Millie was no relative, but her bond with the deceased had been a firm one and her sense of bereavement was intense. When he took her into the room where the body lay, therefore, Keedy stood close to her with a supporting hand under her elbow. Millie gave him a

207

pale smile of gratitude.

By a cruel twist of fate, the model and the student had changed places. As a rule, it was Millie who was nude and Olive Arden who was fully clothed as she sketched her friend in a life class. Millie was now dressed and the murder victim was completely naked under the shroud. The difference between the police morgue and that of Josiah Keedy and Sons, Funeral Directors, was that the latter handled, for the most part, people who had died a natural death. There had been those killed in traffic accidents or by some mishap at work but foul play was never involved. Olive Arden, by contrast, had apparently been throttled by a powerful man either after or during the time that he'd taken his pleasure. The autopsy, Keedy believed, might well confirm that intercourse had taken place. It was a sickening thought. What had probably begun as a passionate experience for a compliant young woman had ended in her death.

Millie was not going to be rushed. She needed time to prepare herself. She breathed in deeply several times and ran her tongue over dry lips. Only when she felt completely ready did she nod at the assistant standing beside the trolley. The man drew back the shroud to reveal the face. Millie let out a gasp of horror.

'It's Olive!' she cried.

Then she collapsed into Keedy's arms.

CHAPTER THIRTEEN

Ellen Marmion reached a decision. After brooding over it for a long time, she resolved to take action there and then. If she held back, she feared, there would be another newspaper stuffed through her letter box with nasty intent. Because Ellen could not rely on bumping into Lena Belton accidentally in the near future, she put on her hat and went off in the direction of the woman's house. It was not a long walk but she'd worked up her indignation fully on the way. The bedroom curtains were closed and, although it was a sunny day, the place had an air of gloom about it. Ellen lifted the knocker and banged it down hard twice in succession. The sound echoed throughout the house but it brought nobody to the door. Ellen was disappointed. A neighbour then walked past on the other side of the road and called across to her.

'Lena is definitely in,' she said. 'Knock harder.'

'Thank you, Mrs Jackson.'

Ellen took her advice and used much more force on the knocker. Nobody inside the house could possibly have failed to hear it. After a few seconds, the frowning face of Lena Belton appeared in the downstairs front window. She glared angrily then came to the front door. Ellen heard a bolt being drawn before the door opened a few inches.

'I'd like a word with you, Lena,' she said, purposefully.

'Go on, then. Say your piece.'

'Aren't you going to invite me in?'

'No,' said Lena, truculently.

'Well, at least let me see you properly.'

'I can hear you perfectly well from here, Ellen Marmion.'

'Why are you hiding like that?'

'It's because I've got nothing to say to you.'

'No,' said Ellen, 'you prefer to make your point by delivering newspapers to us, don't you?'

'I did warn you. Your turn would come.'

'That's spiteful, Lena.'

'I just want you to know how I feel,' said the woman, defensively. 'When you get in my position, you don't want people bothering you all the time, offering you cups of tea, saying they're sorry, trying to interfere.' Her tone hardened. 'And, most of all, you don't want them banging on your front door. You just want to be left alone. What do I have to do to get that message across?'

'Anybody else in your position would turn to their friends.'

'I've got no friends around here.'

'You did have – but you've driven them away.'

'I hate being pestered. Can none of you understand that?'

'Well, I can't,' said Ellen, spiritedly. 'I can't understand why anybody can throw people's sympathy back in their faces. It's atrocious behaviour and you should be ashamed. All right, if you want to lock yourself away, you're entitled to do so, but you're not entitled to take your grief out on me.'

Lena was unmoved. 'Have you finished?'

'What's got into you?'

'Oh, you'll soon find out.'

'No, I won't, because I value my friends and neighbours. If I have bad news, I'll turn to them for comfort in the same way that they'd turn to me. It's what normal human beings do, Lena. They help each other in the bad times. As for Patrick,' she added, 'he will, in time, be called up. The law is the law.'

'I'd expect a copper's wife to say that,' rejoined Lena with contempt. 'A couple of years ago, policemen were people who helped children and old ladies across the road. Now they're part of this plan to control everything, telling us where to go and what to do, saying what we can eat and drink, sending our sons off to be killed in some terrible battle and making our lives a misery.'

'The government had to step in,' said Ellen, reasonably.

'It didn't have to bully us the way it does.'

'Everybody's in the same boat, Lena.'

'No, they're not. Look at you, for instance. You're one of them. Your husband is a policeman and so is your daughter. You side with the bullies. You're part of this plot to murder our children by forcing them into uniform.'

'Nobody forced your sons into uniform,' said Ellen, furiously. 'Norman and Gregory both volunteered. There was no conscription when they joined up. It was the same with Paul. He answered the call straight away. Your sons were proud to fight for their country – and so is Paul.'

'Then Paul will be proud to *die* for his country,'

211

said Lena with a sly grin.

The noise of shellfire continued. Paul Marmion was only feet away from Colin Fryatt yet he couldn't hear his friend's mouth organ. Both had been part of a football team that joined the army in its entirety. Only four of them were left and the ferocity of the battle threatened to wipe out the rest of the team. During a momentary respite, Fryatt sought comfort in the evocative songs that had become so familiar to the troops. Paul thought about his family and his slim chances of ever seeing them again. As the whistle was blown to signal another attack, he clambered out of the trench after Fryatt and felt as if the gates of hell were about to open in front of him.

After a long sequence of bad news, Harvey Marmion was heartened to hear something more positive. Derek Reid called to see him at Scotland Yard.

'My father-in-law finally gave in,' he said.

'He and Mrs Christelow will attend the funeral?'

'Yes, Inspector. The parish priest came to my aid. He pointed out that – no matter what Charlotte had done – she was still their daughter and deserved a Christian burial with all her family there.'

'I'm very pleased to hear that, Lieutenant,' said Marmion. 'In essence, all that your wife did was to go to the cinema with another man. Her parents seem to have magnified that into some sort of terrible crime whereas Mrs Reid is the victim here.'

'They came to accept that in the end.'

'Have you made any arrangements yet, sir?'

'Mrs Bond is helping me do that,' said Reid, gratefully. 'She's setting everything in motion and telling all the neighbours.'

'I'd like to know the date as well. If I may, I'd like to be there.'

Reid was touched. 'Thank you, Inspector.' He straightened his back. 'Are you any closer to catching the man who killed her?

'We are pursuing him with vigour, sir, and have been given extra resources to do so. There has been a disturbing development, however, and before I tell you what it is, I must ask you to treat what I say as confidential because we've not yet released full information to the press.'

'Yes, yes, of course.'

'Earlier today, we were called to an incident in St James's Park. A young woman was strangled to death,' explained Marmion. 'We've reason to believe that there's a connection between this crime and the death of your wife.'

Reid blanched. 'Are you sure of that, Inspector?'

'The similarities are too close to be a coincidence.'

'Does that mean you have fresh clues?'

'Yes, sir.'

'May I know what they are?'

'I can tell you the most important one, Lieutenant. The second victim was a student at the Slade School of Art. We know for a fact that she was befriended by a man during her visits to the National Gallery.'

'Then that's where Charlotte could have met

him,' said Reid. 'She said in her letters how much she was enjoying her art classes. The teacher had advised her to visit art galleries to develop her appreciation. That must be how she met this fellow.'

'That theory is supported by a description we have of him. The second victim had confided to her friend that she was seeing the man yesterday evening. He was said to be handsome, well dressed and in his thirties. It tallies with what we already know of him. He's a professional man and he's a predator.'

'He's a vicious swine, Inspector.'

'That, too, naturally.'

'The wonder is that he's got away with it twice,' exclaimed Reid. 'How on earth can he kill two young women with impunity?'

'Oh, he'll be punished, sir,' Marmion said with emphasis. 'As I promised you once before, we'll catch him and I fancy that we're taking some significant steps in that direction.'

'Do you have any idea who or what this fellow is?'

'He told his second victim that he worked in the art department of an auction house so it's not surprising that he visits the National Gallery.'

'Then all you have to do,' said Reid with excitement, 'is to go to every auction house in London and comb through their staff.'

'At this moment,' said Marmion, 'my detectives are doing just that.'

The search was swift and exhaustive. When the detectives reported back to Scotland Yard, it was

214

Joe Keedy who collated their research. Having secured a positive identification of the body of Olive Arden, he'd sent her friend, Millie Duxford, back to her lodging to recover from the shock. In spite of himself, Keedy still had warm memories of seeing the model in her full glory in the nude and regarded it as an incidental bonus of the investigation. A team of detectives had either rung or visited all of the city's auction houses. Only two of them employed a man named Lionel in their respective art departments. One employee could be discounted at once because he was well into his fifties and had an alibi for his movements during the time that each of the victims had been killed. That left one possible suspect.

Terry Jellings, an eager young detective constable, delivered the news.

'He's the right age, sir,' he said, 'and his colleagues tease him about his good looks. He's single, dresses well and is known as a ladies' man.'

Keedy was taken aback. Jellings had just described his sergeant with a fair degree of accuracy. He felt guilty that, until he committed himself to Alice Marmion, he'd had a series of girlfriends that made him the butt of his colleagues' humour. Those days, he vowed, were well behind him.

'Did you meet him, Constable?' he asked.

'He was not there, sir.'

'Then where is he?'

'Lionel Narraway – that's his full name – is an appraiser for a prestigious auction house. He's very experienced and always puts an accurate guide price on any paintings that come in. He's out of London for most of the day but should be

215

back home before long.'

'Do you have his address?'

'It's here,' said Jellings, handing him a piece of paper.

'Thank you.'

'I took the trouble of going there to size it up. Mr Narraway must have a good salary. He lives in a fine house in a street off Pall Mall. You couldn't afford that on our pay scales, sir.'

'Our job gives us rewards of the heart,' said Keedy with a grin.

Jellings was a realist. 'I'd rather have hard cash, Sergeant.'

'So would I.'

'One other thing – it's an easy walk to the National Gallery from the house.'

'You've shown initiative – well done!'

'Thank you, sir.'

'You and I will pay Mr Lionel Narraway a visit right now.'

Marmion did not wish to arouse the superintendent's wrath for a second time. Should the man call at Scotland Yard again, Chatfield had insisted on meeting the husband of the first murder victim. Accordingly, Marmion sent word to him that Derek Reid was in the building. At their last meeting, the superintendent had been unexpectedly kind to the inspector. Marmion was not counting on his being in such a caring mood again. His instinct was sound. Chatfield was brisk and businesslike. Back upright, he strode into Marmion's office as if on parade. After being introduced to Derek Reid, he expressed his sympathy then rattled off nearly all the information that the visitor had already been given by Marmion. The superintendent eyed Reid's uniform.

'You're in the most dreadful situation, Lieutenant. I'm tempted to say that this is a good time to be in England for any soldier, but that would be tactless.'

'It would be tactless and asinine,' observed Marmion.

'Given the choice,' said Reid, 'I'd rather be with my regiment.'

'Then I admire your courage,' said Chatfield.

'My men rely on me, sir. That's not always the case with my fellow officers. Some are as young as nineteen or twenty. They're nothing more than callow youths. They're learning that war is very different from what they experienced in their playground drills at school.'

'Nobody could have been prepared for a conflict on this scale.'

'I certainly wasn't.'

'The inspector may have told you that his son is at the Somme.'

'Yes, he did, Superintendent.'

'I've been extraordinarily lucky. I have five children but the only two old enough to be called up are my daughters. The eldest of my three boys is fifteen.'

'Hopefully,' said Marmion, 'the war will be over before they're of an age to be conscripted. It's already gone on far too long.'

'I've forgotten why we got embroiled in it in the first place,' complained Reid. 'It's a complete stalemate at the moment. We're sacrificing large

217

numbers of men in the noble cause of winning a few hundred yards of territory that we'll probably lose in the next skirmish. It's soul-destroying.'

'I'm sad to hear a note of cynicism in your voice,' said Chatfield.

'I'm only voicing a general belief among our troops.'

'You should be instilling confidence in them.'

'It's a rare commodity at the front.'

'Lieutenant Reid brought some good tidings,' said Marmion, trying to lift all their spirits. 'With the aid of the parish priest, he's managed to persuade his wife's parents to attend the funeral, after all. They were made to see where their duties lay.'

Chatfield sniffed. 'Quite right, too.'

'They'll be coming down from Yorkshire in due course.'

'That must be a comfort to you, Lieutenant Reid.'

'The only balm we can offer the lieutenant before he rejoins his regiment is the arrest of the killer. That would soothe his mind.'

'It will soothe *mine* as well, Inspector.'

'But you've got his name,' argued Reid, 'and you know what he does for a living. Make an arrest.'

'All that we have is what he told his second victim,' warned Marmion, 'and he might well have been deliberately misleading her. He may, I suspect, have given the same information to your wife as a means of reassurance. He's clearly knowledgeable about art but that doesn't mean he works in an auction house.'

'Oh, I see.'

'We nurse hopes, sir, but ... we shouldn't make hasty assumptions.'

'What will happen if you don't catch him?' asked Reid.

'There's no danger of that,' asserted Chatfield.

'The superintendent is right,' said Marmion. 'As a result of the second murder, we have a much fuller portrait of the man's behaviour. Even though he struck once again in darkness, there may be people who are beginning to realise that they know who he is. It's imperative that we have him in custody soon,' he went on, 'or we may be faced with a third victim.'

Chatfield was categorical. 'That won't happen.'

'It will, if we don't stop him, sir. He's on a spree.'

'The public will be on the alert against him now. That will make it more difficult for him to lure someone else into his trap.'

'But you know that he uses the National Gallery to find his victims,' said Reid. 'Can't you have someone undercover there?'

'Detectives are already at the gallery on the lookout,' Marmion told him, 'but we're dealing with a clever man. Now that he's killed again, he'll realise that we'll put two and two together with regard to the National Gallery. My guess is that he'll avoid it now and search elsewhere for the next victim.'

'We'll get him,' said Chatfield, grimly, 'or the newspapers will crucify us.'

'Then I'll enjoy reading their apologies when we arrest the killer. It's a situation we've been in many times before, sir. The press seems to swing between praise and condemnation with no intermediate stages.' He looked at Reid. 'I'm sorry, Lieutenant. We shouldn't be boring you with our problems. I take it that you'll be staying at your home?'

Reid nodded. 'I will, Inspector.'

'As soon as we have good news, we'll pass it on to you.'

'Thank you.' Reid rose to his feet. 'Well, if you'll excuse me,' he said, 'I have a lot to do, beginning with an appointment at the undertaker's.'

'What will you do when it's all over, Lieutenant?' asked Chatfield.

'I would have thought that was obvious, Superintendent.'

'You'll go back to France?'

'When I've left my wife's funeral,' said Reid, solemnly, 'I'll return to the Somme for my own.'

When Joe Keedy arrived at the house with the detective constable in tow, he had the feeling that he was about to make more than a routine enquiry. Terry Jellings shared his excitement. It was clearly the home of a professional man. Keedy had high hopes that its owner would be wearing a pair of highly polished shoes. As it turned out, his hopes were fulfilled but not in the way that he'd hoped. In response to their knock, the door was opened by a sleek, silver-haired man in his sixties with impeccable tailoring and gleaming black shoes. When introductions were made, the detectives learnt that his name was Edwin Bonner and that he was the owner of the property. Lionel Narraway, they were told, rented

220

two rooms on the first floor. Bonner was polite and cooperative. He invited them into a living room that had exquisite furniture and some fine oil paintings. Keedy stared at a landscape.

'No, Sergeant,' explained Bonner, 'it's not a Constable but it's the next best thing. Lionel tipped me off when it came up for auction. My forte is furniture. Where art is concerned, I always rely on his advice.'

'I see,' said Keedy. 'Is Mr Narraway at home?'

'No, he isn't, not at the moment.'

'We were told that he was likely to be here.'

'He left a short time ago,' said Bonner. 'Might I ask what this is about?'

'We believe that Mr Narraway might be able to help us with regard to an incident that occurred last night, sir. What time did he arrive back here?'

'As a matter of fact, he didn't. Lionel was out of town last night.'

'Do you happen to know where?'

'He was away on business, Sergeant. He doesn't always give me specific details. He's our lodger. He comes and goes as he pleases.'

'Does he ever go to the National Gallery?' asked Jellings.

'If you'll forgive my saying so,' replied Bonner, 'that's a rather silly question. Lionel Narraway is an art expert. He goes to galleries whenever he can. He loves to draw inspiration from them – and, of course, they're a source of income for him at times.'

'Are they?'

'I'm talking about forgeries. You won't see any hanging at the National Gallery but there are some extremely talented artists who copy famous paintings and sell them off as originals. They even provide forged documents about provenance. Lionel,' he said, admiringly, 'has identified fakes in smaller galleries here and abroad. He's saved them a lot of embarrassment. I might also add that he once prevented me from spending a large amount of money on a fake.'

'Is he a sporting man?' asked Keedy.

Bonner laughed. 'Why ever do you wish to know that?'

'It's a matter of interest to me, sir.'

'Then the answer is that he's a very fine cricketer and used to be a racquets champion in younger days.' He looked from one to the other. 'I wish that one of you would tell me exactly what's going on.'

'We're investigating a serious crime, Mr Bonner,' explained Keedy, 'and we have reason to believe that your lodger may be able to help us.'

'Surely, you're not saying that Lionel was *involved* in this crime?'

'All I can tell you is that we need to speak to him as a matter of urgency.'

'Do you know where he is at this moment?' asked Jellings.

'Yes, I do,' replied Bonner.

'May we know where it is, sir?'

There was a long silence. 'We must press you on this, sir,' insisted Keedy.

'I simply refuse to believe that he's done anything wrong,' said Bonner.

'Then you have nothing to worry about. If you're certain of his innocence, you'll tell us where we can locate Mr Narraway and this whole matter can be cleared up very quickly.' Bonner still hesitated. 'Well?'

'He's at the Savage Club,' said the other.

'Thank you, sir.'

'It's in Covent Garden.'

'I know where it is, Mr Bonner.'

After bidding him farewell, the detectives left the house. Jellings was curious.

'What's the Savage Club?'

'It's a place where authors, artists and journalists get together,' said Keedy, breezily. 'For some unknown reason, I've never been invited to join.'

'I've never heard of it, Sergeant.'

'That's because you didn't once have a beat in Covent Garden like me. It's a fascinating area. You get all sorts there.'

As they walked away, another thing troubled Terry Jellings.

'Why did you ask him if Narraway was a sportsman?'

'I wanted to know if he was strong enough to strangle a woman to death.'

Alice Marmion went into the building and headed for Thelma Gale's office. The door was ajar. The inspector was seated behind her desk with a newspaper in front of her. When she saw Alice approaching, she beckoned her in.

'You start on the night shift tomorrow,' she said.

'I don't need to be reminded of that, Inspector.'

'We're engaged in important work. Since the war began, standards have fallen disgracefully. We're the moral conscience of London.'

'I thought we were just there to stop any trouble.'

'Well,' said the other, gently, 'this is not the time to argue over it. I know that you equate a visit to this office with a reprimand of some kind but that's not always the case, Alice. I do have a duty of care towards my officers.'

Alice was about to say that she'd seen very little evidence of it but she stopped herself from doing so just in time. She glanced down at the desk and saw that her superior had been reading *The Times*.

'Have you been able to see this?' asked Thelma.

'No, Inspector, I've been walking my beat with Peggy Lassiter.'

'Then I'm able to reassure you on one matter.' She opened the newspaper and spread the two pages wide. 'Do you know what I have here?'

Alice gulped. 'I think so, Inspector.'

'It's a list of all those who have died so far in the battle of the Somme. *The Times* will be publishing such a list every day.' She smiled at Alice. 'Your brother's name is not here.'

'Thank you for telling me.'

'It must be a worrying time for you.'

'We've been anxious ever since Paul joined up.'

'I share that anxiety, Alice. My nephew is in the Royal Sussex Regiment. He was at the battle of Loos.'

It was the first time that the inspector had ever mentioned her family and it served to humanise her slightly in Alice's eyes. While she could see the value of compiling lists of the fallen, Alice was not sure that she would wish to scour a newspaper in search of her brother's name. It seemed a dreadfully impersonal way to receive bad news. Though the letters being sent out were very formal, with gaps left for the name and regiment of the deceased to be written in, they were infinitely better, Alice felt, than a name in a very long list.

The inspector folded the newspaper again and set it aside. Hands clasped, she sat back in her chair and gazed at Alice with something like her usual disapproval.

'There's been a second murder,' she announced.

'Here in London?'

'A young woman was strangled to death in St James's Park. The rumour is that it's the work of the same killer. Sergeant Keedy will doubtless give you all the details in the fullness of time.'

'I've told you before,' said Alice, 'that neither my father nor Sergeant Keedy ever talk about their cases with me. I'm not a detective and therefore have no right to be included in any discussions.'

'That's as it should be, of course, though I have a sneaking suspicion that the sergeant will divulge some details if only as a means of impressing you.'

'He doesn't need to impress me, Inspector.'

'Men do like to boast.'

'With respect,' said Alice, robustly, 'that's a sweeping generalisation. And no man would want to boast about a murder that remains unsolved and a second killing that may be related to it.' Alice had silenced her for once and she enjoyed her moment of triumph. 'Will that be all, Inspector?'

Covent Garden was caught up in its daily bustle

as the detectives walked along Henrietta Street. Their destination was the long back room of a large house. On the way there, Keedy had told the constable a little more about the club where members met to discuss subjects of common interest. The only club to which Jellings had ever belonged was a football club and the concept of an association where gentlemen of the arts congregated was foreign to him. When they presented themselves to the steward, they were given a cool reception. It became no warmer when they explained that they'd come from Scotland Yard. They were meant to feel like intruders. The steward invited them to sit down then went in search of Lionel Narraway.

'I could never feel at ease in a place like this,' confided Jellings.

'You won't get the chance. The annual fee is too steep.'

'I didn't like the way that steward looked at us.'

Keedy chuckled. 'We'll get an even nastier look if we arrest one of his members,' he said.

The door opened and Lionel Narraway entered. They got up and introduced themselves. He seemed baffled that they should wish to speak to him.

'We went to your lodging,' explained Keedy. 'Your landlord told us that we might find you here.'

'I've been advising the club on the purchase of a painting,' said Narraway.

'We believe that you're an expert, sir.'

'I have written a book or two that have achieved a measure of success in the art world and I'm always ready to share my knowledge with my friends.'

'May I ask where you were last night, sir?'

Narraway tensed. He was a spruce individual in his thirties with curling hair and arresting good looks. Both detectives had noted the shine on his shoes.

'That's a rather impertinent question, Sergeant,' he said.

'I hope that I don't have to repeat it, Mr Narraway.'

'Very well – if you must know, I stayed with friends in Berkshire.'

'And will those friends vouch for your being there?'

'I'm certain that they will if I ask them, but I see no reason whatsoever why I should do so.' A chevron of indignation appeared between his eyebrows. 'Would one of you please have the courtesy to explain why you're here?'

'We're involved in a murder investigation, sir,' said Keedy, 'and we believe that you may be able to help us with our enquiries.'

'What the devil are you talking about, man?'

'Someone answering your description killed a young woman last night.'

'I was in Berkshire, I tell you.'

'That's what you claim,' said Jellings.

Narraway fumed. 'I give you my word of honour,' he snapped. 'Do you dare to question that?'

'It's our job to question everything.'

Jellings was confident that they had found the right man but Keedy was having reservations. He studied the man carefully and left it to his constable to conduct the interview. After reeling off a series of questions, Jellings asked one that came out like an accusation.

'Did you or did you not see a Charlie Chaplin film at the West End cinema?'

Narraway reacted as if he'd just been slapped across the face with a large fish. When he recovered, he looked at the detectives with utter disdain.

'Wild horses would not be able to drag me to a cinema,' he declared. 'I move in the world of the arts. I deal exclusively with pure gold and not with base metal like Charlie Chaplin. The very suggestion that I'd lower myself in that way is insulting. I demand an apology.'

'Then you shall have it, sir,' said Keedy, stepping in before Jellings could open his mouth. 'We seem to have made an unfortunate mistake and we apologise unreservedly. The constable and I will trouble you no further.'

'A letter of complaint will go to Scotland Yard about this,' warned Narraway.

'You're within your rights to send it, sir.' He nudged Jellings. 'Goodbye.'

Keedy more or less pulled his companion away and didn't speak until they were out in the street once more. Jellings was feeling robbed of the chance to make an important arrest. He looked for an explanation.

'It's not him,' said Keedy, flatly.

'How do you know?'

'Because I realised that Mr Bonner is not his landlord.'

'I don't understand, sir.'

'What did you notice at the house?'

'I saw that a lot of money had been spent in that living room. Those chairs must have cost a fortune and that carpet.'

'Something was missing – a woman's touch. I don't believe that Mr Bonner simply rents out a room. He hardly looked as if he'd need the money, did he? The truth is that he and Mr Narraway live alone together.'

'Do you mean that they...?'

'It's not our business to worry about what they do, Constable. We're looking for a man with perverted designs on young women. That's why we left so abruptly,' concluded Keedy. 'Lionel Narraway wouldn't dare to *touch* a woman, let alone lure one into a close friendship.'

Jellings was downhearted. 'In other words, the killer is still at large.'

'I'm afraid so. He's free to find himself another likely victim.'

She was bending over as she moved the items around. The store was closed but the window dresser had stayed on to arrange a display. He was part of a small crowd who watched her at work. While the others were impressed by her skill, he was studying the shapely body and its graceful movements. There was something almost balletic about her. When she finished, she stood with her back against the glass to admire her handiwork. Becoming aware that she was being watched, she turned to face the cluster of people outside. He beamed at her and patted his hands together in a silent gesture of applause.

CHAPTER FOURTEEN

'How ever could you let this happen?'

'Why is this man still free to kill again?'

'Have you made no progress at all?'

'What steps, if any, have you actually taken?'

'Do you have *no* idea who he is?'

'Is there nothing you can say to reassure the public?'

'Are the streets of London no longer *safe?*'

'Will you admit that you've failed abysmally?'

They had anticipated a stormy press conference that evening and there were a few tempestuous moments. The police were variously accused of slowness of response, lack of commitment and – it was hinted – sheer incompetence. On balance, Claude Chatfield was glad that he was not the spokesman this time. He and the commissioner watched from the sidelines as Harvey Marmion took on the hostile reporters, alternately wooing and chiding them until they lapsed into a state of general calm that made them more accessible to reason. He reminded them that the first murder had occurred less than a week earlier and argued that it was unfair to criticise them for being unable to make an instant arrest.

'Let us be practical,' he suggested. 'Millions of people live in this city. Even if we restricted our enquiries to men between certain ages, we would have a huge number with which to contend.

Because of the war, our resources are depleted and are therefore spread more thinly. However,' he went on, 'we have not been sitting on our hands. Since the first murder, we have advised cinemas on ways to increase security and, within hours of the second fatality, we deployed extra men in every park in London. In short, gentlemen, where holes have appeared, we have done our best to plug them. Please give us some credit for that.'

There was a murmur of agreement then a big, assertive man spoke out.

'He's *taunting* you, Inspector,' he said.

'He's certainly laid down a challenge,' conceded Marmion.

'Look at his record. He's committed murder in a crowded cinema then done the same thing in a public park. Where's his next venue – Trafalgar Square during the rush hour?'

'Your guess is as good as mine, Tom.'

'Is that what you're relying on, then – guesswork?'

'We're gathering evidence patiently instead of making the snap judgements that people like you are prone to make. Two young women have fallen victim to the same man and we regret that as much as anyone. But,' said Marmion, 'we must, at all costs, guard against spreading panic. The killer is highly selective. I've explained that he and his victims had a mutual interest in art. That needs to be stressed. Any woman who is approached by a stranger because she has a passion for art should contact us as soon as possible. Please make that clear to your readers.'

231

The questioner narrowed his eyelids. 'There's something you haven't told us, Inspector,' he said as if he had caught Marmion out.

'What else do you need to know, Tom?'

'Did he have sexual relations with Olive Arden before he killed her?'

The murmur of interest became a positive rumble now. Everyone looked up.

'We don't yet have a post-mortem report,' said Marmion, levelly, 'so I'm unable to give you a positive answer at this stage.'

'But it does seem likely, doesn't it?'

'I'm not prepared to so speculate, Tom.'

'That's why so many couples go to our public parks,' said the reporter with a snigger. 'Look behind every bush and you'll usually find some hanky-panky going on?'

Marmion smiled. 'I'm interested to hear that you get your thrills by looking behind bushes.' There was a burst of laughter. 'What happened last night to the victim went well beyond the limits of hanky-panky. Bear this in mind, gentleman. Olive Arden has a family and friends. If you indulge in lurid conjectures about what took place before he actually killed her, you'll be causing them great distress.' He glanced at the clock on the wall. 'That's about it,' he decided, rising to his feet. 'Since the first murder, we've all been working overtime to trace and catch the culprit. Please support us in that endeavour instead of trying to undermine us.'

'One last question,' shouted a man at the back of the room.

'Very well,' agreed Marmion. 'Go on, Peter –

the floor is yours.'

'You have a son fighting in the battle of the Somme. We all know what's happening there at the moment. Isn't it a terrible distraction to you?'

'It's not a happy situation, I grant you, but it's no distraction. My son is not thinking about me when he picks up his rifle. He has far too much on his mind. It's the same with me,' said Marmion, stoutly. 'The moment I arrive at Scotland Yard, I'm wholly dedicated to the task of finding a dangerous killer. Nothing else matters to me. There's your headline, gentlemen,' he said. 'Nothing else matters.'

Alma Bond put her baby down for her morning nap then went to the window and tugged the net curtain. It was the signal for which Derek Reid had been waiting. A minute later, he crossed the road and was let into the house. Alma took him into the kitchen and offered him refreshment. He shook his head.

'I've not long had breakfast,' he said.

'How did you get on yesterday?'

'That's what I came to tell you, Alma.'

'Sit down.'

He was surprised. 'Are we going to talk in here?'

'I think so, Derek.'

They sat either side of the table. There was a tension in the air that he tried to dispel with a smile. Alma shifted uncomfortably in her chair. He took a piece of paper from his inside pocket and referred to it as he spoke.

'The date has been fixed,' he said, 'and I've put details in the obituary columns. They should be in this morning's papers. I've also made a list of people I expect to attend and I'll speak to the vicar about hiring the church hall for some refreshments after the funeral. I'm rather dreading that aspect,' he confessed. 'People will be trying to say soothing things about Charlotte and I just won't believe them.'

'What about her parents?'

'They're coming down tomorrow afternoon and will be staying with me.'

'If there are any other relatives, I can offer you two spare rooms.'

'Thank you, Alma.'

'I want to do all I can to help.'

Their eyes locked and there was palpable embarrassment on both sides.

'I thought you might call yesterday evening,' she said.

'I got back too late.'

'I know – it was almost midnight.'

He was irritated. 'I didn't know that I was under surveillance.'

'I saw the light go on in the bedroom.'

'It was the visit to the undertaker,' he explained. 'It shook me more than I'd expected. All that we did was to go over certain details but I was trembling when I came out of there. I went to the club. A lot of my old friends weren't there, of course, because they'd either joined up or been conscripted but there was still a good crowd.' He shrugged. 'I suppose the truth is that I got horribly drunk.'

'That's not a crime, Derek.'

'I walked all the way home as a penance.'

'Was that really necessary?'

'The fresh air revived me. It helped me to think straight, Alma.'

'About what?'

'Do you need to ask that?'

They both felt profound discomfort. For a few minutes, neither of them could speak. In the end, Reid felt obliged to offer an apology.

'I'm very sorry,' he said. 'It was a mistake.'

'You didn't think that at the time.'

'No, that's true. I was carried away with...'

'I hoped that it was with love,' she said, reprovingly, 'but it wasn't that at all. You never used to be so rough with me, Derek. I still have the bruises.'

'I still have your bite marks on my chest,' he told her as if that cancelled out his treatment of her. 'You could have asked me to stop.'

'I did, I asked you several times. You just didn't hear.'

He flicked a hand. 'Well, it's all over now. It's best to forget it, Alma.'

'Is that all it meant to you?' she demanded

'No, no, of course not – it was ... very nice.'

She flared up. 'You *are* in the mood for passing compliments, aren't you?'

'I didn't mean it the way it sounds.'

He tried to reach out to her but she pushed his hand away and pouted.

'Look, I've said that I was sorry, Alma.'

'That's not what I wanted to hear. I thought that you cared.'

'I do, you know that.'

'All I know is that you took me like a wild animal

235

then left me here and sneaked off back home. I felt *used*, Derek. When it happened before, it was special. You were tender. Not this time – I felt ashamed.'

'How do you think *I* felt?' he yelled, jumping to his feet.

Alma recoiled and put up both hands to protect herself. Reid hovered between anger and apology. He made a supreme effort to relax.

'Perhaps we should have this discussion at another time,' he said, quietly.

'I think that's a good idea.'

'We both need time to ... nurse our wounds, so to speak.'

He went out and Alma followed him, though she took care not to get too close. She was frightened of him now. Adversity had drawn them together but they had now split apart decisively. Reid was shamefaced. After opening the front door, he turned to her and made an incongruous parting comment.

'Inspector Marmion may come to the funeral.'

News of the second murder provoked an immediate response. A series of assorted people turned up at Scotland Yard, claiming to have seen the couple together in St James's Park two days earlier. Most of the descriptions given of them were markedly at variance with what the detectives knew of Olive Arden and so they could be eliminated at once. In the case of Charlotte Reid, they'd been able to release a photograph of the deceased to the press and it had prompted a few memories among the public. Unfortunately,

Marmion had found no photographs of the second victim during his search of her room. Reporters had simply repeated the verbal description that he'd given of her. Anonymous letters also came in, some with extravagant claims of knowing exactly who the killer was and others from people who'd seen or heard something suspicious but who preferred to hold back their names.

As with the first murder, it was tiring and tedious work. When they had a break and a cup of tea, Joe Keedy had some praise to pass on.

'I hear that you were on good form at the press conference yesterday.'

'Well, you didn't hear it from Tom Bowring of the *Daily Mirror*,' said Marmion. 'He's always the one to ask awkward questions. He didn't like it when I made them laugh at his expense.' He stirred sugar into his cup. 'What exactly did the commissioner say?'

'Oh, it wasn't Sir Edward who told me – it was Chat!'

'You're pulling my leg, Joe.'

'It's as true as I'm standing here,' said Keedy. 'Chat reckoned that you gave a master class in defusing the situation. They came in search of your head and you sent them out as fully paid-up members of the Harvey Marmion Appreciation Society.'

'All except Tom Bowring, that is – he refused to pay his dues.'

Keedy changed tack. 'Why is the post-mortem taking such a time? We asked them to give it priority.'

'You, of all people, should know that they can't rush these things, Joe. They want to do a thorough job.'

'What if they discover that intercourse *did* take place on the night in question? Are you going to tell the press?'

'I'll do my best to play that element down, Joe. As and when we catch this devil, the full details will come out at the trial. They'll be splashed all over the papers then. It's such a pity!' said Marmion. 'I'm afraid that Olive Arden's family will be in for a very rough time – and so will that friend of hers.'

'Millie Duxford will be able to cope,' said Keedy with confidence. 'She's a woman of the world. I don't think that anything will shock her.'

'You told me that she collapsed at the morgue.'

'That was different. The horror of her best friend's death hit her very hard. Millie recovered very quickly. That lady is made of steel.' There was a tap on the door and it opened. 'Here we go – another bogus witness, I daresay.'

When the policeman ushered a man into the room, the detectives smelt him before they actually saw him. The newcomer was a tramp who seemed to possess little beyond the ragged clothes he was wearing. He was a stooping man in his fifties with a face so hirsute that his eyes seemed to be peering at them through a hedge. When they introduced themselves, he gave his name as Alaric Griffin in a voice that had an educated ring to it. He spotted the tea at once.

'I don't suppose you've got a spare cup, have you?'

'That depends on what you have to tell us, Mr Griffin,' said Marmion. 'If you've just come in here to cadge some tea and stink the place out, then you can leave right now.'

Keedy opened a window to let in fresh air. 'It's a terrible pong, Alaric.'

'Ye get used to it,' said Griffin.

'How long have you been a tramp?'

'Please, Sergeant!' said the other with righteous indignation. 'I'm a gentleman of the road. I'm an adventurer, an explorer, a man of independent spirit.'

'What have you got to tell us?'

Griffin screwed up one eye. 'I may have seen something.'

'Don't you dare tell us a cock-and-bull story,' warned Marmion. 'We've had enough of those already.'

'I'll tell you the truth, Inspector.'

'What did you see?'

'Two nights ago,' Griffin began, 'I was in the park when it was dark and I saw this man with a young woman.'

'How could you see them in the dark?'

'My eyes had grown accustomed to it, Inspector. If you live the kind of life I do, you have to develop eyes like a cat. Darkness is when danger comes. Nasty things can happen to you at night.'

'What age would the man have been?' asked Keedy.

'I'd say he was about your age, Sergeant.'

'Did you hear his voice?'

'I couldn't hear him properly but he seemed to be saying the sorts of things men say when they want to ... misbehave with a woman.' He gave a snort. 'I put that whole world behind me, ye see. I live alone. I've no time for women now.'

'And no time for a bath either,' said Marmion as the stench hit him again.

'Let me finish, will you?'

'I'm sorry, Mr Griffin.'

Their visitor hit his stride. Though he didn't say so, it was clear to the detectives that he spent the night in St James's Park and was a regular denizen of such places. Griffin explained that two figures had crept past his hideaway and he'd been able to see them well enough to guess at their ages. They had disappeared into some bushes not far away and Griffin had tried to go to sleep. He was awakened after a while by sounds that made him cringe in disgust. Most of the disgust was reserved for the young woman and he made no bones about his being a confirmed misogynist. Griffin had assumed that the moans of ecstasy were the faked pleasure of a prostitute, trying to drive the man on by giving him the impression that she was enjoying full satisfaction. Then, all at once, the crude noises had stopped dead. After a few minutes, a man hurried past the tramp in the dark, pulling his jacket on as he did so.

It was all very plausible but the detectives felt they were being misled.

'Do you have any evidence to support what you've told us?' asked Marmion.

'I've the evidence of my own eyes and ears, Inspector.'

'That's not what I meant, sir. What you've de-scribed is an encounter that might have taken

240

place between any man and woman. In warm weather like this, prostitutes sometimes use a park as a place of assignation. Isn't that what happened in this case?'

'No, I've told you it wasn't.'

'What makes you so certain it was the killer and his victim?'

'It was the way he ran off,' said Griffin, irritably. 'Most men pull up their trousers and put their jackets back on before they sneak out of the bushes. This one didn't. He was in a rush. That's how it happened, you see.'

'How *what* happened?' said Keedy.

'He came to lose this, of course. I saw it glinting in the morning light and picked it up. I didn't realise at the time, of course, who it belonged to. It was his, Sergeant,' said Griffin, thrusting a hand into his pocket. 'And he's got a few bob if he can afford a pair like this.'

He opened his palm to reveal a gold cufflink. He chortled at the look of astonishment on the face of both detectives. They had suddenly started to take him seriously.

Griffin beamed at them. 'Is that enough to get me a cup of tea?'

'Yes,' said Marmion, gratefully, 'but you'll have to stand by the open window while you're drinking it. We'd like to be able to breathe again.'

Since she didn't have to start work until later in the day, Alice Marmion called on her mother and suggested that they did some shopping in the West End. Alice hoped that it would be a relief from the constant worry that both women had about Paul.

On the tube train to Piccadilly Circus, they ignored the jolting rhythm and raised their voices above the clamour. Both of them had searched the lists in *The Times* and were pleased that the name of Paul Marmion was not among them.

'It could be a mistake, of course,' said Ellen with concern.

'Paul is still alive, Mummy. You should be reassured.'

'They don't always get the names right.'

'No,' said Alice, 'they certainly don't. After the battle of Mons, Mrs Dyer's two sons were listed among the dead yet a few months later they were home on leave, as large as life. Someone had confused the names.'

Ellen revived slightly. 'Yes, that's true,' she said, managing a smile. 'Good news does come along occasionally. I just wish that the same thing had happened to Lena Belton.'

'Is she still being rude to you?'

'It's gone beyond that, Alice.'

Ellen told her daughter about the confrontation she'd had and how Lena Belton had refused to apologise. When she heard what the woman had said, Alice was seething with fury.

'Proud to die for his country!' she repeated. 'That's a wicked thing to say.'

'What hurt me was the tone she took.'

'Mrs Belton never used to be like that in the old days.'

'She had three sons alive then.'

'Her tragedy is not your fault, Mummy. It's appalling that she's made you the scapegoat for her grief. I've got a good mind to go round there

242

and tell her what I think of her.'

'Don't do that, Alice,' said her mother. 'That was the mistake I made. In any case, she sees you as one of the enemy.'

'What enemy?'

'You and your father are agents of the government, giving us orders all the time and making sure that we obey them. That's what Lena thinks, anyway. And she says that I'm tarred with the same brush.'

'How does she think we can fight a war *without* government control?'

'It's pointless trying to argue with her.'

Alice pulled a face. 'I discovered that outside the recruiting office.'

'And fair's fair,' admitted Ellen, 'Lena's not alone in what she thinks. You probably saw that letter in *The Times* today. It was from a man who claims we're living in a police state.'

'Oh,' said Alice, laughing, 'I think exactly the same thing when I look at Gale Force. She's a one-woman police state.'

The train hurtled into Piccadilly Circus Station and slowed down before coming to an abrupt halt. The two women got off together. 'What are you going to buy?' asked Ellen.

'Oh, I've come to *look* rather than buy, Mummy. Looking is cheaper.'

'And it's always good fun.'

Their first destination was Swan & Edgar, the famous store which had sprung to life a century earlier and been enlarged and developed over the years. Recent extensions had broadened its basis and allowed it to sell an even greater range of

243

items. When the two of them came up the steps into Regent Street, the first thing they saw was a window display that featured a range of summer dresses. A young woman was scrutinising them from various angles.

'Oh, look,' said Ellen, pointing. 'Doesn't that look wonderful?'

'Yes, Mummy – I'm almost tempted to buy something by that display.'

'Thank you,' said the young woman turning to them. 'I do appreciate what you both said. I'm the window dresser responsible, you see.'

Claude Chatfield read the post-mortem report with a mixture of interest and uneasiness. When he looked up from his desk, he frowned at Marmion.

'This is exactly what some of those reporters were hoping for,' he said with a click of his tongue. 'Especially Tom Bowring and his like. They revel in anything remotely sleazy.' He put the report aside. 'Well, they're not going to know what's in here until details of the autopsy emerge at the trial.'

'It's good to hear you say that, sir,' said Marmion. 'Miss Arden – it's now clear – does appear to have succumbed to the killer's advances. If we reveal that she had intercourse in the park, there will be lots of narrow-minded people who say that she deserved it for being so promiscuous – and that's far from the truth.'

'Nobody could describe *me* as narrow-minded, Inspector, but I strongly disapprove of what the victim did.'

'We can't be sure if sexual relations were forced

or consensual.'

'We can be sure that strangulation was not consensual,' said Chatfield, smiling at what he thought was a clever debating point. 'The warning we must give loud and clear is that women should be extremely wary of strangers.'

'I'm afraid it won't have the impact that it should do, sir.'

'Why ever not?'

'War has broken down many barriers,' said Marmion. 'That's all to the good in some cases, mind you, but not in the way young men and young women relate to each other. Meeting a complete stranger gives an added excitement to some people. They actually prefer easy, casual, short-term attachments.'

Chatfield stood up. 'Well, I think that's wholly reprehensible,' he said as he straightened his tie. 'Respect should be at the basis of every relationship and that takes time to build up. I courted my future wife for four and a half years before we moved on to a more formal arrangement. In that time, we'd learnt to love, respect and honour each other.'

'I had a similar experience, Superintendent, but the present generation is living in a far less secure world. They don't have the unlimited time that we enjoyed. When so many young men are being conscripted, there's a general feeling that people should grab their pleasure while they can.'

'And this is the result,' said Chatfield, snatching up the report. 'Not to mention the alarming rise in the number of illegitimate births.'

'You can't blame Olive Arden for what happened,' maintained the inspector. 'She was certainly not promiscuous and, in fact, she had very few male friends at the Slade. After breaking up with her boyfriend, she was very chary about starting a new relationship there. When I said that people sometimes grab their pleasure, I did not include her. She was a conscientious art student who simply had the misfortune to be picked on when her defences were down.'

'It's very gallant of you to speak up for her but I have to remind you that she was sadly lacking in moral principles. How else can you explain the fact that she agreed to have sexual intercourse in a public park with a man she barely knew?'

'She may have agreed to it at first, sir – though we have no proof of that – but it turned into her death warrant. Unlike Charlotte Reid, however, she did fight back. The report makes that clear,' argued Marmion. 'There was skin under her fingernails that could only have belonged to her attacker. Either she scratched his face or – much more likely, in my view – she was trying to pull his hands away as he asphyxiated her. That must have been how she tore the cuff of his sleeve.'

Chatfield waved the report. 'There's nothing here about a torn sleeve.'

'It's one very possible explanation, sir.'

'Explanation of what, may I ask?'

'This,' said Marmion, putting the gold cufflink on the desk. 'I believe that it belonged to the killer and that it came adrift when he fled the scene.'

Joe Keedy had been left on his own to cope with any other self-appointed witnesses who turned up in person or left notes at Scotland Yard. The volume of information flooding in suggested that a sizeable section of the population of London had been in St James's Park on the night in question. Shocked by the first murder, people had been horrified to hear of the second strike by the same killer. Even if they had nothing useful to offer, they wanted somehow to be a part of the investigation. Keedy was checking the latest statement when a visitor was shown into his office. He produced a broad smile of welcome when he saw that it was Millie Duxford.

'Can you spare me a moment, please?' she asked.

'I can spare you much more than that, Millie. Do sit down.'

'Thank you, Sergeant.'

While she lowered herself onto a chair, he got to his feet and came round his desk. Millie looked striking. She was smartly dressed and had used cosmetics to great effect. Her hair was swept up as it had been when he'd first seen her posing in the nude. Keedy got close enough to catch a whiff of her perfume.

'I read some of the papers,' she complained. 'They gave completely the wrong picture of Olive. She wasn't anything like the way she was described.'

'We can't control everything they write, I'm afraid.'

'Maybe not, but you can ask them to be more accurate. When the inspector told me that he couldn't find any photographs of Olive in her room, I was surprised. I know that she had some taken. There was one with *me*, for a start.'

Keedy smiled. 'Did you have your clothes on at the time?'

'Yes,' she replied with a laugh. 'I only pose for artists, not photographers. Anyway,' she went on, burrowing into her handbag, 'I remembered that I had a few photos of Olive. I don't know if they'll be of any use,' she said, taking them out and handing them over, 'but here they are.'

'Thank you, Millie. These will be a great help.'

'The first is the one I told you about – me and Olive at the Slade.'

Keedy leafed through them. There were four in all. One was of Olive Arden and her late father, standing beside one of his sculptures. The other three were taken at the Slade. In two of them, Olive was more or less obscured in a group photo. The one taken with Millie was the most suitable for use in the press.

'We may have to cut you off,' he warned. 'I don't mean that we'll damage the photo. We'll just use a close-up of Olive.'

'Do you have any news?' she asked, eagerly.

He chose his words carefully. 'We've gathered some useful evidence, Millie.'

'Has anyone suggested the killer's name?'

'Oh, yes, lots of people have done that. The problem is that it's never the *same* name. So far the suggestions have ranged from Ivor Novello to George Bernard Shaw. Inevitably, we had someone who insisted that it was Jack the Ripper.'

'Well, he was never caught, was he?'

'Criminals don't change their modus operandi,' he explained. 'That's their way of doing things.

Each crime has a signature on it. In the case of Jack the Ripper, the signature consisted of a dead prostitute with horrific mutilations carried out with a sharp knife. Olive's killer is addicted to strangulation and he chooses victims who are respectable young women.'

'What about the post-mortem?'

'I'm not at liberty to disclose the details of that, Millie.'

'It must have shown that Olive fought back,' she said. 'She was a strong girl. They lived by the sea on the Isle of Wight and they kept a boat. Olive rowed me out in it when I stayed with her. She pulled on the oars as if she knew what she was doing.'

'She was obviously a versatile young lady.'

Mille sat back, disappointed. 'I'd hoped for an arrest by now.'

'So did we,' said Keedy, 'but that information about a man named Lionel working for an auction house led us up a blind alley – as it was intended to do.' He handed three of the photographs back to her. 'Thank you for these. I'll let you have the other one when we've finished with it.'

'There's no hurry, Sergeant.'

'I'll need your address so that it can be posted to you.'

'Or you could drop it in if you happen to be passing,' she said, looking him in the eye. 'I'm so glad to see you again. I wanted to thank you for what you did when I identified the body.'

'I acted by reflex,' he said. "When you fainted, I reached out to catch you.'

249

'That wasn't what happened, Sergeant Keedy.'

'Yes, it was.'

'I didn't really faint,' she confessed. 'It upset me to see Olive like that but, as it happens, I've looked at a dead body before. My father was run over by a bus and I saw him in his coffin. Because his face was mangled, I did pass out that time.'

'Are you telling me that you collapsed on purpose at the police morgue?'

She grinned. 'I knew that you'd catch me.'

Swan & Edgar was so large and so full of items of interest that Ellen Marmion and her daughter let an hour go past without even noticing. They felt as if they were in an Aladdin's cave of delights with something new to marvel at wherever they turned. Diverting as it all was, however, Alice's mind strayed back to the latest murder.

'You must have seen that Daddy was quoted in the paper,' she said.

'I'm never sure if what they print is what he actually said.'

'They took it down word for word this time, Mummy. I recognised his way of speaking. It's very different to how Joe talks.'

'It was an important warning to spread,' said Ellen, glancing at a display of handbags. 'Young women need to be reminded that this man is still at liberty. Your father doesn't want another victim turning up.'

'There's just one problem,' said Alice. 'A lot of young women don't read the morning papers some of them can't even *read*. How do you reach people like that?'

'I don't know, dear.'

Having seen a handbag she liked, Ellen picked it up and opened it to look inside. Her birthday was not all that far away and Marmion was already asking for ideas of what he could buy. Ellen looked up to ask the assistant the price of the item and realised it was the person they'd seen earlier outside the store.

'Oh, hello,' she said. 'You're the window dresser, aren't you? My daughter and I told you how much we admired that display of dresses.'

'Thank you,' said the young woman. 'I remember you now. Though I'm not really the window dresser, you know. They're just trying me out while Mr Alexander is away. He's a real artist. I've learnt by watching him. When Mr Alexander had to join the army,' she went on, 'they let me have a trial.'

'Well, you've passed through with flying colours,' said Alice, peering at the name tag on the assistant's dress. 'Miss Fuller, is it?'

'That's right. Irene Fuller. I'm normally on handbags or shoes.'

'Well, I hope we see more of your work in the windows.'

Irene was thrilled by their praise and hinted that they might help her by passing on their comments to the manager. They did as she hoped. On their way to the exit, they accosted a man who was a senior member of staff and made a point of saying that they'd been drawn into the store by the excellence of a particular window display. He shot an approving glance in the direction of Irene Fuller.

'Well,' said Alice as they moved off, 'we've done our good deed for the day.'

'All I have to do is to persuade your father to buy me that handbag.'

'I'll tell him that you simply *must* have it.'

When they got to the exit, a well-dressed man in his thirties came through the door and raised his hat in a token of greeting before walking past them. Ellen and Alice went out and strolled up a busy Regent Street. They were soon speculating on what was happening at the battle of the Somme and expressing a fervent wish that the name of Paul Marmion was kept out of the newspapers.

Somebody else, meanwhile, congratulated Irene Fuller on her window display.

CHAPTER FIFTEEN

It was not often that Joe Keedy was caught off balance. Where the opposite sex was concerned, he'd always flattered himself that he could cope with any situation which arose. If anything, his engagement to Alice Marmion had strengthened his emotional fortifications and brought a welcome stability to his private life. Yet the revelation that he'd aroused the admiration of Millie Duxford had taken him unawares and he'd been made to feel very uncomfortable. As he sat alone in his office, he reflected on what had happened. He now understood why his visitor had taken such pains with her appearance. Delivering the photographs was her main reason for coming to Scotland Yard but there'd been a secondary purpose. She wanted to see him again and turn what had so far been a purely official relationship into a real friendship.

Keedy was honest with himself. When he'd recovered from the initial embarrassment, there had been a fleeting temptation. Millie was an attractive woman with her clothes on and, as he'd inadvertently discovered, even more attractive with them off. In earlier days, he might have wanted to develop a friendship with her but two things held him back. The first was his commitment to Alice, a decision that had brought him nothing but pleasure and a sense of fulfilment. Regardless of how appealing she was when naked, no woman could entice him away from Alice even for a brief dalliance. Keedy had turned over a decisive new leaf. His transgressions were in the past. He was deeply in love with Alice and that had enabled him to ward off Millie Duxford.

The other strike against the model was the macabre situation in which she'd first expressed her interest in him. They'd been in a police morgue at the time. When she'd gone through the harrowing process of identifying a best friend, the last thing she should have been thinking about was the handsome detective sergeant standing right next to her. Yet she'd not only pretended to faint, she'd clung onto him when she seemed to be recovering. Keedy knew from his experience as an undertaker that loss could have extraordinary effects on bereaved relatives. Millie was not the first woman he'd had to catch when a shroud was pulled back from a face. One man had had such a violent heart attack when viewing the corpse of his wife that Keedy's father had been compelled to arrange two funerals instead of one. What had never happened before, however, was that a young woman had taken advantage of such fraught circumstances to fling herself into his arms. While Millie's grief was undoubtedly genuine, it was clearly fringed with desire.

Since he was troubled by the incident, he felt the need to discuss it with someone else if only to laugh it off and flush it out of his mind. The obvious person was a close colleague but it was hardly a topic he could broach with his future father-in-law. In matters like this, Marmion could be very old-fashioned and he wouldn't be pleased to hear that Keedy was the recipient of an amorous approach from a woman he'd only met once. Whatever happened, Millie's declaration of interest had to be kept from the inspector.

Keedy's meditations were soon interrupted by the arrival of company.

'Sorry to leave you on your own, Joe,' said Marmion, striding into the room. 'Chats with Chat seem to get longer and longer.'

'What did he think of the autopsy report?'

'The same as me – parts of it need to be suppressed.'

'I'd agree with that, Harv.' Keedy handed over the photograph. 'We've got a photo of Olive Arden at last.'

'Good.' Marmion examined it. 'Isn't that her

254

friend, Miss Duxford?'

'Yes, it was Millie – Miss Duxford – who dropped it off here. She had some other photos but this was the best for our purposes.'

'You saw her, then?'

'She left not long ago.'

'How is she bearing up?'

'She's very resilient,' said Keedy with feeling.

'It's a strange way to make a living – taking your clothes off, I mean. I'd hate to have a group of art students staring at me.'

Keedy chuckled. 'I'm not sure that you'd qualify somehow, Harv.'

'Don't they use male nudes?'

'I wouldn't know.'

'Well, I suppose you could call it an honourable profession. Women have posed in the nude for the greatest artists in the world. Some people – Chat, for instance – would say that it was a form of prostitution but I don't think so,' said Marmion. 'Artists' models are not taking money for sexual favours.'

Anxious to get off the subject, Keedy moved the conversation elsewhere.

'What did the Superintendent have to say?'

'He became very religious when he discovered that intercourse had taken place between Olive Arden and her killer. It may not have been in the park, of course. It could have occurred before they even got there. But,' Marmion continued, 'some sort of sexual encounter took place behind those bushes and that was enough for Chat. I had to listen to details of his courtship.'

'That must have been exciting!'

'It took him four and a half years to pop the question.'

Keedy laughed. 'I'm surprised he was that quick.'

'A little more respect, please! I know that we mock him but, underneath all that pomposity and Roman Catholicism, he's a good detective. He came up with a suggestion that you and I should have thought of, Joe.'

'And what was it?'

'Do you remember the name that the killer gave to Olive Arden?'

'Yes,' said Keedy. 'It was Lionel, supposedly working in the art department of an auction house. That was a name he plucked out of the air to trick her into believing that he had a respectable job.'

'Chat's argument is that he didn't pluck it out of the air.'

'I don't follow, Harv.'

'What happened when you ran Lionel Narraway to ground?'

'We ended up with red faces,' admitted Keedy. 'Actually, the person with the reddest face was Terry Jellings. When he realised the kind of man we'd just talked to, his face turned the colour of beetroot. He's never come across two men living together in a close relationship. Meeting Mr Narraway and his friend was a revelation to him.'

'I daresay that this Lionel chap was embarrassed to be confronted.'

'Yes, but he was also hopping mad.'

'It could have been the killer's intention,' said Marmion. 'That was Chat's suggestion, anyway.

The fact is that there was a man called Lionel and he did work for an auction house.'

Keedy pondered. 'I see what the superintendent was getting at,' he said at length. 'Having given the name to Olive, the killer could count on her passing it on to a friend who would, in turn, mention it to us. We would follow up the lead and there would be a very humiliating moment for Lionel Narraway.'

'In other words, the killer doesn't like him.'

'I can't exactly say that *I* took to him either, Harv.'

'Well, you're going to have to see him again, I'm afraid. If the killer knows Lionel Narraway then the reverse applies. The art expert – without realising it – must know the killer.'

'It's a possibility but I'd put it no higher than that.'

'When evidence is thin on the ground,' said Marmion, 'we have to grasp every possibility that comes along and this is one of them. Lionel Narraway must be asked if he has any enemies.'

'He does,' said Keedy. 'I'm one of them.'

'Be serious, Joe. Someone could be settling an old score with him.' He sensed disagreement. 'You obviously have doubts about that.'

'Not at all – it's a logical supposition and Chat deserves a pat on the back for pointing us in the right direction. The problem lies with Mr Narraway. I've met him before, remember. Gentlemen of that ilk are extremely discreet. For legal reasons, they have to be. Yes, he'll have enemies – we all do – but we may never get him to divulge their names.'

'We will if we apply gentle pressure.'

'All right – though I can't say that I'm looking forward to a second meeting with him.'

Marmion grinned. 'Don't worry, Joe. I'll be there to hold your hand.'

'My fear is that Lionel Narraway might try to do the same thing.'

They'd been misled. Paul Marmion knew that now. The week-long barrage was supposed to have destroyed German entrenchments, inflicted huge losses on the enemy's manpower, cleared away the miles of barbed wire laid to ensnare the British troops and made the result of the battle of the Somme a foregone conclusion. The plan had failed disastrously. German fortifications were too strong and deep to be removed by shellfire, enemy losses had not been significant and the barbed wire had remained to trip, snag, sting, hamper and draw blood from soldiers like Paul Marmion and Colin Fryatt. Both had their battle scars but the most painful were not on their bodies. As they crouched side by side in the trench, Fryatt sought solace in his mouth organ. Halfway through 'It's a Long Way to Tipperary', he broke off and turned to his friend.

'Promise me one thing, Paul.'

'What's that?'

'Stay close,' said Fryatt. 'If we're going to die, let's do it together.'

A morning spent with her daughter had been a real tonic for Ellen Marmion. While she'd bought only a few small items there, the visit to the West

End had cheered her up a great deal. Ellen was reassured to see that big stores and small shops alike were open for business. In some cases, stock was limited because of the difficulty of getting imported goods but that didn't lessen her pleasure. The main bonus – apart from time spent with Alice – was that she'd found the ideal present that Marmion could buy her for her birthday, thus depriving him of his annual panic.

When she left the tube station, her walk home would have taken her down the street where Lena Belton lived but she was keen to avoid a chance meeting with the woman. She therefore made a detour, adding a couple of hundred yards to the journey but sparing her the unpleasantness of another confrontation. Part of her felt ashamed that she had to resort to such a device. It smacked of cowardice. But another part of her argued that she was right to take sensible precautions. If a problem could not be solved, it was better to walk around it and pretend that it was not there.

Unhappily, the diversion did not take her safely past danger. As she came around a corner, she was jolted by the sight of Lena Belton, coming out of the greengrocer's shop with a bag in her hand. Ellen's immediate thought was that she was now condemned to say something to the woman, if only to make a vacuous comment about the weather. In the event, however, she was not called upon to speak at all. Patently, Lena Belton believed that actions spoke louder than words. Turning on her heel, she walked off in the opposite direction and disappeared down a street to the left. Ellen was torn between relief and annoyance, glad that no argument had taken place but exasperated by the other woman's behaviour. It was difficult to feel sorry for Lena now. She'd used up all of Ellen's compassion. The fortunes of war had turned a friend into an embittered neighbour with an evil tongue.

A thought suddenly hit Ellen and brought her to an abrupt halt. Is that what would inevitably happen to *her?* In the event of her son's death, would *she* turn into a sour and unsociable hermit like Lena? Was that going to be her fate?

Ellen rushed home and let herself into the house. The first thing she did was to grab the newspaper and open it on the kitchen table. Then she went through the alphabetical list of dead soldiers to make sure once again that Paul Marmion's name was not among them. Thankfully, it was not but her suffering was not over. When another list of the fallen arrived in the newspaper next day, her searing pain would start all over again.

Lionel Narraway kept them waiting. They had no idea if it was deliberate or not but they were left alone in his office for the best part of ten minutes. They used the time to look at the plush environment in which he worked. It was impeccably tidy. Every book was in place, every painting hung with care. There was also a wonderful balance of colour and Keedy was reminded of the house where Narraway lived. It had the same subtle shades. Marmion was impressed by the amount of money on display. The paintings were by talented artists and he knew how expensive the books of colour reproductions were. On the desk was a facsimile edition of *Très Riches Heures de Duc de Berry*, a book of hours produced early in the fifteenth century. He could not resist opening a page and looking at a beautiful illuminated manuscript.

'What is it, Harv?' asked Keedy.

'It's a Christian devotional book. Around the illustrations are texts from the Bible.'

'We'll have to buy a copy for Chat.'

'Not on the money we get paid, Joe.'

'What sort of wage will Narraway be on?'

'I fancy that he'd call it a salary,' said Marmion, 'and it would make our eyes water with envy.' He closed the book. 'The art world is a wealthy one.'

He heard someone coming down the corridor outside and stepped away from the desk. The door opened and Lionel Narraway came in. As soon as he saw Keedy, he tensed. Marmion sought to make him relax a little.

'Before we go any further, Mr Narraway,' he said, smoothly, 'we need to give you an apology. I'm Inspector Marmion and I was distressed to hear that one of my officers caused you any upset. It was not intentional and I've brought Sergeant Keedy with me so that he can express his regret.'

'That's right,' said Keedy, solemnly. 'I'm very sorry, sir.'

'It all arose from a misunderstanding.'

Narraway was only partially appeased. 'It was very unpleasant, Inspector.'

'Unfortunately,' explained Marmion, 'we're

dealing with a very unpleasant situation. I daresay you've seen reports in the newspaper of the two murders. What happened was this.'

Marmion was succinct. He told Narraway how the killer had told his second victim the name that had led them to the auction house. He emphasised that Narraway was not a suspect but that it seemed more than a coincidence that there was someone called Lionel who worked in the art department of an auction house.

'It may be that the name and profession were not picked at random, sir.'

'The killer *knows* you,' added Keedy.

'I don't consort with murderers,' said Narraway, peevishly. 'I have a small but highly selective group of friends.'

'We're not talking about friends, sir. This man wanted to hurt you.'

'Why should anyone want to do that?'

'We're hoping that you might tell us, sir. Is there anyone you've ... offended in the past? It might be one of your former clients, for instance.'

'What an absurd suggestion!' said Narraway. 'I'm always excessively polite to my clients. I have a good professional relationship with everyone who seeks my help.'

'Think hard,' urged Marmion.

'I don't need to, Inspector. There is *nobody* – full stop.'

'Far be it from me to correct your grammar, sir, but let's make it a semi-colon, shall we? When it's first put to you in the blunt way that we've had to resort to, you probably find it impossible to remember every word of criticism levelled at you or every person who might – just might – have taken umbrage at something you did or unwittingly said.'

'My answer remains the same, Inspector – there's nobody.'

Keedy indicated a painting. 'I assume that's an original, sir.'

Narraway was scornful. 'I'd never hang anything else in my office.'

'Supposing – just for the sake of argument – that an art expert walked in here and told you that the painting was, in fact, a fake. How would you react?'

'I'd tell him that he didn't know his job and kick him straight out.'

'What happens when *you* are the expert and you pick out a fake?'

'I'm invariably right, Sergeant.'

'And does that happen often?'

'Not often, perhaps, but it does occur from time to time.'

'If I paid a large amount of money for an original Gainsborough,' said Marmion, 'and you examined it and declared it a fake, I'd be very angry.'

'Granted,' said Narraway, 'but you'd be angry with the dealer who sold it to you and not with me.'

'If I was trying to sell it at auction – and I *knew* it was a fake – then the person I'd turn on would be the man who revealed that it was not an original. That would be you, sir. Fraudsters hate being exposed as fraudsters.'

'My reputation goes before me, Inspector.

Artists know better than to try to smuggle a forged painting past me. I'd soon find them out. It's a game and they know that I'd win.' He walked to the door and opened it. 'I don't wish to detain you from the search for this killer. Look elsewhere, gentlemen. You won't find him in my address book or in my client list.'

'Don't be so certain about that,' said Keedy.

'Someone or some incident may have slipped your mind, sir,' said Marmion. 'We ask you to reflect on what we said.'

'Good day to you, Inspector.'

'We are investigating two heinous crimes, Mr Narraway, and it may be in your power to give us some significant assistance. You may claim that you don't know this man but we believe that he knows you. Why else would he send the police to your door,' asked Marmion, 'unless he wanted to unsettle you?'

'Goodbye, sir,' said Keedy, going out.

'You know where to find us,' said Marmion following him.

Narraway shut the door firmly behind them before crossing to his desk. Inclined to dismiss the visit as an inconvenient distraction, Narraway stopped for a moment to think. Something stirred at the back of his mind. Crossing to the desk, he began to leaf his way slowly through his appointments diary.

Alice Marmion did not enjoy her first night shift. A persistent drizzle fell as she and Peggy Lassiter started their beat. Nocturnal bombing by Zeppelins had forced the capital to dim its lights appreciably so that it did not present an easy target. Areas felt to be especially vulnerable – those with munition factories, for instance – were subjected to a total blackout. The subdued lighting meant that Alice and her companion carried powerful torches. They were also accompanied by a uniformed constable. He offered them protection against rapacious drunks or angry servicemen on leave who took exception to the fact that the beam of a torch was shone on them when they were in flagrante with one of the city's many prostitutes. The darkness hid the blushes on the cheeks of the two policewomen. Walking around central London at night was an education for both of them.

One young woman trawling for custom was furious when she was moved on by the trio. She responded with a mouthful of abuse before slinking away.

'That was another French prostitute,' said Peggy.

'Actually,' said Alice, 'I think she was Belgian. That sounded like Flemish.'

'How do you know that?'

'I used to belong to the Women's Emergency Corps. We dealt with huge numbers of Belgian refugees.'

'There are far too many of them,' complained the tall, gangly PC Mike Searle, strolling along beside them. 'Belgians are everywhere.'

'We could hardly turn them away,' said Alice.

'I think that's exactly what we should have done. We should have taken so many then said "Okay, that's enough. Go somewhere else." That's my view.'

'There *was* nowhere else.'

'What about Ireland or Scandinavia or one of a dozen other countries?'

'They don't have the treaty obligation with Belgium that we have.'

'Alice is right,' said Peggy. 'It was our duty to help them, PC Searle.'

'It doesn't mean that we should let them flood in the way they did. If we get any more Belgians,' said Searle, 'we'll all end up speaking Flemish or Walloon.' He grinned in the dark. 'And by the way, you can call me "Mike". The same goes for you, Alice. By the end of this shift, we'll be good friends.'

Alice was uncertain about that. Searle had been pleasant company at first and they were glad that he was there to assert his authority during the confrontations that inevitably arose. But he'd clearly singled out Alice as the more attractive of the two policewomen and started to make suggestive remarks to her. She dealt with them by studiously ignoring his innuendoes. When their shift came to an end, however, he made his move. Putting an arm around her shoulder, he produced what he believed was a winning smile.

'I've really enjoyed looking after you,' he said, winking at her. 'Both of us sign off now. Why don't I see you safely back home?'

'That won't be necessary,' said Joe Keedy, emerging from the shadows.

Searle squared up to him. 'And who might you be?' he demanded.

'I'm Detective Sergeant Keedy and I don't like anyone pestering my fiancée. Please bear that in

266

mind, Constable.'

'Yes, yes, of course, sir,' said Searle, backing away.

'Good night.'

Keedy's farewell was a brusque dismissal. Searle quickly vanished and Peggy Lassiter went into the building after him. When Alice had signed off, she and Keedy walked arm in arm through the drizzle.

'Thank you so much, Joe,' she said. 'You came to my rescue.'

'Has he been a nuisance?'

'He was just starting to be.'

'Well, he can shift his attention to Peggy Lassiter instead.'

'Oh, I don't think he'll make any headway there. Peggy disliked him almost as much as I did.'

'So this is what you get up to, is it?' he teased. 'When I'm not there, you arouse the interest of amorous constables.'

'I didn't do it deliberately.'

'I'm sure you didn't, Alice. And, in a sense, it makes us quits.'

'What do you mean?'

'We've both been the target of unwanted admirers,' he said. 'Unfortunately, in my case, you weren't there to leap out and frighten Millie off.'

'Who's Millie?'

'Millie Duxford – she's the best friend of the second victim, Olive Arden. They met at the Slade.'

'Oh, they're both art students, are they?'

'No, Millie is a model. She poses in the nude. That's what she was doing when I first clapped eyes on her.'

'Since when have you been looking at naked women?' she demanded.

'She wasn't naked,' he temporised, 'she was nude.'

'It comes to the same thing, Joe.'

'Not if you're an art student. Anyway, this lady seems to have taken to me. When she turned up at Scotland Yard this morning, she made that very clear.'

'Did she have any clothes on at the time?'

He laughed. 'Don't be silly!'

'Well, you can hardly expect me to be glad. You told PC Searle that you didn't like anyone pestering your fiancée. I could say the same thing about you.'

'She wasn't exactly pestering me, Alice.'

'Then what was she doing?'

'Millie was ... expressing an interest, that's all.'

'What – on the strength of knowing you for only a couple of days?'

Keedy smirked. 'My charm has an instant effect.'

'Then you shouldn't be turning it on for the benefit of naked women.'

'She was a nude model.'

'And you were staring at her.'

'I couldn't help it. When I walked into the room, she was *there*. Look, I didn't have to tell you about it. I hoped that we could have a good laugh together. Why are you being so narrow-minded all of a sudden?'

Alice looked away. 'It doesn't matter.'

'Yes, it does,' he said, turning her to face him.

'I've never seen you in this mood before. What am I supposed to have done wrong?'

'I don't think you're telling me the full story, Joe.'

'Of course, I am.'

'If this woman has shown an interest in you then you must have given her some encouragement.'

'That's not true at all.'

'You did it without even realising it,' she argued. 'That's why I'm upset. You gave the impression that you were ... well, available.'

'Then you must have done the same to that constable earlier on.'

'I did nothing of the kind!'

'He seemed to think that you did, Alice. What does it matter, anyway?' he asked, pulling her close. 'I can't see what the argument is about. If I hadn't popped up when I did, you'd have given Constable What's-His-Name the cold shoulder and that's exactly what I did to Millie Duxford. Neither of them is going to come between us, Alice.' He kissed her. 'Didn't you *want* to see me tonight?'

'Yes, Joe,' she said, hugging him.

'Then let's have no more bickering, okay?'

It was her turn to initiate the kiss this time. Afterwards, she smiled at him.

'Being in love can be so difficult at times, can't it?' she said.

They had attended a piano recital the previous evening, then gone on to the home of some friends. It was not until they were having breakfast next morning that Lionel Narraway was able to raise a topic that had been niggling him.

'I had another visit from Sergeant Keedy yesterday,' he said.

'Why on earth is he still bothering you?'

'The situation is more complicated than I imagined.'

'I don't see why,' said Edwin Bonner, reaching for the marmalade. 'It was a clear case of mistaken identity.'

'It was and it wasn't, Edwin.'

Narraway gave him a brief account of what had happened in his office on the previous day and explained that he'd found Inspector Marmion far more amenable than his sergeant. At the end of it all, Bonner shrugged.

'It was just an unfortunate coincidence that the killer used your name.'

'Was it?'

'Yes, Lionel. You know it was. You have no enemies.'

'There are none that I can think of, anyway.'

'Then you can stop worrying about it.'

'That's what I've tried to do,' said Narraway, 'but the possibility – remote as it is – refuses to go away from my mind. I went through my appointment diaries for the last two years and, I have to admit, there were a few people whom I upset.'

'You simply told them the truth about their worthless paintings, Lionel.'

'One of them might have harboured a grudge.'

'Do you honestly believe that anyone would murder an art student as an act of revenge against *you?* It's risible.'

'I agree,' said Narraway, pouring some coffee, 'but that isn't what happened, Edwin. Why else should someone give my name and profession to the young woman he intended to kill? The chances were that she was bound to pass on the details – and so it proved. The next thing we know, the egregious Sergeant Keedy is banging on the door.'

'Distance yourself from this whole business, Lionel.'

'I wish that I could.' He added milk and sugar to his coffee before stirring it. 'Some clients have been very angry with me. The worst was that American who thought he owned a genuine Whistler.'

'That was years ago,' said Bonner, airily. 'You haven't been to America since the war started. Part of your job entails giving bad news and there are lots of people who were disappointed when your valuation of their paintings was considerably lower than their expectations. But that's not a motive for two murders and a determination to involve you in the second of them as a putative suspect.'

'You're probably right, Edwin.'

'Let the whole thing blow over. You'll never have to see either of those detectives again.'

'That's true,' said Narraway, confidently. 'I won't, will I?'

Harvey Marmion had his head in a copy of *The Times* when Joe Keedy came into the inspector's office. He looked up at his visitor and shook his head.

'Paul's name is not in the list – thank God!'

'I'm glad to hear it, Harv. Why don't you ring Ellen and tell her?'

'She insists on seeing it herself in print. As soon as the newsagent opened this morning, she was probably waiting on the doorstep.'

'One thing is certain,' said Keedy. 'Judging by the reports that I've read, the battle of the Somme is going to last quite a while.'

'It will,' agreed Marmion, putting the newspaper aside. 'That means terrible casualties on both sides. So far, I fear, the British army has had the bigger losses. It's a bloodbath over there.'

'You have my sympathy.'

'Thanks, Joe.'

'The worst thing is having no idea what's going on in France. That's what Alice told me, anyway.'

Marmion was surprised. 'You've seen her?'

'Since I worked late last night, I picked her up at midnight after her shift and saw her safely back to her digs.'

'That was good of you.'

'It was the only chance I had of seeing her.'

'How is she?'

'Alice was much happier on the day shift. But there was one advantage of starting much later. She and her mother were able to go shopping in the West End.'

'So I heard. It was an expensive trip for me. I've been lined up to buy a handbag at Swan & Edgar.'

Keedy sniggered. 'I didn't know you carried a handbag, Harv.'

'Ellen's birthday is coming up soon,' said Marmion. 'That's what she wants.'

'Then you're lucky that Alice didn't take her to Harrods or to Selfridges. You'd have needed a mortgage to buy a handbag there.'

'The best possible present for Ellen would be good news from Paul. We couldn't put a price on that. It's the best present for all the family.'

'That includes me.'

'Yes, Joe. When he was home on leave, Paul gave his blessing to the engagement. He used to joke that nobody would ever marry Alice because she was too opinionated. You destroyed that myth.'

'I have to explode a few myths about me now,' said Keedy, meaningfully. 'Is Ellen still having some hassle from that neighbour of yours?'

'Yes, Joe.'

'Alice told me about an argument *she* had with Mrs Belton.'

'Lena Belton is her own worst enemy. There are dozens of people willing to help her through the long period of mourning, but she's erected a wall between her and them. Ellen has walked straight into it and bounced off.'

'Is this woman still poking newspapers through the letter box?'

'No, she's stopped doing that. And Ellen has stopped offering her friendship and consolation. She's trying to avoid Mrs Belton altogether. Ellen can't bear to see that smile on the woman's face again.'

'What smile?' asked Keedy.

'It was more of a sly grin, apparently,' said Marmion. 'That woman is brimming with ill will. She actually *wants* Paul to be killed in action.'

The whistle sent them off once again. But it was not a referee's whistle to signal the start of a football match in which they were playing. It was a command to send them running at the enemy across uneven ground. The noise of shellfire and gunfire was continuous. Paul Marmion did his best to catch up to Colin Fryatt but his friend stayed yards ahead of him. Then the rattle of a German machine gun was heard and Fryatt was hit with a hail of bullets that stopped him in his tracks, doubled him up in an unnatural position then made him slump forwards onto the ground. Letting out a cry of horror, Paul tossed his rifle aside and dived down beside his friend, cradling him in his arms and promising to carry him back to safety. But there was no time for Paul to move. A shell smashed into the ground not too far away and exploded with such ferocity that it sent debris flying in all directions. As he was hit from behind by an avalanche of earth, stone and shrapnel, Paul didn't see the crater that was gouged out of the ground by the shell.

He'd plunged headlong into oblivion.

CHAPTER SIXTEEN

He took sensible precautions. Because the newspapers were appealing for witnesses who'd seen a well-dressed man in his thirties with gleaming shoes entering St James's Park in the company of a pretty female in her twenties, he changed his

274

appearance slightly. He now wore a crumpled but still serviceable blue suit, an old pair of shoes and a hat pulled down over his forehead. Pinned to his lapel was a badge to show that he was in a reserved occupation and therefore excused national service. When he went into Swan & Edgar that morning, he headed straight for the handbags and was dismayed to see that Irene Fuller was not there. A podgy middle-aged woman had replaced her. When he asked casually after Miss Fuller, the woman told him that she'd been transferred to the shoe department.

He smiled to himself at his luck. His task had just become much easier. Instead of standing incongruously in front of a display of handbags, he could sit down and have Irene attend to him. A more intimate relationship could therefore develop. When he walked across to the shoe department, she was handing some money to an elderly lady and thanking her for her custom. He stepped into Irene's line of vision and lifted his hat.

'Good morning!'

'Oh, hello,' she said, only half-recognising him.

'Yes, it's me again. I praised you for that amazing window display.'

She smiled sweetly. 'I remember you now.'

'Then you can do me a favour, Irene, and help me to choose some shoes.'

'Yes,' she said, pleased that she had another customer so soon. 'What did you have in mind, sir, and what size are you looking for?'

She conducted him to the section where men's shoes were arranged on a series of racks. He examined some of them, asked the price then replaced them. Eventually, he decided to try on two different pairs of black shoes. Irene invited him to sit down then went off into the storeroom to find the right size for him. He'd already untied his laces so that he could slip off the shoes he was wearing. Kneeling down, Irene eased his feet gently into the new pair.

'They look very nice on you, sir.'

'Thank you,' he said, getting up and walking to and fro. He paused to stare in a mirror and was impressed. The shoes were a perfect fit and looked good on him but he pretended otherwise in order to extend the amount of time with Irene. 'They feel a little tight across the instep. Let's try the others instead, shall we?'

When he sat on the chair again, she bent down to untie and remove the first pair of shoes from his feet. He savoured their brief proximity once again, ogling the contours of her body. Irene was wearing a cheap scent. He inhaled it deeply.

'That's a delicious perfume,' he complimented her. 'Is it French?'

'No, it's nothing special, sir.'

'It suits you, Irene. I'm sure that your boyfriend says the same.'

Her face clouded. 'I don't have a boyfriend any more.'

'I can't believe that. Someone as attractive as you must have dozens of suitors chasing after you. If I was younger, I'd be one of them.'

'Thank you,' she said with a half-smile. 'My boyfriend was killed in action earlier this year. There's been no one since Martin.'

'Oh, I'm so sorry to hear that, Irene. What a pity he never had the chance to see what a talented window dresser you are. He'd have been so proud of you. When I saw you at work in the window the other day, I could see that you had real flair.'

'You're very kind, sir.'

'I know talent when I see it,' he said. 'Right, let's try on this other pair. I can't leave the store until I find some new black shoes. I need them for a funeral.'

Since their argument, Alma Bond had neither seen nor spoken to him, but she could not keep out of his way indefinitely. Joint decisions had to be taken. Gathering up her daughter, therefore, she walked across the road and knocked on his door. She was reassured when he opened the door and gave her a smile of welcome.

'Hello, Jenny,' he said, tickling the baby under the chin.

'Is this a good moment, Derek?' she asked.

'Yes, yes, please come in.'

They went into the living room and sat opposite each other. She kept the baby on her knee. He offered her tea but she declined with a shake of the head.

'We've got a lot to discuss,' she said.

'Yes,' he agreed. 'Look, I'm sorry about–'

'Let's forget that, shall we?'

He was relieved. 'Well, all right, if you say so.'

'This is about Charlotte, not about us.'

'You're quite right, Alma.'

She was pleased that the tension between them had now eased. He seemed as keen as her to put their differences behind him. Whatever mistakes they'd made were minor irrelevancies when compared to the funeral. That took precedence.

'I've got a rough idea of numbers,' she said.

'Excellent.'

'It makes the catering so much easier.'

'Have you spoken to the churchwarden?'

'Yes, Derek, he'll arrange for tables and chairs to be laid out in the church hall. Everybody has offered their help. Mrs Cinderby was the first, of course. She was so fond of Charlotte that she'd have willingly dug the grave, if need be.'

Alma winced as if from a stab of pain. 'Oh, that's a terrible thing to say!'

'It sums up Mrs Cinderby perfectly,' he said, tolerantly. 'She's a wonderful neighbour – and so are you, Alma.'

As their eyes met, she felt a frisson but it soon passed because the baby jiggled about on her knee and had to be adjusted to a different position. He made no comment but she had the feeling that he was grateful for Jenny's presence. It made him look at Alma as a married woman with a child and not as anything else. That suited her.

'What have you said to the vicar?' she asked.

'Very little – he knew Charlotte extremely well so needs little prompting from me. The only favour I asked was that he wouldn't dwell on the circumstances of her death. It would create the wrong mood altogether.'

'I'm glad to hear you say that. As it happens, I bumped into the vicar when I went to the church hall. It was a bit embarrassing, really. He asked –

in the politest possible way, of course – why I hadn't been to church for a while.' Alma bit her lip. 'I felt so guilty when I used Jenny as an excuse.' She rearranged her daughter again. 'When are Charlotte's parents arriving?'

'Later this afternoon – I'll meet them at the station.'

'If there's anything that you–'

'I'll manage,' he said, interrupting. 'You've done more than enough.'

'The flowers have been ordered. They'll be delivered to the undertaker's.' She thrust a hand into her pocket. 'I've brought the bill.'

'Thank you,' he said, taking it from her.

'What hymns did you decide on in the end?'

'I picked Charlotte's favourites. It only seemed appropriate. The order of service has been printed so everything is in hand.'

'Then we need to talk in more detail about what happens *after* the funeral,' she said, briskly. 'Oh, there was one thing I meant to ask you, Derek. Have you contacted Scotland Yard?'

'No, I haven't.'

'I thought that Inspector Marmion wanted to be there.'

'Well, *I'm* not going to invite him,' said Reid, sharply. 'When he first suggested it, I was touched but I've had second thoughts. He has no place at the funeral. I want to remember Charlotte as she was when we were married in that church. If the inspector is there, all I'll be able to think about is the way that she died.'

When he ran his eye over his appointments diary,

Harvey Marmion noted that the funeral of Charlotte Reid was on the following day. The date had been published in the obituary column of *The Times*. He was surprised that her husband had not contacted him directly to remind him. Reid was not the sort of person to forget things like that. He could only surmise that the lieutenant had reservations about Marmion's attendance and he could imagine what they were. Other families of murder victims had been unsettled by the presence of detectives at the funerals of their loved ones. It reminded them of unfinished business.

Marmion was closing his diary when Claude Chatfield came into the room.

'How did you get on with that art expert?' asked the superintendent.

'I can't pretend that he was glad to see us, sir.'

'He could provide us with valuable clues.'

'He could have done so,' said Marmion, 'but I'm afraid that he didn't. Mr Narraway insisted that he had no enemies and could therefore give us no names. On reflection, I hope, he may change his mind. We all step on someone's toes from time to time, often without realising it.'

'There has to be a reason why the killer gave his name.'

'I agree, sir, and it was important to speak to Mr Narraway again. That was done on your excellent advice.'

'You shouldn't have needed telling, Inspector.'

'We were exploring other avenues.'

'And they all turned out to be cul-de-sacs.'

'We don't know that for certain, sir,' said Marmion, defensively. 'Having a photo of Olive Arden will be a help. It was in all the papers this morning. *Someone* may have seen her with this fellow. The National Gallery has a lot of regular visitors.'

'I suspect that the killer won't be one of them. He'll be lying low.'

'I doubt that, Superintendent. He'll want fresh blood.'

'Will he – even though every policeman in London is on the lookout for him?'

'That's part of the attraction. He likes humiliating us.'

'Well, I don't like *being* humiliated,' snarled Chatfield. 'The press have very sharp teeth. They seem to enjoy sinking them into me.'

'I've come in for a fair amount of criticism myself, sir.'

'That's as maybe.' His eye fell on the newspaper beside Marmion. 'I see that you've been going through that list in *The Times*.'

'Happily, my son's name is not there.'

'I hope it continues like that, Inspector.'

'Thank you, sir.'

'It must be imposing a terrible strain on your wife and daughter.'

'It's a trying time for all of us, sir.'

'Then I must congratulate you on the way that you put your private concerns aside when you come to work. Other officers in your situation would be hopelessly distracted. You're not,' said Chatfield. 'From the moment this fiend came to our attention, you've kept your nose to the grindstone.'

'I want him caught, sir,' affirmed Marmion.

'We all want that.'

'It's the reason I'll be going to Charlotte Reid's funeral tomorrow.'

'I don't understand.'

'He may be there, sir.'

Chatfield was taken aback. 'Would he take a chance like that?'

'I think it's more than likely, sir,' said Marmion. 'He takes souvenirs from his victim so that he can gloat over them. He likes to wallow in what he probably sees as his triumphs. The funeral will give him the opportunity to do just that.'

When she'd been born, Ellen Marmion had only ever seen horse-drawn vehicles on the roads. Many of them had now been supplanted by motorised transport but she still liked to hear the clip-clop of hooves and the rattle of carts. It was one of the reasons she enjoyed a visit from Steve Seymour, the baker, a diminutive man in his fifties who always had a half-smoked cigarette tucked behind his ear. The horse needed no direction from Seymour. As soon as it reached the Marmion house, it pulled up at the kerb and waited. By the time that the baker had hopped down onto the pavement, Ellen was walking towards him with a purse in her hand.

'Good morning, Mr Seymour,' she said.

'Good morning, Mrs Marmion.'

'You're always so punctual.'

'I do my best.' He opened the door at the rear of his carriage. 'The usual, is it?'

'Yes please.' The aroma of fresh, warm bread

wafted out to her. 'Oh, I love that smell. I'm so grateful that you come to me early on your round.'

'You're one of my first customers, Mrs Marmion. I'd have been here even earlier if I hadn't been flagged down by Mrs Belton.'

'What did Lena want?'

'She wanted more than I was able to give her,' he replied. 'She doesn't seem to realise that I have to share the loaves out among my customers. Wheat imports have been badly hit so the prices of home-grown wheat have gone up. We have trouble getting enough of it. Needless to say, I get the blame on the doorstep for that.'

'Not from me, you don't,' she said. 'Food shortages are the fault of the war.'

Seymour had taken out a loaf and wrapped tissue paper around it. As he handed it over, she paid him and he found some change in the leather bag around his neck. She popped the coins into her purse then frowned.

'Why did Lena want extra bread when she only has one mouth to feed?'

'It's a very big mouth,' he said, ruefully. 'When I told her what I could spare, she started to yell at me. I had half a mind to give her nothing at all. It was only because of her situation that I relented.'

'She's been rude to just about everyone.'

'There's no call for it. I lost a grandson at Mons but I don't use that as an excuse to call people names. It's something I've had to accept,' said Seymour. 'You mourn in private. I have other customers whose sons and fathers have been

283

killed in action. They don't rant and rave.'

'It's very sad, Mr Seymour. Lena Belton spurns all of us.'

'It doesn't cost anything to keep a civil tongue in your head. That's what I told her in no uncertain manner. She just turned her back on me.'

Ellen remembered the moment when the woman had done the same to her. The insult still rankled. She hoped that it would never be repeated. Seymour climbed back up onto his seat.

'Is there any news about your son?' he asked.

'We've heard nothing.'

'People have been searching lists in the paper.'

'I'm one of them, Mr Seymour. You've no idea how relieved I am when I see that Paul's name is not there. A black cloud suddenly vanishes – until the next day, that is. It will be back again tomorrow.'

'I'll keep my fingers crossed for you,' he said, putting the cigarette between his lips and lighting it. 'But always remember this – no news is good news.'

Paul Marmion recovered consciousness very slowly. What first struck him was that he was in pain and unable to move freely. All over his body, his limbs and his face, he could feel soreness and sharp twinges. When he gathered up his energy and shook himself, he dislodged much of the earth under which he'd been half-buried. He then became aware that he was not alone. Paul was lying across the body of his best friend. He remembered trying to help Colin Fryatt but that was all. His mind was otherwise a blank. When he

284

opened his eyes, he reeled from the shock. Although he could feel the bright sunshine on his face, he could see absolutely nothing. The battlefield was in complete darkness. He hugged Fryatt impulsively for comfort but there was no response. His friend was dead. Paul was left alone in no man's land, unable to get up and aghast at the prospect that nobody would ever find him and that he'd perish from lack of food and water. He felt something digging hard into his chest and feared that he'd been shot. When he moved slightly, however, he understood what had caused the pain. It was his friend's beloved mouth organ. Paul groped around frantically until he could find the pocket. Undoing the button, he pulled out the instrument and put it to his lips.

Then he blew and blew as hard as he possibly could.

The photograph of Olive Arden in the newspapers brought in a fresh wave of correspondence. Much of the information was too hazy to be of any use but some of the notes and letters handed in at Scotland Yard were more promising. Joe Keedy put one letter aside for further use. He then picked up an envelope addressed to him personally. The handwriting was very spidery. Wondering who had sent it, he opened the letter and took out a photograph that made him sit back in surprise. It was of Millie Duxford, standing beside a marble column as she posed in the nude for the art students. Keedy was both alarmed and – against his will – fascinated. Able to study her body at leisure, he realised just how voluptuous it was. When he was finally able to take his eyes off her, he turned the photo over and read the message on the back.

'Remember me?'

Unsure what to do with it, he thrust the photo into a drawer in his desk and sighed. Millie Duxford was not going to give up easily. She had to be stopped before she became even more of a problem. He was trying to work out a strategy to get rid of her when Marmion came in.

'I've just been talking to one of the attendants at the National Gallery,' he said. 'He remembers seeing a couple who may well have been Olive Arden and the killer.'

'How close did he get to them?'

'Fairly close, I gather. He was on duty in the gallery where Olive – if it really was her – was sketching a painting. I should imagine she's not the only student who does that but this man was adamant. It was the girl in the photo. When he saw it in the paper this morning, it jumped out at him.'

Keedy was still trying to adjust to the impact of a photo that had jumped out at him. It was now hidden in his desk. He wondered what Marmion would have said if he'd caught the sergeant poring over the body of Millie Duxford. He shifted guiltily in his seat. Marmion peered at him.

'Are you all right, Joe?'

'Yes, yes, I'm fine.'

'You look rather liverish.'

'Late nights are catching up with me, Harv.'

Marmion laughed. 'At your age?' he asked. 'Wait till you're as old as me.'

'I may not live that long.'

'Alice will have something to say about that.'

Marmion went on to describe what he felt was a reliable sighting at the National Gallery. The attendant had been struck by the man's expensive suit and gold cufflinks. What he also recalled was the slight awe with which Olive looked at him.

'Did he hear what they were talking about, Harv?'

'He only caught snatches of their conversation. The killer – and it sounds very much like him – was instructing her about the painting. He sounded authoritative.'

'That takes us back to the art department of an auction house.'

'Perhaps he *used* to work there,' suggested Keedy.

'That's more than possible, Joe, but his name is certainly not Lionel. Anyway, the attendant had a second sighting of the two of them. It was the day on which Olive was killed. He saw her and the man meeting up outside the gallery and thought no more of it until he opened this morning's newspaper.' Marmion looked at the correspondence on the desk. 'You've had a lot of love letters this morning. Is there anything interesting?'

'There are a few faintly possible leads we might follow up.'

'What we need is something more concrete.'

'We just don't have it.'

'Then we must find it before we run out of time.'

'Do you think he's lined up his next victim already?'

287

'Yes, I do,' said Marmion. 'It was not long after the first murder that he broke cover and struck again. He won't want to lose momentum and may already have a third young woman in mind.'

Keedy snapped his fingers. 'I looked up the details of that case you mentioned.'

'Which one was that, Joe?'

'It was the case involving the Lambeth Poisoner,' said the other. 'I looked for parallels. The method was different but the results were the same – women ended up dead and there was some sort of sexual pleasure for the killer. It was Thomas Neill Cream's lust for publicity that interested me. As you pointed out, he kept on attracting attention to himself when he should have been doing the exact opposite.'

'That's what our man has been doing.'

'Then he must be furious at the Battle of the Somme. It's monopolising the headlines. He can't compete with the death toll there.'

Marmion winced. 'Let's leave the Somme out of this, if you don't mind.'

'Oh, yes – I'm sorry.' Keedy cursed himself for his lack of tact. 'The man we're after has a streak of daring in him. He simply has to taunt us. That's why I fancy he'll be at Mrs Reid's funeral.'

'It's precisely the reason I'll be there myself.'

'Do you need me?'

'Yes, Joe – you can watch from a distance. It's what he'll probably do.'

'Dr Cream made things easy for the police. Those cross-eyes of his meant that he'd be recognised at a glance. I wish that our man had a nasty squint, a pair of outsize ears, a missing nose or something that makes him easy to pick out.'

'His malformations are inside his head, Joe.'

'Would it be worth contacting mental hospitals in London to see if anyone with dangerous tendencies has recently left one of them?'

'I don't think so. If they realised what was going on in that mind of his, he'd never have been released. Dr Cream had a passion for women but at least he didn't steal their underwear or get some weird thrill by looking at their paintings. You can't blame a man for loving art,' said Marmion, 'until it drives him to these extremes.'

'I can't wait to get him,' said Keedy, bunching a fist. 'He's a monster.'

'He wasn't born like that, Joe.'

'Then he's developed into one.'

'I'll be interested to know where his perversion first started,' said Marmion. 'I wouldn't be at all surprised if he used to belong to one of those so-called camera clubs. They're supposed to be for serious photographers but they're often nothing more than groups of dirty-minded old men who like taking pictures of naked women.'

Keedy leant forward as if to stop the desk drawer from shooting open to reveal his nude photograph of Millie Duxford. He was writhing with embarrassment at the secret he was hiding. It was one he could share with nobody. Marmion's next comment only intensified his discomfort.

'When we finally arrest him,' said the inspector, 'we'll be able to reclaim the portfolio he stole from Olive Arden. I think that we should return it to her best friend. Miss Duxford will be very grateful, I'm sure. You can have the pleasure of giving it to her, Joe,' he continued. 'You know the woman much better than I do.'

In the course of his day, Lionel Narraway had met five different people who'd brought paintings for auction. The first four had been interesting enough for him to recommend their being accepted but the fifth was of such poor quality that he felt it would damage their reputation if they included it in their catalogue. Accordingly, he told the owner that it had little value and might not sell at all. The man had been outraged by Narraway's appraisal and insisted that the painting was worth far more than the estimate. During the row that ensued, the art expert was frightened at one point that the man might attack him. Instead, the thwarted owner rid himself of some foul language then charged out and slammed the door behind him. The incident had upset Narraway so much that he had to sit down to compose himself. Unpleasant as the confront-ation had been, however, it did unlock a memory that he'd deliberately pushed to the innermost recesses of his mind.

It could not be rushed. He'd won Irene Fuller's trust but it would take time before their acquain-tance could blossom into friendship. Meanwhile, he needed to know more about her. He'd changed into a different suit from the one he wore when he bought the new shoes and he now wore a cap. When she eventually came out of the store at the end of her shift, he was invisible in the crowd thronging the tube station at Piccadilly

290

Circus. Irene walked within yards of him without suspecting for a moment that he was there. He loitered near the ticket office to see what ticket she was buying then he joined the queue and purchased one for the same destination. In a packed compartment, he could just see the top of her hat. For her part, she was too short to see over the heads of the intervening passengers. When she finally got off the train, he followed her at a discreet distance, going up the escalator with his back turned to her.

It was a relatively short walk to the house. Situated in a narrow street off the Caledonian Road, it was a small villa with a flower basket hanging outside on a metal bracket. He watched her take out a key and let herself into the house. She'd told him she lived at home so he was able to assess the family's social position by giving the house a rough valuation. Her parents were not wealthy and he suspected that she earned only a modest wage at Swan & Edgar, even when it was supplemented by the additional money from her window-dressing exploits. The similarities with Olive Arden were obvious. She was young, appealing, wounded by the loss of a boyfriend and susceptible to flattery. Irene Fuller was an ideal choice.

'You were lucky, Private Marmion,' said the doctor. 'The fields were littered with so many corpses that you could easily have been mistaken for one of them.'

'I blew Colin Fryatt's mouth organ,' explained Paul.

'That probably saved your life.'

'What about...?'

'I'm sorry. There was nothing they could do for your friend. They had to leave him and concentrate on wounded soldiers like you. Stretcher-bearers carried you back for half mile or more.'

'I can still hear shellfire and machine guns.'

'That's a good sign. Lots of patients in your condition have gone deaf.'

Paul Marmion was lying on a camp bed in a field hospital. The conditions were poor. He was only a foot from the next patient and dozens of other camp beds were crammed into the tent. There were cries and moans all round him and the stink of horrific wounds and medication invaded his nostrils. When they'd brought him in, he'd been stripped and examined. His back was covered with shrapnel wounds but there were, miraculously, no lost or broken limbs. Relief that his body was still whole was, however, offset by the fact that he'd gone blind. Heavy bandaging encircled his head and covered his eyes.

'Will I ever see again, Doctor?' he asked.

'It's too soon to tell,' replied the other. 'A common condition of shell shock is that sight does come back but you lose it again from time to time. Don't ask me the reason why that happens. I'm not a specialist.'

From his voice, Paul could tell that he was a relatively young man who lacked the experience of a mature doctor. He sounded as weary as Paul felt. Hearing him get up to move to another patient, Paul reached out to grab his arm.

'What will happen to me?'

'You'll spend a short time here to be properly assessed, then a decision will be made. The chances are that you'll be shipped back to a hospital in Blighty. Before that, one of the officers in your regiment will write to your parents to explain what happened to you.'

'Don't let them do that!' begged Paul.

'There's nothing I can do to stop them.'

'I don't want my parents to see me like this.'

'They're bound to do that sooner or later.'

'No, they're not,' said Paul. 'I might regain my sight and there's nothing wrong with my body. I'm strong – I'll soon recover.'

'You need a long, long rest, Private Marmion. It's no good having impossible dreams. You must accept hard fact. Your war is over.'

'But it isn't. Crawling back home would be cowardice. I want to *see* again and hold a rifle in my hands. Can't you understand, Doctor?' he pleaded. 'I've got to go back there and kill the bastards who shot my best friend.'

When he got home late, Marmion found his wife waiting up for him with his supper in the oven. He gave her a hug of gratitude then fell on the meal with relish.

'What kind of a day have you had?' she asked.

'It was a very long one, Ellen, with meetings, more meetings and endless frustration.'

'Then it's just like any other murder investigation,' she said, resignedly.

'The killer is not doing us any favours, if that's what you mean.'

'They never do.'

293

'But I'm hoping to get a first sighting of him tomorrow.'

'Really – where will he be?'

'I have a feeling that he might be at Mrs Reid's funeral. For everyone else, it will be a very sad occasion but he'll revel in it. He'll be like an artist viewing a painting when it's finally finished and enjoying every brushstroke.'

'What a horrible man!'

'He's sick in his mind, Ellen.'

'Are you sure he'll turn up?'

'No – but the temptation will be very strong.' He munched his food. 'What have you been doing today?'

'I did what I do every day, Harvey – I worry about Paul.'

'He may well have survived, love. The early casualty lists were enormous and he wasn't on any of those. It's turned into a battle of attrition now.'

'My nerves are frayed, that's all I know.'

'I have my moments when my stomach lurches but I try to hide them.' He nibbled a slice of bread. 'This is delicious.'

'Mr Seymour called this morning.'

'Was he as chirpy as ever?'

'Actually,' she said, 'he was rather annoyed. It seems that Lena Belton waved him down and demanded more bread than he was able to give her. She didn't mince her words. She'll be lucky if he ever gives her *any* bread from now on.'

'That woman has achieved the impossible. Steve Seymour never gets upset. He's the most even-tempered man around here. If Lena angered him then she must have said something very unpleasant.'

'She did, Harvey, and it made me think.'

'Go on,' he said through a mouthful of food.

'Well, you're not the only detective in the family, you know.'

'I agree – there's Alice, of course, and Joe Keedy.'

'Don't forget me,' she warned him, tapping her chest. 'I've been putting all the evidence together and I may have the explanation for the way she's behaving.'

'It's called despair. Because *she's* in mourning, she can't bear to see people like us who've had to cope with no terrible losses in war.'

'There's more to it than that, I fancy. Why did she want an extra loaf when she's there on her own?' asked Ellen, thoughtfully. 'Why does she hide herself away in a house with the bedroom curtains drawn all day? Why does she keep all her friends at bay?'

'You tell me, Ellen.'

'It's because of Patrick.'

'He's working on a farm in Warwickshire, isn't he?'

'That's what Lena wants us to think,' she said, 'but I believe it's a lie. When he's her last surviving son, she'd hardly want to get rid of him to some distant farm. She'd want to cling on to Patrick even more tightly. That's what I'd do and that's what Lena is doing behind those drawn curtains. Her son is still there.'

'Then why has nobody seen Patrick?'

'She's holding him captive.'

295

Once again, it was locked. When he tried the door of his bedroom, Patrick Belton could not open it. He was a big, muscular youth with the strength to force the door open but that would arouse his mother. It was well past midnight and she'd be fast asleep now. He lived in fear of her but his frustration was even greater than his fear. He lifted the sash window and looked down into the garden as he'd done every night that he'd been imprisoned in his room. This time it was different. He had to get away. All that he had to do was to swing across to the roof of the shed then drop down to the ground. His weight was the problem. To reach the shed, he had to hold on to the drainpipe and he was afraid he'd prove to be too heavy. If the drainpipe came away from the wall, he could be injured in the fall. Yet he couldn't stay locked in his bedroom like a dog chained in his kennel. He simply had to break free.

Pushing the sash window right up, he got a leg over the sill and reached out for the drainpipe. When he gave it a tug, it rattled ominously but it was too late to turn back now. Taking a firm grip on the pipe, he brought his other leg over the sill and swung towards the shed. There was a loud, rasping sound as the pipe came away from the wall but he landed safely on the roof of the shed and realised that he'd escaped at last. He was suffused with a sense of achievement. Since it was a little over six feet to the ground, he decided to jump, landing on the little patch of grass and rolling over on his back. When he tried to get up, however, his mother stood over him, brandishing a walking stick.

Lena Belton was not going to lose another son.

CHAPTER SEVENTEEN

They were far too preoccupied to notice that it was a beautiful day with bright sunshine gilding the roofs of the houses. The funeral pushed everything else from their minds. Derek Reid had just shared breakfast with his guests. Philip Christelow was the image of a man doing something disagreeable to him under sufferance and his wife, Esther, a stringy, nervous woman with grey hair, moved between a battered silence and an intermittent flood of tears. When the meal was over, there was something that had to be raised.

'What about the inquest?' asked Reid.

'What about it?' said Christelow, almost belligerently.

'I can't be there. Someone from the family should be.'

'Well, it won't be me.'

'Don't you want to know exactly what happened?'

Christelow scowled. 'I know far too much already.'

'Now, now,' said his wife, reproachfully. 'You did promise.'

'I only promised to attend the funeral – nothing more.'

'Well, I'd like to attend the inquest. I'd also like to attend the trial of the man who killed our daughter but I don't think I've got the strength to do that. In fact, the doctor advised me not to come to the funeral.'

'Neither of us should have come, Esther.'

'Well, you're here,' said Reid, crisply, 'so let's make the most of it, shall we? Whatever private reservations we may have must be kept to ourselves. All eyes will be upon us and we mustn't let Charlotte down.'

'It was Charlotte who let *us* down,' asserted Christelow.

'Philip!' scolded his wife.

'Why deny it?'

'Can't you stop thinking about your own pain for a second?' said Reid. 'This is an ordeal for all of us, Mr Christelow – for me, for my family and for Charlotte's many friends. We don't need you to make it even worse.'

His father-in-law was penitent. 'No, I agree,' he said. 'I apologise.'

'And I apologise for him, Derek,' said Esther, getting up from the table. 'If you'll excuse me, I need to go upstairs for a few minutes.'

She shot her husband a look of dismay that compelled him to go with her. Reid sat back in his chair, glad that he finally had a moment alone. When there was a knock on the front door, he went to open it. Alma Bond was standing there.

'Hello, Derek,' she said. 'How is everything going?'

'Things are rather fraught, to be honest.'

'Is there anything I can do?'

298

'Yes, please. I desperately need the sight of a friendly face.' He moved aside to let her step past then closed the door. 'It's been grim in here.'

'Is Mr Christelow still being awkward?'

'He's trying to be. Luckily, my mother-in-law is on hand to chide him.'

'I hope he's not going to do anything untoward at the funeral.'

'He'll just sit and sulk. It's his wife who concerns me.'

'I thought that she insisted on being here.'

'She did, Alma, but she's not in the best of health. When she first heard the news, she had another angina attack. The funeral may be too much for her.'

'I'll sit close to her,' she said. 'I was trained as a nurse before I married.'

'I'd forgotten that.'

'It seems like an age ago, doesn't it?'

They looked at each other with unexpected pleasure as they recalled the moment when they'd first met. Reid had been engaged to Charlotte Christelow at the time and Alma had just started walking out with her future husband. Yet there had been an instant attraction between her and Derek Reid. It had later led them astray and given them a satisfaction that neither was getting from their respective spouses. But it had been an illicit attachment that brought guilt in the wake of pleasure and it had finally ended. The smiles they exchanged were an acknowledgement of something that had been meaningful to them.

'What about Inspector Marmion?' she asked. 'Did you relent?'

'No, Alma, he got no invitation from me.'

'You told me that he wanted to come.'

'If he turns up, I shall ask him to leave.'

She was disturbed. 'You mustn't create a scene, Derek.'

'A funeral is for family and friends only.'

'Perhaps he just wants to show his respects.'

'Then he can do that by staying away alto-gether,' said Reid, vehemently. 'I don't want any policemen there. They should be too busy trying to catch Charlotte's killer.'

He spread the paintings and the drawings out on the table so that he could compare them. Charlotte Reid's work showed a raw talent but it could never have flowered into the effortless brilliance evinced by Olive Arden. Even when sketching an Old Master, Olive had an eye for detail that was remarkable. In her paintings, there was a stunning use of colour and signs of an extraordinary imagination. In every way, Olive gave him more pleasure than Charlotte, though his friendship with the latter remained a delicious memory. After studying the work of his two victims, he reached for the photograph he had taken one evening. It showed a window display at Swan & Edgar and he had now begun to reel in the young woman responsible for it.

Charlotte Reid, Olive Arden and Irene Fuller – each one of them was an artist of sorts. He liked to think of himself as an artist as well. His canvas was the female body and he left his indelible signature upon it. Instead of hanging in a gallery, his work occupied the front pages of national newspapers.

Publicity was the source of his inspiration.

'What do you want me to do?'

'Stay well out of sight, Joe.'

'The best way to do that would be in the car.'

'No,' said Marmion, 'it wouldn't. Your vision would be restricted and, if you do have to give chase, you'd waste time getting out of the vehicle.'

'What about you, Harv?'

'I'll drift in at the last moment and sit right at the back.'

Keedy was dubious. 'He'd never actually go into the church, would he?'

'I'd put nothing past him.'

'Have you had any word from Lieutenant Reid?' Marmion shook his head. 'Then he'd obviously prefer it if you stayed away.'

'He can't stop me going, Joe. The chances are that he won't even notice me. He'll have his parents and his in-laws to contend with, remember. Mrs Christelow wanted to come but her husband was ready to wash his hands of his daughter altogether.'

'I can't understand that.'

'Wait until you're a father yourself.'

'How do you know I'm not one already?'

It was a feeble joke and it fell flat. Marmion glowered at him and made the sergeant wish that he'd never blurted out the stupid comment. They were coming out of Scotland Yard and walking towards the car parked at the kerb. Opening the door to get into the rear of the vehicle, Marmion paused.

'Will you be seeing Alice tonight?'

301

'Yes, I promised to take her home when she came off her shift.'

'Then I've got some news you can pass on about Lena Belton.'

'What's that woman been up to now?'

'Well,' said Marmion, seriously, 'if Ellen is right – and it sounds as if she may be – Lena's been telling the most outrageous lies. Her son, Patrick, is not toiling away on a farm in Warwickshire. He's locked up in the house.'

Everyone knew that she ran the household. Even when her husband was alive, it was Lena Belton who made all the important family decisions. In spite of their age and their physical bulk, her three sons had been frightened of her. Disobeying their mother brought cruel sanctions into play so they made sure they did what they were told. It was Patrick Belton's turn for a reprimand. As he sat on a chair in the kitchen, his face was still bruised and his head still aching from the beating his mother had given him. She'd wielded the walking stick with real force. He could still feel the blows. He could also feel the pangs of hunger.

'When can I have some food?' he bleated.

'You don't eat until I say that you can.'

'I'm starving.'

'It serves you right.'

'Haven't you punished me enough?'

'No, Patrick,' she said, 'I haven't. You need to be taught a lesson.'

'I won't do it again, I promise.'

'You won't get a chance, my lad. From now on,

you'll be under lock and key whenever I leave this house.'

'That's unfair!'

'It's your own fault. What on earth possessed you to do what you did?'

'I just wanted some fresh air.'

'You can get that by opening the window. You didn't have to climb out of it the way you did. Where did you think you were going?'

He hunched his shoulders. 'I don't know.'

'You wouldn't dare to *leave* me, would you?' she asked in a voice laden with threat. 'You're my flesh and blood, Patrick. I need you here.'

'I ... know that now.'

'You can never desert me.'

It was exactly what he'd tried to do. The situation was intolerable. Forced to give up a job he liked, he was confined to the house during the day and locked in his room at night. It was as if he never actually existed. Because the house was overlooked, he was forbidden to use the privy at the end of the garden during the day and had to resort to the chamber pot beneath his bed. His mother made him empty it out after dark. Patrick Belton was a prisoner in his own home.

'It's wrong, Mother,' he complained. 'I have friends but I'm never allowed to see them. I liked working at the brewery but you won't let me anywhere near it.'

She was scornful. 'Sweeping up and doing odd jobs – that's all they let you do. Instead of moving barrels, you should have been making them. But they said you weren't clever enough for an apprenticeship so they treated you like a drudge. I saved

303

you from that, Patrick. You ought to be grateful.'

'I must do *something*.'

'You're doing it – you're living here with me. That's how it's going to be from now on. And if the war is still on when you turn eighteen, I'll tear up any papers they send you and tell them that you've run away. Whatever happens, they're not going to put you into uniform. That was how Gregory and Norman died. They'll not have you as well.'

'But I *want* to join the navy,' he said. 'I want to fight the Germans.'

Lena slapped him so hard across the face that he almost fell off the chair.

'Don't you ever think that again, let alone say it out loud. You're all I've got left, Patrick Belton, and nobody will ever be allowed to come between us.'

Head down, he rubbed his face gingerly. The truth suddenly slipped out.

'I was going to the farm,' he confessed.

She gaped. 'What do you say?'

'You told everyone that's where I was so I thought I'd go there. They'd take me in. There'd be work for me there. I'd enjoy it.'

'And what about me?' she cried. 'What am I to do without my son beside me? You can't run off to Warwickshire. How would you have got there? You don't know the way and you haven't got any money.'

He glanced up at her then turned away shamefaced. Lena exploded. Going to the dresser, she took down the pot in which she kept all her money. It was empty. She ran into the hallway and came straight back with the walking stick in her hand.

The carriage arrived to pick up the chief mourners. When the driver got down and opened the rear door, Esther Christelow was the first person to get in. She was followed by her husband and by her son-in-law. Derek Reid had toyed with the notion of asking Alma Bond to join them in the vehicle but he felt that it would be misconstrued by some people. Alma had, in any case, made it clear that she preferred to go to the funeral on foot. Having left the baby with her mother, she was free to mingle outside the church with the other friends of Charlotte Reid. To arrive with the husband of the deceased would, in her view, have been unseemly.

It was a slow drive to the church of St Matthew, Bayswater, not far north of Kensington Gardens. Curious pedestrians stood still, men removing their hats, and stared at the hearse as it rattled past, drawn by four black horses with black plumes. Reid kept his eyes closed, his mother-in-law was weeping into a handkerchief and Philip Christelow was a marble statue. When the cortège finally arrived at the church, the vicar stepped forward to welcome them. The torment had begun.

Having watched from a distance, Joe Keedy sauntered towards the church and looked in all directions. Several people had stopped to stare at the mourners who were now filing in after the coffin but none of them aroused the sergeant's interest. The killer was certainly not lurking out-

305

side. He signalled the information to Marmion who was in the queue moving towards the church door. If the man they were after had turned up, he had to be inside and that seemed unlikely. Keedy paced up and down the pavement in case the killer made a late appearance but the only people who came into view were two women and a policeman on his beat. The sight of the uniform was enough to frighten any criminal away. The vigil was therefore over. Keedy went back to the car.

Since neither Inspector Marmion nor Sergeant Keedy was available at Scotland Yard, Lionel Narraway was referred to the superintendent. Claude Chatfield was pleased to meet him, offering him a seat with due solicitude and making an initial assessment of him. What he saw was a highly educated, well-spoken, well-paid professional man with an accomplished tailor.

'I'm very sorry that you've been caught up in this business, sir,' he began. 'It's just unfortunate that your name was mentioned by the killer.'

'I'd hoped that it was a complete fluke, Superintendent. But I've come round to the view that perhaps it was not.'

'What's happened to change your mind?'

'I've been thinking.'

Chatfield waited until his visitor was ready to unburden himself. Narraway needed time to prepare himself. When he finally spoke, it was with some rapidity as if anxious to discard as quickly as possible something unpleasant from his past.

'I was reminded of an altercation I once had

with a client,' he said. 'It must have been over two years ago now which is why I didn't at first recall the incident. A lady brought a painting to the auction house where I'm employed and asked for a valuation. She told me that it had been in the family for generations and was reputed to be an original Moroni. That's Giovanni Battista Moroni,' he explained with a touch of condescension. 'He was one of the most talented portraitists in Lombard painting in the sixteenth century. The lady had documentation which seemed to verify its provenance. What she did not have, however, was a genuine Moroni. It was a clever forgery and I had to turn the painting down.'

'I daresay that she was very upset.'

'She was pulsing with rage, Superintendent, and she became abusive.'

'Why take out her disappointment on you?' asked Chatfield. 'All that you did was to tell her the truth.'

'It was a painful truth. Her high expectations had been dashed.'

'Forgive me saying so, Mr Narraway, but I'm not sure that this is in any way germane to the case. The one thing that is incontrovertible is that the killer is male. However upset this lady was, she wouldn't use your name out of spite and embroil you in a murder investigation.'

'You didn't let me finish, Superintendent.'

'Oh, I do beg your pardon.'

'She was not alone. A gentleman was with her – a *younger* gentleman. The nature of their relationship was not difficult to see,' said Narraway with frank disapproval. 'Wanting to ingratiate himself, this gentleman gave me a warning look.'

'Is that all?'

'His eyes were blazing. The lady called him "Hubert", but he had a faintly Mediterranean cast of feature. You know how hot-blooded such foreigners can be.'

'But this all happened over two years ago.'

'Malice can lie dormant for longer than that, Superintendent.'

'Do you think that this man is *capable* of murder?'

'The stare he gave me was like a death sentence,' said Narraway with a shiver. 'It took me days to recover from it. I made an effort to bury the memory and – but for the visit of your detectives – there it would have lain buried.'

'Can you describe this man?'

'In almost every detail, he resembles the killer. The description in the newspapers fits him like a glove.'

Chatfield was irritated. 'I wish you'd told us this when my detectives first made contact,' he said.

'I was too incensed at being taken for a murderer. Sergeant Keedy was very heavy-handed. As you've now realised, I'm wholly innocent.'

'You are, sir – and I'll speak to the sergeant about his treatment of you. What you've told me may turn out to be extremely valuable in spite of the lapse of time since your clash with these two individuals. I'll need their names.'

'I only know the man as Hubert but here's the name and address of the lady.'

Taking out his wallet, Narraway extracted a piece of paper and handed it over. He watched as an expression of total amazement spread slowly over Chatfield's face.

'Are you *sure* about this, sir?'

'That was the lady in question,' confirmed Narraway, 'and she taught me that elderly members of the peerage could swear disgustingly if minded to do so.'

All that Keedy could do was to wait until the funeral service was over. He passed the time by studying the church itself. Built over thirty years earlier, it was a fine example of the gothic revival with a basic design worthy of a cathedral and with a multitude of perches to attract birds. Keedy counted a dozen or more different species who called the place their home. The coffin eventually reappeared and the bearers slid it gently into the hearse. Mourners came out in a steady, unhurried procession and got into various modes of transport to go off to the cemetery. Emerging towards the end of the queue, Marmion joined his colleague in the rear of the car.

'What was it like, Harv?'

'It was very moving.'

'Did you spot anyone suspicious?'

'No, I didn't.'

'That makes two of us – he's not here.'

'It's not over yet, Joe.'

'Do you think he'll turn up at the burial?'

'He might do.'

'Well, I don't. I think we'd be spitting in the wind.'

'It's a funeral,' said Marmion. 'We can't leave until it's all over.'

He didn't belong there. That's what Paul Marmion kept telling himself. He wasn't just another blind soldier stumbling along towards a future of total darkness. Somehow he knew that he would recover his sight in time. Paul was going to will himself better. At the moment, however, he needed a period of recuperation under the military doctors. That was why he was part of a long line of uniformed soldiers with a hand on the shoulder of the man in front of him. They formed a sad crocodile, picking their way uncertainly over rough ground towards the waiting trucks, knowing that they'd escaped the battle of the Somme but that it had left them for ever with its mark. The soldier in front of Paul was trembling uncontrollably and making strange noises. The man behind him was digging his fingers into Paul's shoulder as if hanging on to a life raft in a turbulent sea. They were doomed to lives of misery and recrimination. Paul was different. He was convinced that he would be back. Instead of leaving the war, he was only taking a short rest from it. With his free hand, he felt in his pocket. The mouth organ was still there. It would always remind him of a lost friend and keep Paul's fire crackling away inside him.

Harvey Marmion remained on the fringes, close enough to hear the vicar but far enough back to be ignored by everyone else. The funeral had drawn a large and sympathetic congregation. When the coffin was lowered into the grave, there was a general sigh and the shedding of silent tears. Marmion looked around the cemetery but

310

could see nobody else in view. Joe Keedy had a very different perspective. Detached from the funeral, he took the path that led around the perimeter of the cemetery and stopped beside a headstone as if to pay his respects. He knelt down and read the lettering chiselled into the marble. It was the grave of a young woman who'd died many years ago. A sentimental verse had been added. Although it looked trite, he was touched by the feeling behind it and he paused to wonder what had robbed the woman of her adult life.

When he rose up again, he did so carefully and peered over the top of the headstone. The funeral was breaking up in the middle distance and a new mourner had appeared. He was a gravedigger, dressed in rough garb and an old hat, leaning on his spade and watching from the shade of a tree. Keedy was about to turn away when he took a closer look at the man. The ugly face of Horrie Waldron came into the sergeant's mind. Waldron had been a murder suspect in a previous investigation and was a gravedigger by trade. Keedy remembered his dishevelled clothes, his weary trudge, his indifference to respect for the dead and the way that the spade grew out of his hand as if it had been born there. None of those things was evident in the man Keedy could see now. He was no employee at the cemetery. He was an intruder in disguise.

Not wishing to frighten him away by sudden movement, Keedy began to walk in his direction with an apparently aimless gait. The gravedigger was alerted at once. He pulled back behind the trunk of the tree so that he was out of sight, then took to his heels. Keedy went after him, dodging between the gravestones and increasing his speed until he was actually sprinting. The man was fast but the sergeant was slowly gaining on him and the closer he got, the more convinced he was that the killer had come to the funeral after all. That lent speed to Keedy's legs and gave him an upsurge of determination. When the man disappeared in a stand of yew trees, Keedy went in after him. It was a mistake. He was knocked to the ground from behind by the flat of a spade. It hit him so hard that he was completely dazed, eyes misting instantly and head pounding.

When he dragged himself to his feet, he realised that he'd failed. The man had got away and Keedy had no idea where he went. Marmion came into the trees and saw his colleague swaying unsteadily.

'Are you all right, Joe?' he asked, taking him by the shoulders.

'I think so.'

'What happened? I saw you haring across the grass.'

'I almost caught him, Harv.'

'Who was he?'

Keedy bent down to retrieve his hat from the ground then he set it gently on his head. Even that light contact with his skull made him wince.

'I think it was him,' he said, gritting his teeth. 'The killer was here.'

Ellen Marmion sensed that she had found the explanation. Lena Belton's behaviour was designed to keep everyone at bay. Nobody was allowed to

312

get close and she would never invite anyone into the house. Trapped inside, Ellen decided, was the woman's youngest son, hidden away in the mistaken belief that his mother was saving him. It was an unhealthy situation for Patrick Belton. A boisterous, outgoing youth was being deprived of a normal life. It made Ellen feel more sympathetic to Lena. What she was doing suggested that the woman had serious mental problems. Since Ellen was no doctor, she wondered if she should alert her general practitioner because she knew that Lena was also a patient at his surgery. Marmion had advised her to ignore the woman altogether but Ellen felt that she ought somehow to help. First, however, she had to be sure of her facts. At the moment, she was working on instinct and she knew that firm evidence was needed.

On her way to the library that afternoon, she went out of her way so that she could walk past the Belton house on the other side of the road. As before, the curtains in the front bedroom were drawn. Ellen stopped to look up at them. There was a small gap between them and it suddenly disappeared as the curtains were pulled to overlap. Someone was in the bedroom, keeping the street under surveillance. As she walked on to the library, Ellen wondered if it was Lena Belton or her son.

Before they returned to Scotland Yard, they called in at the hospital so that Keedy could be examined. The X-ray of his head showed no skull fractures so – after he'd been given some painkillers – he was released. Back in the car, he felt

313

much better.

'What made you suspect that man?' asked Marmion.

'It was Horrie Waldron. Remember him?'

'Yes, I do. You had a tussle with him as well, didn't you? It's obvious that gravediggers just don't like you.'

'The point is that he wasn't what he pretended to be,' said Keedy. 'I got so used to seeing Waldron's slouch and his abiding sense of boredom. He never took the slightest interest in a funeral unless he was waiting to fill in the grave. The man I saw today was a spectator. From the way he leant on his spade, I had the feeling that he'd never handled the implement before.' He felt the bruised rear of his head. 'I must admit that he used it to good effect on me, though.'

'It could have been worse, Joe. He might have hit you full in the face.'

'I'd have preferred it if he hadn't hit me at all.'

When they reached their destination, they got out and went into the building. As soon as they appeared in the corridor outside his office, Claude Chatfield came out and pounced on them.

'What kept you so long?' he demanded.

'We had a spot of bother, sir,' replied Marmion. 'The sergeant had to be treated in hospital.'

Keedy gave him an abbreviated account of what had happened, insisting that it had made him even more determined to catch the man. Glad that the killer had apparently come out of hiding, he was sorry that he'd been unable to apprehend him when he had the chance.

'You've probably frightened him away from

314

attending Olive Arden's funeral.'

'We hope to catch him before that takes place, sir.'

'Then I might have information to help you do just that, Sergeant.'

Taking them into his office, he told them about Lionel Narraway's visit and took the opportunity to rap Keedy over the knuckles for upsetting the man at their first meeting. Marmion was very pleased that Narraway had come forward.

'It must have taken an effort of will,' he observed. 'As you saw, the gentleman is rather repressed. He's not inclined to release any details of his private, or indeed, his professional life. Mr Narraway likes to live a calm, untroubled existence. A sensitive man like him would be very upset by a death threat.'

'It wasn't actually put into words, though,' said Keedy.

'Yet it was definitely there,' said Chatfield. 'He impressed that upon me.'

'So this man named Hubert was a sort of gigolo, was he?'

'That's what he implied.'

'It's that aspect that raises doubts for me,' said Marmion. 'Someone who takes money from an older woman for sexual favours does not sound like the man we're after. It may be worth checking on him but I'm not sanguine.'

'Follow it up,' ordered Chatfield. 'If nothing else, you may help to put Mr Narraway's mind to rest.' He handed over the sheet of paper given earlier to him. 'I was rather surprised to see the lady's name.'

Marmion read it with astonishment. 'So am I, sir.'

'Where do we have to go?' asked Keedy.

'It's an address in Berkeley Square.'

Patrick Belton was torn between terror and bravado. Cowed by his mother, he wanted to break free but, whenever he got as far as the door, he drew back for fear of the consequences. She had always been strict but her regimen was even more austere now. He'd lost everything he valued and was reduced to an arid existence with a mother whose maternal instincts seemed warped. Belton was a youth of fairly low intelligence. His elder brothers had done reasonably well at school and taken up apprenticeships in good trades. Belton lacked their abilities and their discipline. He was content to do menial chores at the brewery. Even though he'd earned a pittance there, it was a world in which he felt comfortable.

Seated at the kitchen table, he'd been playing cards by himself. It staved off boredom but it didn't still the nagging urge to smash down the front door and run. He was shuffling the pack when he heard a key being inserted in the lock. His mother had returned and the quiet terror resurfaced. Belton hoped that he would escape further punishment with the walking stick. He still had its marks on him.

'What have you been doing?' she asked, coming into the kitchen.

'I've been playing cards, Mother.'

'Is that all?'

'Yes, it is.'

'You haven't been out in the garden or done anything stupid, have you?'

'No, I haven't,' he said. 'I swear it.'

'Has anyone come to the door?'

'It was only the postman. There's a letter for you.'

'What about the neighbours – have they been prying again?'

'Not anyone from this street,' he said, 'but there was someone who stared at the house for a bit. I saw her through a chink in the curtains.'

She smacked his head. 'I told you to keep out of my bedroom!'

'I was only in there for a few seconds. Honestly.'

'So who was this woman staring at the house?'

'It was Mrs Marmion.'

Beneath Lena Belton's growl of anger was a sudden uneasiness.

Berkeley Square comprised long ranges of large houses. It offered some of the most exclusive addresses in London yet, when the detectives stepped into one of them, they were not met with the opulence they expected. There was scant furniture and some of the paintings had been removed, exposing lighter patches of wallpaper. The only person in residence was Mrs Croft, the housekeeper, a watchful woman in her forties. Information had to be dragged slowly out of her.

'And where might Lady Ingleside be?' asked Marmion.

'Her Ladyship is staying with friends, Inspector. I'm not at liberty to tell you exactly where they live.'

'When will she be returning?'

'I've yet to be informed of that.'

'The house is curiously empty. Is it going to be put on the market?'

'That's not for me to say,' replied Mrs Croft. 'The only decisions that fall to me are concerned with the upkeep of this place.'

'What about Lady Ingleside's country pile?' said Keedy. 'Aristocrats always have a mansion somewhere, don't they? This is merely a town house.'

'Sir Esmond died less than a year ago, Sergeant. It was rather unexpected. Her Ladyship is still in mourning.'

'I'm sorry to hear that.'

'Is there any way that we can get in touch with her?' asked Marmion.

'If you'd care to give me more details,' said the woman, loftily, 'I can write a letter. You still haven't told me why you wish to contact Lady Ingleside.'

'Actually, we're more interested in speaking to a friend of hers. We really came in search of an address for the gentleman.'

'And who might this gentleman be?'

'That's the problem. We only have a Christian name – but we understand that he was a close friend of Lady Ingleside at one time. His name is Hubert.' She was startled. 'I see that you recognise the gentleman.'

'You're wrong, Inspector,' she said, recovering her poise. 'I've never heard of him. I'm afraid that I can't help you.'

'And I'm afraid that you're not *trying* to help us,

318

Mrs Croft. We are not here to make idle enquiries. Sergeant Keedy and I are leading a murder investigation and if you insist on hiding things from us, we'll have to take you to Scotland Yard for a more searching interview.'

Her poise disintegrated. 'I know nothing of a murder,' she said, anxiously.

'But you have heard the name Hubert before, haven't you?' pressed Keedy. She gave a reluctant nod. 'Then perhaps you'll tell us his full name and where we'd be likely to find him.'

'I don't know where Mr Gazzi lives now. He hasn't been here for a very long time. I'm not even sure that he's still in London.'

'But he was a close friend of Lady Ingleside, wasn't he?'

'I'd prefer to call him an acquaintance.'

'Was her husband aware of this acquaintance?'

'That's immaterial,' said Marmion, quickly. 'We're not concerned with Lady Ingleside's private life. All that we're after is an address for Hubert Gazzi.'

Mrs Croft pursed her lips. 'You could try his studio, I suppose.'

'What studio?'

'The one where he worked, Inspector – Mr Gazzi is an artist.'

CHAPTER EIGHTEEN

Paul Marmion fretted at the delays. The trucks had taken them to the railway siding and there'd been a long wait until they were helped into their compartments. Because they were crammed in together, it was hot, sticky, uncomfortable and reeking of unwashed bodies. The constant noise was an additional trial. Urgent conversations took place all around him as other wounded soldiers speculated worriedly about their future. The man next to Paul treated him to a long diatribe against the government for sending him to war in the first place. He didn't seem to realise that Paul made no comment in return. The monologue rolled on, rising above the rhythmical tumult of the train and the routine clicking of the points. Someone tried to start a sing-song but there was too much desperation in the compartment and nobody had enough spirit to join in. Paul thought fondly of the many times when Colin Fryatt's mouth organ had serenaded them in the trenches. The instrument now lay silent in his pocket.

There were stops and starts and indistinguishable noises of all kinds. When the train finally reached the coast, they were unloaded and put back into their line. There was a long, perilous walk through the docks and more than one of them tripped and fell, making the line concertina as the blind men bumped helplessly into each other. Paul could smell the sea and hear the waves slapping against the side of the harbour. Another long wait followed. Preference was being given to more serious cases, they were told.

'What can be more serious than losing your sight!' protested one man.

'Losing your legs and your balls,' yelled someone in reply.

'Get us on board and take us home.'

'Wait your turn, chum.'

Paul tried to be patient but it was difficult. As long as he couldn't see, he was a prisoner in a chain gang. He moved only when everyone else did. A pleasing sound eventually drifted into his ear. It was the clack of shoes on stone as nurses worked their way along the line, distributing tea and words of comfort. Someone had taken notice of them at last. When a cup was thrust into his hands, he wanted news.

'Where are we going?'

'The ship will dock at Southampton,' said a lilting female voice. 'You're on your way to Netley.'

'What's there?'

'It's the Royal Victoria Military Hospital. They'll look after you.'

'I just want them to give my eyes back to me,' said Paul, earnestly.

But she'd already moved to the next man in line.

The address was in a part of London that someone had once called Little Venice and, though it fell ridiculously short of its counterpart, it seemed an appropriate home for a man with an Italian name. When the detectives arrived there by car, they saw a line of barges moored in the canal. Opposite was a row of houses. They searched for the number they'd been given. An old man with a straggly white beard was seated beside the canal with an easel set up in front of him. When he saw the two newcomers, he called out.

'Who are you looking for?'

'Hubert Gazzi,' replied Marmion.

'Who wants him?'

'We do, sir. I'm Inspector Marmion of the Metropolitan Police and this is Sergeant Keedy.'

'Why are you after Hube?'

'We need to speak to him.'

'Then you'll need a loud voice,' said the old man with a chortle, 'because the poor bugger is dead. The Huns got him. He's buried somewhere in France.'

The detectives crossed the road to talk to him. 'Did you know Mr Gazzi?' asked Keedy.

'I know all the artists round here because I own that house opposite and rent out the rooms as studios. Hube had the front bedroom,' said the man, pointing. 'He worked there and sometimes slept there. He painted some wonderful things in that room. When the sun hits the bay window, there's good light for an artist.'

'Could we see inside, please?'

'You can, if you wish, but it's in a hell of a mess. I haven't had time to clear it out properly. Hey,' he added, thrusting his chin, 'I don't want you taking anything. It's private property. It'll go to Hube's family when they finally come and get it.'

'We just want to look inside,' explained Marmion.

'Hang on, then.'

The man clambered into a barge and vanished inside. When he reappeared, he was carrying two keys on a ring. He tossed them to Keedy who caught them.

'Do you make a living as an artist?' asked the sergeant.

'I try to,' said the other. 'Artists always manage to rub along somehow.'

'What about Mr Gazzi?'

'Oh, he was different. Hube had other talents.'

'We heard that he had friends in high places.'

'He had lady friends all over the shop,' said the old man, enviously. 'If you have a mug like mine, the most you arouse in women is a feeling of pity. Hube took after his father. He was handsome in that kind of flashy way Italians are – though his mother was English, of course. Anyway, he knew how to use his good looks. That's how he attracted what he used to call his "sponsors".'

The detectives understood. Lady Ingleside had obviously been such a sponsor.

'He had expensive tastes, you see,' the old man continued. 'That was the way he paid for them. His paintings always sold well to his sponsors.'

'We'll go and take a look at them,' said Marmion.

When they'd crossed the road, Keedy unlocked the front door and they went in. There was an overpowering stench of oil paint and mustiness. Fresh air had rarely penetrated the house. They went upstairs and into the main bedroom.

323

Sketches and unfinished paintings lay everywhere in companionable chaos. Artists' materials were scattered on a variety of surfaces. It was a hopelessly cluttered environment in which to work but there was no doubting Gazzi's talent. Judging from the examples they could see of it, the artist was very gifted. Marmion singled out one particular example. It was the portrait of a tailor, poised over his table and about to cut some cloth with a pair of shears. After examining it with interest, Marmion showed it to Keedy.

'This is a copy of a portrait by Giovanni Battista Moroni,' he said.

Keedy was stunned. 'You recognised it?'

'Yes, Joe.'

'I didn't realise you were an art expert.'

'I'm not,' said Marmion with a grin, 'but I did learn to read.' He turned the painting over and showed his colleague the name scrawled on the back. 'I fancy that this is the forgery shown to Mr Narraway. Lady Ingleside owned the original and got her young friend to paint a version of it. When they tried to pass it off as Moroni's work, they were rumbled.'

'Now I can see why she was so irate.'

'And so was Gazzi. He thought his work was good enough to deceive an expert. No wonder he turned the evil eye on Mr Narraway.'

'He and Lady Ingleside were trying to perpetrate a fraud.'

'That's the way it goes in policing sometimes,' said Marmion, philosophically. 'You lose a potential killer and get an art forger in return – a dead art forger, as it happens. Gazzi is beyond the law now.'

'What about Lady Ingleside?'

'Let's forget about her, Joe. She's not our problem. My guess is that she's in deep enough water as it is. You saw the house in Berkeley Street. She's selling the contents off to keep it going. And she must have been in dire straits if she'd stoop to fraud.' Marmion took a coin from his pocket. 'Heads or tails?'

'What do you mean?'

'Hubert Gazzi is dead. Someone has to tell Mr Narraway. He'll be thrilled.'

'I'm not sure that I want to see him thrilled, Harv. He's bad enough when he's quiescent. Okay,' agreed Keedy. 'Heads, *you* go and break the good news; tails, we both go together.'

While resenting yet another visit from the detectives, Narraway was so pleased by the news they brought that he actually shook each one of them by the hand. Breaking off work early, he rushed off to the antiques shop run by Edwin Bonner to tell his friend what had happened.

'I don't think you were ever in real danger, Lionel,' said Bonner.

'Gazzi was vengeful. I somehow persuaded myself that it was him.'

'It was nobody. This whole business is the result of a grotesque coincidence. I suggest that we put the thing right behind us.'

'I wish I could, Edwin.'

'What's stopping you?'

'I don't know,' said Narraway. 'It's just that I have these ... lingering doubts.'

'They're utterly without foundation.'

'Why was it *my* name? That's what I keep asking myself.'

'It was purely accidental.'

'I wonder.'

'Enough of this,' said Bonner, clapping him on the back. 'You've just been given some excellent news and your spirits should be sky high. Instead of that, you're still looking over your shoulder for someone who never even existed in your life. You're in the clear, Lionel.'

Narraway smiled nervously. 'Yes, I am, aren't I?'

'I think that dinner at our favourite restaurant is called for, don't you? After all, we have something to celebrate.'

'We do, Edwin. We can celebrate my peace of mind.'

Claude Chatfield was realistic enough to know that the pursuit of Hubert Gazzi was very much a long shot. Just because the man had expressed hostility towards Narraway, it didn't mean that he'd entangle the art expert in a double murder in order to settle an old score. When he heard the report of their findings from his detectives, the superintendent was resigned rather than disappointed.

'I've not been idle in your absence,' he said.

'We never imagined that you were,' said Marmion, with a sarcasm too mild to be recognised as such. 'You are always a whirlwind of activity.'

'What have you found out, sir?' asked Keedy.

Chatfield unfolded the full extent of his researches. Lady Ingleside, it turned out, was the

326

widow of Sir Esmond Petrie Ingleside, late of Ingleside Manor in Leicestershire. Having inherited substantial debts, Sir Esmond had cheerfully added to them by a life of profligacy. He and his wife had spent very little time together, allowing her to have the freedom of living alone in London. An interest in younger men meant that she was never short of company but indulging them had eaten into her own depleted funds. Lady Ingleside was now effectively living off old family friends while her town house was being prepared for sale. In retrospect, it was clear that her bungled attempt at art fraud had been conceived as a way to get money.

'The inspector worked that out, sir,' said Keedy.

'It was an interesting diversion,' said Marmion, 'but it took us away from the killer instead of towards him. It did, however, offer Mr Narraway some much-needed reassurance. We asked him to let us know if he recalled any other clients with whom he had serious difficulties but he insisted that there were none. Yet we cannot get away from the fact that the killer pointed us in his direction.'

Chatfield puffed his cheeks. 'That's what makes this case so baffling.' He brought an end to the discussion. 'You can get back to work now. Oh, not you, Inspector,' he added as they moved to the door. 'I'd like a word in private.'

Keedy went out and Marmion closed the door behind him.

'Yes, sir?' he asked.

'I spoke with the commissioner earlier. He asked me to pass a comment that I should have made earlier on my own account. We've both scanned the list in this morning's *Times* and we were delighted that, once again, the name of Paul Marmion was not included. Your son must have a charmed life.'

'I wouldn't call fighting in a desperate battle evidence of a charmed life, sir. A name that *did* appear in the list this morning was that of Private Colin Fryatt. He was my son's best friend. That would have hit Paul hard. So while I'm grateful to you and to Sir Edward for your comments,' said Marmion, 'I make no assumptions about my son's apparent invincibility.'

Ellen Marmion had been shocked to hear of the death of Colin Fryatt. As soon as she'd read his name in the newspaper, she went straight round to his mother to offer her condolences. Unlike Lena Belton, who'd refused her offer of help, Barbara Fryatt was extremely grateful. Her son had been very close to Paul Marmion. They'd done everything together, including volunteering to join the army with the other patriotic members of the football team. Ellen spent well over an hour with her, making tea, listening to her recriminations and offering unconditional sympathy. It was late afternoon when she finally got back home. She was unlocking the front door when she heard footsteps behind her and saw a telegraph boy in uniform. Her heart congealed. Had Paul been killed as well? Had the enormous list of dead in the morning paper been inaccurate?

Hand shaking, she took the telegram that came from the boy's leather pouch then went straight into the house to open it. The contents had the force of a poleaxe. Ellen simply flopped into a chair, unable to think, speak or move a single inch. The telegram floated down to the carpet.

Joe Keedy's attitude towards Millie Duxford was ambivalent. While he had no intention of renewing her acquaintance, he found himself taking a peek at her photograph from time to time, marvelling at her nude body and reminded of classical sculptures he'd seen in a museum. Unhappily, Millie was not a marble figure from antiquity. She was very much alive and eager to see him. The photograph was unambiguous. Millie was ready to put herself at his disposal. As a means of shunting her out of his mind, Keedy tore temptation into shreds and tossed them into the waste-paper basket. The timing could not have been better because there was a knock on the door and it opened enough for Terry Jellings to pop his head in.

'That young lady is here to see you again, Sergeant.'

'Tell her I'm not available,' said Keedy.

'I've already told her that you are.'

'Then say that I'm in an important meeting.'

'Miss Duxford insists on seeing you,' said Jellings. 'She claims to have remembered something else about the man who befriended Olive Arden.'

'I bet she does,' muttered Keedy to himself, certain that it was simply a device to see him again. 'All right, send her in. But if she's not out of here in ten minutes, bring a message that Chat wants to see me urgently.'

'I will, sir.'

Jellings went out and, soon afterwards, showed Millie Duxford into the room. She was disappointed that Keedy remained behind his desk instead of coming to greet her. Left alone with Millie, he offered her a chair and she sat down, crossing her legs in a way that was flagrantly provocative. Keedy maintained eye contact with her.

'Did you get my photograph?' she asked with feigned coyness.

'Yes, but I didn't think that it was appropriate.'

'I can't think of anything more appropriate, Sergeant Keedy.'

'This is a murder investigation,' he reminded her. 'That takes up every minute of my time.'

'Oh, I'm a very patient girl. I can wait.'

'Then you'll have to take your turn in the queue behind my fiancée. She, too, is patient and had been waiting a long time to see me.' Millie was deflated. 'While I thank you for your interest in me, I'm unable to return it. Bluntly, I'm spoken for.'

'In that case, I'd better have that photograph back.'

'That's ... no longer possible.'

She was horrified. 'You've *destroyed* it?'

'It was the honourable thing to do.' Her shoulders sagged. 'Now, what's this new evidence you have for us? Does it concern what the killer said to Olive?' She nodded. 'Let's hear it.'

'Didn't you *like* looking at the photo?'

'I'm more interested in catching a very dangerous man,' he said. 'If we don't arrest him soon,

330

another young woman might meet a very unpleasant death. To be candid, *that's* what occupies my mind at the moment – not looking at photographs.'

'Of course,' she said, sobered by the severity in his manner. 'I'm sorry If I've been a nuisance to you, Sergeant. I just thought ... oh, well, never mind.'

He was polite but firm. 'It's very good of you to help us,' he said, 'and I'm grateful but that's as far as our relationship can go. Olive should be at the forefront of our minds now.'

'Oh, she is – I never stop thinking about her.'

'And you've remembered something else?'

'Yes,' she replied. 'It's only a small detail but it might tell you something about the man you're after. Olive wasn't naïve. When an older man took an interest in her, she was bound to wonder if he was married and just seeking a mistress. But that wasn't the case at all. He told her that he'd been widowed a couple of years ago. One of the reasons he was attracted to Olive was that she reminded him of his wife.' Millie gave a wan smile. 'I don't know if it's true but it's what Olive believed. It's why she trusted him so much.'

'Thank you for telling me.'

'He obviously took care to win her confidence.'

'And having won it,' said Keedy, sadly, 'he promptly killed her.'

Harvey Marmion returned from a meeting with the commissioner to find a note on his desk that asked him to ring home as soon as possible. Only a serious development would have made his wife make contact so he lifted the receiver and dialled the number. At the other end of the line, the receiver was snatched up the moment that the instrument began to ring. Ellen had clearly been waiting beside the telephone. She started to gabble unintelligibly and he had to ask her to slow down and start again. When she repeated the news, she was still in a state of agitation.

'Calm down, love,' he advised. 'Paul is still alive. That's reassuring.'

'Yes, but what sort of state is he in?'

'Didn't the telegram give any details?'

'No,' she replied, anxiously. 'It simply said that he'd been wounded in action and was being transferred to the Royal Victoria Military Hospital.'

'That's at Netley in Hampshire. They'll probably bring him back to Southampton.'

'What if he's lost an arm or a leg or even worse?'

'Don't even think that, Ellen.'

'But there are so many of them on crutches these days. When Alice and I went shopping, we saw so many wounded soldiers in the West End. One had no legs at all. It was a pitiful sight.'

'Paul is our son and, whatever's happened, we'll love him just the same.'

'I know that, Harvey, but–'

'Listen to me,' he said, cutting her off. 'You're running towards problems that might not even exist. "Wounded in action" can mean anything. Let's find out the full details first.'

'We can't visit until tomorrow and only between certain times.'

'That's fair enough, Ellen. It will take time to

settle them all in. Paul won't be the only one being sent back. Netley is a huge hospital. There are somewhere in the region of two thousand patients there. And in some cases,' he recalled, 'they're only there for a recovery period. I read an article that said they sent as many soldiers back to the front as they could.'

'I don't want Paul going back there again.'

'The decision is not up to us. I'd just be relieved that he'd be fit enough to fight again. What I'll do is this,' he suggested. 'I'll get in touch with the hospital and see what I can find out.'

'Oh, thank you,' she said. 'I'd rather know the truth than drive myself to distraction, fearing the worst.'

'How much they'll tell me over the telephone, I don't know. Paul is only one of lots of soldiers, all of whom will have concerned parents and friends. Everybody will be desperate for the details. Make yourself a nice cup of tea, love,' he said, 'and try hard not to torment yourself. Paul is alive.'

'Yes,' she agreed, rallying. 'He's alive and he's safely back in this country. We must be thankful for that.'

After clearing his desk, Joe Keedy set out the police photographs of Charlotte Reid and Olive Arden. Since they both lay sprawled in unbecoming positions, there was an obvious similarity but it didn't extend far beyond that. Accustomed to looking at corpses without flinching, he scrutinised the faces in detail. Death had distorted both of them. Even allowing for that, he could see nothing that might link them in the eyes of the killer. He reached for the photograph that Millie Duxford had given him of Olive and herself. Keedy felt a pang of embarrassment. Beneath his desk, another photo featuring Millie lay in pieces in the waste-paper basket. At least he was now able to see Olive as she had been, a happy, committed art student standing beside her friend. The differences now became apparent. Olive was plump while Charlotte had been slim. One had thick eyebrows while the other woman's were carefully plucked. The art student wore no cosmetics but the errant wife had applied them with subtlety.

There were other features that set the two victims apart. The information that Millie Duxford had brought seemed to be false. If the killer had befriended Olive because he was reminded of his late wife, the chances were that he'd selected Charlotte for the same reason. Yet they bore no resemblance. For that reason, Keedy dismissed the remark made to Olive as simply a means of assuring her that he was not married and of arousing her sympathy. He was still staring at the display when Marmion came into the room. Keedy glanced up at him and saw the apprehension in his face.

'Is everything all right, Harv?' he asked.

'No – as a matter of fact, it isn't.'

'What's up?'

'Ellen rang earlier on,' said Marmion. 'Paul has been wounded and sent back home. You can imagine the state she's in.'

'Did they say what sort of injuries he sustained?'

'They didn't, Joe, and that made it all the more worrying.'

'Where have they sent him?'

'He's at the Royal Victoria in Netley. I managed to get through to them but there was very little they could tell me. They were still in the process of sorting out the latest intake and assigning them to wards. Paul's name was on a list of soldiers suffering shell shock.'

Keedy was disturbed. 'I see.'

They both knew about the effects of shell shock. In extreme cases, it could reduce men to deformed animals, unable to walk without quivering all over, for ever haunted by the moment when a violent explosion ended normal life for them. Among the more usual results were blindness, deafness, severe impairment of movement, loss of articulate speech and brain damage. Shell-shocked soldiers were often mere remnants of the fighting men they'd been. They would never be the same again. Marmion could see what the sergeant was thinking.

'We don't know how serious Paul's condition is,' he said. 'Some lads have been known to recover and go back to France. Others...'

He didn't need to put it into words. Keedy understood only too well.

'How did Ellen take it?' he asked.

'It's knocked the stuffing out of her, Joe.'

'Has Alice been told yet?'

'No, she's already started her shift.'

'Then let me get out there and find her,' Keedy volunteered. 'I know her beat. It shouldn't be too difficult to track her down. You'll want to go

335

home, I daresay.'

'I would like an hour with Ellen. Chat said that I could take as long as I like. And I'd be grateful if you locate Alice. There's no visiting until to-morrow so there's nothing we can do in the short term except ... prepare ourselves.' He looked down at the photographs. 'What's been going on here?'

Keedy told him about the visit of Millie Dux-ford and about the remark made to one of the victims by the killer. Marmion thought it might be important.

'Only if both women reminded him of his wife,' argued Keedy, 'and there's no way they could do that because they have nothing in common. Also, why would he want to kill someone who looked like the woman he married?' Marmion was study-ing the photos. 'You see what I mean? They're opposites.'

'There is *one* glaring similarity.'

'Well, I can't see it.'

'Look at their necks.'

'If you mean that both necks are badly bruised, then they do share a single feature. That's what happens when someone throttles you.'

'I'm not talking about the bruising, Joe. Both these women have unusually long necks. You can see it clearly in this picture of Olive Arden,' he went on, picking up the photo of the art student and her friend. 'Millie Duxford's neck is much more in proportion to her body but Olive's is slightly elongated.'

'You're right,' conceded Keedy. 'There *is* some-thing that connects Olive with Charlotte Reid.

Perhaps the killer has a preference for long necks – it makes it easier for him to get his fingers on them.'

As he pretended to search for a card in the stationery department, he was able to look across at Irene Fuller without being seen by her. She was in the act of fitting a shoe onto the foot of an elderly lady. As Irene turned her head, the man could see her in profile and the sight of the long, slender neck sent a buzz of pleasure through him. At that moment in time, Irene looked so much like his wife that it was almost uncanny. When he could see more of her face, of course, the resemblance vanished instantly. She was in every way different. The neck was enough in itself. It had first attracted him to Charlotte Reid and then to Olive Arden. Other women – more beautiful than either – had crossed his path but his victims were the ones chosen. Irene Fuller had now been selected to follow in their footsteps, an apposite path for someone who worked in a shoe department.

As he replaced a card in the rack, he was nudged by the woman beside him.

'Oh, I do beg your pardon,' she said with an apologetic smile.

'That's quite all right.'

'I'm not always this clumsy.'

She bared her teeth in a smile and held his gaze. She was a woman in her thirties with fading good looks underneath the liberally applied cosmetics. Well dressed and brimming with a vulgar confidence, she touched his arm gently.

337

'Do you have the time, sir?' she asked.

'No, I do not,' he said, the words escaping from his mouth like a hiss of steam. 'If I ever see you in this store again, I shall report you to the management and have you thrown out. I'm a married man leading a respectable life and I want no truck with despicable creatures like you. Get out of here!'

Recoiling from him in fear, the woman headed swiftly for the exit.

He soon found her. Alice Marmion was walking along the pavement with Peggy Lassiter beside her. PC Mike Searle was a few paces behind. When he saw Joe Keedy hurrying towards them, Searle thought for a moment that another reprimand was coming his way, but the sergeant simply wanted a private word with Alice. Detaching her from the others, Keedy took her aside and told her about the telegram concerning her brother. She was dazed at first but recovered quickly.

'I must go and see him at once,' she said.

'Visitors are not allowed until tomorrow, Alice. Besides, you have a shift to finish. I'm sure that Gale Force will give you time off tomorrow but she won't be impressed if you leave your colleagues in the lurch today.'

'No, that's true.'

'Your father rang home and did his best to calm your mother down,' said Keedy, 'but she's still terribly upset.'

'Shell shock can be a life sentence, Joe.'

'Only in certain cases – and there are many exceptions.'

'Paul wouldn't have been sent back here unless it was serious.'

'We don't know that.'

'This is so frightening,' she admitted, closing her eyes tightly for a second and tensing her body. 'When I saw that Paul's name was not in this morning's list, I almost cheered. Then I saw that Colin Fryatt had been killed in action and I was shaken. He and Paul were like brothers. They were best friends since they first started at school. In addition to everything else,' she said, 'Paul will be mourning the loss of Colin. He'll be in despair.'

'He's also well away from the war zone, Alice, and getting expert medical care. Take some comfort from that.'

'You read such terrible things about shell shock.'

'You'll be able to see your brother tomorrow. Be strong for him. Paul may need a lot of help from all of us.'

Alice fell silent. He put an arm around her to give her a squeeze. She replied with a weak smile of gratitude. After a few moments, she looked up at him.

'Will you be there at the end of my shift?'

'Try stopping me,' he joked.

'I'd like you to take me home. I'll spend the night there.'

'That's the best thing to do, Alice. And don't worry about Gale Force. Your father was going to explain the situation to her.'

'Good.' She realised that her colleagues had disappeared. 'I'd better catch them up,' she said. 'They'll wonder what's happened.'

'I could have waited until midnight but I felt you'd want to know right away.'

'Thank you, Joe – that's very thoughtful of you.'

'Try not to brood on it too much. You're still on duty, remember.'

'Yes, I am,' she said. 'I'll have to catch the others up.'

Alice gave him a token kiss then marched smartly off. As Keedy watched her go, he wondered about her brother's condition and about the effect that it was going to have on the whole Marmion family.

There were so many wounded soldiers aboard that Paul Marmion had had to sit on deck with the other men in his group. The choppy sea made them feel queasy. When they docked in Southampton, there was an interminable wait as the patients were disembarked in turn. There was one heartening piece of news. When they walked to the railway station, they were told that there was a line that went directly to the hospital. Packed into a compartment with the others, Paul had no sense of joy at being back on British soil. He was musing about Colin Fryatt, one of the countless soldiers from his regiment buried back in France. Paul gave an involuntary giggle. The man next to him was puzzled.

'What's so funny?'

'I was thinking about my friend, Colin,' said Paul. 'He was a wizard on the mouth organ. Colin could play anything you asked for. If he was still alive, I know what tune he'd be playing right now.'

'Oh – and what's that?'

'"Three Blind Mice".'

There was ironic laughter from those within earshot. The train powered on until it reached Netley. The Royal Victoria Military Hospital had been the first custom-built hospital for wounded soldiers. It had been set up in the wake of the Crimean War and it had grown steadily in size over the years as successive conflicts brought increasing numbers of wounded men back to Britain. What Paul and his group could not see as they were unloaded from the train was the sheer scale of the place. Rows and rows of long stone buildings stretched out across the Hampshire countryside. The church at the heart of the military community had been used over the decades for worship and for an endless series of burial services.

Forming their familiar line, Paul and the others were led to one of the Red Cross huts that had been erected to cope with the additional numbers flooding into the hospital. A female hand guided Paul to a bed and he was told to sit down.

'What's your name?' asked the nurse.

'Paul Marmion.'

'Yes, you're here on the list. Welcome to Netley, Private Marmion.'

'Thank you.'

'When you've settled in, we'll give you a different uniform. Since you won't be able to see it, I can tell you that it's blue. That's what convalescent soldiers all wear – Hospital Blues.' She touched his shoulder. 'How are you feeling?'

'I feel as if I want to get out of here,' he said, purposefully.

'That may take time,' she said, softly, 'a lot of time.'

It was perfect. The building had taken a direct hit during a night-time Zeppelin raid. What had once been a thriving department store was now, for the most part, an empty shell, its stock either looted or removed to the warehouse and its windows reduced to fragments. Large signs warned the public to stay clear as the building was not safe. Against the main entrance was a board to which was pinned a notice announcing that the store was scheduled for demolition. Ignoring the various warnings, he let himself in and used a torch to guide him in the darkness. Wrecked shop fittings and abandoned cardboard boxes lay everywhere. He had to pick his way through the debris with care. Eventually he came to a large window with some tailor's dummies standing forlornly in a circle as if speculating on the fate of the bright new dresses they'd once worn. Shards of glass lay at their feet.

This was the place to bring Irene Fuller. Where better to take a window dresser than to a window that had once been famous for its striking displays? When the chance came, he would offer the public something else to arrest their gaze.

It was perfect.

CHAPTER NINETEEN

'They're having another go at us, Sir Edward.'

'It was ever thus, Superintendent.'

'Anybody would think we'd simply been twiddling our thumbs.'

'The press want an arrest,' said the commissioner, gravely, 'or, at the very least, a glimmer of one. This morning's *Daily Mail* is the worst. Beside photographs of the two murder victims, they have a blank space with a question mark in it.'

'I saw it,' said Chatfield, gloomily. 'WILL YOUR DAUGHTER BE NEXT? It implies that we're incapable of safeguarding the young women of London and that's grossly unfair.'

'In one respect, we're blessed. Most of the young women in the capital are well able to look after themselves. It's one of the fruits of the war. Women are now more competent, more aware and more assertive than they were in my day.'

Chatfield sniffed. 'I can't say that I've watched those developments with any pleasure. The contribution of women in general to the war effort has been admirable but we don't want to breed a race of viragos.'

The commissioner laughed. 'There speaks a man with daughters.'

'Femininity is important, Sir Edward. I'd hate to see it disappear.'

'So would I, Superintendent.' He glanced down

at the newspapers spread out on his desk. 'Though, I have to confess, that I'd be delighted if some of the damaging headlines here would disappear.'

The two men were feeling embattled. When reporting events in the war, the press was subject to a degree of censorship. Some of the newspapers and magazines full of trenchant articles attacking the government's decision to enter the conflict had been suppressed altogether. The major daily newspapers restricted themselves to a recitation of salient facts from the front. There was little editorialising. When it came to crime on the home front, however, editors were more outspoken, ready to call the police to account and to expose what they perceived as shortcomings. It meant that Sir Edward Henry and his men routinely collected more criticism than praise.

The commissioner opened a copy of *The Times* and grimaced.

'Look how many names there are,' he said. 'The columns go on forever.'

'The Grim Reaper is stalking the Somme,' observed Chatfield, darkly. 'Over nineteen thousand British soldiers died on the first day and fifty-seven thousand plus were wounded. The numbers are incredible. In a single day, we had three times the losses incurred during the whole of the Boer War.'

'In comparison with what we're engaged in now, those events in South Africa are starting to look like a veritable sideshow.' He perused the list of names. 'I don't see the inspector's son here.'

'No, Sir Edward, it's something I meant to tell

you. Paul Marmion escaped death but he was wounded in action and brought back yesterday to Netley.'

'Was he *badly* wounded?'

'All that the inspector knows is that his son is suffering from shell shock.'

'Oh dear!'

'Since the first murder, he's been working all the hours that God sends. Given his extraordinary commitment, I didn't feel that I could refuse his request for time off today to visit the hospital.'

'No, no, you had to let him go, Superintendent.'

'The Inspector and Mrs Marmion are probably on their way to Netley.'

'There's a daughter as well, isn't there?'

'Yes, and she also wears a police uniform. Her name is Alice Marmion.'

'Women police!' said the commissioner with a wry smile. 'Such a phenomenon is unimaginable to people of my generation. Girls were taught to be docile and domestically oriented. Running a home and bringing up a family often marked the height of their ambition. Now they actually go on patrol as auxiliary constables – Alice Marmion is a case in point.'

'Her superior, Inspector Gale, tells me that she's an exemplary officer.'

'I like to think that *all* our officers – male or female – are exemplary.' He closed the newspaper. 'So they've gone to the Royal Victoria, have they?'

'They have, Sir Edward, and they'll have to face up to the grim truth about their son. It could be

345

very distressing.'

They couldn't remember the last time when the three of them had had a family outing. Marmion was always too busy and Alice always had commitments elsewhere. Ellen was lucky if she got to spend any length of time with her husband and her daughter. The fact that they were all together brought her great solace. Having taken a train to Southampton, they changed to one that served the station at Netley. It was full to the brim with people like themselves, anxious family members doing their best to keep up their morale. Some had been to the hospital before and their overheard comments offered a degree of reassurance. Doctors and nurses were universally praised and the strict regimen was accepted as a necessary imposition. On the debit side, however, Marmion heard of overcrowded wards and of intolerable pressure on the staff. The number of patients was daunting. It would be an achievement simply to find out where Paul Marmion actually was.

Their first sighting of the military hospital was through the window of their compartment. It looked vast and its grounds occupied a huge acreage. They could see one-legged patients struggling along on crutches and more severely wounded men being wheeled in bath chairs by nurses. There was a surge for the exits as the train finally came to a halt and the platform was soon covered by urgent visitors. Marmion and the two women joined the noisy procession to the hospital.

'What are we going to say?' asked Ellen.

'We say very little,' replied her husband.

'Daddy is right,' said Alice. 'We must let Paul do the talking. And we must try not to be shocked by the condition he's in.'

'That's good advice, Alice.'

'It's not mine, Daddy. It was Joe's suggestion. If we react in horror, he said, it will only upset Paul.'

'I agree. We're here to offer love and comfort.'

They were disappointed to learn that Paul Marmion was not in one of the large wings on every side of them. Instead, he'd been put into a hut whose facilities were, by definition, inferior to those of the wards in the main buildings. Armed with a list on a clipboard, a sister was waiting to greet them at the door. They waited their turn in the queue then finally reached the woman.

'Paul Marmion?' she repeated, scanning her list. 'Yes, you'll find him in the last bed on the right. Please bear in mind that we don't want our patients to get too excited. And when the bell rings, that really is the end of the visit.'

She stood aside so that they could open the door and enter the ward. All three of them were stunned by what they saw. Bed after bed was occupied by a soldier with his eyes heavily bandaged. Some had additional wounds and a few had missing limbs. All of them looked young, broken and defenceless.

Ellen was the first one to pick out Paul, sitting patiently on his bed.

'My God!' she gasped. 'He's *blind*.'

Patrick Belton prowled the house relentlessly. Desperate to get out into the fresh air, he was held back by an invisible rein that jerked him to a halt whenever he got close to a door. Even though she wasn't there, his mother was controlling his movements and stifling his spirit. When he came into the living room, he paused to look at the photographs of his two brothers on the mantelpiece. Gregory and Norman Belton had also been kept under the maternal thumb and their only means of escape had been to join the army. Sadly, they had died in action, a fact that Lena Belton kept repeating to her youngest son. His safety consisted of staying hidden like a refugee in his own house. Patrick found it demeaning.

When he saw her through the window, he retreated to the kitchen and filled the kettle before putting it on the gas. Expecting his mother to be as grim, stern and unforgiving as usual, he was surprised to hear her laughing for once. She swept into the kitchen and dumped her shopping bag on the table.

'It's happened at last!' she said, cackling. 'I heard the news at the post office. Paul Marmion has been wounded in action and shipped back home. It's the turn of the Marmion family to suffer now. I hope he's hurt bad.'

Paul Marmion had been tugged in opposite directions. Eager for the support of his family, he hated the thought that they'd see him in such a terrible condition. They'd been proud of him when he signed up, but there'd be no sign of that pride now. Instead, they'd be shocked, repelled and anxious about his future. Given the choice, Paul decided that he'd prefer it if they delayed their visit until his

'How nice to see you again!' she replied.

'I never thought I'd bump into you out here, Miss Fuller. I thought you'd be toiling away in the shoe department.'

'They let me off for half an hour over lunch. I always try to get some exercise if I can. I hate being cooped up.'

'I'm the same,' he said. 'A daily walk is vital.'

She lowered her voice. 'Have you worn those shoes you bought from us?'

'No – I chose something else for the funeral.'

'Was it someone in the family?'

'No, Miss Fuller,' he replied, thinking fondly of Charlotte Reid, 'it was just an acquaintance. I wanted to pay my respects.'

'I've never been able to do that,' she said, biting her lip. 'My boyfriend was killed in France. I don't even know where Martin is buried.'

'That must make it very difficult for you. When the war is over, it might be possible for you to find out exactly where his grave is and visit it.'

'I haven't looked that far ahead.'

'You deserve to know, Miss Fuller. It may help to soothe your mind. Grieving over a loved one is a painful process. I found that out when my wife passed away. However,' he went on, smiling, 'let's not spend this brief time together talking about death. I want to know if you've been asked to do any more window dressing?'

'Yes, I have, though it won't be for a matter of weeks.'

'I'll make a point of walking past to admire the results.'

'That's very kind of you.'

'Perhaps I should let you in on a secret, Miss Fuller,' he said, lowering his voice. 'I have more than a casual interest in retail, you see. We're not big enough to rival Swan & Edgar, perhaps, but we did establish a place in the market. If I told you that my name is Goddard, you might understand.' Irene was puzzled. 'Join it with the name of Iddlesleigh.'

'Oh, of course,' she said with a grin of realisation. 'Iddlesleigh and Goddard. I applied for a job there once and they turned me down. And you are...?'

'My grandfather helped to found the store. I've worked there since I was sixteen. Unfortunately, my career was interrupted by a German bomb. The whole store was gutted. However,' he went on, 'we'll rebuild in due course and I'll resume my role in senior management. I can guarantee one thing, Miss Fuller. You won't ever be turned down by our store again. In fact, I shall come searching for you so that I can offer you a post as a full-time window dresser. How does that sound?'

Irene gave a laugh of disbelief. 'Do you *really* mean that, Mr Goddard?'

'Yes, I do. I'm deadly serious.'

On the crowded train back to London, it was virtually impossible to have a proper conversation so they waited until they reached Waterloo Station. Marmion led his wife and daughter to the refreshment room and they found a table that gave them enough privacy to allow for an honest exchange of opinions over a cup of tea.

Ellen was melancholy. 'Paul frightened me,' she

352

admitted. 'He's going to be blind for the rest of his life but he just won't accept it. All that talk of going back to France frightened me.'

'He *might* recover his sight,' said Marmion, hopefully. 'It does happen, Ellen. Soldiers with far worse injuries have made amazing recoveries. In some cases – and we can only hope that Paul's is one of them – shell shock does slowly wear off.'

'The important thing is that he *wants* to go back,' observed Alice. 'I don't like the idea myself but I took it as a good sign. When he was home on leave, Paul wasn't looking forward to rejoining his regiment at all. It wasn't cowardice, it was sheer fatigue. He'd lost all of his old fighting spirit. Somehow he's got it back again.'

'Yes, Alice, I felt that.'

'I listened to some of the other visitors at that hospital. The patients they'd been to see were down in the dumps. They'd given up. They'd resigned themselves to living as permanent invalids.'

'Paul may have to do that as well,' said Ellen.

'He's not going to give up, Mummy.'

'We have to be realistic.'

'It's the only sensible thing to be,' said Marmion. 'Even in the short time we were allowed to spend with him, the changes in Paul were obvious. We must accept them without comment. But he's regained his sense of conviction and that's something we can hold on to.'

'What if his eyesight never improves, Harvey?'

'Then the army will send him to a place where he can be taught to adapt to his disability. They won't just cut him loose, Ellen. They have a duty of care to wounded soldiers. Paul will come through this somehow. We must be careful that he never hears despair in our voices.'

Ellen shuddered. 'That doesn't stop me feeling it.'

'Paul was so much better off than some of the others,' said Alice. 'There was one man whose face had been shot away and lots who'll be disfigured for life. Paul was lucky. When he recovers, he'll be fit and healthy.'

'He may also be blind.'

'That's not the end of the world, Mummy.'

'No, it isn't,' said Ellen, trying to shake off her pessimism. 'If that's what he has to cope with, we'll be right behind him.' About to sip her tea, she put the cup down again. 'There's one thing that worries me.'

'Only one?' teased her husband. 'You usually have a list.'

'I'm serious, Harvey.'

'Sorry – go on.'

'What did both of you make of Paul?'

'I was relieved to see him alive,' said Marmion. 'Once I'd got used to all that bandaging, I realised that he wasn't as bad as he looked.'

'Yes,' added Alice, 'there were flashes of the old Paul. I loved that.'

'What was the one thing worrying you, Ellen?'

'If neither of you noticed it, then I must have been wrong.' This time she sipped her tea before speaking. 'I had the horrible feeling that ... well, that Paul didn't really want us there.'

Joe Keedy still had the photographs of the two

murder victims. When he laid them out on his desk again, he wondered what had persuaded two intelligent women to be lured into the killer's web. In the case of Charlotte Reid, he'd exploited her loneliness while her husband was away. According to Alma Bond, the marriage had already had some underlying problems. Short of male attention and approval, Charlotte had been won over by someone who'd offered both. She'd been attracted by the notion of meeting him inside a cinema, a place of darkness where nobody would recognise her. The killer had not only chosen the venue because it enabled him to strike in public without being seen, he had sought its anonymity as well. Inside the cinema, his identity had vanished. In courting another man's wife, was he also hiding from his own spouse? It was a question that Keedy returned to time and again.

A different approach had been adopted with Olive Arden. The relationship had been closer to that of master and pupil at first. The killer had praised her work then impressed her with his knowledge of art. As they got closer, the age gap between them had slowly shrunk and Olive was flattered that she'd found an admirer. Keedy looked at the photograph of the art student and the model. The killer would never have chosen Millie Duxford in preference to Olive. Millie was too well acquainted with the ways of the world to be taken in so easily by the man. Something else would have deterred the killer. She was a strong, red-blooded woman who would not have been easily subdued. Millie would have fought back. Olive, it appeared, had been seduced then strangled when she was at her most vulnerable.

There was nothing vulnerable about Millie. As he thought about the other photograph of the artists' model, Keedy was tempted to tip everything out of the waste-paper basket so that he could put her together again like a jigsaw. The impulse soon passed. He was grateful that it did because Harvey Marmion sailed into his office and would have caught him at an awkward moment. Keedy was interested to know how the trip to the hospital had gone and, in particular, how Alice had coped with the experience.

'Alice was as positive as I tried to be,' explained Marmion. 'She didn't allow herself to get upset. Ellen found it a little more difficult to adjust to Paul's injuries. Because he was blinded in the explosion, she's convinced that it's a lifelong condition, but that's not certain at all. The specialist has told Paul that there's a chance he may regain some, if not all, of his sight. He's clinging to that as if it's a firm promise.'

'Alice told me that Gale Force had given her the day off.'

'Yes, she's spending another night at home. I'm glad of that, Joe. I didn't want Ellen to go back there by herself and mope. Alice will stop her doing that. However,' he went on, 'that's enough of family matters. Let's get back to work.' He glanced at the photographs. 'I see you've been busy again.'

'I noticed their long necks this time.'

'What else did you notice, Joe?'

'He picks women that he knows he can overpower physically.'

'I fancy that he overpowers them emotionally beforehand then attacks them when they're least prepared.'

'Did you see the *Daily Mail* headline today?'

'Yes, I did, and it definitely won't be *my* daughter next.'

'So who will it be, Harv – another lonely wife or another art student?'

'He'll find someone,' said Marmion, uneasily. 'I just hope that we can track him down before he gets those evil hands around another female neck.'

He stood behind her so that he could look at her neck and run his gaze down her back. Irene Fuller was too preoccupied to realise what he was doing. The two of them were standing in front of the charred vestiges of Iddlesleigh and Goddard, one of the oldest department stores in London. She was horrified to see how much damage could be done by a direct hit from a German bomb. Window after window had been shattered and left staring at the street like eyeless sockets. To someone who worked in a similar department store, it was a depressing scene.

'I had no idea that it was as bad as this,' she said, pulling a face.

'It would have made my grandfather weep to see this.'

'I'm not surprised, Mr Goddard.'

'By the time we've finished rebuilding,' he boasted, 'it will be bigger and better and we'll be back in business.'

'How soon will that be?'

'Oh, it will take a long time, Miss Fuller, but you'll know when it's ready because I'll be chasing you with a contract.'

'I can't believe that you'd take me on when you know so little about me.'

'Well, I'm not offering you the top job,' he warned. 'You'd be an assistant to our chief window dresser and learn from him. In any case, I don't believe that what I saw at Swan & Edgar was a first effort. You've done it before, haven't you?'

'Yes, I have,' she confided. 'It's my third attempt, as it happens, and I don't just get into the window and make it up as I go along. I prepare sketches at home so that I have a concept to work from.'

'That's exactly what I hoped you'd say, Miss Fuller. You take a professional approach. I'd like to see your sketches, if I may. That will give me a clearer idea of your scope and your imagination. Could you bring them to work some time?'

She was eager to please. 'You can see them tomorrow, if you wish, Mr Goddard.'

'Excellent, Miss Fuller – I'll meet you after work.' He began to walk and she fell in beside him. 'I'll see you safely to the tube station then I must get back home.'

As they strolled along in silence, she felt completely at ease in his company.

'There's something I've been meaning to ask you,' she said, tentatively.

'Go ahead.'

'It's rather personal.'

'We're friends, aren't we?'

'Yes, we are,' she said, reassured. 'I've been wondering. Your wife must have been quite young when she died. Is that true?'

'Sadly, it is,' he replied. 'Diphtheria is no respecter of age. Marion died before she reached the age of thirty. It was a tragedy. We'd only been married for five years.'

Newspapers were delivered to the island on an irregular basis and she'd been there for three weeks without ever seeing one. It had not troubled her in the least. She wanted to be cut off from events in England. The past had too many unpleasant associations and she didn't wish to revive them by reading national newspapers. Anything of real importance, she believed, could be picked up from the gossip in the island's only shop. The Battle of the Somme had been the dominant topic for some time now and she'd heard the same pointless words of pity being uttered on a daily basis. When she went to buy some groceries that morning, however, the focus for the discussion had changed. Instead of talking about the war, two women were reacting with alarm to an article on the front page of a newspaper. Discussing the murders, their voices were raised to a pitch of hysteria. The newcomer heard enough to make her curious.

'Where did this happen?' she asked.

'It was in London, of course,' replied one of the women with disgust. 'Terrible things happen there. He strangled two young lassies and got awa' scot-free. One of them was found wi' hardly a stitch of clothing on her poor body. They reckon there'll be a third victim in a wee while. If you ask me, it's monstrous. What sort of a man is driven to kill and kill and kill again?'

The newcomer put an involuntary hand to her neck.

Lena Belton could not contain the perverse pleasure she felt. As darkness slowly wiped all of the light out of the sky, she told her son that she was going out for a walk. Patrick was surprised but made no objection. After pulling the curtains in the living room, she went out and walked to the Marmion house some streets away. She took a moment to compose her features into a semblance of compassion, then she knocked on the door. It was opened by Alice Marmion, astonished to see who the caller was.

'Oh, hello, Mrs Belton,' she said. 'What can I do for you?'

'I wanted a word with your mother.'

'Then you'd better come in.'

She stood aside to let the visitor in then shut the door. Alice took her into the living room where Ellen was even more amazed to see Lena Belton.

'I heard about Paul,' said Lena, quietly. 'I felt that I had to come.'

Ellen was suspicious. 'Did you?'

'Have you been to see him yet?'

'Yes, Alice and I went to Netley with my husband. We saw Paul.'

'How bad is he wounded?'

'He's suffering from shell shock,' explained Alice, taking over from her mother, 'but his life is not in danger in anyway. Paul is very resilient. He was chatting away as if there was nothing wrong with him.'

Lena was disappointed. 'He's not going to be an invalid, then?'

'We hope not, Mrs Belton, but he'll be in hospital for some time.'

'Ah, I see. Well, I just wanted to ... say how sorry I was by the news. I know that I've been rude to your mother in recent weeks and I came to apologise for that.' She turned to Ellen. 'This war has really got me down and made me do things that I regret now. Losing my two boys was like having limbs cut off. Now that Paul's been injured, you'll have some idea how I felt. It eats into you.'

'It was good of you to come,' said Ellen, keen to get rid of her, 'and I think we should forget any little disagreements we had in the past.'

'I didn't know what I was doing.'

Ellen and Alice said nothing but they were both convinced that the other woman had known exactly what she was doing when she'd stuffed newspapers through the letter box then turned her back on Ellen in the street. They sensed that Lena was not there to offer genuine sympathy but to enjoy the anxiety they were bound to feel about Paul. Alice changed tack.

'How is Patrick getting along on the farm?' she asked.

'Oh, he's ... doing very well,' replied Lena.

'Have you heard from him?'

'Yes, I had a letter only yesterday. Patrick loves working with animals.'

'It must be very lonely for you – living alone, I mean.'

361

'I must put my son first. He's safer in Warwick-shire.'

'Hasn't he been back to see you?' said Ellen.

'No, he hasn't.'

'That's funny. When I passed your house the other day, I had a feeling that Patrick might have come home for a while.'

'Well, he hasn't,' snapped Lena, abandoning her attempt at politeness. 'So you can stop peering at my house, Ellen Marmion. I live there alone. My son is a hundred miles away from here.'

Patrick Belton didn't need to climb through the bedroom window at night this time. He was able to leave by the front door because he'd at last found where his mother had hidden the spare key. His bag was already packed and hidden under the bed. After another raid on his mother's money, he was ready to break out of his prison at last. Knowing the route she must have taken, he went off in the opposite direction. Freedom had an uplifting effect on him. Having been locked up, body and mind, for so long, he felt the urge to celebrate. His walk became a trot then quickly turned into a joyous sprint. It was all he could do to hold back a yell of triumph. Within a matter of seconds, he'd been swallowed up by the gloom.

As the car dropped them off outside the house, Marmion noticed the figure of a woman scurrying away. He nudged Keedy.

'That's Lena Belton.'

'Is she the trouble-maker?'

'Yes, Joe. I've half a mind to go after her and tell

362

her to stop treating Ellen so badly. She needs a stern word.'

'Why don't you set Chat on to her?' suggested Keedy. 'All that he has in his vocabulary are stern words.'

They traded a laugh and went into the house. Ellen and Alice gave them a welcoming hug. All four of them adjourned to the living room.

'I daresay that you spotted Mrs Belton,' said Alice.

'What did she want?' asked Marmion.

'Ostensibly, she wanted to offer sympathy. She's heard about Paul and pretended that she was sorry. The only thing she was really sorry for was the fact that Paul hasn't come back in pieces.'

'She's such a venomous woman,' said Ellen. 'Lena will never forgive me for having a son who somehow has managed to survive at the front.'

'Harvey was telling me about your theory,' remarked Keedy.

'It's more than a theory, Joe. It's hardened into a fact.'

'She's got her youngest son hiding in the house?'

'I wasn't certain until she came here just now,' said Ellen, 'but she gave the game away. As soon as we mentioned Patrick, she got very defensive. And when I said that I had the feeling he'd come home for a visit, she turned on me.'

'Yes,' confirmed Alice, 'it was very unpleasant. I was glad when she left.'

'Why tell everyone that her son is working on a farm?' asked Marmion. 'It doesn't make sense.'

'It does to her, Daddy.'

'Then she's soft in the head,' said Keedy. 'There's nothing illegal about what she's doing but there will be when the lad is old enough to be conscripted. Is that the idea? Does she really believe she can keep him out of uniform by hiding him away?'

'In spite of all she's done,' said Ellen, 'I still feel sorry for her. Her mind has been warped by what happened to her eldest sons. Lena is as much a victim of the war as they were. It's had a dreadful effect on her.'

'What about the effect on Patrick?' wondered Marmion. 'Being locked away in that house with a madwoman is bound to take its toll. He's the one *I* feel sorry for.'

Keedy was perplexed. 'Why does the lad put up with it?'

'He's terrified of her, Joe. His mother rules the roost in every way so Patrick will do exactly what she tells him to do.'

Lena Belton was furious. Her stratagem had failed. Instead of being able to gloat inwardly over the misfortune of the Marmion family, she'd been told that Paul was not as badly injured as she'd hoped and might even recover completely. It had made her seethe with annoyance. What had really caused a stab of pain, however, was the suggestion that Lena's youngest son was staying at the house. Having taking such elaborate precautions to convince everyone that Patrick had been sent away, she was mortified that her ruse had been uncovered. Searching for someone to blame, she decided that Patrick was the culprit.

He'd seen Ellen Marmion looking at the house. In order to do that, he must have been disobeying his mother by peeking through the curtains in the front bedroom. He deserved another hiding. It was his fault that his mother had been forced to leave the Marmion house with her tail between her legs. Lena would give him a beating that he'd never forget.

Letting herself into the house, she grabbed the walking stick from the umbrella stand and went to the bottom of the stairs. After shouting for Patrick to come down, she waited impatiently. When he failed to appear after a second command, his mother went storming up the stairs and flung open the door of his bedroom. It was empty. Taken aback at first, she realised that he must be in the outside lavatory because it was now dark enough for him to slip out there unseen. Descending the stairs at speed, she let herself into the garden and hurried across to the lavatory, using the walking stick to hammer on the door.

It swung open immediately. He was not there.

The chance of being able to sleep properly was almost non-existent. Apart from the constant discomfort from his wounds, Paul Marmion was disturbed by the groans of pain from other beds and by the rat-tat-tat of shoes on the wooden floor as nurses went up and down, tending patients in distress. The pungent smell of sickness and disinfectant was another thing that kept him awake. Death was hovering over some of his companions. Some had come back to England to die. Paul had a stronger reason to fend off sleep.

It was fear of the recurring dream of the gruesome moment when Colin Fryatt had been sliced apart by machine-gun fire. Paul had seen him buckle, twitch then fall head first to the ground. The scene was replayed endlessly to him in his dreams. He was not tormented by memories of the shell that rendered him useless as a soldier. What haunted him was the cruel death of his best friend.

He still wished that his family had given him time to get better before they visited him. He'd felt exposed. Though they were unfailingly tactful, he knew what they must be thinking and hated being in such a helpless condition. On the other hand, he'd drawn comfort from the sound of their voices. The worst was over now. They'd seen him at his lowest. He would slowly improve. Paul was convinced of that. Even though his eyes were closed beneath a thick bandage, he believed that he would one day see again and be able to avenge the murder of his friend. The mouth organ was in the palm of his hand. He tightened his grip on it.

The man in the next bed reached out to tap his arm.

'You still awake, Paul?' he whispered.

'Yes, I am.'

'It's so creepy in here. I've got no idea what's going on.'

'It will get better.'

'It may do for you,' complained the other, 'but not for me. I've lost my nose as well as both eyes and half of my teeth are gone. What girl would look at me twice now? I've been robbed. I've

366

been robbed of a real life. That's what war's done for me,' he moaned. 'I went off to be a hero and I came back as a wreck. I must have been raving mad to volunteer.'

'It was our duty,' said Paul, stoutly. 'If I had my time all over again, I'd do exactly the same.'

'Then you're stupid. No sane man should ever want to be a soldier.'

'I do.'

When the driver saw him in silhouette, he changed gear and slowed the lorry down. The figure ahead of him stopped and turned. As the vehicle juddered to a halt, the driver leant across to open the passenger door. A sturdy youth clambered in and thanked him for the lift. He pulled the door shut behind him. The lorry moved off.

'How far do you want to go?' asked the driver.

'Take me as far as you can.'

'Where are you heading?'

'The navy,' said Patrick Belton. 'I want to join up.'

CHAPTER TWENTY

As a result of the appeal in the newspapers, information was still dribbling in to Scotland Yard. Most of it could be ignored completely. Some people felt able to identify the killer, their wild guesses taking them into the realms of fantasy. One person even suggested that the murders were committed with the help of an accomplice. When the same name was put forward independently by two people, however, the detectives had to investigate. Harvey Marmion sent two of his constables off to interview the man in question. He and Joe Keedy were wondering if they'd tracked down the killer at last when Claude Chatfield came into the room. The superintendent looked glum.

'I blame the war,' he said. 'It's depleted our manpower yet given us a much wider area of activity. We now have to do far more with fewer men. As well as looking for spies and hunting deserters, we have to enforce the dictates of DORA.'

'The Defence of the Realm Act was a necessity, sir,' said Marmion. 'I know that it's made policing more difficult but it's also acted as a deterrent.'

'Without the war, we wouldn't have needed the legislation.'

'It's changed the nature of our job,' observed Keedy. 'We now have to pry more closely into people's private lives and they don't like that at all. They think that we interfere too much.'

'It's for safety's sake, Sergeant,' said Chatfield. 'The fact is that, with a full complement of men, we'd have cleared up these murders days ago. We might even have prevented the second one.'

'That's wishful thinking, sir,' argued Marmion. 'It's not simply a question of needing more detectives. It would help us to gather evidence more quickly, maybe, but sheer numbers would not by themselves solve the crimes. The killer is a very clever man. He operates in darkness in public places that offer him a ready means of escape. After the first murder, security was tightened in every cinema in London, so what does he do?'

'He murders his second victim in a park.'

'Because we've now set up surveillance in all the parks, you can guarantee that he'll change the location of his next attack.'

'There mustn't *be* a next attack, Inspector.'

'Perhaps you could tell us how to prevent it, sir,' said Keedy, mischievously.

Chatfield rounded on him. 'You do that by arresting him.'

'But we have no idea of his identity or his whereabouts.'

'We've learnt more about him every day,' said Marmion, stepping in to save Keedy from the superintendent's ire. 'We have a good idea of what he looks like and a definite insight into his character. He craves attention. He can only get that by finding yet another victim.'

'Imagine the headlines if that happens,' said Chatfield, ominously.

'The press don't realise how hard we're working behind the scenes, sir.'

'I keep telling them.'

'Shout a little louder,' suggested Keedy.

'We can do without your inane comments, Sergeant.'

'Yes, sir – I'm sorry I spoke.'

'Is there *any* way to appease the newspapers?'

'We've had a name for the killer put forward by two quite different people, sir,' said Marmion. 'I've sent men to interview the person identified. We could be lucky but I'm not investing too much hope in the exercise. For obvious reasons, we shouldn't release the name at this stage.'

'*Somebody* out there must know who this fellow is,' Chatfield emphasised. 'It may even be that they are deliberately shielding him.'

'I don't think that's the case, sir.'

'Neither do I,' said Keedy. 'The killer is definitely working alone. Nobody could possibly condone what he's done, still less help to conceal his crimes. Ask yourself this, sir. Who would want to stay close to a man like that?'

The boat took her to the mainland and she went straight to the railway station. Getting all the way to London would involve a change of trains at two points along the line. It would be a long, exhausting and tedious journey and part of her wondered if it was entirely necessary. What if she was mistaken? Why not find some way to contact Scotland Yard by telephone? Or should she simply think of herself and, in the interests of self-preservation, stay where she was? She took the newspaper from her bag and read the article once again. The description was accurate. It *had* to be him. Whatever the discomfort, she had to go back. Somebody's life might depend on it.

When they visited him at the hospital, Paul Marmion had told them that he was to undergo a thorough examination on the next day so it might be better if they stayed away. Like her husband and daughter, Ellen suspected that it was a white lie but she understood her son's desire to be left alone. Now that she'd seen and talked to him, she felt much better. A second visit to Netley could be postponed. Busying herself with housework, however, she never stopped thinking of Paul and planning ahead for all eventualities. If his blindness turned out to be permanent and he was condemned to live forever in darkness, changes would have to be made at the house. It might even be necessary to sacrifice a room on the ground floor so that Paul didn't have to negotiate the stairs. In spite of the upheaval, they would manage somehow.

Ellen was cleaning the inside of the living room windows when she saw Lena Belton bustling along the street. Realising that the woman was coming to see her, she was tempted to ignore the knock on the door. If Lena wanted to ask after Paul again, his mother did not want to let her in. There had already been too many upsetting confrontations with the woman. What persuaded Ellen to change her mind was the agonised look on Lena's face. She was in evident distress. This time she'd not come to gloat. There was a definite crisis. Ellen went to the door and let her in.

'Thank goodness you're here!' cried Lena, embracing her clumsily. 'You've got to help me. Patrick has disappeared.'

'How do you know?'

'I had a letter from my cousin. Patrick ran away from the farm.'

Ellen refused to believe it. Before she challenged her visitor, however, she took her into the kitchen and calmed her down. They sat either side of the table.

'Why come to me?' asked Ellen.

371

'Your husband is a detective. Get him to find my son.'

'Harvey is investigating two murders. They take priority.'

'Then make him order someone else to search for Patrick.'

'If he has run away,' said Ellen, 'then it's something that should be reported to the police but they'd need the full facts. You claim that he disappeared from the farm but we both know that isn't true.' She looked Lena in the eye. 'It isn't, is it?'

Lena lowered her head. 'No, it's not.'

'He was living at home with you, wasn't he?'

'It was the only way to keep him alive,' protested the other.

'What sort of a life could he have being locked away from his friends?'

'He accepted it. When I explained it to him, Patrick accepted it.'

'That's what he said, I'm sure, but only because he was frightened of you.'

'He's a good boy – he does what he's told.'

'I think you pushed him too far.'

Lena flared up and seemed on the verge of losing her temper. Instead, she broke down and burst into tears. Ellen got up to put her arms around her. It was minutes before her visitor dried her eyes.

'When did you find out?' asked Ellen, releasing her.

'It was after I'd been to see you. When I got back...'

'And are you *certain* that he's run away? He might just have wanted to see his friends or

372

spread his wings.'

'He's gone,' said Lena. 'He took his bag with him and he...' There was no point in hiding the truth. 'Patrick stole some of my money.'

Ellen was shocked. 'That doesn't sound like him at all.'

'I've spent the whole night trying to find him. I walked and walked until I was ready to drop. In the end, the only thing I could think of was to come here and ask your husband to help. Patrick is all I have. I *need* him.'

'Do you have any idea where he might have gone?'

'No, I don't.'

'What about the farm in Warwickshire?'

'He wouldn't go there because they'd send him back home.'

In view of recent events, Ellen had come to dislike Lena Belton intensely and sought to avoid her company. Seeing the woman in such a pitiful condition, however, she was filled with sympathy. A grieving mother needed help.

'Patrick must be reported as a missing person,' she said, decisively. 'I'll come with you to the police station, if you like. But you must tell them the truth. It's no good pretending that he ever went to that farm. Is that clear?'

Lena nodded. She was compelled to face the truth. Her plan had not only failed, it had driven her son away.

They had drawn another blank. The man who had been named by two different people turned out to be completely innocent of the crime and not a little aggrieved that he should have been suspected in the first place. Marmion and Keedy received the news without surprise. Inured to disappointment, they didn't even voice a complaint. They simply went over the available evidence once again.

'There's something we're missing,' said Marmion, rubbing his chin, 'and I don't just mean an arrest.'

'We could be looking in the wrong direction, Harv.'

'Why is that?'

'Instead of concentrating on what he *has* done, we should be thinking about what he's planning to do next. Which victim will he choose this time and when will he strike?'

'I've been cudgelling my brains to answer those questions.'

'Since the murders, there's been a much bigger police presence in London. Is there a chance that we've scared him off?'

'I don't think so, Joe. Nothing scares him.'

'No,' said Keedy, feeling the back of his head, 'not even the sight of me running towards him at the cemetery. That's a point,' he added. 'Is he going to turn up at Olive Arden's funeral as well?'

'I doubt that. It will be on the Isle of Wight. Her body's been released for burial now. I can't see how he'll find out details of the event. Besides,' said Marmion, 'he'd be worried that we'll be on the lookout again.'

'Will we?'

'There's no point. He'll stay away. He'll be too busy.'

'Doing what, Harv?'

'My guess is that he'll be cultivating his third victim somewhere. I know that we issued a warning in the press but some young women never read the newspapers. And even if they do, they don't believe that it could happen to them.'

Keedy grunted. 'How many times have we heard that?'

'Far too many, Joe,' said Marmion. 'The chances are that some gullible and unsuspecting young woman has already been caught in his net. The maddening thing is that all that we can do at the moment is to react to events.'

Irene Fuller had been tingling with excitement all day. When her colleagues at Swan & Edgar commented on her high spirits, she fended them off with an excuse about going to a birthday party afterwards. She was careful not to confide in any of them. Irene was not the only shop assistant with ambitions to be a window dresser. If she told them about her offer from another store – albeit in ruins at the moment – they'd be simmering with envy. So she kept it a secret and let it glow quietly inside her.

She was among the first to leave when the store finally closed and she hurried to the place where they'd arranged to meet. Under her arm was the sketchbook in which she kept her ideas for eye-catching window displays. Expecting to see him waiting for her, she was cast down when he was not there. Had she got the wrong time or the wrong place? Had he changed his mind? The confidence she'd been exuding all day slowly began to fade. Irene started to feel like a jilted lover. People were rushing past her in both directions but there was no sign of the man she knew as Mr Goddard. It was almost twenty minutes before he came panting up.

'I'm so sorry to keep you waiting,' he said, touching her arm in apology. 'I had a meeting with the insurance company and it went on into the evening.'

'That's all right. I knew that you'd come in the end.'

'Have you brought that sketchbook you mentioned?'

She held it up. 'Yes, it's right here, Mr Goddard.'

'Then let me atone for my lateness by buying you a drink. I can't look at your work out here in the open. I know a nice, quiet bar we can go to, Miss Fuller.' He smiled disarmingly. 'Since we've become friends, may I call you Irene?'

'Please do,' she said.

'And you must call me by my Christian name – it's Edwin.'

Edwin Bonner had locked up his antiques shop and was counting the day's takings. It had been a profitable day. He'd not only sold three expensive items of furniture, he'd bought a set of Chippendale chairs from someone who didn't know their true value and who could therefore be gently exploited. The man had come to his shop on the recommendation of Lionel Narraway. It was not the first time that his friend had guided customers in his direction. He needed especial thanks in this case because a handsome profit had been made. Bonner would be able to sell the chairs for well over twice the amount he paid for them. Keen to pass on the news, he was delighted when the bell rang and he looked up to see Narraway outside the glass-fronted door. Bolts had to be drawn back and two separate keys used in the locks before he could let his visitor in. After locking the door securely again, he took his friend into the room at the back of the shop. Narraway sensed his elation.

'I see that he came.'

'He came, sold and departed. It was the bargain of the month for me.'

'I had a feeling that it might be, Edwin.'

'It's all thanks to you,' said Bonner, clapping him on the shoulder. 'But I thought we'd agreed to meet at the club this evening.'

'Something came up.'

'Nothing unpleasant, I hope.'

'I'm afraid that it could be very unpleasant.' Narraway glanced at a drinks cabinet. 'A glass of your excellent sherry would be most acceptable. To be honest, I feel that I need it.'

'Then you shall have it at once, dear fellow.'

Bonner took a bottle and two glasses from the cabinet. When he'd filled the glasses, they took one each and adjourned to the sofa. After lifting his glass to his friend, Narraway took a long sip. His friend was concerned.

'You look rather flushed, Lionel. Are you un-well?'

'No, no, it's nothing like that.'

'Then what's your problem?'

377

'I'm afraid that the problem may be *yours*, Edwin.'

'Really?'

Narraway had another fortifying sip. 'I've been thinking about that business with the police,' he began. 'And I refuse to believe that we can dismiss the fact that my name was used as an unfortunate accident.'

'Don't start all that again,' said Bonner, jocularly. 'I thought we'd put that misunderstanding behind us. The world is full of Lionels – though, admittedly, they don't all work for an auction house.'

'You haven't let me explain.'

'If you're going to tie yourself in knots over what was obviously a weird coincidence, then I'm not going to *listen* to an explanation. Forget the whole thing. It's not like you to let something prey on your mind.'

'It's not my mind that worries me, Edwin – it's yours.'

Bonner drew back. 'I don't follow.'

'When I searched for someone in my life with a reason for such malicious behaviour, I could only produce one name. That person, it transpires, died in action at the front. When I learnt that, I felt liberated.'

'I know. We celebrated the occasion in style.'

'But supposing that I wasn't the real target? The object of the exercise was to cause maximum embarrassment. Nobody likes to be questioned by detectives as a suspect in a murder investigation. It really jangled me.'

'It affected both of us, Lionel.'

'That was the intention,' insisted Narraway. 'It was a means of causing us mutual discomfort, not to say humiliation. But the main target was not me, Edwin. I think that it might have been you.'

Bonner shrugged. 'How did you arrive at that conclusion?'

'It's because there's someone in your past who'd be more than capable of the kind of malignancy that's been shown. Because *my* name reached the ears of the police, you were drawn into the general awkwardness. We both suffered. That was his aim. He was too cunning to use your name and profession. If he'd done so, then it would have been obvious to you who might be the culprit.' He had a third sip of sherry. 'Are bells starting to ring?'

'Yes, they are,' said the other, pensively, 'and I agree that he might wish to strike against me out of spite. But I simply can't believe that someone in his position would commit two hideous murders.'

'Neither could I – at first, that is. Then I remembered that look of hatred he gave you in court. It upset you for days.'

'It still does, occasionally.'

'He *knows* you, Edwin, and he knows about us. That's why he used my name as a means of getting back at you. Can't you see that? By inflicting pain on me, he was doing so to both of us. It's him – I'm certain of it.'

The thought made Bonner quiver with apprehension.

It all happened so easily. Irene Fuller was enjoying a drink with her new friend and lapping up the praise he was showering on her work. She was a competent artist and each of the sketches in her books showed a different window display. On every single one, his comments were positive and encouraging. His voice was so authoritative and his artistic instinct so apparent that she didn't dare to contradict him. Almost without realising it, she moved from the bar to a small, dimly lit restaurant. Over an excellent meal, washed down by a bottle of wine, he talked about her future as his employee. Irene was overjoyed. Out of the blue, she'd acquired a friend, a patron and a guide to her career. In time, she believed, she'd be rescued from being a mere assistant in a department store. She'd have a new status and real scope for her talents. As the evening wore on, she worried about the time.

'I mustn't be too late,' she said.

'We have to visit the store first.'

'We won't be able to see much if it gets too dark, Edwin.'

'We can see everything in the mind's eye, Irene,' he assured her, pouring more wine into her glass. 'And you mustn't worry about getting home safely. I'll take you back in a taxi.'

'There's no need to go to all that trouble.'

'Oh, I insist. I always take good care of my staff.'

After a journey lasting most of the day, she arrived in London. The trains on which she'd travelled had been noisy, smelly and filled with passengers. The last stage had been the most un-pleasant because she'd shared a compartment with a group of inebriated soldiers on leave.

Aroused by the sight of an attractive woman in her thirties, they'd ogled her and made suggestive remarks. She'd been grateful when they'd left the train in Watford. After queuing for a taxi, she was taken to Scotland Yard. When she explained why she was there, she was shown at once to Harvey Marmion's office. He introduced himself and Joe Keedy to the visitor. They learnt that her name was Rebecca Forrester and that she'd come all the way from Scotland.

As soon as she sat down, she took out the folded newspaper from her bag.

'I believe that my husband is the man you're looking for,' she said.

'What makes you think that, Mrs Forrester?' asked Marmion.

'The description given in the press alerted me, Inspector, but there was something else as well. It concerns ... the way that the victims were killed.'

'Why travel all this way to tell us?' said Keedy. 'There are police stations in Scotland from which you could have rung through the information.'

She shifted uncomfortably in her seat. Rebecca Forrester struck them as a handsome, educated, middle-class woman. But there was a haunted air about her and, even in a building filled with officers of the Metropolitan Police, she was patently ill at ease. She needed time before she could reply to Keedy's comment.

'I agree, Sergeant,' she said at length. 'It would have saved me a lot of trouble. But this is not something I can discuss over the telephone. In fact, I'm not even able to talk freely about it now. The truth is that ... I'd rather confide in another woman. Since I came all this way to see you, it may sound rather cowardly of me but it's a delicate matter and – no disrespect to either of you – I'd find it difficult to broach the topic in here.'

'I fully understand,' said Marmion, considerately. 'Fortunately, we do have women police officers. I'll arrange for you to see one right away.'

In retrospect, Paul Marmion wished that he'd allowed his family to visit him again. It would have interrupted the tedium. The hospital day seemed interminable and the noise was constant. Nurses took them out for a walk in the grounds at one point and he was able to inhale fresh air again but it was only a brief respite from the sharp odours and the enduring clatter of his ward. Darkness reigned. It became oppressive. Determined to regain his sight somehow, he wanted to tear off the bandage around his eyes. The only thing that stopped him was the warning voice of the doctor. Paul needed time to recover. He had been told not to expect too much too soon. Patience had to be his watchword. Some of his companions, however, had already lost their patience. They were crying in pain, demanding attention, yelling for the sake of it or railing against the vicissitudes of fate. Paul was in a pit of desperation.

He was sitting on the edge his bed when he heard someone approaching.

'Is there anything I can get you, Private Marmion?' asked the nurse.

'Yes – I'd like some peace and quiet.'

'We'd all like that,' she said with a laugh, 'but it's not possible in here.'

'Yet it's not as bad as it was,' he noticed. 'When we first came in, the noise was ear-splitting. It's a little better now. Have some patients been moved out?'

'You've got good hearing. We have lost patients. In fact, a number of the beds are now empty. That won't last, I'm afraid. They'll soon be filled.'

'What's happened to the men who've left?'

'They went to a specialist hospital for the blind.'

It took a supreme effort of will to take Edwin Bonner to Scotland Yard. Apart from the residual resentment he felt against the police for upsetting his friend, Lionel, there was the fear of being dragged into a murder investigation and of being exposed to unwelcome publicity. Two things finally persuaded him to overcome his objections. The first was a sense of public duty. If he didn't disclose what he felt might be vital information, someone else could fall victim to the killer. The second reason was even more powerful. He might be in danger himself. The man had already expressed his loathing of Bonner by embroiling him indirectly in the case. While trying to comfort Lionel Narraway, it had never crossed Bonner's mind that he himself had been the killer's real target. Now that the notion had taken root, it unsettled him at a deep level. His enemy had already committed two murders. Bonner feared that he might be next on the list.

When he got to Scotland Yard, he insisted on seeing Marmion alone.

The inspector was curious. 'Is there any particular reason, sir?'

'Yes,' said Bonner. 'I couldn't speak freely in front of your sergeant.'

'Sergeant Keedy is an experienced and discreet officer.'

'I wouldn't question his experience, Inspector. Where I would take issue with you is over the question of his discretion. When he called at my home, there was something about him I just didn't trust. Mr Narraway had the same reaction.'

'I'm glad that you put your trust in me,' said Marmion. 'How can I help you?'

'I believe I can name the person you're after.'

'That would be very gratifying, Mr Bonner. As it happens, someone has already come forward with a similar claim. It will be interesting to see if you both identify the same man.' He waved a hand. 'Please go on.'

Bonner cleared his throat. 'Until eighteen months ago,' he said, 'I've been fortunate to enjoy excellent health. In fact, I've been the curse of doctors because they didn't get a single penny out of me. Then ... a disconcerting problem arose and I was forced to see a consultant. While his diagnosis was accurate, the medication he prescribed was not a success. In fact, it caused me considerable discomfort yet he refused to change it. I am not one to suffer in silence, Inspector.'

'Did you ask for a second opinion?'

'That's exactly what I did. I won't go into tiresome details but the upshot was this. Because of the unnecessary pain I'd undergone, I demanded an apology from the first consultant. He not only resolutely refused to admit he'd been at fault, he was frankly abusive. That angered me more than anything,' said Bonner with a steely smile, 'so I took him to court.'

'What was the outcome?'

'He won the case. I'd been warned that it was a lost cause. When an individual member is under threat, the medical profession always closes ranks. I did have the satisfaction of seeing the man rebuked by the judge but I was the one who ended up paying the legal costs. That rankled.'

'I can see why this consultant might dislike you, sir,' said Marmion, 'but a doctor takes a vow to save lives. The man we're after takes them.'

'It's him, Inspector. That's why he used Lionel Narraway's name, you see. It was deliberate on his part. He knew that it would cause profound embarrassment to my friend and, as a result, to me. You have to arrest him at once.'

Marmion was interested in the story but not entirely convinced by the conclusion that Bonner had drawn. Another disappointment seemed to beckon.

'Who was this consultant, sir?'

'His name was Forrester – Dr Vincent Forrester.'

Rebecca Forrester was daunted by the sight of her at first. Thelma Gale looked so stern and redoubtable in uniform that her visitor almost flinched. As soon as they began talking, however, the initial doubts soon faded away. The female inspector turned out to be kind, attentive and highly sympathetic. Rebecca was able to reveal details to her that she'd be unwilling to divulge to a man. For her part, Thelma was pleased to be involved in a murder investigation for once instead of being confined to more peripheral areas of policing. She was very grateful to Marmion for drawing her briefly into the team and hoped that her assistance would be decisive.

'Your husband seems to be a rather strange man, Mrs Forrester,' she said.

'He wasn't like that when we first met. Vincent was a brilliant doctor with a glittering future in front of him. We were very happy together. Then, all of a sudden, he announced that he was going to join up.'

'A qualified doctor would be like gold dust at the front.'

'But that was the odd thing, Inspector,' said Agnes. 'He didn't join the medical corps. Vincent wanted to be an ordinary soldier and serve in the trenches. I couldn't believe that he'd turn his back on his career and take such risks.'

'How long did he last in the army?'

'Less than six months – then he was discharged.'

'What was the nature of his injuries?'

'He didn't appear to have any,' explained the other. 'To the naked eye, he looked the same as before. But it soon became apparent that there was something wrong with him. It was his mind that had been damaged and not his body.'

'How did that damage express itself, Mrs Forrester?'

'He became obsessive. He'd always had a passion for art in his life but it turned into a mission. He dragged me off to galleries here, there and everywhere. And he built up a huge library of books on art.' Rebecca had reached the point beyond which she couldn't go with a male detective. Even with a woman, she had to force the truth out. 'Vincent became obsessive about something else as well...'

The detectives didn't hesitate. As soon as the information had been passed on to them by Thelma Gale, along with a house key, they dashed out of the building, got into a waiting car and sped off. Marmion was quietly confident that the breakthrough had come at last. Keedy was ripe for action.

'Gale Force deserves a medal,' he said.

'She certainly earned one, Joe. Like every other old-fashioned copper, I didn't take to the idea of female police officers and I certainly didn't like it when my daughter volunteered to be one of them. Now, however...'

'Mrs Forrester told her what she couldn't tell us. When her husband was invalided out of the army, he became obsessive about sexual intercourse. He not only made excessive demands on her, he started to do something he'd never done before.'

'He strangled her,' said Marmion. 'He applied enough pressure to her neck to make her black out because, he claimed, it was a way to intensify his pleasure.'

'What about his wife's pleasure?'

'Mrs Forrester didn't have any, Joe. No wonder she ran away to that island cottage owned by her aunt. If she'd stayed at home, it was only a matter of time before he squeezed too hard and actually killed her. What he was doing to his wife borders on necrophilia.'

'Dr Forrester is obviously a very nasty man.'

'That was Mr Bonner's opinion.'

'Something happened to him in the army to turn him into a killer.'

'They're *all* turned into killers, Joe,' said Marmion, sadly. 'Killing is what soldiers are trained to do. My son is a good example. He knows how to kill with a bullet, a bayonet or with his bare hands. The tragedy in Forrester's case is that he was a gifted doctor. Hands that were sensitive enough to save lives in the operating theatre had been turned into murder weapons.'

Keedy had a momentary doubt. 'Are we *sure* it's him, Harv?'

'I'd say the evidence was conclusive.'

'Chat won't like the fact that we charged off without telling him first.'

'He'll forgive us, Joe.'

'Only if we make an arrest,' said Keedy.

'We will.'

Since the house was within easy reach of a fast car, it didn't take them long to get there. They leapt out and hurried to the front door, using the doorbell and the knocker simultaneously. There was no response and the house was in darkness. Keedy used the knocker again, applying more force this time.

'He's not there,' he decided after another wait.

'Then we let ourselves in,' said Marmion, putting a hand in his pocket. 'Mrs Forrester is a sensible woman. When she fled the house, she remembered to take her key with her.' He inserted

388

it into the lock and opened the door. 'Switch the light on.'

The two of them entered the house and conducted a swift search. The passion for art about which Rebecca Forrester had spoken was apparent. Art books were in abundance and every wall had tasteful paintings on it. But it was in the master bedroom that they found the most telling evidence. Paintings from the portfolio of Charlotte Reid lay scattered among the stolen items of her underwear. Examples of Olive Arden's skill as an artist were on the dressing table. Photographs of both victims were side by side on the bed itself.

'Do you still have any doubts, Joe?' asked Marmion.

'Oh, no – Forrester is our man.'

'All we have to do is to wait until he comes back. We don't want to spoil the surprise, do we? I'll send the car away and turn the lights off. Then we can sit quietly in the darkness.'

As he spoke the words, he realised how appropriate they were for his son. He and Keedy could create darkness by flicking switches. Paul's individual switch had already been flicked. Whether or not it would work in the opposite direction was an open question. Marmion felt a pang. As they went downstairs, Keedy detained him with a question.

'Remind me how they finally caught Dr Cream,' he said.

'He tried to kill the wrong woman,' replied Marmion. 'She was a prostitute with the sharpened instincts of someone who worked in the oldest profession. When he offered her tablets, she only pretended to take them. She later testified in

389

court against the Lambeth Poisoner. Had she taken the tablets, she'd have died. That's what we need in Forrester's case, Joe,' he went on. 'We need a designated victim with enough sense to realise what he's doing to her before it's too late.'

The combination was irresistible. Drink, delicious food and unending praise conspired against Irene Fuller. She was lulled into a state of compliance. It was dark when they left the restaurant and took a taxi to the remains of the department store. Forrester pointed out to her that his name – or that of Goddard, anyway – still stood proudly along the front of the building. Guiding her alone past the empty windows, he told her what items would be on display in each one and how real artistry would be needed to capture the interest of the passing public. When Irene offered her suggestions, he seemed pleased with her ideas. She warmed to him even more.

'Let me show you your office,' he said.

'I'm to have an office?' she gasped.

'Well, you'll have to share it with your superior, of course, but it will be far better than anything they can offer you at Swan & Edgar.'

'I share a changing room with well over a dozen girls there.'

'You'll be promoted when you come here, Irene.'

She giggled. 'I just can't believe this is happening to me, Edwin.'

'Let's go inside.'

If anyone else had tried to entice her into a bombed-out building in the dark, Irene would have refused point-blank to go. Yet she cheerfully followed him as he picked his way through the rubble with the aid of a torch. When they came to a small office at the rear of the store, he used the beam to explore its four walls.

'This is it, Irene. Ignore the mess. It will look very different when restored.'

'I never expected anything like this.'

'You deserve it.'

'Do I?'

He shone the torch at her face and Irene blinked. He was reminded how appealing she was and let the beam travel slowly down the shapely body that had first attracted him. He'd only been able to snatch some pleasure from Charlotte Reid before he strangled her. Olive Arden, by contrast, had yielded up everything. He'd ravished her in the park and killed her while he was doing so, achieving a heightened ecstasy that he'd not even managed to attain with his wife. While he lusted after that special feeling again, he had to accept that he was not in the most propitious place. He could take her up against a wall or even on the table that stood in the office. But there was no chance of having her on the floor where he could exert full dominance. The rubble erased that option. As he considered what to do, he let the torch fall to his side.

Irene was worried. 'Why has it suddenly gone dark?'

'What?' He realised what had happened and directed the beam at her face again. 'I'm sorry, Irene. My mind wandered.'

'I'd like to go home now, please.'

'There's no hurry. The night is young.'

'My parents will be expecting me. Take me back to the street.'

'We have some business to transact first,' he said, switching off the torch and lunging at her. 'Come here, Irene.'

Muffling her scream with the palm of his hand, he dropped the torch so that he could get the other arm around her. Irene fought back. She was no defenceless woman in the back row of a cinema. Nor was she a half-naked art student seduced into believing that she had a new lover. Irene was intent on survival. Shaking off the effects of the alcohol, she sank her teeth into the hand over her mouth and forced him to pull it away. Then she screamed as loud as she could until a blow sent her reeling against a wall and made her drop her sketchbook. He blundered after her in the dark and got his hands on the long neck so reminiscent of his wife's. And he squeezed.

But Irene was not caught off guard like his other victims. She was a strong young woman with a rising anger at the deception he'd practised on her. Her attacker, she now knew, had nothing what-soever to do with the department store and she was never destined to work there. As fury surged through her, she reached out to grab his genitals in her hand and exert every ounce of pressure that she could muster. It worked. Releasing his grip, he howled in pain, giving her a priceless moment to duck his flailing arms and to stagger off through the rubble. He was enraged. Falling to his knees, he groped around for the torch but he couldn't find it. All that he managed to do was to cut his hand on a shard of glass. Hauling himself to his feet, he went after her, trying to follow the sound of her footsteps. But the chase was futile. Irene was already screaming at the top of her voice and passers-by could be heard calling out to her. It was all over. He'd failed.

The wait lasted just under an hour. Harvey Marmion stayed at the window so that he could keep the street under surveillance while Joe Keedy stood beside the front door, complaining about being hungry and wondering if there was anything in the larder. He was told that the time to eat was after an arrest had been made. There would also be drink by way of celebration. The promise helped to still his rumbling stomach. Marmion eventually saw a figure emerging from the darkness.

'Stand by, Joe,' he said. 'Here he comes.'

Hurried footsteps approached the house then a key was jabbed into the lock. When the door swung open, Forrester plunged in and reached for the switch but the light came on before he could even touch it. The door slammed shut behind him and he found himself faced by a stranger.

'Who the devil are you?' he demanded.

'I'm Inspector Marmion, sir, and the gentleman behind you is my colleague, Sergeant Keedy. We've come from Scotland Yard.'

'How on earth did you get in?'

Marmion held up a key. 'Your wife kindly provided this.'

'Rebecca? But she's not even in London.'

'She is, Dr Forrester, and she won't have to stay

in hiding now that we've taken you into custody.'

Forrester seemed bewildered. 'What are you talking about?'

'We're arresting you for the murders of Charlotte Reid and Olive Arden.' He saw the blood-stained handkerchief around Forrester's knuckles. 'I hope that there isn't a third name to add.'

'I don't know what you mean, Inspector. I'm afraid that there's been a terrible misunderstanding and I can see exactly how it arose. Don't believe anything that my wife has told you. Rebecca is so prone to ridiculous fantasies that she had to be sectioned.' Forrester heaved a sigh. 'Did my dear wife tell you that she'd been in a mental asylum?'

'She told us enough to let us know that you'd say anything to talk yourself out of this situation,' said Keedy, stepping forward. 'Why go on pretending, sir? We've seen Mrs Reid's underwear and we've seen Miss Arden's portfolio. Or are you going to suggest that, unknown to you, your wife brought them into the house after escaping from a straitjacket in the asylum?'

Forrester looked from one to the other. He was caught. Putting back his head, he let out a peal of laughter that was filled as much with relief as with triumph. Then he moved with surprising speed, grabbing Marmion and pushing him hard against Keedy to create some precious seconds. Before they could stop him, he darted upstairs, dived into the main bedroom and locked the door behind him. Annoyed at being tricked, Keedy went after him, putting his shoulder to the door and making it shudder. He stood back to take a run at it and hit the timber with full force, breaking the lock and making the door fly open. Forrester was crouched beside the bag from which he'd taken a syringe. Peeling off his coat, he was about to inject himself through the shirt when Keedy knocked him flying. The syringe went spinning across the room. When Marmion came in, he picked it up and held it.

The fight was one-sided. Though Forrester had the frantic energy of a man trying to escape a death sentence, he was no match for Keedy. The sergeant held him down, took all the fight out of him with a relay of punches then banged his head on the floor until Forrester finally gave up. When he was pulled unceremoniously to his feet, Forrester was expertly handcuffed.

'Well done, Sergeant!' said Marmion. 'The superintendent will be delighted.'

Keedy grinned. 'That's a novelty I long to behold, sir.'

The Battle of the Somme was released in August. It was a film unlike anything that had ever preceded it. Day after day, cinemas all over the country were packed. In the first six weeks, it was estimated, somewhere in the region of twenty million people saw the film. It pulled no punches. It was an honest, straightforward, documentary account of what had actually happened. Real soldiers were seen being killed by real bullets and real shells. Stretcher-bearers risked their lives to retrieve wounded men. The full horror of conditions in the trenches was laid bare. Instead of feeding off rumours and press reports, people saw the ugly truth at last. This is what was happening to the nation's soldiers.

They went as a family soon after the film appeared. Relieved of the bandage over his eyes, Paul Marmion sat between his parents and listened to his father's whispered commentary on what was on the screen. There was no soundtrack but Paul, like other soldiers in the audience, could hear the noise of gunfire and the screech of shells. He could smell and taste the battlefield. He could also hear his friend, Colin Fryatt, playing the mouth organ once more. Holding hands, Alice and Keedy sat with the others, aghast at what they were witnessing and amazed that Paul had somehow survived the bloodbath and returned home.

It was an experience that burnt itself into the memory of everyone there. Not far behind the Marmion family were the unlikely figures of Claude Chatfield and his wife, conquering their disdain for the film industry for once. An even more unlikely patron at the West End cinema was the Reverend Matthew Hearn, actually venturing into a place that he'd earlier viewed as one of the circles of hell. Like everyone else sitting in the darkness, he was at once enthralled and humbled, realising that the visceral power of cinema could be a force for good.

When it was all over, hardly a word was spoken. The lights came up and the audience began to disperse in a daze. They'd been enlightened rather than entertained. They'd finally been allowed to see the carnage and the futility. Darkness remained for Paul Marmion, however, yet it was now pierced by a tiny spectre of light, flickering slowly before him like the flame of a minute candle. It was as if *The Battle of the Somme* had lifted – albeit slightly – some of its terrible burden from him.

'I can see,' he murmured. 'I can see something.'

The publishers hope that this book has given you enjoyable reading. Large Print Books are especially designed to be as easy to see and hold as possible. If you wish a complete list of our books please ask at your local library or write directly to:

Magna Large Print Books
Magna House, Long Preston,
Skipton, North Yorkshire.
BD23 4ND

This Large Print Book for the partially sighted, who cannot read normal print, is published under the auspices of

THE ULVERSCROFT FOUNDATION